SUMMER SYMPHONY:

A NOVEL IN FOUR MOVEMENTS

SUMMER SYMPHONY:

A NOVEL IN FOUR MOVEMENTS

COLIN DUCKWORTH

For Jefferson & Ireny
with love & best wishes,

Colin Duckworth

Melbourne
Nov '06

MONGREL JAZZ

Melbourne, Australia

Mongrel Jazz
An imprint of Black Pepper

First published by Mongrel Jazz
403 St George's Road, North Fitzroy, Victoria 3068

National Library of Australia
Cataloging-in-Publication data:

　　　　Duckworth, Colin
　　　　Summer Symphony

　　　　ISBN 1 876044 99 3

　　　　I.　Title

　　　　A823.3

Cover design: Gail Hannah

Colin Duckworth is known internationally for major works on the 18th century, especially Voltaire and French counter-revolutionary espionage, and on modern theatre, with particular reference to Samuel Beckett. He is now a freelance academic, writer and occasional television actor and theatre director. He holds an M.A. in Modern Languages from Birmingham, where he studied singing at the School of Music. He also has a Ph.D. from Cambridge and a D.Litt. from Melbourne University, where he is an emeritus professor and professorial fellow. He is a Commander in the Ordre des Palmes académiques.

His theatre and book reviews, essays, stories and articles have appeared in journals and newspapers in England, the U.S.A., Canada, Australia, New Zealand, France, and Germany. As writer, actor and director, he has been involved in works for radio, television, and stage (including writing libretti for two very successful children's operas). He holds British and Australian nationalities, is married, lives in Melbourne, and has two children.

Summer Symphony, his third novel, grew out of a short story, 'Summer Lark', which won the inaugural Melbourne *Uni News* short story competition.

The story of Alan Scott is dedicated to all young people who overcome obstacles so that their artistic and creative talents can flourish, and to the older people who help and encourage them.

CONTENTS

First Movement
'I sigh the lack of many a thing I sought.'
WHITE: C major > RED: G minor

Second Movement
Mysteries
PURPLE: B flat major

Third Movement
Revelations
GREEN: F minor

Fourth Movement
Resolutions
BLUE: E major

First Movement

'I sigh the lack of many a thing I sought.'
WHITE: C major > RED: G minor

By means of music the passions enjoy themselves.

F. Nietzche, *Beyond Good and Evil*

Music has powers for evil as well as for good

Dr Howard Hanson, *The American Journal of Psychiatry*

TEMPO 1

Duo - Trio

Bloomsbury, London, Monday, 4 January 1971

Dearest Rebecca,

It's a long time since I wrote, sorry. Not been at my best, one thing and another, but something has happened that I must tell you about, because it brought you back into my mind like a flood, instead of just the usual constant stream. Last week I spotted an announcement in the paper about a concert — odd for me to do that, as you know I'm not an arty person. It was a symphony that caught my eye, because it was called a symphony of healing, and it was by... Alan Scott! There might have been another musical Alan Scott but I thought it unlikely. So I bought a ticket to the Festival Hall (on the south bank of the Thames, you wouldn't know it, after your time, alas).

I've just got back, and must tell you what happened before the details fade. It was a very strange experience, I must say. The music had a curious effect on a lot of people, even me. When it ended, there was an odd stunned silence for a bit, and one or two people got up and said how the music had affected them, which was of particular interest to me. One woman proclaimed to the world she'd had the first orgasm since her boyfriend left her! The conductor gestured to the composer, and Alan, looking as if he was having to be encouraged by the woman sitting next to him, stood up to acknowledge the applause, shyly, as though uncertain it was really for him. I recognised him straight away, even after twenty-five years. A bit chubbier, a bit balder, but still Alan.

The man sitting next to me said, 'He looks as if he's expecting to be lynched,' which was true. He seemed reluctant to claim responsibility for that very strange music that had affected the audience mysteriously deeply.

On the way out of the auditorium (which has funny boxes as if they have to be pulled out like drawers) I looked round and saw Alan accepting congratulations from several people with a

3

vagueness that seemed aloof but was probably euphoric. Always a bit donnish, even then, old Alan. I approached him in the foyer, then thought better of it and turned away.

Alan, up in the clouds, did not even notice me, but he did do something rather odd at that point: he put his fingers in his ears and stood still for a moment, with his head on one side, as if listening. Then he briefly looked round rather anxiously, like a sparrow on the *qui vive* for a cat. I watched him take the arm of the slim dark-haired woman walking beside him, and heard him say to her, 'They seemed to like it.'

She seemed remotely familiar, and then, in a flash, as she smiled at her companion, I placed her. Bella Cassell! You never met her, but Alan must have mentioned her. I made up my mind.

'Excuse me... Alan Scott?'

Alan paused on the stairs and faced me. All he saw, no doubt, was a stockily built, greying, bearded man, shabbily dressed, but not from poverty (though I'm pretty near the bread line), more from indifference to outward appearances. A musician, Alan probably surmised, or a programme autograph-hunter. Rather a creep, maybe, I don't know, I try to read people's minds but usually get it wrong.

He said, 'Yes, that's right. How do you do?'

I said, 'I'm well, thank you.'

He paused again and went on staring at me. I started to feel uncomfortable. I felt my mouth twitching slightly, that smile you used to call enigmatic, or sneering, or harbouring a secret. Maybe he thought I was a blackmailer? Good luck to him if he had something to hide.

I said, 'Your Mum will be proud of you.'

Alan frowned, looking unsure if he had heard me properly, and said, 'I beg your pardon? My mother? She's dead.'

I was sorry, and said so, and thought I'd better introduce myself before he turned away. 'You don't recognise me, of course, with the beard. Excuse me. Keith Maxted.'

For a moment Alan stood open-mouthed while the cogs in his head ground away. They finally meshed.

'Of course! Keith! Forgive me — Good heavens! — it must be...'

'Twenty... twenty-five years, give or take.'

I extended a hand, which Alan took reluctantly. As we examined each other's face for vestiges of youth, a quarter of a century melted away, and we were momentarily young men about to face a hostile world in our very different ways.

Out of the corner of my eye I saw Bella was watching us carefully, as if guessing what was going on in our minds as we scanned the years. Alan turned to her.

'Bella, this is Keith Maxted. We were at school together. Keith, my wife, Bella.'

I felt more relaxed now, with my unshared knowledge.

'Yes,' I said, 'we have met, actually.' I didn't mean to say it, it just came out, and immediately I regretted it when I saw Bella's startled look.

'Oh?' she said. 'Have we?'

Had she really forgotten? Anyway, I hastened to repair. 'But only once, I think, briefly. Alan preferred to keep you to himself, and I don't blame him. We all thought he'd gone bonkers till we realised he was going through the agonies of first love.'

To Alan's obvious consternation her expression turned warmly welcoming, as if she had made a sudden decision to be friendly. She took my hand in both of hers.

'How do you do, Mr. Maxwell,' she said (clever, that). 'I remember now. You're right — a beard is a great disguise! What have you been...?'

Up to? Doing? Her question hung on the air as Alan broke in. 'Darling, we really should go and meet the others.'

She went to take my arm as if she was just about to invite me to join them, but Alan forestalled her.

'I'm sure you understand, Keith,' he said, waving his arms about, 'lots of musical colleagues, friends and foes, terribly boring for outsiders.'

As he moved away to chat to other people, music fanatics, Bella said to me rather conspiratorially, 'Sorry about that, Keith, it's been a tense time.'

I tried not to look offended. No, not offended. Hurt. 'That's all right, Bella. I'm used to it!'

'What have you been doing all these years?'

'Oh, nothing much. When I was finally released I got into medical school. Then International Red Cross, WHO, Médecins sans frontières stuff. Anywhere where innocent people are getting torn to bits by warmongers.'

Bella peered over my shoulder; I turned and saw Alan making frantic gestures at her.

'Look, Keith, must go, give me — give us a ring, please, tomorrow. I'm sure Alan would really like to catch up. Our phone number's ex-directory, so...'

I took the card Bella held out to me, looked at it, and carefully pocketed it.

'Yes, Bella, I will. You are being very kind. I'd like to talk to Alan about his curious music.'

I'm not sure, Rebecca dearest, if I shall follow it up. Alan was evidently not too pleased to see me again. He always was a bit of a prig, but I'd like to put things right with him, just as I've tried over the years to put things right with you, my poor love.

I'll sleep on it. Let it lie for a few days. But somehow I feel it is important to link up again with Alan. Something to do with the music. To think that rather colourless boy you and I both knew long ago has turned out to create such disturbing and powerful stuff! Disturbing and possibly dangerous. I wonder where it came from? I suspect the brilliant Bella has had a lot to do with it. No need for you to be jealous about her, by the way. She was before your time. So why am I lying to you? Of course I recognised her right away.

A kind of mission is forming in my mind, but I must move carefully.

You are always with me. You will never die.

Keith

Hammersmith, London, 4 January 1971

Several hours later: the Scotts are lying in bed, pleasantly exhausted, back at the small flat they keep on in Hammersmith as a base for their frequent but brief visits to London.

Bella opens the concert programme. 'Will you autograph it for me, please, Mr. Scott?' she asks shopgirlishly, 'it reads ever so lovely!'

In fact she has previously — frequently — told him she thinks his programme note ill-advised. 'The music speaks for itself, so let it!' she begged, but Alan decided 'the listener' (singular) would need some guidance.

She now reads out loud what he wrote, hoping to make him agree with her at last:

'"Each movement is a different reaction to the seemingly inexhaustible powers of belligerence and destructive hatred possessed by the collective mind of the human species. The last movement is a threnody of despair in the void, resolved by the most complex and mystical of the six harmonies that end the movements."'

As Alan seems determined not to respond — indeed, he is feigning sleep — she reads on, quietly tut-tutting to herself. To reassure 'the listener', Alan has promised 'some wallowing in hopeful idealism' in the first movement, 'frankly sentimental lyricism' in the *Adagio*, and 'a rollicking macabre gallop over the bodies on the battlefield that Voltaire would have appreciated' in the *Scherzo*. As for the fourth movement, Alan has commented that it 'defies definition by tempo, since this varies horizontally and vertically from one bar to the next. Hence the indication *Orgia, ma con amore.*' Into the last two 'healing' movements, he wrote, 'I have poured my soul, without regard for the practicalities of performance or the likelihood of favourable reception'.

Bella heaves a great sigh. 'You really didn't want this to be performed, did you, darling?'

Alan opens his eyes and looks shocked. 'What can you mean? Of course I did. It's what I've been wanting for years. Do you

7

remember that day you tricked me into playing for Professor Walker? I told him I used to dream of a vast orchestra and choir, and they were playing wonderful music that I'd written. Well, this was like those dreams come true.'

'Of course I remember it, darling. It was the second time we'd met, and I'd also just tricked you into kissing me.'

'No I didn't! *You* kissed *me!* Regular little Jezebel you were.' He shuts his eyes again, a smile on his lips.

'It's a bit late to complain now, thirty years later. But don't change the subject, Alan my love. I was saying, it's just that — except for the bit about being horizontal in the Orgy movement — you seemed to go out of your way in the programme note to make the symphony sound dreary, and it's not at all dreary.'

'Well, thank you, Dr. Scott! That's mighty generous of you.'

'The orchestra did you proud, darling,' Bella says, now in truce mode.

'Thanks to Sir George. Great conductor. Held everything together wonderfully. Did I tell you he's encouraging me to write an opera for Covent Garden? Someone's sent him a libretto based on *The Insect Play*. An anti-war play by some Czech chaps.'

Bella says it sounds promising.

Alan goes on, 'I made sure he realises this is *our* symphony, not just mine.'

Bella leans over and kisses his cheek. 'Nice but untrue. You did the donkey work. I just applied the whip now and then.'

'And supplied the map for the journey.' He thinks for a couple of seconds, then adds, 'In a way, you're my Lilly.'

Bella blinks. 'Oh? Who's this Lily? Of Laguna?'

Alan laughs. 'With two Ls. Debussy's Lilly. She said *Pelléas et Mélisande* was partly her work, because she encouraged him when he despaired of ever finishing it.'

'Just a minute, darling. Didn't he ditch her and she committed suicide?'

'She tried to shoot herself, poor thing. But...'

Bella looks him firmly in the eye. 'Well, let's get this straight, Mr. Composer. If you ditch me, it's not me I'm going to shoot!'

'I'm not likely to be doing any ditching,' Alan says uneasily.

They pause. He knows what's coming next.

'By the way, why were you so hostile to your friend, Keith Whatsit?'

'I wasn't hostile! Well, not very. I suppose he brings back so many memories, most of them painful.'

Bella turns so that she can see Alan's face. 'Including me?'

'No, not you, of course not. He was part of my life you missed out on, remember? Thanks to Mr. Hitler.'

'Oh, yes.' She lies her back on the pillow, biting her lower lip. Then: 'So he was. Well, he seems to be a good man. He's a doctor, you know. Goes around the world working for the International Red Cross.'

'Still trying to ease his conscience, I expect. He was a conscientious objector. A conchie.'

She hopes the contradiction between his idealistic programme note and his hostility to Keith the Pacifist will strike him, but she senses he is too emotionally close to both, so she spares him and does not press the point. For the time being.

'The moment I saw him hovering there,' Alan goes on, 'before I remembered him, I disliked him. Something creepy, I thought.'

'Pure unfounded prejudice!'

'He has a sly look about him.'

'Haunted, I thought. Hunted.'

'Ah, possibly. By the police.'

'I thought he was rather dishy. Sort of hairy Dirk Bogardish.'

Alan snorts. 'Dishy! You sound like a teenager.'

'You don't need to be jealous, you know! I don't want an affair with him.'

'I'm not jealous. Of what? Oh, this is getting silly. All right, let me try and explain why I feel so strongly. Think of the circumstances. 1944. I was about to go off, as all our pals had, and get killed for all I knew. I'd lost you, apparently for ever, because of the war; my darling old gran had been blown up in her bed; and my mother was behaving very badly. And Keith Maxted suddenly announces he just wants the luxury of nursing his precious conscience.'

He opens a book; end of conversation. But not for Bella.

'Yes, but... I've never known you so vehement, darling. I wasn't too happy either, when you first knew us. After what mummy went through — was still going through — and the agonies daddy was suffering all that time, not knowing about mummy. And the domestic enemy was quite willing to kill daddy and me, remember? It was a terrible time for all of us. But it was so long ago.'

Alan lowers his book and takes the opportunity to plump up his pillow while he considers. 'All right. I'm overreacting. I'm willing to concede that he might be a sensitive soul.'

'I think,' says Bella, 'there's something desperately sad about

9

him. As if he has missed a chance in life and still bitterly regrets it.'

Alan feels his eyes drooping. It's been a long, exciting, but exhausting day. 'Perhaps he never got over Rebecca. Any more than I'm ever likely to get over you.'

First flash of her brown legs, first stroke of cheek, first touch of lips.

*

They wake up late the following Sunday morning. Alan has been determined not to read any of the reviews in the dailies, but when friends and colleagues begin telephoning, referring to comments in magazines and Sunday newspapers, some kind and some dismissive as always, he can no longer keep up the pretence of airy indifference to opinion. By ten o'clock he is at the newsagent's in Hammersmith Underground station, picking up the most likely culprits.

Bella, still in her dressing gown, has made coffee while he is out, and takes hers to the bathroom with her, leaving Alan free to give vent to his feelings in private. What interests and appalls him, above all, is the almost universal ability of professional critics to miss the point. Some have done the academic analysis thing — key relationships, inversions, modulations, recapitulations.

'Anyone would think I'd said to myself, 'Ah, now I'll pivot on the mediant and move from E flat major to C sharp minor,' he grumbles, then remembers that they probably studied analysis with him during his brief stint on the staff at the Royal Academy of Music.

Other reviewers have gone in for the source-hunting game: Models and Influences. 'A distinct homage to Debussy...', 'Echoes of Messiaen...', and to Alan's great surprise, 'An obvious debt to Conrad Beck's Fourth Symphony'.

Beck? He vaguely recalls the name, but is sure he has never heard anything by him.

'Bella!' She's in the shower and can't hear him, so he opens the bathroom door and speaks through the steam and plastic curtain. 'Who's Beck?' he yells.

Bella screams and sticks her head out. 'Alan! Don't ever do that!'

'What? For heaven's sake...'

'I told you I didn't want to see that terrible film again, but you had to drag me along, didn't you?'

'Oh!... *Psycho*? Yes. Sorry.' He did, indeed, drag her out to see

10

the Hitchcock classic again — much against her will as she remembered vividly the nightmares it had given her ten years before — a couple of evenings ago, mainly because of Bernard Herrmann's wonderfully atmospheric music.

'Listen, this critic says...'

'Can I *please* finish having my shower?'

Alan retires to the kitchen and finds a pair of scissors, with which he cuts two of the reviews out.

The Musical Times (**London**)
10 January 1971

THE FESTIVAL HALL REDUCED TO SILENCE

The final harmonies fade gently into the distance, as if reluctant to abandon us. For fully one whole minute no one moves. No applause. No hissing or booing either. Indifference? It quickly becomes obvious this is far from being the case. Tears are running down the cheeks of several listeners, but of joy, not sadness. Gradually a hum of conversation begins; the unthinkable is happening to an English audience — strangers are talking to one another like old friends! And the subject is not so much the music as the curious effect it has had on them. This can be described only as a generalised euphoria. One elderly woman stands up and exclaims she has not been able to do that without help for years, despite two visits to Lourdes. Another, much younger, admits without embarrassment that during the fourth movement she experienced her first orgasm since she and her lover split up, and this opens up a flood of accounts (astonishing even for the Swinging Sixties), from both sexes, of unaccustomed wellbeing and unashamedly intimate sensations.

Mystifying

Reviewers are already commenting on the extraordinary reception given to the longawaited *Symphony of Universal Healing* by Alan Scott. The work was mystifying enough without the unparalleled collective phenomenon that followed its first performance on this enigmatic composer's forty-fourth birthday.

As most music lovers already know, each of the six movements of this, his second symphony, lasts seven minutes. Each ends with an unnervingly haunting chord that has been slowly built up, Sibelius-like, from fragments, like the slow unfolding of one of those artificial shell-flowers in water Proust wrote about. This should be but preparation for a transcendent harmony that closes the symphony, an ineffable amalgam of impenetrable complexity and imponderable mystical power. There is something mysteriously unfinished about this work.

Nevertheless, tried, tested, battle-hardened against sensational musical assaults on the emotions as I am, I was not immune to the effects of this new work, but I decided to delay my comments until I had had the (rare) opportunity to speak to the elusive Mr. Scott about his own reactions to the public's reception...

How did he explain the bizarre scene we all witnessed when the final notes of his *Symphony of Universal Healing* had died away? Was he surprised by it?

'Surprised? Not really. I've already experienced the power of those particular harmonies, and this was the most powerful mustering of sonic forces I've ever had at my disposal to share them with the public.'

Sublime outpouring

Certainly the combined effect of the new Moog synthesiser and large symphony orchestra was so overpowering it made Scriabin's *Poème d'Extase* and Messiaen's *Turangalîla-Symphony* seem insubstantial by comparison. But it was not just a question of volume. This was a texture never before heard. It was as though Scriabin, Debussy, Ravel, and Messiaen's ecstatic, free-floating chords, had all been a mere preparation for this sublime outpouring.

This symphony must surely be the work of a (still young) composer who received some mystical revelation, no doubt the fruit of an ascetic, aesthetic and intellectual life of a high order dedicated to music following on a precocious musical childhood and artistic background. Always reticent about his private life, little is known about his background before the evocative *Paris Symphony* of 1955. In this he managed to seize the transient impressions of a dream city, in ways reminiscent of Delius but with a voice of his own. Since then he has shunned publicity, flitting between California, London and Paris, while producing (in Los Angeles) a regular stream of well-wrought film scores, and (in Europe) respected but unconventional chamber, orchestral and synthesised works — rather more accessible than those of his contemporaries, Berio, Stockhausen and Boulez.

Would he have preferred all the sound to be synthesised?

'I've always,' he told me, 'regarded our traditional ways of making music, by plucking, blowing, tapping, scraping and banging, as rather primitive, and find the new electronic instruments exciting. But I realised that perfect frequen-

13

cies are not everything. A human element had to be provided in a healing work by fallible, warm musicians doing their thing as best they can.'

Revelation

Alan Scott then spread his hands in what turned out to be a typically self-depreciating way. 'As for explaining the effects of those chords, my wife and I have been trying to do this for years, without much success. She's a psychologist, or rather a cognitive neuroscientist, specialising in music therapy research. The six harmonies defy analysis, even though they are basically just vibrations, like all music. Their range is enormous, of course, going from far below the lowest note on the Albert Hall organ to notes only a dog can hear. They were revealed to me many years ago, and it's taken me all this time to find out how to harness them and disseminate them for the good of mankind — if that doesn't sound too pretentious.'

He went on: 'The universe is all vibration, you know. Music, colour, matter, and the fundamental life-force are inseparable.'

So the process is very eso-teric? Again, that half-amused, half-bemused look. 'I'm wary of terms like that. They tend to put people off, alienate them. It's really no good asking me, I'm just a medium. I simply hope that one day musical vibes might be able to cure our ills, both individual and social.

Otherwise, quite frankly, I think we're all done for. But,' he adds sombrely, 'even white objects throw a dark shadow. There are some very destructive, evil and harmful things going on in the musical world too.'

— **Carl Hanslick**

14

WEIRD MUSIC, WEEPING WIMPS

Some very dangerous music was heard emanating from the hallowed walls of the Festival Hall last night. You've heard about Wagner inspiring Nazis to greater than ever nationalist fervour and disco music turning nice young people into crazy junkies, well forget it! That's kid's stuff compared to what we heard.

Alan Scott (anyone heard of him?) has written a so-called *Healing Symphony* that reduced well-dressed people from Kensington and Hampstead Garden Suburb to tears and had them all but hugging one another and dancing in the aisles with arms outstretched like New-born Charismatic nut-cases.

This is a new low in mass brainwashing, and must be stopped before we become a nation of defenceless wimps and weeping willies incapable of saying boo to a mouse.

This Scott apparently spends most of his time in California and France. He has obviously been knocked silly by Flower Power! He should remember what defeatism did to the French in 1940. The longer he keeps his debilitating ideas and music out of England, the better!

15

During breakfast, as Bella reads the reviews, making appropriate noises, tut-tutting here, hear-hearing there, Alan suddenly remembers: 'I had such a vivid dream last night. About the first time I spoke to you, when you invited me to your birthday party. I really felt I was there again. Flung back in time.'

'Because of your friend turning up out of the blue, I suppose,' says Bella and, not wishing particularly to be reminded of those days, immediately goes on to admit she has never heard of Conrad Beck, even though Grove reveals that he's Swiss and still alive. 'Is it important?' she asks. 'Music's full of accidental similarities.'

'Yes, of course it is,' Alan agrees, 'but we need to know if he's aware of the harmonies.'

That has not occurred to Bella.

He's seventy now,' she works out, 'so he's not made much of a splash with them if he was aware.'

At about noon, as Alan is putting on his coat to go out to meet a young conductor who wants a few contacts in the U.S., the phone rings. Bella answers it. She stands silently holding the handset to her ear for about a minute, then slowly replaces it, staring at nothing.

'What is it, darling?' Alan asks, alarmed.

'It's the answer to Beck, I think. Somebody said "Tell Alan Scott he has released something and he'll wish he hadn't".'

'Released something? Did you recognise the voice?'

Bella shakes her head. 'No. It was male, but strange, muffled. False. But it means that Beck hasn't used the harmonies, if you're being credited with 'releasing' them. Funny word to use: releasing. Like a plague of locusts.'

'Or letting something out of Pandora's box,' Alan murmurs. He takes off his coat again and goes to the desk. 'Maybe it's got something to do with this kind of reaction,' he says, showing Bella the review in *National Pride*.

'"...a new low in mass brainwashing..."' she reads, '"...must be stopped before we become a nation of defenceless wimps and weeping willies incapable of saying boo to a mouse." Why did you buy this drivel?'

'Well, Mortimer Englehart said on the phone there was something 'sinister' in that new tabloid called *National Pride*. I suspect he reads it every day before raising the Union Jack in his back garden.'

Bella reads through the review again. 'It is a bit sinister, isn't it? Creepy. Can you find out who wrote it?'

Alan thinks about that for a moment, then says, 'I don't think I'll bother. It's not a musician, that's obvious.'

Bella is not so sure about discounting the writer of the *National Pride* review as the phantom phoner — or any other possible cowardly culprit. The ferreting instinct is much more developed in her than in her dreamy let-sleeping-dogs-lie husband. Perhaps it's because she feels more physically vulnerable; perhaps it's plain feminine inquisitiveness; or perhaps because she has her mother's instinct to resist coercion. Whatever, she decides she is not going to let that creep turn her into a reactive victim.

Alan is not in the mood for looking on the black side of anything. 'The woman who had her first orgasm for years is on our side.'

'Did she?' cries Bella. 'Poor woman.'

'I thought you liked orgasms.'

'Yes, of course, you know that! I mean her not having one for years. We could get Decca to market the L.P. as 'Music to Make Love to.'

It is not until the following week that Keith telephones. Alan is momentarily surprised to hear his voice, but can't quite figure out why. By this time he has calmed down enough about his old school friend to invite him to a pub lunch.

'Come to the flat first,' he suggests, 'it's quite close to Hammersmith underground station. Bella is out for the day, so we'll be able to chew the fat.'

'Oh. Well, yes, that will be nice,' Keith replies. Alan cannot make out whether his audible disappointment is because Bella won't be there, or because he fears a hostile encounter. Or because he feels guilty?

When Keith arrives at twelve-thirty, panting heavily, the pile of letters on the desk catches his eye.

'Your lift's out of order,' he complains. 'Phew!'

'Again. Yes, it's all a plot to keep me fit.' Alan begins to sweep up the letters into a basket. 'Look at all this lot! The perils of fame!' he jokes, but Keith can see he's really enjoying a bit of celebrity. 'The trouble is, these blessed journalists keep on asking such stupid and irrelevant questions. How did I feel? Did I want to brainwash people? Do I have a guru, am I a...?'

Keith shoots him a look and asks sharply, 'Do you?'

'...am I a... What?'

'Do you have a guru?'

17

'No, course not.'

'And...' His voice is softer now, '...do you want to brainwash people? Think about it, Alan.'

'Brainwash? Certainly not. Music from Bach to the Beatles can change moods and bring serenity or excitement, but that's not brainwashing.'

'Not quite the same, is it?' Keith persists.

'But not quite different either. At least, that's what Bella and I are trying to find out. But these silly people,' he picked up a handful of letters, 'want to know, Am I a hypnotist? Can I do miracle cures? And so on. I ask you!'

'They're not necessarily silly. More like desperate. You're not a catholic angling for sainthood, are you?'

'Heavens, no!' Alan is amused at the idea. 'I'm still totally impervious to organised religion — power-hungry priests and pious fraud. But I'm not a supernatural sceptic, like Bella. She'd have been one of the first on the pyre.'

Keith looks round the room, then out of the window at the courtyard below with its sprinkling of snow. 'Nice place you've got here. Apart from the lift. A bit different from the suburbs of Brum.'

Alan goes into the little kitchen and Keith follows him, noting the décor.

'Everything white? Walls, doors, tiles. Ceilings.'

The observation strikes Alan as slightly odd, coming from a man. He opens the fridge. Also white. 'Yes, all white. We find it easier to live with. Less obtrusive, doesn't clash with anything, and it actually changes colour — during the day, at different seasons. Even different moods. It's white white today, with the snow outside.'

He takes a bottle of riesling out of the fridge. 'Will this do for apéritif?'

Keith looks at the bottle with faint longing, then shakes his head. 'Do you have any mineral water? Anything will do.'

Alan is always disconcerted by teetotallers, and searches half-heartedly in the fridge. 'Tonic water do?'

'Fine thanks. I have a bit of a liver problem.'

Alan makes sympathetic noises. 'I once had to think about whether it would be worse to go blind or go deaf. A more frivolous dilemma would be whether to have to forgo wine or baked beans.'

'Speaking as your medical adviser, since I'm not,' Keith says with mock seriousness, 'I would frankly advise: Both in moderation!'

Gradually, Alan finds bits of the old Keith coming to the surface as he visibly relaxes. As they both relax.

'You go to a lot of concerts, do you, Keith?'

'No, not at all. You may remember I'm not a great music-lover, although I always envied you your talents, Alan. Remember at school how you tried to shame me into coming to those bloody Classical Music Club meetings of yours?'

'I once put on a bit of Gershwin especially for you, and you went to sleep.'

'Sorry about that. Anyway, I've been wandering round strange foreign parts most of my working life, so symphony orchestras weren't thick on the ground. Records of *My Fair Lady* and *Salad Days* are about the limit of my tolerance. But when I saw in the paper they were going to perform a symphony by Alan Scott, I guessed it must be you.'

'And you couldn't resist taking a *bain de nostalgie*? Did you regret it? Did you find my music boring? You can be quite honest, because if you say Yes, I can put it down to your tin ears.'

Keith looks round the room and walks over to the window again, with an expression not of envy exactly, but certainly of regret at something missing in his own way of life.

'Nice quiet haven, this,' he murmurs. He turns back to the piano; clumsily, his fingers hit a couple of keys. 'But not ideal for a noisy musician like you, I'd have thought.'

'Noisy? I said you had tin ears!'

'Oh, I didn't mean those strange chords in your symphony, Alan. Although... I have a feeling you didn't invent them yourself.'

So this is what he's been leading up to.

'Are you accusing me of plagiarism?'

Keith looks taken aback. 'No! No. Not at all. It's just that they seemed... how can I put it?... out of this world. Sort of... I'm not very good at this... a different dimension. Mystical.'

Keith says the word as though he's ashamed of it.

Alan sits in one of the two armchairs and points to the other. 'Sit down, Keith. Why do you ask?'

Once again, Keith answers with a question. 'Did you know the kind of effect they would have on people?'

'I asked you why you're so interested,' Alan pursues, 'as you're so unmusical.'

'I'd have thought that was obvious. My life has been devoted to healing. It was as much the title of your symphony that intrigued

19

me as its composer.'

Alan takes up his glass and drinks. Reflects. Makes up his mind. 'All right, I'll be honest with you. You know, Keith, for years I've been plagued with strong emotional reactions to certain moments in music. And I don't mean swooning over Bing Crosby. This will all be meaningless to you, I suppose.'

Keith seems genuinely interested, so Alan goes on. 'A particular change of key or of rhythm for instance. Privileged moments that bring tears to my eyes. Debussy, Ravel, Rachmaninov — they're full of them. Powerful emotional triggers. Many non-musicians feel that, of course, but I've tried to analyse these moments in the scores. I understand intellectually and technically exactly what's going on, but I still can't explain the link between the sounds and the reaction.'

'You do mean tear-jerkers, then?' Keith provocatively suggests.

Alan realises he will have to refine his language. 'It's more than a question of degree. They're not just tear-jerkers. Tears can be jerked out of eyes by a punch on the nose or a soppy song or the end of *King Lear*, but no one would equate them. It's hard to think of an analogy without seeming to be condescending... That's all leading to my answer: the harmonies were... how can I say?... revealed to me. I knew they could actually cause certain physical changes in some people.'

'How did you know that?' Keith cuts in, almost aggressively. At least he has been listening closely, vague and non-scientific though Alan's discourse has been.

Alan pauses, slightly taken aback. 'Ah, now that's a long story that Bella and I share. It isn't just mine to tell, because she's doing research in that area. We've had a couple of hate phone calls, you know.'

Keith expresses concern. 'Hate? Why would anyone do that?'

'There are some out there who think we're out to warp people's minds.'

Keith is about to say something but shuts his mouth and appears to regard nuisance calls as unworthy of attention. He moves on to another thing that puzzles him. 'Have you ever wondered... I don't mean this in any critical way... But, why *you?*'

'You mean I'm nothing special?'

'No, I didn't mean that.'

'But it's true, Keith. Why me indeed? I was a very ordinary bloke with no connections or background. Yet I really feel I was entrusted with some precious esoteric knowledge. I don't know why. It's as if many, many small causes went into that one big effect, but I didn't recognise them at all along the way. Only now, in retrospect. I expect that all sounds like prophetic nonsense to you.'

'Oh, no, on the contrary,' Keith says with perfect seriousness. 'I don't believe anything happens to us for no reason.'

'Good! The reason you're here is lunch. Let's go and eat at my favourite pub round the corner. They have jolly good mineral water.'

As they don their coats and go out into the crisp January air, Alan says, 'Actually, I did hear about you, a few years back. From an old flame of yours. Ours, I should say. Joy.'

'Joy! The impressively pneumatic Joy! Good heavens, that's going back a few years!'

Wartime. The lights have gone out all over Europe. If a young lad had not been cutting a garden hedge on that Saturday afternoon; if a pretty girl had not chosen that moment to walk by — this symphony, this story, would not have come about. The harmonies might still be unknown. Not that the path between small cause and large effect was smooth, or straight, or painless. Only at the end could one say that it was inevitable, and even then one might be wrong. Where, indeed, did the path begin? Fragments of a half-forgotten past are about to become inextricably bound up with the present, now that Keith Maxted is installing himself again in the lives of Alan and Bella.

From the white of hope and aspiration
to the red of fire
   blood
     anger.

TEMPO 2 — ALLEMANDE

barbaro - tragico - amoroso - marziale

Birmingham, England 1930s-1940s

Through the bomb sight of a Dornier or Heinkel it appears like the curved finger of a giant glove with a bulbous tip, poking into a layer of spinach and sauerkraut. Worth a few incendiaries, perhaps, to keep them on their toes, nothing more. Closer inspection, still from above barrage balloon altitude, reveals the finger to be a residential road, a cul-de-sac in an outer suburb stretching its tentacles through the green fields Falstaff had babbled about, in the Warwickshire countryside towards Stratford upon Avon. One of those fields gave the road its name: Fallowfield Avenue.

Down at ground level, none of its inhabitants think to ask themselves why it was fallow, or whether its fallowness was the reason for its being sold for development about ten years before, in the early 1930s, and carved up into little leasehold blocks for a hundred semi-detached, identical houses.

The only relief from this uniform anonymity is one older large house at the bulbous end of the cul-de-sac. The name of the house which will shortly become an important location in this story, is painted elaborately on its big red gateposts:

The Firs

But the locals, with characteristic deflationary Brummagem humour, call it 'The Fire Station', or more precisely, 'The Foir Styshun'. The estate developers responsible for the avenue's encroachment upon nature tried to buy it in order to demolish it, but the owner, an old man who was quite happy vegetating in its rambling solitude, refused all offers, despite having his driveway constantly and deliberately blocked by lorries for weeks on end. Eventually the developers had to build round the house and its large, unkempt garden.

Several years later the old man died, and for many months the house had remained empty. His grown children had rushed down from London, cleared it out with indecent haste, and disappeared again without making the acquaintance of any of the neighbours occupying those horrid, horrid, horrid little houses littering the meadows that used to surround the old house in the happy days of their childhood and youth there.

If those cut-and-run descendants from the capital had ever strolled along the bumpy asphalt pavement instead of riding in their purring Daimler, insulated from reality, they would have learned that the architectural uniformity of these little semi-detacheds masked profound private, domestic differences, hiding from public view the daily enactment of many petit-bourgeois tragicomedies. Mr. Hose, for example, befuddled and unemployed, sitting discreetly in the upstairs back bedroom while his wife entertained that swarthy man with the camel-hair overcoat and the black Vauxhall every Wednesday afternoon; Mrs. O'Reilly, pregnant yet again, squinting through the latest black eye and wondering if she dare ask for more credit at the corner shop; sweet young Mrs. Pratt, recently married to Corporal Pratt, rushing to the door every morning when she saw the postman through the net curtains. Mr. Greasely, setting off with his window-cleaner's ladders on a home-made cart, hoping to beat T.B. with fresh air. Mr. Brampton, wondering if his uncontrollably rising blood pressure will soon force him out of his job as a P.T. teacher.

The visitors from London might have been surprised to hear incongruous sounds emanating from Horrible Little Suburban Box Number 27: someone playing Chopin or Debussy on a piano, or a contralto voice singing *Softly awakes my Heart*, or a wireless set playing Beethoven. Had they peered through the bay window they might have glimpsed a copy of Muther's *History of Modern Art* on the window sill, or an easel bearing an unfinished canvas. Then they might have paused to wonder at the disparity between that unprepossessing, nondescript habitat and the improbable artistic activities being pursued there.

At the back of Number 27 Maddy Scott looked out from her kitchen window and sighed, a half-mouldy wartime potato in left hand, scraper in right. The fence round the little suburban garden was nothing but a row of stakes, waist-high and held together by twisted wire; but they might as well have been ten-foot iron bars.

The mound of sandbags at the far end, covering the Anderson

shelter, made her think of the Black Hole of Calcutta. At night, as she lay down there on her narrow bunk when there was an air raid, she would imagine herself buried with the other bodies, all getting hotter and sweatier, till the air gave out. Then, ignoring Bill's protests and the danger of falling red-hot shrapnel, she would clamber up, breathless and panic-stricken, out to the flashes of bombs and gunfire.

Out, as well, to the oily, cloying smell of paraffin hanging in the air, for the whole city was surrounded by burners like great Valor stoves that belched out smoke at night to try and mask it from the Heinkels and Dorniers. That never worked, but just added to the catarrh and bronchitis that were essential features of life in England's second largest city. The raids had been a humiliating shock to several worthies on the City Council who had stoutly maintained, *on the highest authority*, that Birmingham was beyond the range of German bombers, so there was no need to spend ratepayers' money on air raid precautions.

Maddy had three regular ways of escaping from the drab world around her: playing the piano; painting flower-studies; and daydreaming. Today, as she stood there on the cold red Mansion-polished kitchen tiles, she daydreamed back in time to the little worker's cottage of her childhood. Such warmth, such company, so much laughter! Always someone tapping on the kitchen door and coming in unheralded with needs or stories. Whereas here, in outer suburbia, there was more space but nothing in it. Just a small undifferentiated box enclosing her spirit.

My home. My prison. And now my shelter, which might smother me.

Nobody knew why, one day, she had laughed, a deep but mirthless laugh, when she learned that the Home Office was in charge of prisons.

Quickly she shook off the cloud of self-pity trying to envelop her. Things could be a lot worse. They could still be cooped up in a couple of rented rooms in depressed Coventry, banned from the house during the daytime because the baby's crying annoyed the landlady. They could be living closer to the bombs at night, like Mom. She could have married a brute, and Bill was not that, whatever his weaknesses. She could have not had Alan...

Alan... That boy! The symmetry of chronology appalled her. She had been fourteen when the last lot began, the war to end all wars. Now her son was fourteen and here it was again. Only much worse, by the look of things. She looked round at the *Daily Express* map stuck up on the kitchen wall, showing the armed might of

Germany that had spilled out beyond the Siegfried Line, and the puny beleaguered offshore island that alone stood in the way of Nazi domination of the civilised world. The whole of Europe had been taken over. *Just twenty-two miles of sea between us and those monsters with their Panzers and Messerschmitts!* Her ears found even the words horrible; she couldn't bear to hear Richard Tauber any longer — the ten-inch record of songs from *Das Land des Lächelns* had been chucked into the dustbin.

Thank God this one couldn't possibly last long enough to involve Alan. Surely the Americans must come in soon? Or, she wondered, would they sit on the sidelines until near the end like last time and then claim all the credit?

She turned from the sink, ear straining, potato peeler poised to gouge another eye out of the rotten King Edward's cowering in the bowl. They had tried to grow their own, but the heavy clay was a tuber graveyard.

'Alan! I can't hear you!'

Alan Scott was peering through the window of the front room as her voice reached him. Bother! He was sure *she* was about to appear, striding lithely past his house as though it and he did not exist, her dark curls fringing her forehead, that mysterious smile on her lips. Slowly he walked, backwards, to the piano.

'It's O.K. Mum, I was thinking. About this fingering. Trying to work it out.'

'Don't say O.K.'

'O.K. I mean, all right.'

Why should All Right be all right, he wondered, *and O.K. all wrong? Funny stuff, language.*

'Do you want me to help you, Alan?'

Oh no! That would be not all right, not even O.K. There would be no chance of even a sideways glance at the road outside if she was breathing down his neck showing him how easy it was if only he would concentrate.

'No thanks. I'll work it out.'

Yes, I bet he will, his mother smiled grimly. Any moment now he'll be playing that tuneless rubbish he says comes out of his head, instead of mastering scales and ledger lines and key signatures. He pushed back the wave of hair that flopped down over his right eye and squinted at Swinstead's *Step by Step to the Classics*. Then he closed it again and opened Czerny. Boring old Czerny.

Caesar, who had been lying under the piano stool with one paw on the loud pedal, groaned, got up, and flopped down by the door with a plaintive whine, ears spread out.

'You look like a hairyplane, Ceez,' the reluctant pianist laughed.

They were unusually long ears for a springer spaniel, which raised doubts about his pedigree. 'There's a bit of cocker in there,' Alan's father reckoned, 'a sprocker, that's what he is.' He was a failed gun dog who disliked fetching gory twitching birds and rabbits, and had been rescued from Uncle Reg, who was about to have him put down, by Maddy's offer to give a home to what her brother-in-law called 'that useless bloody animal'.

However much Caesar's suspect heredity might have reduced his chances at Crufts, Alan would not have had him any other way. Especially endearing was his expression, the result of an accident of nature or of something that had happened before he entered the Scott family: one eyebrow was noticeably higher than the other, which gave him a look of permanent, quizzical disbelief. This made him the ideal confidant: non-judgemental, amused, and resigned to the inexplicable illogicality of human behaviour.

'I know how you feel, Ceez,' Alan sighed as he launched into arpeggios. 'Music first, walkies soon.'

It was seven o'clock before Bill got home, in his Special Constable's uniform. The war had so far been good to Bill Scott. Better than he knew, in fact: Robin Hood Jams and Jellies had been on the brink of sacking him for poor performance in August 1939; then all the younger men were called up. So instead, he had been made an Area Sales Manager. The promotion had had a slight galvanising effect on him for a while, but Maddy saw with disquiet that he was sinking back into his old ways. Late starts, back home for lunch at one, snooze and dither till three, make a few phone calls to grocers glad to lay their hands on anything edible, get an order for a couple of dozen jars of jam or lemon curd if he was lucky, then change into uniform and play at policemen. His amiable lethargy, a source of constant irritation for his wife, did nevertheless have a positive quality: he never pushed his customers or tried a hard sell, and so they often gave him an order because they liked him.

'I'll have to go over to Mom's tomorrow and give her a hand at the shop,' Maddy announced over the sausage and mash and sundry overcooked vegetables.

'When I grow up,' Alan announced, 'I'm going to be Minister of Agriculture, and I'll ban parsnips, turnips, cabbage, cauliflower, and brussels sprouts.'

'You should be glad of what we get,' said Maddy, 'there's a war on.'

'Can I come to the shop?' Alan asked, knowing the answer already. He loved going to granny's shop, with its shelves full of gaily-coloured packets and tins.

'No, of course you can't. Why do you ask silly questions like that when you know it's a school day?'

'It's only a half-day tomorrow. I think they're running out of teachers.'

'Then you can catch up with some piano practice, can't you? You're becoming very lazy, Alan. I can't think where you get it from.'

She glanced over at Bill, whose gaze remained fixed upon the *Birmingham Post*.

'London again last night,' he announced.

'And us too,' Maddy said.

Bill frowned at her. 'Better watch your tongue, love! We've just had a directive down at the station about rumours and careless talk.'

Maddy laughed. 'Oh yes, walls have ears and all that. You don't think Alan's a fifth columnist, do you?'

Alan started on hearing his name. 'What?'

His mother shook her head. 'There, you see, even if he was he wouldn't hear anything. Too busy dreaming about that girl.'

Bill stared at his wife, then at his son, who had gone pink. 'Girl? What girl? He's too young for girls.'

'Just shows how much you remember about being fourteen. Or notice. He's not too young for girls, but he should be too busy to be wasting his time on them.'

Alan shifted uncomfortably and mumbled, 'I don't know what you're talking about, Mum.'

'Right. That's O... that's all right then.' She let the matter drop. He had been warned. 'You'd better get on with your homework. And don't leave the room empty-handed.'

'O.K. Mum.'

Maddy opened her mouth and shut it again when she saw the slight provocative smile on his lips. She recognised it only too well as her own when she was his age, rebelling much more strongly than he against the various forces of authority — teachers and parents — with which she had always seemed to be in conflict.

When Alan had left the little dining room with his plate, knife and fork, and had stomped up the stairs to his room, Maddy said, 'I worry about Mom so much. I wish she'd sell up the shop and come and live next door.' She had always called her mother Mom.

Bill put down his paper. 'Yes, I know you do, love. I do too. But she can be so darned obstinate. I really think to her mind moving out now would seem like she was giving in to Hitler. Anyway, who'd want to buy it now?

It was a corner grocer's shop in Sparkbrook, part of Birmingham's grimy bomb-torn inner slums, but it had been a little goldmine since Elizabeth-Ann Rogers had taken it over in 1930: an act of defiance and desperation. For years she had struggled to make ends meet on Joseph's meagre wages as a lithographer. Much of what he earned went on paints and canvases, but his own old-fashioned genre pieces never sold for much.

Then his sister Alice, who had married well and had recently been comfortably widowed, came up with a proposal: she would set them up in a business if they would have her to live with them as a non-paying guest. Without even consulting Joseph, Beth-Ann had agreed, on condition that the business would be in her hands and in her name. Alice thought that was very sensible. She had always admired Beth-Ann for her hard-working determination; not for nothing did she come from good farming stock, believing you only got out of life — and the earth — what you put in.

Joseph, on the other hand, had never overcome the disadvantages of privilege. By the time he was thirty he had somehow gone through the small fortune inherited at his majority, travelling round Europe, painting in the Paris of *la belle époque*, playing his violin and singing jolly songs in Bavarian beer-gardens. A very important link in the chain of events, is Joseph Rogers, Esquire.

Beth-Ann was flattered when he turned up regularly at *The Spread Eagle* and began courting her. Her, a country-girl turned barmaid! He was bowled over by her lovely strong features, firm mouth, rich chestnut hair, saucy green eyes, and beautiful figure. He told her she would make a fortune in Paris, but she didn't know what as, and didn't like to ask. She refused point-blank to sit for him in the nude, so he asked her to marry him instead. That was in 1896. He never wanted to talk about his life as an artist on the continent, and she never pressed him. Whatever indiscretions he might have committed before he knew her were none of her business; so long as some little French tart didn't turn up on the doorstep with a child. Her friends and family told her he was a good catch despite his lack of money and his age (a venerable thirty-two): handsome with his waxed moustache, cultured, gentlemanly, frequently in demand to give a rendering of *The Lost Chord* or *Roll on, thou Dark and Deep Blue Ocean* in his deep baritone voice.

He had died shortly after she bought the shop, unable to face the humiliation of failure, the shame of being kept by a wife in *trade*. Not once had he condescended to serve a customer or check the stock.

'We should have opened an art gallery,' he used to say. 'I wouldn't have minded that. I could have sold some of my own paintings, perhaps.'

'And perhaps not,' she countered, always the realist, seeing little scope for selling paintings during a national depression. 'A pawnbroker's would make more sense.'

Joseph shuddered.

A born trader, she rapidly built up goodwill among the local workers' wives. She could read despair on a mother's haggard face, and would slip a few sausages or slices of York ham into a near-empty basket. Generous to the needy, maybe, but she could be ruthless with anyone who tried to cheat her — and there were plenty of them in those hard times. One ploy was to ask for something they knew was on a bottom shelf, then whilst Beth-Ann was squatting down they popped things in their bag hoping she hadn't seen. She soon cottoned on, and would say, 'That's two and tuppence, and then there's the milk in your bag.'

If any item was requested and she did not stock it, she would promise to have it next day. She never failed, even if it meant walking or cycling for miles to find it. Often it was Maddy who made this possible by either looking after the shop or going out herself, collecting and delivering, wheeling baby Alan through the dismal streets in his pram which did double service as a trolley.

Maddy and her mother made a formidable team, despite periodic clashes of their strong wills. With her father, on the other hand, Maddy had never quarrelled. He was her idol, and she never saw his faults. He taught her to paint before she could write; for hours she sat beside him while he patiently made suggestions, taught her perspective and brushwork. For her he bought a battered old piano and encouraged her to learn so that she could accompany him when he sang. Only once did he raise his voice in anger, and that was over Maddy's choice of future husband. She was being courted in the early 'twenties by two young men: Eric, a well-off man who spent his spare time riding motor cycles in T.T.

30

races; and William Scott, a salesman without two pennies to rub together.

'Take my advice,' said Beth-Ann, 'Marry a man who has to make his own way in the world. I know what I'm talking about,' she added darkly.

Joseph stood up, moustache quivering. 'Yes, I know I've been a failure,' he said, 'but Eric's got some fine qualities, even if he has got money. Above all, he isn't an artist, so chances are he won't be a bad as me!'

Eric solved the problem a short time later by getting himself killed in a race on the Isle of Man. At the Registry Office, just after Maddy and Bill were married, Joseph whispered to his daughter, 'If it doesn't work out, you know you can always come home,' an offer not calculated to inspire confidence.

By 1933, despite the Depression, which was very hard on the inhabitants of Sparkbrook — mainly factory and railway workers — the corner shop had prospered so well that Beth-Ann opened a second one just far enough away to avoid taking custom from herself. When Alice died, being childless, she left Beth-Ann with enough money to buy not only the shop, but a couple of houses being built in Fallowfield Avenue. One house she sold to Maddy for a nominal five pounds, and the other she kept for herself to retire to, whilst assuring Maddy's agitated sister that it would be hers one day. In the meantime it was rented out and Maddy kept an eye on it for any signs of midnight flits by the tenants — a frequent activity in those depressed times.

Throughout this time Bill Scott drifted through several jobs as a travelling salesman. Fatherless since the age of seven, with two brothers and two sisters, he had left school at fourteen, like Maddy. He had come out of the 1914-18 war with the stripes of a sergeant driving-instructor but no other skills. However, being — thanks to a disciplined if brief education — literate and numerate, having a charming manner and some powers of persuasion, he managed to avoid returning to the world of manual labour from which he had barely escaped, by selling wrapping paper. It suited his strong dislike of being stuck in one place, such as an office, with a supervisor breathing down his neck. Then the bottom fell out of paper and he searched desperately for some other way to keep his new wife and child.

One Tuesday morning he came home at lunch-time announcing he had found a job 'on the road'. Maddy threw her arms round his neck and kissed him.

31

'Oh good, I'm so glad. What it is? Do you get a car?' The question really meant, 'It's not door-to-door selling brushes, is it?'

'Well, transport, yes. It's outside.'

She ran to the front door and opened it. There, before her, stood a large van with LYONS TEA and a coat of arms painted on the side.

'What's *that?*' she asked.

'I'll be selling tea. Instead of paper.'

Maddy said nothing. Just stared at the van.

'It's quite good pay,' Bill said. 'And a bonus at Christmas if I do well enough.'

Maddy turned to face him. 'It's not staying there.'

'What?'

'That van. It's not being parked in front of the house. You'll have to leave it at the bottom of the road.'

And so it was. Every night Bill would park the van where it would not be an eyesore and a perpetual reminder to Maddy that her husband was not, as she told everyone, a 'company representative', but a delivery man. It was not really snobbery that dictated her reaction, it was fear. She had a vivid and unsettling dream about her father, standing at the bottom of the bed, saying, 'If it doesn't work out, you can always come home.' But she was not one to admit defeat. Somehow or other, they would make their way.

Alan, now seven, loved the van, and spent many days during school holidays travelling in the back, helping Bill to carry packets of tea into the corner shops that smelled comfortingly, like Gran's, of Lifeboy carbolic soap and a paraffin stove. The van's shelves were packed with many-coloured labelled teas, going from gold and white (the most expensive) to green and red (the most popular). He would stretch out on an empty shelf at the end of a good day and breathe in the exotic aromas, thinking of India and China and Ceylon and wondering what they were like, and how one became a tea planter.

During all those years Maddy had been bringing in a few extra shillings by exercising the musical talent she prized as much as painting. Piano-playing had been a useful source of pocket-money ever since she was still at school. When the silent films gave way to talkies she looked to the dance halls, formed her own little band, and could have been out playing the quick-step and slow foxtrot, veleta and St. Bernard's every night had her father, and then baby Alan, permitted it. As soon as Alan could be left with Bill in the evenings, she started getting engagements for dances again, but Bill was far from happy about it. It was obvious a lot of men found her attractive, with her rich auburn hair and vivacity.

Then, in 1938, came a breakthrough. In the euphoria following Neville Chamberlain's return from Munich waving a piece of paper and promising 'peace in our time', Robin Hood Jams and Jellies advertised for another commercial traveller. Bill went to Evesham in his best suit and trilby hat, impressed them, and drove back home in a dark blue Morris 8.

Dolly Wise lived with her husband Harold at number 23. They had moved there, from London, only about five years before, but she and Maddy immediately became firm friends because of their common interest in dancing. Dolly had been a Tiller girl in the 'twenties, but Harold had put a stop to that; not that she minded giving it up, it was extremely demanding. Nevertheless, she was delighted when the idea came up (neither could remember who thought of it first) in the summer of 1939, of opening a dancing school. Maddy had been playing most Saturday nights for local dances, and regularly for another school, but it catered mainly for children. There was nothing for adults who wanted to catch up on the latest dances, or learn new steps to old ones, or indeed make up for the sad lack of a misspent youth and start from scratch.

The programme was worked out, a hall was booked, and fliers were printed announcing the *Grand Opening of the Dolly and Maddy School of Dancing* on Saturday the second of September 1939. Alan delivered hundreds of them, pushing them through letter boxes and running the same risks of digital amputation as the postman. The opening was neatly, but quite inadvertently, sandwiched between the German invasion of Poland and the beginning of World War Two.

*

By some quaint sociological happenstance, although the houses in the avenue were identical, prime examples of nineteen-thirties suburban ribbon development, the families living in those at the bottom, open, end of the avenue were much worse off than those in the upper half. The main reason was unknown to them, but it was simple: most of the lower-end families rented; the upper half ones were owners. So as soon as anyone said they lived in the 'upper' or 'lower' half their class was effortlessly established. The

Scotts lived, one might say, right on the cusp; in constant danger of being dragged down, but hopefully ascendant. Number 27 was a No Man's Land in a social limbo, its inhabitants having no allegiance to working-class solidarity or access to middle-class affluence.

Tom O'Reilly and Gordon Wiggins lived in the lower end. Since they were the only two boys of Alan's age in the avenue, they were all inseparable friends even after Alan went on to grammar school in 1938, while the others stayed at the senior school. Maddy, for all her aspirations, had no objection to this. Somehow she felt it would be important for Alan to know people from all walks of life. There were no Little Lord Fauntleroys around, but you never knew, he might have to mix with them too one day, and be at ease with them, which meant not having a Brummy accent and not leaving school at fourteen.

There is no more natural and exciting playground for lively young boys than a building site. For more than a year, just before the outbreak of war, the fields behind the odd numbered houses of the avenue were turned into a battleground of mud and holes, and uprooted trees, followed by the rapid construction of yet another road. The exhilaration of clambering over half-built houses was enhanced by three vivid juvenile imaginations at work. Games of Cowboys and Indians, Cops and Gangsters, Tommies and Jerries, all became real with the help of the builders. Fortunately no parents were aware of the risks being blithely taken as the boys learned to walk, then run, over the floorboardless joists of upper storeys. Both Sadlers Wells Ballet and Aston Villa would have noted the rapid improvement in their sense of balance and timing, and would undoubtedly have sent their dancers and players to practice on building sites had they known.

But near-tragedy struck one Saturday afternoon. Tom and Gordon were cowboys escaping from a prowling Indian. They found a panful of soft cement up on the first floor. It felt just like the filling of a custard tart, the sort that Laurel and Hardy and Charlie Chaplin repeatedly got thrown at them. They called Alan, he came, looked up, saw them sitting on the joists... and received a large dollop right in the eyes. What a shot! But the concrete contained slaked lime, which began to burn. Laughter quickly turned to concern and they climbed down, found a bin full of water and tried to wash the cement out. Alan could see nothing, so they led him, with smarting, burning eyes, home.

The doctor ordered him to lie still with his festering eyes bandaged for days, and no one knew whether he would be blind or not. During those days, as he listened to the wireless, he tried to imagine what it would be like if he had to depend solely on his ears for the rest of his life.

'Mum, if you had to go blind or deaf, which would you choose?' he asked — a question he would recall only too well in the not too distant future.

She was desperately worried, but tried not to show it. How could a boy manage with no sight? She imagined her son with a white stick, stumbling along, bumping into things, falling down open manholes, unemployable, selling matches in the street.

'It's morbid to think about things like that,' she said to him.

'I'm just trying to work out which would be more useful to keep,' he insisted, 'eyes or ears, that's all.'

'Well,' she pondered reluctantly, 'it's a terrible choice to have to make.' She had no doubt it would be worse to be blind, totally dependent on others in a dark world, but that would scarcely reassure the boy. Finally she said, 'I just can't imagine not being able to hear music. It'd be awful to have to live with total silence round you. Pity poor old Beethoven.'

'Why?' he asked, 'what happened to him?'

'He went deaf, that's what. Right in the middle of his life, with years of music still to write. But he went on, he didn't give up. Wrote wonderful symphonies and quartets that he never, ever heard.'

Alan said nothing, trying to imagine Beethoven's plight. Then he said, 'That wouldn't be so bad, would it? He'd have heard the music in his head, and it might have sounded better than anybody played it.' Then his voice sank so low that his mother hardly heard what he said: 'No one could play the music I have in my head.'

That was really all he wanted to do, harness the music in his head. At the moment it was like a wild horse, refusing to be caught and tamed. But there were always other, irrelevant things getting in the way, obstacles in his path: air raids, maths, chemistry, shopping, and endless household chores Maddy insisted he help with ('Everybody does his bit in a family,' she would say, eyeing her menfolk just as her mother had eyed her daughters): tidying his room, sprinkling carpets with tea leaves then sweeping them up with the entrapped dust, polishing lino, weeding and digging the clay-bound garden... Admittedly there were self-imposed distractions he enjoyed: roller skating at breakneck speed down the hill, playing games, making things out of wood from *Hobbies Weekly*, working out elaborate practical jokes. He wondered if composers always had things happening to them that interrupted their music. A composer's life was altogether a bit of a mystery to him: did he just write music and someone with an orchestra would take it away and play it?

How long would it be, he wondered, before he would be able to say to the world, 'Leave me alone!' What else was fate going to drag him into before he could get on with the one thing he felt worth while? What, for instance, was the point of this accident that was reducing him to bored inactivity? Perhaps it should be character-forming or something? There had been a talk on the radio that morning about the moral value of suffering, which he had disagreed with violently, as far as he had understood it. Probably, he decided, it was intended to make people feel good when they had their homes and families blown-up.

After a couple of weeks, his sight was back to normal. His pals came round, full of contrition, with a small brown paper bag of humbugs, most of which they ate themselves.

The new road was finished, the houses soon occupied, and the battleground was divided up into fenced back gardens. But the God of Active Boys intervened again. The 'Fire Station' became empty. During those months in the spring and summer of 1939, the last summer of sanity Maddy called it, the vast garden surrounding the now empty old house gracefully let Nature have its way, and it became once more part of the fallow field of old. For Alan and his friends Tom and Gordon it was a haven, an untamed playground beyond their dreams, where they were free for a while from the irrational strictures imposed by adults in the crazy world they were creating.

Maddy fretted about evacuation.

'We shouldn't have brought him back from Hereford,' she moaned as they struggled up the garden with the all-clear heralding the dawn. Back in September 1939 Alan had been separated not only from home, but also from his friends, and evacuated to stay with Uncle Reg and Aunty Emily. Maddy had had doubts about their — her — decision not to send him to North Wales with the grammar school he'd been lucky enough to get into the previous year, but she could not bear to think of her boy being mothered by some unknown woman to whom he might become attached. Her sister, Emily, she knew, would not capture his affection; she had never wanted a child of her own, being too self-centred to experience maternal feelings.

Then like thousands of evacuated children, Alan had returned home towards the end of the Phoney War, but Adolf and Hermann had changed tactics in September 1940 and started to bomb the industrial Midlands.

On Thursday 14 November the sirens went at 6 p.m. again, and the Scotts trooped down to the Anderson through the drizzle, Alan clutching his satchel full of homework. Wave after wave of bombers throbbed heavily overhead, but the bombs seemed to be falling on the other side of the city.

At about half past two in the morning, Bill, with his steel helmet on, called from the shelter entrance.

'Maddy, come and look at this.'

Wearily she climbed out, past the sandbagged entrance, and gasped. The sky was ablaze with light.

'My God, somebody's catching it tonight,' she said.

'I think it's Coventry. That direction anyway.'

Alan called sleepily from the shelter. 'Dad? What's the matter?'

'Come and look, lad.'

'Put your slippers on,' his mother commanded.

Alan gazed upwards, awestruck by the red glow, brighter than any sunset. 'Cor! You could read a newspaper! That's over Coventry way, isn't it? More than twenty miles away.'

Coventry it was. That night they had heard five hundred bombers — more than in any single raid on London — rain down fire and death from the heavens: five hundred tons of high explosives and nine hundred incendiaries. A third of the homes, and the magnificent cathedral, were destroyed. Five hundred and fifty-four of its 250,000 inhabitants were killed; many of them children as only three thousand had stayed out of danger in evacuation areas.

Maddy did not have any sentimental feelings about Coventry, recalling the years spent in rented rooms — only one at any one time — fending off carping, rapacious landladies and predatory landlords. Sometimes she had had to walk in the rain all day, pushing the pram, because the baby made so much noise crying with apparently incurable colic. She hoped Mrs. Jex had been bombed and her groping husband had been wounded in his vital parts. Alan, on the contrary, felt immensely sad at Coventry's destruction: for one thing, it was the site of a profound revelation he did not yet understand: one day, when he was about four, he remembered standing at the bottom of a big — to him — garden, listening to the birds singing and the breeze soughing, and the grass growing, and the sun humming its glorious sounds, and the crackling of the earth drying out under his bare feet. He remembered rushing back to the house, shouting, 'Music, mummy! Music! Come and listen!' She had tried to tell him there was no music, only the wind, but he knew she had simply not been able to hear. Indeed, he could still remember what the music of nature had sounded like.

During that winter of 1940-41, bleary-eyed, clutching blankets and thermos, hoping there would be either gas or electricity (rarely both) for a cup of tea, Elizabeth-Ann and Maddy and Bill and Alan and a million other inhabitants of Birmingham had already forgotten life had once been different. The dark, dreary, Midland months crept by. Christmas... Happy New Year! Some hope. There was some hope, quite irrationally. Nobody spoke of defeat. Many feared it. Before Dunkirk, the Chiefs of Staff had told the Prime Minister, Winston Churchill, in a secret paper, that 'Germany could gain complete air superiority unless she could not knock out our air force, and the aircraft industries, some vital portions of which are concentrated at Coventry and Birmingham.'

'His school-work's suffering,' Maddy said as she tried to make porridge on the one-bar electric fire — no gas this morning, 'and he's got School Cert. next year.'

Alan sat up with a start. 'What! No, Mum, July, 1942. Eighteen months away yet. You gave me a fright!'

'Yes, and you'll need every day of it the rate you're working. He should have stayed with Reg and Emily.'

Bill disagreed. 'He was miserable there. Reg didn't treat him well, always telling him off. 'Spare the Rod and Spoil the Child,' as he's always saying. That's the sum total of Reg's idea of being an ideal parent. The boy's school reports were terrible, but they're fine now he's back. It's best we all go up together.'

Maddy told him not to be morbid. Alan said he would run away and escape back home if they sent him off again. 'Uncle Rod was horrible to me,' he protested.

'Well, maybe,' said Bill, 'but you shouldn't call him Uncle Rod. And you oughtn't to have blown him up.'

'I didn't blow him up. I'd have liked to, but I didn't really.'

He had done in his mind, there was no dispute about that. He had been reading quite by chance the death notices in the local Hereford paper when the idea came to him. Carefully following the prescribed wording, he had written and sent in the following:

THEOBALD, Rodinald, of 35 Park Road, Hereford. *Accidentally killed by enemy action, when sitting on an unexploded bomb having his photograph taken. Will be sadly missed by his friends Adolf and Hermann. Rest in Pieces. No flowers.*

Greatly to his surprise, his little flight of imagination had been printed without question by a junior typesetter. Things got a trifle out of hand after that, mainly because Alan had not been able to stop laughing. Finally, tears of joy streaming down his cheeks, he confessed. 'I only did it for a joke!' Reg was not mollified by this admission and immediately phoned Maddy to complain about 'your menace of a son — he had me blown up in the paper and even got my name wrong! Can't even spell! Nobody's called Rodinald'.

Back in Birmingham, his head singing with joyful music, Alan rejoined the remnants of non-evacuated boys at his own school. Back home, in his own room with his books, listening to old gramophone records of Elgar, played by an tuneless orchestra in a railway tunnel. Back, with Caesar, who had constantly moped around the house while he was away in Uncle Rod's safe and horrible house. He was delighted Caesar had missed him.

The three boys, Alan, Tom and Gordon, were reunited on their return from brief evacuation, and for months came to regard the wilderness around 'The Firs' as theirs. Their shock and rage knew no bounds one day in early 1941 when they found the driveway blocked by an enormous furniture van.

'What are you doin' 'ere?' Tom asked the driver.

Without removing the sodden Woodbine from the side of his mouth, the ancient removalist mumbled, 'Wot's it look like, yer cheeky young devil. Evacuatin' Buckinnam Palace, o' course.'

'You're from London, aren't you?' Alan asked. He was developing an ear for accents, thanks to inveterate cinema-going (he could 'do' Ronald Colman and was working on George Raft). That, and enforced bilingualism: at home he was not allowed to speak Brummy (which Maddy called 'lazy yob English'), whilst with his pals he fell naturally into their patois, which he had perfected for self-preservation at his previous school servicing a council estate where, according to Bill, the baths were used to keep coal in.

"Sright lad. Wot's left of it. 'Ad bleedin' Jerry over 'ere, 'ave yer?'

Gordon was about to launch into a gory and highly exaggerated account of blown up buildings and bodies in bits when Alan remembered the posters about careless talk, nudged him and cut him off.

'Not much,' he said. He didn't know it, but the national press had been ordered not to report anything about the extensive damage to the industrial Midlands.

The new occupants created great interest. Mr. Slater, a retired auctioneer with direct intelligence links on such matters, maintained down at *The Fox and Hounds* that the furniture included many valuable items 'of foreign origin'. Everyone took this to mean 'suspicious'. Then the family arrived, and rapidly became a source of gossip and speculation; for not only was there Mr. Castle, whose name turned out to be spelled Cassell, who Mrs. Watkins said ought to have been locked up with all the other forinners, and Mrs. Cassell, who was too blonde to be natural, but there was also *another woman,* whose function exercised the collective imagination of Fallowfield Avenue for weeks.

This man Mr. Cassell was observed to leave every morning in an Austin 16 camouflaged a flat grey-brown, and the brassy Mrs. Cassell chugged out in her Morris 8 (until she mysteriously disappeared altogether) leaving the house in the care of the Other Woman. A two-car family with petrol, at a time when everyone else was reduced to bicycles, caused unkind comment. Everyone else, that is, except Bill Scott, who was allowed a petrol ration as his job depended on being able to do what a commercial traveller did: travel commercially.

None of this speculation and gossip concerned young Alan Scott until one morning, when he was bringing Caesar back from his walk, he saw the camouflaged Austin approaching slowly and majestically as he was about to cross the driveway of The Firs. He glanced inside without much interest, and saw a vision through the open window, sitting in the back. It was female, young, with dark curly hair and soft brown eyes which transfixed him. He stopped in his tracks, to Caesar's puzzlement, and continued to stare, paralysed. He might well have stayed rooted until someone carted him away; but the girl looked back at him, and waved a tanned bare arm. The blood rushed to his face. He was just about to return the wave when Caesar got impatient and tugged him on to the next vital smell, marring the intended effect of his salute. He walked on, transformed in his mind into Romeo awakened by the herald of the morn and beating it back to Mantua (a set text for next year's School Cert.).

He had not seen her since. Not for weeks. Frequently he stood at his parents' bedroom window, whence he could observe the site of the vision. He palely loitered outside The Firs, to Caesar's annoyance and the amusement of neighbours peeping behind lace curtains. He became obsessed with the beautiful face and shadowy figure he had merely glimpsed, dreaming and day-dreaming of her, staring into space at meal times, refusing food, making even more violent and noisy improvisations on the piano until his mother threatened to lock it if he didn't stop driving her mad. His mother was certain he was Coming Down with Something, but Gran shook her head and said to leave the lad alone, he was just growing up.

He was, quite simply, pining away, and for someone he had not even spoken to. How had she suddenly materialised? Was she just a visitor? How, when, would he ever see her again? He imagined a hundred different scenarios, mostly taken from films, with himself as Ronald Colman. He would be dropped as a secret agent into Germany, and would kill Hitler, and when the King knighted him she would coming looking for him and would beg to be his girl friend.

When it did happen, he was totally unprepared. He had been trimming the privet since noon. Rivulets of dusty sweat trickled into his smarting eyes. He hated this job. So did Caesar, who sighed mournfully at his feet, occasionally swatting an importunate fly off his nose with a furry paw. Although the boy argued, always ineffectually, that time spent on domestic chores took him away from his real work thinking about music, and he might die tomorrow, and then everyone would be sorry, he had finally agreed to cut the hedge for a reason intimately connected with the fact that this activity increased the chances of his seeing *her* passing by. Across the small dry lawn came snippets of the one o'clock news on the B.B.C. Home and Forces Programme: 'air raids', 'casualties', 'enemy aircraft shot down'.

He surveyed the hedge. 'Nearly done, Ceez. Walkies after lunch.'

Caesar raised one eyebrow and wagged the other end as his small spaniel brain registered Walkies, one of the O. K. — All

Right — words.

'After lunch, stupid. Go back to sleep.'

He snipped and swept heaps of leaves into the home-made wheelbarrow, gazing periodically up at the old house, dreaming tunes. Strange tunes, like nothing he had ever heard on the radio or when his mother played the piano. He sometimes tried to pick them out on the upright, but he needed an orchestra, and before long his mother would always complain: 'If only you'd practise properly, you'd soon play proper music. We could play duets. Handel's Hallelujah and Beethoven's Minuet.'

But that prospect never appealed to him. To Hell with Handel! To Blazes with Beethoven! His own inner music soared and swooped, free above the earth, like a solitary flute or violin floating effortlessly, with ethereal shimmerings and dark swirling menacing rumbles coming from below. You could stuff Schubert's *Marche militaire* for four hands up your jumper.

In the small paved back yard, separated from the scarcely larger lawn by trellis Bill and Alan had put up together, Bill Scott poured the last of the beer into Harold Wise's glass.

'Thanks, Bill.'

Harold drank, set down his glass, and wiped his bushy moustache with the back of his hand.

'Good lad, that Alan o' yours. If he wants to earn a tanner, he can come and cut my hedge next.'

Bill laughed. 'You'll be lucky! When old Watkins asked him to collect some horse manure in the barrow for sixpence, he said, "I'll sell you the barrow for a shilling, and you can get your own manure."'

Harold chuckled and finished off his beer. 'Reckon he'll be at the Stock Exchange before the Labour Exchange.'

'No,' Bill shook his head, 'he lives in another world, that boy. We never know what's in his head. He'd die for that dog, though. Like brothers, they are. It's being an only child, I suppose.'

Harold pulled his watch out of his waistcoat pocket, looked at it, and rose.

'Like me. It's swings and roundabouts, like everything else in life I reckon. Better get back for dinner or the missus'll be round after me. By the way, have you set eyes on that new lot moved into the Fire Station? Rum feller. Supposed to be clever, though. Must be, to afford that house and car. Something very hush-hush, they say.'

It was at that moment, in the front garden, that She descended upon him — unexpectedly from the opposite direction, before he could compose his face more like Errol Flynn's. In fact, he was angrily trying to remove a persistent fly from his right ear. She mistook his gesture.

'The last time you waved at me you got carried off by your dog.'

His thighs, encased in long baggy shorts cut down from a discarded pair of his father's trousers to save clothing coupons, felt weak. Never had he been so close to such breathtaking beauty. He studied her face intensely, as if to treasure it. Involuntarily his eyes lowered to her neck, and slowly downwards. He caught his breath: her blouse was diaphanous. *He could see her bra! It stood out white against her tanned skin below.* Alan's knowledge of female anatomy was limited to surreptitious nocturnal porings over the coyly airbrushed artwork in the stained, tenth-hand copy of *Health and Efficiency* he had bought for sixpence off another boy. This lack of experience did not, however, lessen the impact of the vision before him; fortunately, the hedge was hiding him from the waist down. Caesar, who seemed intent on humiliating him, began humping the young lady's leg. His father always maintained that Caesar was a reincarnation of Casanova and threatened to have the vet do something to him. The girl pushed him down off her short skirt with some irritation, but the ice had been broken.

'My name is Bella,' she said, holding her hand out over the privet.

Alan looked down at his own grimy hand, wiped it on his shirt, and said, 'It's a bit dirty, I've been... cutting... the hedge.'

This inadequacy made him bite his lip. Her brown hand was smooth and cool in his. He had a sudden urge to raise it to his lips the way Clark Gable would have done, just to see what it felt like, to savour it, Bella's fingers, her soft palm... but he would never have dared.

'So I see,' she said, inexplicably.

'Sorry?'

'You're cutting the hedge, Alan.'

'You know my name!'

'Of course. It wasn't easy — mummy and daddy don't like me mixing with the neighbours I can't think why because I like people and I love chatting to boys but I never get the chance being at a girls' boarding school it's absolute misery but I liked you the moment I saw you.'

She seemed to have said all that without breathing, and he

listened entranced to her beautifully modulated voice, like Jessie Matthews's. As he was clearly not going to contribute to the conversation, she cast her eyes demurely downwards and went on: 'You looked... cute.'

'Cute?'

'Yes. You have a nice smile.'

This was the first time he had been made aware of the impression he made on a girl. He felt obliged to respond, but he wanted to tell the truth.

'I think you're...'

He scratched his leg.

'...Yes?'

Everything was going too fast. He blurted it out.

'I think you're beautiful.'

They looked at one another. Then Bella said 'Thank you' as though she was used to compliments. He was sweet, she thought, with his mop of sandy hair flopping into his blue eyes, freckles, and glistening chest. And a nice voice.

'I must go. It's my birthday today. I'm giving a party this afternoon.'

He wanted to ask how old she was, but simply wished her many happy returns.

She paused, then said: 'Would you like to come? It's terribly early, half-past two. Several of my friends have to leave early to get home miles away before the sirens go, so it's a garden party. You will come? Don't be late, I should never forgive you!'

She raised her eyebrows at him. 'He's hooked,' she thought, 'it will do Jamie Fortescue good to have some competition.'

'I'd love to...' Alan's brain was racing. *Crikey! A garden party! There really was a world where people had garden parties!*

'...only, you see, I've p... p...' (he had never stuttered before in his life) '...promised Caesar I'll take him to the country for his Saturday afternoon walk.'

Her expression changed. She compressed her lips to half their size, and narrowed her eyes.

'Please yourself.'

She tossed her head, her short dark curls bounced, and she walked towards the red gate posts. Alan stared after her hopelessly. His perceptions had suddenly changed. The slim tanned legs that were now going out of his life revealed a new function for legs. Not just for walking; their smooth firmness existed to be touched, stroked.

'I'll be there when I get back from the walk!' he called after her, but it was too late. She did not even look round. Caesar was hopefully wagging; he had heard *that word* again.

'You don't know the sacrifices I make for you, you spoilt spaniel, you cock-eyed springer.'

He stumped into the house, brandishing the shears.

At lunch, he broke the news.

'I've been invited to a party.'

Maddy was pleased for him. At forty (admitting to thirty-nine), more attractive than ever, she could still get excited by the thought of a party. She vaguely recalled that once upon a time in her distant youth there used to be tennis club parties, and socials... Ah, well... There was a war on.

'That's nice. When is it?'

'This afternoon.'

'Good heavens, that's short notice. Where?' she asked.

'You're taking Caesar out,' his father reminded him.

'Yes, I promised him. I'll go over the road afterwards.'

'Over the road?'

Alan examined his plate.

'Bella's having... giving... a birthday party.'

'Bella?'

'At The Firs. She lives there.'

'Oh! The Fire Station,' Bill chortled.

He ignored that. The old house could never again be an object of ridicule. 'She invited me while I was cutting the hedge. Caesar liked her.' He immediately wished he hadn't said that.

'She must be a good looker then,' Bill commented drily.

'You'll have to take a present. I'll try and find something suitable while you're out,' his mother offered. 'One of your Auntie Emily's Christmas presents, I've got a drawerful of them.'

He couldn't imagine taking one of those horrid green and purple scarves, or a box of those useless little lacy handkerchiefs, and resolved to lose them under a hedge on the way over. How could he get hold of a diamond bracelet or a pearl necklace by half-past two, he wondered? Cary Grant would have managed it.

When Alan set off with Caesar it was already after one and the sun was high. The windmill was their favourite place: in a large field, surrounded by hedgerows and ditches. Caesar always investigated interesting smells while Alan climbed the rickety stairs inside. Each time he went there, another stair or floorboard had rotted away, but once up he could see for miles, to the hills in the

45

west, the smoky town to the north, and suburbia swallowing the countryside.

That afternoon he felt the meadow had prepared itself to be perfect. He leaned on the old five-barred gate, at peace with the world, as if in some little rural Shangri-la untouched by the carnage and terror threatening it.

'In fifty years time,' he said to himself, 'when you've been round the world and seen everything, come back up here and ask yourself if anything was as perfect as this.'

If the world had come to an end there, he would have been content. The waving grass, the rustling oaks, the fluffy inoffensive clouds, all conspired to create this hazy, lazy, expectant midsummer atmosphere. The old mill, like a feudal lord, protective but stern, surveyed the fields.

Gradually Alan became aware of another presence. When everything seemed perfection, this came to crown it: far above them, a lark was singing. Its music became transformed in his mind; flute, violin, piano, oboe, took up the melody and played with it. He joined in, whistling, and the lark seemed to respond. But this was just his fantasy. Wasn't it?... So engrossed was he that he failed to notice another sound in the sky, a lower, menacing rumbling, humming, sound. Maybe, also, he had become so accustomed to the thrum of heavily-laden bombers every night that a lone Dornier on a bright afternoon didn't impinge on his inner warning system fast enough. Caesar, however, did react in a manner appropriate to his species. He interrupted his sniffing and fixed his brown eyes on the shadow running across the field, slightly ahead of the plane. His hunting instinct roused, he dashed off after the shadow, barking joyfully. When Alan saw the swastika and black crosses just above him he froze. This was the closest he had been to the enemy. Paralysis swiftly turned to anger as he heard the rat-a-tat of the machine-gun in the nose and saw bits of turf fly up behind Caesar. They were shooting at his dog!

'Caesar! Come back! Heel! Come back!' His shouts could barely be heard over the noise of the engines, no more than two hundred feet above their heads. Now panic-stricken, Alan began to chase after his beloved friend, stumbling along, tripping over tufts, his voice shrill, screaming obscenities at the Dornier he had never uttered before. Then suddenly Caesar stopped, yelped, and rolled over on to his side. The bomber was now way in front, banking left, trying to climb fast. A few seconds later a cloud of smoke rose in the air, followed by an explosion. It had fouled a barrage-balloon cable.

'Serves them bloody well right,' he whispered as he sank down beside the inert Caesar. He guessed it had been the front gunner's desperate attempt to inflict some damage on the *Englische Schweinhunde*. 'I'll pay you back for this!' Alan wept. 'One day I'll drop bloody great bombs on the lot of you!'

The skylark was still singing.

The party was swinging. Bella was ecstatic, surrounded by her friends, who had put themselves out to come, overcoming parental arguments about travel problems and the risk of getting caught in an air raid. Fallowfield Avenue had never known so many cars, disturbing the peaceful Saturday afternoon and leaving smart-looking noisy young people at the big house. There had been a momentary panic when the air raid siren started to wail, but the all-clear sounded immediately after, so order and party-spirit were quickly restored. It must have been a false alarm, some clown had pushed the wrong button.

The garden looked beautiful; Bella consoled herself that with its tall hedges you couldn't tell you were surrounded by those awful little boxes called semi-detacheds.

Bella was walking up the stone steps from the lawn to the french windows when the door bell rang.

'May, answer that, will you?'

The Other Woman complied, and looked down at an unkempt boy standing on the step: dirty face, stained shirt, uncombed gingery hair, and traces of... *blood?* Ah yes, one of the neighbours. She smiled primly.

'Yes?'

Alan had not foreseen that the door might not be opened by Bella herself.

'Yes?' the Dragon Woman repeated.

'Can I speak to Bella, please?'

'She's busy with her guests. Can I help you?'

To his relief, Bella came, looking at him crossly.

'It's all right, May. This is Alan. I invited him to the party, but he's late...'

May retreated, grumbling.

'You might have got cleaned up a bit,' said Bella. 'A garden party doesn't mean you do the gardening.'

An elegant young man with plastered hair like Clark Gable's sidled up behind her and encircled her waist.

'What's that, darling? A local yokel?'

Bella rounded on him.

'Shut up, Jamie. This is Alan, a new friend. He's just been... digging for Victory, and now he's going home to get changed for the party.'

Alan felt reassured. 'It's Caesar.'

'Who?'

'My dog.'

She raised her eyes skywards. What a bore with his silly dog, the smelly rude creature!

'He's been injured.'

'Oh. I mean, Oh dear. Run over?'

'No. Machine-gunned.'

Jamie snorted. 'Don't tell me the Germans have landed!'

A bespectacled girl with a brace on her teeth overheard Jamie's remark, and dashed into the garden, screaming:

'THE GERMANTH HAVE LANDED!'

Hubbub ensued, most of it excitement; but one girl, pale and anxious, ran to the door crying 'I want to go home. It's the invasion!'

Bella glared at Alan.

'Now look what you've done, ruined my party!'

'*I* didn't say the Germans had landed, your smarmy friend did. I said Caesar's been machine-gunned, and it's true!'

Bella then saw how stricken he was and, to her astonishment, began to feel sorry for him.

'Jamie, go and calm everybody down, say it was a mistake, put a record on.'

Reluctantly, he obeyed. She held out her hand, and Alan took it, soft and electric. He felt a shiver go right through him.

'Come in, Alan.'

She led him into a study lined with more books than he had ever seen outside a library. He spotted a couple of titles: *Mathematical Physics*, and *Theory of Relativity*. Bella closed the door.

'I'm sorry. I didn't realise you're so upset. What happened?'

He told her.

'It must have been a stray bomber. Caesar got a bullet in his leg. Luckily I was able to stop the bleeding by making my handkerchief into a pad and tying it with a piece of string. Dad's taken him to the vet. He says he'll be O.K. I mean, all right. That's why I'm such a mess. I just came as soon as I could and forgot to change.'

She put a hand on his shoulder.

'He was very brave,' Alan went on, 'as I was carrying him he licked my face as if to say thanks.'

Bella thought this overly sentimental, but when Alan burst into tears and sobbed she stroked his head as he leaned against her shoulder. Then he pulled himself together, ashamed.

'I'm sorry,' he sniffed, 'I couldn't help it.'

'It's all right, it's the shock, I expect. But you are soaking my blouse. Here...'

She pulled a dainty handkerchief from her sleeve, and dabbed his eyes, smiling. She leaned forward and kissed them, like a butterfly, very gently. Then her lips rested on his. He felt his hands go round her slim pliant waist. When the tip of her tongue lightly touched his lips, he trembled and wanted to pull away, but she held him. Time stopped. There was no more war, no more killing, the melody in his head soared to the clouds with a thousand violins.

At last, she stood back. They smiled at each other, but differently. A shadow had passed from him, and she had gathered it up with a gentleness she had not known was in her.

'Thank you, Bella.'

'Now,' she looked into his eyes, 'you must dash home, smarten up, and come back to tell me how Caesar is. It'll help take your mind off things. Meantime, I'll get rid of Jamie, who has become very boring. That will be a lark, won't it?'

By the time Alan returned, the party was almost over. Just a few stragglers who didn't have far to go, and only bits of food and drink left. He shook hands with Mrs. Cassell, who seemed very absent-minded and spoke with an odd accent, then Bella took him into another room. A grand piano stood in the bay window.

'This is the music room,' she said unnecessarily.

'Golly, a Steinway!'

'Oh, yes, of course. Do you play?'

'My mother says I mess about. Never on a Steinway though.'

'It's just the same as any other. Still only eighty-eight keys, I think. I've never counted.'

'Could I just see what it feels like?'

'Well, you can see what it sounds like.'

He sat down on the long piano stool, pushed back the lock of hair, and tentatively played a chord. So suave. Then an arpeggio. The old Murdoch never sounded like this. Without thinking he began a bit of Chopin he had never succeeded in playing before, and it came out perfectly, as if it had been waiting for the right instrument. Then his mind went into its usual dreamy state, and he found the presence of Bella receding as the keyboard responded to his touch. His fingers followed the sounds in his head as well as they could: curious chords in the bass that he simply could not sustain for as long as he wished, and a melody that would not stay in one key the way he knew it should. The richness of tone enthralled him.

As if coming out of a trance he heard applause behind him. Turning round, he was appalled to see not only Bella but a tall, good-looking man in his forties, sitting in large, soft armchairs.

'Alan, this is my father. Daddy, Alan, um...'

'Scott. How do you do, Mr. Cassell.' He had only seen his head and shoulders previously, through the car windscreen.

'It's *Doctor*, actually,' said Bella.

'It doesn't matter, Bella,' her father smiled, 'I don't mind dropping handles with a musician.'

Alan thought he was teasing him and began to blush.

'I'm sorry, I didn't know you were there, I was just...' His voice trailed away.

'You mustn't apologise, Alan,' said Dr. Cassell, 'so long as you tell me what you were playing. I didn't recognise it.'

'Oh, I was just messing about. Like Mum always says I do. Sorry.'

'You mean... you were improvising? Making it up?'

'Yes. I was improvising.' He knew what it meant, thank you.

Dr. Cassell stroked his chin, nodded, and smiled again. 'Very interesting. Thank you. I hope we meet again. Soon.'

Back home, Alan blundered blithely on to a patch of Maddy's unpredictable and widespread minefield of envies.

'...and they've got a Steinway, and they let me play it!' he enthused.

'Really?' Maddy pointed to the dish containing three fat British sausages, extracted with much difficulty from the butcher. 'Take those in, will you? And call dad, he's in the garden. So you won't be wanting to play our old Murdoch again, will you, after a Steinway? We might as well sell it.'

That night there was no raid. At eleven o'clock the next morning, Sunday, there was a knock at the front door. Alan was in the back garden comforting Caesar, who was being very brave on three paws.

Maddy was wrestling in the kitchen with half a pound of mince for dinner, thumbing through the *Wartime "Good Housekeeping" Cookery Book*. Ah! Mince with parsnips — no, Alan refused to eat parsnips. Minced meat Risotto — no, no rice, no tomatoes. Minced Meat Savoury: bread, parsley, ketchup, dripping, thyme. Possible. Only thirty minutes in the oven. Right!

Gran was upstairs having a lie down; so as the visitor knocked a second time Bill put down the paper and answered the door. He was surprised to find a tall, fair-haired, athletic-looking gentleman standing there. After a second he recognised him; as a Special it was his job to keep an eye on people, surreptitious like.

'I hope you'll excuse me,' said the visitor, 'I'm Henry Cassell, from The Firs, at the top of the avenue.'

'Yes, I know,' said Bill. 'Er... is there a problem?' He wondered if he should have his uniform on.

'No, not at all. It's about your son.'

'Oh. Oh? Come in, won't you?'

Bill showed him into the front room, which was always tidy, but smelled damp. There was not enough coal to keep two rooms heated. 'Not been a nuisance, has he?'

'No, of course not. He does play the piano, doesn't he?'

'Yes... well, he mainly messes about, my wife says. She's the real pianist round here.'

'Ah, really? Now that is interesting. The thing is, I'm having a couple of friends round this afternoon to listen to music, and I was wondering if Alan would care to come?'

'That's very nice of you. I suppose we'd better ask him. I'll go and get him.'

'Who's that?' enquired Maddy, lifting a steaming saucepan lid and letting loose the aroma of overcooked cabbage. Bill told her, and she rushed upstairs to take off her apron and tidy herself up a bit.

Bill replaced Alan on canine comfort duty, and Alan went into the front room. He found Dr. Cassell looking through the pile of sheet music on the piano.

'I was very sorry to hear about your dog, Alan. How is he?'

'He'll live, thanks. It was a lone Dornier. He crashed not far away.'

'You recognised it?'

'Oh yes, I'm going into the R.A.F. — if the war isn't over in four years time. I'm keener than ever now. Aircraft recognition is one of the things we'll have to know. I don't get it — why shoot a dog? Perhaps because he's a springer spaniel, not a dacksee or a rottenwheeler!'

'Or perhaps it was you he was really after. You were lucky.' He turned back to the music. 'Who plays the Grieg?' he asked.

Alan wasn't used to this kind of rapid conversational switch. 'Pardon? Oh, Mum. My mother. It's beyond me, I'm afraid.'

'Would you like to be able to play it?'

'Yes... Well, frankly, no. It doesn't interest me.'

'What does interest you? Apart from my daughter. I mean musically.'

Alan said nothing. For one thing he didn't know how to read the remark about his daughter: was her father disapproving? And as for musically...

'Nothing. I mean, nothing I've come across musically is like what I think music ought to be like. I... I can't explain it.'

'Do you listen much to music?'

'On the radio, yes. But it's mainly Bach and Mozart and Beethoven. Germans. Even if they weren't Germans I wouldn't like it. It's dull... Oh!' He gave up, unable to express the inexpressible.

'If you come this afternoon, you might hear something that will interest you,' said Dr. Cassell.

The door opened and Maddy came in. She had taken off her apron, clipped back her auburn hair and put on some lipstick.

Alan did the introductions pretty well. My mother... Dr. Cassell.

'How do you do, Dr. Cassell?' said Maddy, lowering her eyelids.

He noted that she didn't offer her hand, or say 'Pleased I'm sure' or 'Nice to meet you.' She was an attractive woman, he thought. A cut above her husband.

'My daughter asked me to invite your son over to listen to some music this afternoon,' he explained. 'As you are a musician, perhaps you would care to come too?'

Alan silently prayed she would say No.

'That's very kind of you, Mr.... Dr. Cassell,' she replied. 'But my mother is with us for the day and I'd better stay with her.'

Alan gave silent thanks.

Bill was on the *qui vive* as Alan showed Dr. Cassell to the front door, and joined him on the front path. He had been thinking hard about this Dr. Cassell's accent while tickling Caesar's tummy. Perfect, but too perfect.

'Excuse me asking, but you're not English, are you?'

Dr. Cassell looked at him and smiled. 'I know I'm rather a mystery round here. And these are suspicious times. My father was English, my mother Swiss. They went to live in Switzerland before I was born, so I was educated in Zurich, and have spent most of my working life here in England. But I returned to Switzerland for three years in 1935 for my daughter's sake. Unfortunately she contracted T.B. and had to get better in a sanatorium there.'

This intimate revelation made Bill feel very uncomfortable. 'I'm sorry. I didn't mean to pry. But as a Special Constable...'

Dr. Cassell shook his hand. 'Very commendable, Constable Scott. We all have to be careful in these terrible times. We shall expect Alan at three.'

Bill was thoughtful as he went back inside, with several questions on his mind. Why had a man like him, obviously well-off, who had lived in Switzerland, come to a place like Fallowfield Avenue when he could be living in a posh area like Solihull? If he was a doctor, where did he work? At a hospital? No one had ever seen any patients going to the house. Where was he educated — Zurich, did he say? Was that in Germany? Sounded German. And the girl with T.B. — was that infectious? Was it safe for Alan to go to the house?

Alan went to the kitchen when he had shown Bella's father out, to make sure parsnips were not on the menu, and picked up the *Wartime Cookery Book* his mother had been trying unsuccessfully to follow.

'Hey! Caesar! Listen to this!' he called. The dog limped obediently into the kitchen. 'This advertisement says Chappie is in short supply — that's because we're eating it, I expect — but they say here, *'Cheer up, old chap. Bark for the downfall of Hitler. Then, when peace comes, see that your master puts you on Chappie.'* How about that, eh? Worth getting shot for, wasn't it?'

It never even occurred to him that it was odd to find an advert for dog food in a cookery book.

His schoolfriend Edwin Morley lived in the new road, just behind the Scotts. His mother was in her kitchen when a bomb went through it. It didn't explode, but it carried her down with it. Only a cricket-ball's throw away, closer to the Scotts' air raid shelter than to their house. Somehow, Alan found the thought that she was down there in one piece was worse than if she had been blown to smithereens. As the bomb disposal squad couldn't work out if it was delayed action or just unexploded, they couldn't dig her up in case they set the bomb off.

No one thought to wonder about why the bomb had landed there, in an outer suburb miles away from the industrial area. No more bombs ever landed anywhere near, apart from a few incendiaries intended to light up a flight path for the raiders. No one linked it up with the daytime marauder that had flown low over the windmill. If a connection had been made, the new arrivals at The Firs would have been moved out as fast and mysteriously as they had moved in.

'A fat lot of good that bit o' tin and sandbags you call a shelter would've been if that had landed a hundred yards closer,' Beth-Ann grumbled. She always came to stay with them at weekends. 'I'm not going down into that hole any more. I'll die comfy in my own bed.'

Alan began to wonder what it would be like to be blown up. Did you feel anything as your arms and legs and head flew off in different directions? But he stopped worrying about it. No point, as Gran said. He just hoped that if Caesar went, he would too. When he listened to Gran talking of her own childhood back in historical times, when Queen Victoria was on the throne, he wondered if he would remember all this when he was old, if he lived. In fifty years time, say? In 1990. Would there still be a world then? Or would it have all been sent sky high, with nobody left to bury the dead? Who would there be to listen to his music? Only wild animals, and ants, and flies. And birds. The skylark certainly wouldn't need anyone else's music.

*

The next time he called on the Cassells after the garden party weekend, it was Bella herself who answered the door, and not the Dragon Woman. They shook hands formally and then laughed. He was glad to see there was no one else in the music room. He turned to face her.

'By the way, Bella, there's something I wanted to ask you...' he began.

'Yes, you may kiss me.' She was almost as tall as he was, but tilted her chin up slightly. From so close up he saw her soft dark velvety eyes were flecked.

He felt momentarily like a derailed train. 'Oh. Thanks. Good. I mean...'

Bella stopped his inept mumbling with her soft, slightly open lips, one hand resting lightly on his cheek. Fortunately, he thought, it was not the one growing the unsightly pimple. She released him and, to his surprise, took his hand and led him to an armchair, sitting him in it and perching on the arm.

'Well?' she asked, her head pertly on one side.

He just wanted to go on looking at her, but managed to splutter 'That was very... nice. Thank...'

She rolled her eyes, but not unkindly. 'I meant what did you want to ask?'

That kiss, to him electrifying and hair-raising, had evidently had less impact on her. Was he a disappointment, he wondered? Or did such things not affect girls the way they did boys? Perhaps she was just a little flirt, a coquette, notching him up as another conquest like Jamie? His ignorance about the realm of experience he was being introduced to became increasingly, worryingly clear to him. With an effort he wrenched his mind back on its track.

'Bella, you said you're at boarding school. Does that mean you're going away?'

She stood up and did a joyful little pirouette, her short summer skirt billowing out. 'I was, but we've just heard the school's been taken over by the army and so they're moving the girls to Wales. My parents didn't want us to be apart any more, so as they'd had to move from London, I've joined them here. I'm going to Bruton.'

She sat on the arm of his chair again, crossing her tanned legs in a way that revealed to him an awful lot of thigh. He tried to concentrate on the happy news. She was staying! Going to a local girls' grammar school. Bliss.

He said, 'I hope they don't change their minds now bombing has begun here. My parents are talking about evacuating me again, but I'd rather die. Especially now.'

'What do you mean, especially now?'

'Well...' *Careless talk, oh dear.* 'Now... Now I've met you.'

She jumped up. 'Good. That's all right then.'

He found something unnerving about her matter-of-factness, as though she had been expecting him to say that and took it for granted. Like being called beautiful. And kissing him like that. Once again he felt out of his depth with her. But when she turned her limpid dark eyes upon him, he forgot all that. 'Will you please play something for me?' she pleaded.

'Oh no, I'd rather not. There'll be other people in a minute.'

'No, they'll be late. Some hold-up on the road. Please, *please*,' she took his hand in hers, 'improvise something again for me.'

Irresistible, that. 'Well, I'll try, but it doesn't come to order, just like that, you know.'

'Yes, I know,' she said airily, 'like love, *cela ne se commande pas.*'

What, he wondered, could she know of love, this cajoling girl who treated him so casually? He took a couple of minutes to relax and settle down, then he began to forget her presence, where he was, everything except the lovely sounds coming as though from some mystical source and passing through his fingers. A simple sequence of notes led to more — complex developments, not contrived or academic, but mysterious, following unwritten and unpredictable patterns. Finally they ceased, and so he stopped.

Bella clapped enthusiastically and said 'Lovely!' just as the half-open door opened fully. In walked Dr. Cassell, followed by a short, rotund man with a pink face and a crown of straggly grey hair round his bald pate, who was introduced as Professor Frank Walker. Alan retreated to neutral ground and sat next to Bella, thinking he would now be hearing the music he had been promised. Instead, Dr. Cassell began to question him, and the other professor chap, whose name Alan hadn't heard properly, seemed to be taking a great interest in his answers.

'Alan, have you heard of a composer named Debussy?'

'Yes, I think so. I think Mum plays something by him, something to do with a golliwog.'

'*The Golliwog's Cake-walk.* Nothing else?'

'No.' What was this, some sort of exam?

'And what about Ravel? Maurice Ravel? Or Schoenberg?'

No to both.

'Good.' Dr. Cassell seemed to be pleased by his ignorance. 'Now I'd like to ask Professor Walker what his impression is.'

'His what? His impression of what?' Alan was now feeling very uncomfortable, like an animal being scrutinised in a cage.

The professor cleared his throat. 'Alan, you must be very puzzled by this, but I think you are really quite remarkable. Your music, I mean. I couldn't help hearing you when you were playing. I did enjoy it.'

Alan began to relax a bit. 'Thanks. But it's nothing I have to be proud about. It just happens.'

'And the music you play isn't like anything you've heard? As far as you know.'

'I might hear it in dreams sometimes. I dream I'm conducting a vast orchestra and choir, and they're playing this wonderful music that I've written. That's what I try to play, but it's nothing like it.'

'I know the feeling, Alan. It's very frustrating, isn't it?'

That was exactly the word. Frustrating.

The professor went over to the piano. 'You see, Alan, what I find quite surprising, to say the least, is the sophistication of your harmonies. You don't seem to like diatonic scales — do you know

56

what they are?'

Alan's brain dragged up something from his theory book. 'Um, they're the usual sort of scales, aren't they?'

'Yes, major and minor.' He played the obvious one in C. 'But your music is full of defective scales...'

'Oh.' Alan looked hurt.

'There's nothing pejorative in that, it just means scales like the whole-tone and pentatonic.' He played them, and Alan recognised them as the kind of note sequences he liked. 'Together with lots of unresolved chords of the seventh and ninth, complex harmonies rather than pedal points, and sonorities based on the second and fourth.' He illustrated each one as he spoke, and Alan was immediately at home with what he heard, even though the technical terminology was new to him.

He put up his hand. 'Excuse me, but how could I use all that when I've never heard any of those terms before?'

The professor laughed. 'There's a play written by a French dramatist called Molière about a man who calls in a professor — like me — to teach him how to use language properly, and he's surprised to find he's been speaking prose all his life without realising it. You've been doing all these complicated things without realising it, without ever having been taught how to do it. That's what is remarkable, you see?'

'Yes, I see.'

'Now, you said that you dream about conducting an orchestra, not about playing the piano. Is that right?'

Alan nodded, wondering where all this was leading to. Did he have an orchestra out in the garden so that he could make a fool of himself waving his arms about the way he did in the privacy of his room, to his records?

'I'm not surprised,' the professor went on. 'The richness of your harmonic palette and texture indicate you are striving to attain an *orchestral* effect.' He turned to Dr. Cassell. 'I think we could begin with...'

He said a word Alan didn't catch. Bella took Alan's hand and squeezed it. 'Isn't this wonderful?' she whispered. 'He thinks you're very clever.'

To his relief he didn't blush, just felt a warm glow. Dr. Cassell went over to a large radiogram with *two* loudspeakers and turned it on. There was a record already on the turntable. 'What do you think of this?' he asked.

The music seemed to come from two directions at once, with a richness of quality he had never heard before. As for the music itself... Alan closed his eyes and was transported. Far away in the heavens a flute played a swaying melody, while violins shimmered and below the cellos and double basses made a ground you could walk on. Then came voices, no words, just a chorus of gods or angels emitting pure sound, and the whole blended into glorious multicoloured harmonies. Then it stopped. He opened his eyes as Dr. Cassell lifted the pickup from the record.

'One day soon we shan't have our music broken into four-minute chunks,' he laughed. 'The Americans are working on it.'

While he turned the record over, the professor asked Alan, 'What did you think of that?'

Alan was too stunned to say. Finally he blurted out, 'It was like I'd written it myself. It was just so beautiful. Like a wonderful sunrise over the sea, with a million colours sparkling on the waves and the calm sky overhead going from dark blue to gold.'

The professor nodded, rummaged in his briefcase from which he pulled out a book, and murmured 'You're quite right. It was called 'Lever du jour', 'Daybreak'. Now have a look at this book.'

Alan glanced at the cover. It said,

MAURICE RAVEL
Daphnis et Chloë
Symphonie chorégraphique

There were more musical notes on each page than Alan would have believed possible.

'You've not seen an orchestral score before?' the professor asked.

Alan shook his head, fascinated by it. 'The music goes left to right, like piano music, and each line is for another instrument. Is that it?'

He looked at the abbreviations for the instruments running down the page. 'I suppose the highest are at the top — yes, it says 'Fl.', that's flute — and the double basses must be at the bottom but it says 'Cont...' something.'

'*Contrebasses*. French for double basses, yes.'

Alan ran his eye over several pages, trying to translate what he saw into sound. He began to hum without realising it.

The professor found the beginning of the third tableau and invited Alan to follow the same music with the score, right through to the end. He was astounded at the complexity of each strand that

58

went to make up the soundscape, and had difficulty in keeping up when the music became more animated. By the end he felt quite exhausted.

At five o'clock the Dragon-Woman brought in tea, glaring at Alan as though he shouldn't be there. Dr. Cassell said, 'I think you can see why I thought you would like Ravel, Alan. Most of the characteristics of your music the professor pointed out are true for Ravel too, and many of them for his predecessor Debussy. You'll love him too.'

Bella handed rounded tea, and biscuits that must have devoured most of somebody's ration.

'I once met Ravel,' said her father.

Alan choked on his biscuit. 'You *met* him?'

'Yes. It was very sad, actually. He was in a clinic in Switzerland, 1934 I think it was, and very ill. Bella was there too, a little girl getting over a quite serious illness. He was suffering from partial loss of memory and was finding it difficult to speak any more. We had a mutual friend, a French mathematician, who wrote to me and asked me to try and cheer him up. I'll never forget the anguish he went through when he told me, "I still have a mind full of musical ideas, but they vanish the moment I try to write them down." Then he broke into sobs, this cool, elegant, dignified, reserved man, and cried, "I still have so much music in my head. I have said nothing so far, nothing".'

No one broke the silence. The poignancy of that tragedy struck them all. Finally, the professor spoke up. 'You never told me that before, Henry.'

'I thought Alan would understand what it's like to have a head full of music and no way to record it for others to enjoy. Ravel at the end of his musical life, and Alan at the start of his. But Alan can still put things right, which Ravel couldn't.'

'What do you mean, put things right?' Alan asked. That old feeling of being got at was coming back.

'I mean that you won't move forward if you don't buckle to and learn the *craft* of music. Your mother is right if she says you're messing about. It's brilliant, but it's not getting anywhere. Am I wrong, Frank?'

'I'm afraid Dr. Cassell is right, Alan. You have a remarkable gift, but it's untamed. I don't mean it has to be curbed. Debussy and Ravel suffered terribly by being curbed by their stuffy old professors in Paris. Ravel was actually thrown out of the Conservatoire for failing his composition exams. But they both mastered the techniques of piano playing and composition completely, and had enormous respect for tradition and for great musicians of the past: Bach, Mozart, Rameau, Couperin, Schubert, Chopin. Then they were able to build their innovations on solid foundations.'

He delved into his briefcase again and hauled out another book. 'Look at note 3 on the page with the bookmark,' he said.

Alan read: 'Allow your son to assimilate instinctively the elements of music by perfecting the study of an instrument and by becoming acquainted with classical and modern works.'

'That's Ravel's advice to a mother who wrote to him,' said the professor. 'Now, I think it's time my star pupil had some fun.'

For a moment Alan, foolishly, thought he meant him, until the professor beckoned to Bella.

'Come on, my dear, Let's do the Saint-Saëns.'

With whoops of delight, they both sat at the keyboard and gave a rip-roaring rendering of *The Carnival of the Animals*. When he left, Alan was very subdued.

'You're very quiet,' said Bella as she saw him off.

'I feel an absolute fool,' he said. 'You never told me you could play like that. I'll never be as good as you. Why did that professor call you his star pupil?'

'Oh, he was just teasing me. I used to go to him for lessons.'

'Used to?'

'Till they were evacuated and we came down here.'

'Till who was? And why *down* here. I thought you lived down in London?'

'Anywhere else is always *down* from London. He teaches at the Royal Academy of Music. I won a scholarship there. Pure fluke. I think he likes little girls,' she added knowingly.

'That's nonsense. You're brilliant. And you're not little.'

She was about to say that's what she was implying, but spared his innocence; taking his hand she faced him and looked seriously into his eyes. 'Listen, Alan. Being able to play means nothing. It's fun, but idiots can do it pretty well. I can only play other people's music, I can't *create* anything. I wouldn't know how. But you can. You have a kind of... inner spark. Anyhow, we must play some duets soon. That will be fun.'

Alan didn't see why professors should have all the fun of playing with her *and* sitting close next to her.

He was unclear whether it was the traumatic effect of the machine-gun attack, or the emotional impact of Bella's kiss, or the musical revelation wrought by Professor Walker, but soon afterwards Alan began to be subject to a curious phenomenon that could only be described as synaesthetic, but it was not a transposition of sound to colour or vice versa. Rather, it consisted of the whole of reality, his total being and everything around him, for one frozen moment, expressing itself in the form of a block of sound. Then it would die away. These moments were sometimes audible manifestations of his emotions, which he immediately accepted as the sort of thing a musical person would experience. But — and this was more disturbing — they were sometimes premonitions. Warnings accompanied by an odd tingling at the back of his neck, that presaged either imminent danger or pleasure. He would be walking down a road and would be sure someone he knew was coming the other way — but it wasn't. However, that person would come along very soon after. On occasion this new faculty turned out to be useful, as he could employ avoidance tactics in advance. However, the sound just as often presaged something desirable, not to be spurned. It did not happen often.

A month passed and Maddy did not once have to tell him to get on with his practice. He finished Swinstead, tried some Debussy Preludes (without much success) and ploughed through a book on the theory of modern music, but was defeated by its mathematical turgidity. Dr. Cassell told him to read Cyril Scott's chapter on Debussy and Ravel in his *Music: its secret influence throughout the Ages*, which he lent him. Flipping through the pages, his eye almost immediately came to rest on Cyril Scott's statements about the disruptive character of modern jarring, discordant music and the need for future music to heal the wounded psyche of mankind. What he called 'the Dark Cycle', or 'the Age of Destruction' would, he prophesied, *end in 1944*. He looked at the publication date: 1933.

Some of the esoteric language was beyond him, but certain words and phrases fascinated him so much he wrote them down: *clairaudience* (he knew about clairvoyance as his grandmother had been interested in spiritualism), *Nature-music, spirits of the water and the clouds, the Higher Powers*, and *Devas*. The idea of bringing together musical harmony, the occult, and the history of the world was entirely novel to him, and yet it resonated in him in a way that set his mind racing. Somehow he felt it all *applied to him* and what he was trying to do. One effect of this intuition was to increase his sense of impotence, his sheer frustration, like a person bursting with ideas but deaf, dumb, and blind. He begged to have his Christmas present in cash weeks in advance, and bought records of

Daphnis and Chloë and, on Bella's recommendation, Debussy's *Prélude à l'Après-midi d'un Faune*, which he played over and over up in his room, following the scores he'd borrowed, until he knew every note and every instrument. Finally Maddy warned him the needle would go through to the other side. His obsession with music was beginning to perturb her, and finally, she tackled him about it.

'I want you to understand one thing, Alan,' she said, 'I don't mind paying for your piano lessons so long as you practice, and so long as you realise it's not to be taken too seriously. You can never make a living out of music.'

He was struck by the self-contradiction, and surprised by the ferocity in her voice. 'That's all right, Mum. If I'm not good enough, I won't try.'

Maddy shook her head angrily. 'You're not listening, Alan! You are not to even try. Music's all right for fun, to entertain your friends, but no artist's life is worth living. Not unless you're a Duke Ellington, or a Myra Hess, or a Cézanne, or a Laurence Olivier.'

'But,' he protested, 'how can you know unless you try? You can't learn to swim if you never get in the water.'

'Yes, Alan, but you don't throw yourself out of a window to find out if you can fly. Just look at your grandfather, and me. Both of us, good painters, good musicians, and look at what we've achieved. He died of disappointment, and I'm still painting on the dining room table and getting a couple of bob playing for dances.'

Alan still could not understand what had brought on this outburst, and said so.

'It's those people,' his mother replied, 'those Cassells. They're making you take it far too seriously. These records you're playing all the time, never a moment's peace. I don't know how you get any school work done.'

'But I work much better with music on,' he protested. 'I can concentrate really hard.'

'Well, so long as you treat it as background, just an interest.'

'Tell me about grandad,' he went on, anxious to change the subject. 'You never talk about him. He sounds a really interesting chap.'

Suddenly she hated herself and what she had just been doing to Alan, remembering the lengths her father had gone to in order to discourage her own musical aspirations. With bitterness she recalled the day she had come home with news that she could win a scholarship to go and study singing. 'But you can't sing,' he'd mocked, 'you always sing flat.'

'You must talk to Gran about him,' Maddy advised her wayward son.

The next weekend he went upstairs when she was resting.

'Can I talk to you, Gran?'

'Of course, love. We haven't had a chat for a while.'

'I want to ask you about Grandad. What he was like when he was young.'

She gazed up at the ceiling. 'Oh, he was very handsome, with a fine moustache and blue eyes. Swept me off me feet, he did.'

'But before that, what sort of a musician was he?'

'Musician? I'm not sure. I always thought of him as a painter. But he did play the violin. Played in an orchestra in Germany, he told me. I've still got some of his violin music, I think, although he never played it after we were married. Took up singing instead. Lovely baritone, he had. Sang Gilbert and Sullivan a treat.'

'What about that orchestra, Gran? Was it a symphony orchestra?'

'I've no idea,' she answered. 'That wouldn't have been my kind of music, you see. Maybe he gave it up because I couldn't appreciate it. I never thought of that. There might be something in the tin trunk.'

His ears pricked up. 'Tin trunk? What tin trunk?'

'Oh, a battered old thing, not very big, full of papers and books. I've haven't opened it since he died, in fact I think I've lost the key.'

'Could I have a look?'

'Yes, of course, love. It's under my bed. We'll ask your father to bring it over, shall we?'

There was something Alan wanted to know now, however, whatever interesting memorabilia the trunk might hold.

'Why wouldn't he let Mum go on with music?'

She looked at him sharply. 'Has your Mum been complaining about that?'

'No. She's doing the same to me. Trying to stop me taking music seriously.'

Gran's face suddenly became set. 'Well, maybe there's some sense in that, Alan love. Grandad stopped her because it was no life for a girl, being a musician, or a dancer, or on the stage. He'd seen it first hand, you see, he knew what the dangers were. It's different for a boy, but it's still no good to make any money at. Take my word for it. You could be just playing for beer money in pubs in forty years' time. That's no future for a lad.'

'But I don't want to play the piano, Gran. I want to compose music.'

'Compose? Oh, I wouldn't bother, love, there's far too much music in the world already. If you went on playing it non-stop I bet it would go for a thousand years. What would be the point of adding to it?'

Alan found this conversation profoundly depressing. Bill said he would bring the tin trunk back one day from Gran's bedroom over the shop, when he was feeling strong enough, but Maddy took him on one side and told him to let the boy forget about it.

Despite Gran's discouraging response to his musical aspirations, back in his room he went on listening avidly, but now through his cumbersome black earphones, to some of that music that had had the good fortune to be born already, warding off the universal silence of stars and space surrounding earth. But he was beginning to hear a voice — he had to look round, sure there was somebody there, behind him — intent on making him less certain now about the wisdom of wanting to add to more to the world's stock of music. What could possibly be the point? Other than not wanting to do anything else, that is.

Maddy, hearing no more Debussy or Ravel seeping through the door of his room, was pleased that he had taken her advice.

Together he and Bella braved the approaching Midlands winter of 1941 and went for long walks on Sunday afternoons. Caesar accompanied them, but Bella had no patience with his need to ferret out the smelly history of every blade of grass.

Alan sprang to his canine friend's defence. 'It's only his way of trying to make sense of the world.' But she was not impressed and marched ahead resolutely, so Alan had to force Caesar to abandon his inbuilt habits.

'I've heard that if a dog can't sniff he goes crackers,' Alan said.

'I think he's crackers already,' she replied, 'so you don't have to worry. You English, you're so soppy over your dogs.'

'That's great, coming from a Swiss,' he riposted, 'where would you be without St. Bernards? Still trying to dig yourselves out of snowdrifts.'

She wanted to go for walks on Saturdays, but he usually had muddy rugger matches to play, so it had to be Sundays. She declined to come and watch him play that silly English game (unfortunately he was not aware the French were as fanatical about *le rugby* as the English about soccer). All he could think of was, 'Well, it's understandable, I suppose, you don't have any flat ground for rugger pitches', and promised to give her a real thrill and take her to a cricket match when the next season started.

'Thank you,' she responded with a grimace, 'but I think I'd rather watch Wagner sung in German Swiss.'

Whenever he asked about her mother and May, she shrugged and said her mother's work kept her away a lot, and somebody had to look after the house and her. She was amused when Alan said he called her Dragon-Woman.

'I'll tell her, and then she'll breathe fire on you,' she teased.

'And what about your father? Does he work in a hospital?'

'A *hospital!* Good heavens, no!' Bella laughed. 'Whatever made you think that?'

'Because he's a doctor, of course,' Alan said, hurt by the ridicule implied by her reaction.

'Ah, I see. But there are dozens of other kinds of doctor, Alan, not just medical. Science, and philosophy, and literature — and music, too. Maybe you'll be a doctor of music one day.'

Slightly mollified by this encouragement, he asked, 'So, what's he do exactly?'

Bella gave one of her shrugs. 'I don't know, either exactly or vaguely. He is a physicist, but that could mean lots of things.'

Alan thought about school physics — Electricity and Magnetism, Heat Light and Sound, and calorimeters and virtual images, and Doppler effects, and incomprehensible equations scrawled all over the blackboard — and said he wondered how on earth anybody as interesting as Dr. Cassell could spend his life doing physics.

Bella surprised him by saying, 'Music is only physics, you know.'

'What?'

'Vibrations. In the air, on a string, down a tube, in our eardrums.'

'Oh?' He was annoyed by this sudden attack on the mystery of music as he understood it. 'Then why does it sound so marvellous, and make us full of joy or want to weep?'

Another shrug. 'Odd, isn't it? Something to do with the brain, I suppose.'

She went on to talk about places she had been to, Paris, Italy, the Mediterranean, and Brittany, magically exotic places Alan could barely picture.

'Would you like to see some of our French holiday photos?' she asked.

'Happy snaps? Yes please.'

Bella went off to find them, and came back empty-handed. 'Sorry, May says they've been sent away.'

'Sent away? What for?'

'I can't think who'd want pictures of me doing handstands or eating ice cream in places like Cavalaire and Cassis and boring old Normandy beaches,' she said.

She made him speak French with her, which he enjoyed, because at school they only did grammar, which he knew backwards, and never actually used the language.

'When the war's over, the first thing I'm going to do is go to France,' he said.

'We'll go there together,' she promised. And she kissed him again, as they sat side by side on the piano stool, fluttering her tongue against his lips. This time he didn't mind. In fact, he enjoyed it very much, and put his hand on her breast. It felt both firm and soft, and inexplicably exciting. Then May came in with tea and they pretended to be discussing the piece of music they weren't playing.

When the Dragon-Woman had gone out they sat on the sofa. It was while munching a biscuit that Alan dredged up enough courage to ask, 'Have you ever kissed a boy like that before?'

Bella flickered her eyelids and said, 'Pardon? I couldn't hear. You spat a bit of biscuit at me.'

'Oh, sorry.' He took a swig of tea. 'I said, have you ever kissed a boy like that before?'

'A boy like what?'

'I mean... Oh! You jolly well know what I mean! What about that chap at your party — Jamie?'

'Oh, he's just the brother of a girl at school.'

'That's not an answer.'

He could see she was getting restless, but that only served to arouse his curiosity further.

'Well,' said Bella, 'more tea? No? Mind if I do?'

'Well what?' he persisted.

'Well, one does.'

'Oh, "one does", does one?' he mimicked. 'You sound like royalty. "One does go to Paris for the summer, doesn't one?"'

'Airctually,' she riposted, 'one does not go to Paris for the summer. One leaves Paris and one goes to the Riviera.'

He could see clearly what she was doing. 'To get back to the point, did you kiss like that? Did he... touch you... there?'

She pouted and shook her head. 'Really, Alan darling, you are getting very boring. What on earth does it matter now? Anyway, that's my business. It was before your time. I don't ask you about other girls.'

'Because you don't care.'

'No, frankly, I don't. Anyway, your innocence is part of your charm. Other boys are only after one thing.'

'Oh? Are they?'

He judged it best not to ask what they were after, exactly. He knew they *talked* a lot about 'it', but here was a girl saying they *did* it.

Another puzzling thought struck him. 'I thought you were at a girls' school?'

'Oh lord, yes!' she sighed, 'you've no idea how *boring* girls can be. All they're interested in is soppy romance stories, and crushes on mistresses, and giggling behind their hands about boys, and clothes, and parties they've been to and who they met there and snogged with under the Steinway.'

Snogged seemed a curiously crude word, coming from Bella. So that's what she did?

'But with you,' she was going on, 'I can really talk about interesting things.'

He was far from flattered. 'Is that all you like about me — you can talk to me?'

'No, of course not, silly! I think you're intelligent, and fun to be with — and nice to kiss. There! Now are you satisfied?'

He was still troubled. He'd clearly been missing out on something here. 'But... if you've gone further... *snogging* with other boys, don't you want to do it with me?'

She called his bluff, batting those eyelids. 'Do what, Alan?'

Miserably he replied, 'I don't know. Touch your... your...'

'Breast? There?' She placed his hand on her bra. 'Yes, that's nice. You haven't told me why you like me.'

With his hand still there, he said, 'I don't like you, Bella.'

'Oh!' She took his hand away.

'I don't just like you. I love you.' It was the first time in his life he had uttered those words. Except, maybe, for 'I love you mummy' when he was very little. He felt exhilarated and at the same time scared, as if he had just jumped off a cliff with a parachute that might not open. A point of no return. He could not unsay it — but Bella's reaction made him wish he could, as she

67

looked at him almost fiercely.

'Now, that's a very serious word, Alan Scott. I'm not sure we should use that word. Everything is too... topsy-turvy. We can't be sure we'll still be in one piece tomorrow, or made to move somewhere else and never see one another again.' She took his hand and held it in hers, soft and warm. 'Let's not get too serious, Alan,' she said earnestly, but with kindness in her voice, 'it'll only spoil things. But I *do* like you, *really*. In fact, I'm very fond of you.'

It was apparent that Alan's sentimental education was going to make no further progress for the time being, but at least he had not been shown the door or — even worse — laughed at.

Alan spent most of that night in such a state of emotional turmoil that he began to wonder if he was ill. If this is what being in love is like, he thought as dawn broke, chaps ought to be warned. Where was the joy romantic poets wrote about? Then the truth struck him: this was not just love, but *unrequited* love. Until now, it had been a word he could spell and more or less define, but the experience of it was another kind of knowledge, and one he would rather not have. Like death.

*

Concentrated attacks on Birmingham began again in late 1941, and lasted for six months, seventy-three raids later. The longest was on the night of 11 December, when the unremitting thrum of loaded Heinkels, the whistle-crumph of bombs, the hiss-crackle of incendiaries, and the hollow bangs of the ack-ack guns went on non-stop for thirteen hours.

At dawn, the Scotts trailed back up the garden to the house, Caesar still not able to spring as a springer should. Bill came back from making a few calls at noon, an hour earlier than usual, white-faced. Alan had cycled late to school, and Maddy was trying to do something, anything, with two slices of corned beef and some boiled cabbage.

'You're back early,' she said.

'I tried to drive into the city,' he said, 'but the main road's cordoned off, so I took a few side streets, to go and see if your mum was all right.'

He paused. She tore off another cabbage leaf to wash.

'Yes? Well? Go on.'

'It's chaos down there. There was a landmine.' He paused.

She could feel the fear rising inside her like black bile. 'A landmine. Yes?'

'It flattened thirty houses. The shop...' His voice broke. 'It's not there any more.'

In a whisper, she asked, 'And mum?'

He put his arm round her. 'She always said she wanted to go comfy in her own bed.'

Maddy said, 'Oh, no,' and Bill caught her as she slipped to the kitchen floor.

Landmines were the worst. Dropped by parachute, one of them could wipe out a street. The joists bearing the floor of the attic above the shop had fallen across her, crushing the rib-cage and breaking her neck, lumbar spinal cord, and legs. Death was instantaneous, the rescue squad assured Maddy when she went to Henly Street next morning. It was only because Bill was wearing his Special Constable's uniform that she was allowed to get anywhere near the tottering walls. Later, at the frantically busy undertaker's, she saw that fortunately, her mother's head was unscathed, so her last memory of her, lying in her coffin, was of her determined and vaguely amused expression, as if she knew she had died the way she wanted to die, and would move into the next world on her terms.

The funeral took place in the little Spiritualist chapel nearby, surrounded by débris and devastation. More than a hundred people turned up, all numbed with their own griefs.

The grim task of sifting through the stock and private belongings fell to Maddy and Bill. Emily went to the bomb site and quickly decided there was nothing there she wanted to lay claim to; just her portion of the proceeds of sale and insurance money, when Mr. Arkwright had worked it out.

Bill brought home one or two miraculously whole bits of furniture — including an old wind-up gramophone, which had been kept under the steep, dark staircase. On the lid was a picture of a half-draped woman and the word *Bellona* printed underneath. Inside the sturdy oak stand he found a few dusty gramophone records, ten and twelve inch 78s for the most part, but also two that required rotation at 80 rpm. Alan wondered who had decided the unlikely figure of 78 would be the international spinning norm? He cast his eye over the titles, without much hope since they were not HMV Red Label, but tried them out and found some that would make ideal accompaniments to fretsawing in the garage: music hall songs and ballads, *The Lost Chord, Let's put out the Lights and Go to Bed, O For the Wings of a Dove,* and *The Teddy Bears' Picnic.*

As he listened to them he found himself transported back six or seven years, to the sitting room behind the shop, crowded with furniture, where Gran, Grandad with his bushy moustache, Mum and Dad, spent evenings listening to these very records, which he could hear lying in bed upstairs, together with their muffled voices and laughter. Now it was all rubble. Gran was rubble. The world was being turned into rubble. Then he imagined Gran standing beside him, looking at him firmly with her fine dark eyes and telling him to pull his socks up and stop crying over spilt milk, so he put on *Let's put out the Lights and Go to Bed* again to cheer himself up.

'What does Bellona mean, Mum,' he asked.

'Oh, *I* don't know, Alan,' she replied, with acerbity born of grief. 'For goodness sake, look it up if you need to know.'

For some reason, he did need to know, and went straight up to find it in his encyclopaedia:

> BELLONA: *Name of the Roman goddess of war, sister of Mars. By extension, a tall fine-looking woman.*

His mother being rather unreceptive, he took the problem to his father.

'It's rather funny to name a gramophone after the goddess of war, isn't it, Dad?'

Bill had no views on the subject, but saw that the boy needed a response.

'Perhaps they liked the sound of the name, and didn't know who she was?' he suggested.

'Yes,' said Alan thoughtfully. 'It is... an interesting name.'

Another item surprisingly intact was Grandad's violin, which had been stored under the stairs ever since his death, unscathed in its stout wooden case. Alan took it out, tuned it, and scratched a few notes on it.

'Perhaps I should take up the violin,' he suggested, tongue in cheek. 'I could always get a job in an orchestra.'

'If you're going to play that,' Maddy warned him, 'you can do it down in the garage. Perhaps it'll scare the mice out of the Anderson.'

It was only then that Alan thought to ask about the tin trunk — but again it was his father he approached.

'The shop's just a pile of rubble, Alan,' Bill said, 'it must have been blown to bits.'

'But it was under her bed, Dad,' he persisted. 'That could have protected it.'

Bill went back the following day. Corpses and bits of bodies were still being dug out from under tons of bricks and timber. It was just one episode that would go towards the final assessment of Birmingham as the most heavily bombed British city outside London. But that became less impressive alongside the fact that more bombs fell on London than on the rest of the country.

In the pouring rain he clambered over the remains of the shop, ignoring an ARP warden's advice to keep away, as the shattered walls might collapse. It was the upper floor that had caught the blast, but the bed, with its brass bedstead, had gone through the floor. The mattress, since made sodden by rain, still bore traces of blood, and he hesitated to touch it. Bracing himself, he lifted it up, and saw the tin box, dented but unbroken.

He took it straight to the garage at the bottom of the garden, where he and Alan prised open the hasp with a screwdriver. Then Bill left Alan to it, which was just as well as he would have seen his son go into a kind of trance, standing in front of the box on the workbench with the screwdriver still in his hand. He would not have realised that Alan's head had suddenly filled with sound, a sonic complexity denoting something very important to his future.

The box had been fairly water-tight. In it were old letters, a lot of bills, and some brown photographs of formidable-looking men in high stiff collars and ladies in vast hats and veils over their faces. He would ask his mother about them, perhaps, one day, when she was talkable-to again. Most of the books were in German, which he put aside; but one, with a yellow paper cover, was in French: a novel entitled *L'Oeuvre* by somebody named Emile Zola This he placed in a cardboard box to take to his room.

Right at the bottom was another book, or what he took to be a book, bound in dark blue leather, with a lock on it. The hasp, however, was open, and Alan saw it was a diary, notebook, and sketchbook all in one. On the inside cover, neat copperplate writing announced 'Joseph Rogers, Artist and Musician Extraordinary, January 1892.' Page after page was filled with the same fine handwriting, interspersed with drawings, sometimes in pencil, sometimes in pen and black ink, mainly of faces and figures of beautiful girls not wearing anything at all. Alan spent a long time looking at sinuous curves of breasts, waists and hips, his attention particularly drawn to finely detailed triangles of hair which barely veiled the mysteries of the female sex. Had Grandad really seen

71

French girls like this, opening their legs like that while artists drew them? He began to see advantages to an artist's life that were denied to musicians.

Some pages were headed by a place and date: 'Berlin, August, 1892', 'Rome, November, 1892', and finally, 'Paris, February, 1893'. Alan tucked the book under his jacket and crept up to his room with it.

The main problem reading it was the use of abbreviations. Some he could decipher quite easily:

'Vis. the new Tour Eiff. Magnif. views.'

'Took Mitzi to Le Procope. Oldest Café in wld, they say, 1686.'

Was Mitzi the girl with the impressive bosom on the previous page, Alan wondered? He read on.

'Went to 89 rue de Rome. Inv'd to one of Mallarmé's Tuesday reunions by little Henry T-Lautrec. Met there a moody, black-bearded composer, frizzy hair, about my age, Italian-looking but French name, Claude de Bussy.'

Alan's head began to thump, and his breathing became faster, as he suddenly realised what it was he was reading. His eyes focused again on the calligraphic writing.

'He played for us some of his strange music, piano score of his latest piece, a new orch'l prelude about a faun and some nymphs. Never heard anything like it, so sensuous — langour and fury — but such clarity! So diff't from what I've been hearing in Germany. All tunes and big noise there — too many Strausses, from jolly Johann to deathly Richard. But this prelude was like *listening to a painting* and getting lost in it. C de B is still controversial but the company at rue de Rome loved it. Where would you find such a group in England, poets, painters, musicians? I want to spend my life here in Paris!'

Alan looked up, hardly daring to breathe. His own grandfather had actually heard Debussy play! Not only that, but he had been bowled over by the very piece that would have such a tremendous effect upon his grandson on first hearing it fifty years later. Had his mother known anything about this? If so, why had she never said anything? And why didn't he go on living in Paris? He did a bit of mental arithmetic and worked out that he must have got married to Gran, in rotten old Birmingham, only a few years afterwards.

The next page gave him some answers.

'Rec'd terrible news from Arkwright...'

Arkwright! That was the name of the solicitor Mum had been dealing with over Gran's affairs!

'...His letter had been following me round from Berlin and Rome. A says I'm broke, that my credit has run out. I can't believe it. Something v. wrong somewhere. But I must leave tomorrow. I'll be back when I've straightened out this mistake.'

But apparently he did not go back to his beloved Paris. There was little else in the notebook-diary. Just a cryptic entry a couple of pages further on:

'Cannot believe I have been so stupid. Trusted Haraucourt with my letters of credit. If I had a gun I'd shoot Gaston. Must find work.'

And that was it. Lots more blank pages, but no more outpourings, no more sketches of lovely girls. Just an empty life as a lithographer in Birmingham, presumably. Except that he did marry Gran, and have Mum, and she had him. Did that make it all worth while? Was he supposed in some way to make up for two failed generations? He could hardly imagine it ever being possible. Could it be that failure was built into the family heritage?

He decided not to say anything about the diary and the book for the time being. They were his secret link with his grandfather, and it gave him a strange sense of personal reality which he had never felt before. Above all, he wanted to keep those delicious drawings all to himself, to pore over as he lay in bed. These were not *any* girls; they were girls his grandfather had lovingly caressed with his eyes to re-create them for him. There was a link between them. He even felt sad that they would now be old women in their sixties, maybe dead, and that he would never see them himself to tell them how beautiful they were.

He was devastated by his Gran's death, and had nightmares for weeks. It was not just the shock of her not being with them any more, it was the horrendous way he imagined her dying. His parents thought they were sparing him by not saying exactly how she died, so he visualised much worse, seeing her not having a body, dismembered even before she was dead. Maybe the bleeding pieces of her could still feel as they flew through the air, like a chicken running around after having its neck chopped. No death by gentle stages, first the loss of consciousness, the last sigh of relief that liberation was nigh, then the whole physical being lying there still, but as if in sleep; then the final putting to bed in the lined wooden box not unlike a crib, and finally the letting go of the carbon-based envelope, either into the ground or into ashes.

The suddenness had caught him out; he had always expected to be able to spend hours with her when she came to live next door, listening to her talking about the ancient world of her childhood and youth, asking her opinion about things. At least he had had one heart-to-heart with her, and even though she had not said the things he wanted to hear about his musical aspirations, at least she had listened to him quietly and had treated him like an adult.

He lay on his bed, remembering the days when she had been the one he used to run to when he was little with a hurt finger or scraped knee; she had always had comforting words when another child had been nasty to him or stole a toy. It was she who had wisely told him that every boy should have two things in his pocket, just in case: a penknife and a piece of string. Now he bitterly regretted all the time he could have spent with her at weekends, when he had gone off with Bella. Nothing could bring that back. The one wise person he could have shared things with was no more. His parents were too distraught and preoccupied to pay attention to his grief; Bella did her best to comfort him, but even she began to tire of his moroseness.

Bill decided that it would be good for them all to get away for Christmas, which came just a couple of weeks after the funeral. Since Hereford was part of his territory he could justify their going by car in order to stay with Reg and Emily. Then Bill could make calls on shops in the surrounding area for a week or so, and try to get some much-needed orders for jam. Alan thought this was about the worst idea he had ever heard, and voiced strong protests which fell on deaf ears. Maddy was so upset and depressed that a change of scene away from sirens and bombs would help, even though she and her sister could tolerate each other for only a few days without starting to argue. 'At least she's a link to Mom,' she reasoned.

Alan was so distressed by the prospect of being separated from Bella that he completely forgot he had invited a chap from school, Keith Maxted, to come round on Boxing Day, to compare notes on balsawood modelling. Keith was into ships, Alan made aeroplanes.

Overnight there had been about an inch of snow which now lay crisply on roads, pavements and gardens, reducing them all to muted blandness. At 10 a.m. young Keith Maxted paused outside number 27. There was something strange, he thought, then saw why: no footprints in the snow either on the path or the front step, and yet Alan had told him it was always his job to take his dog for a short bladder-relieving walk every morning. He knocked a couple of times and got no response. Just as he was raising the brass

74

knocker again a voice came from the garden gate.

'They're not in, you know. They've gone away for Christmas. For about a week.'

Keith turned and observed his informant. A staggeringly beautiful girl with long dark hair, a distinctly kissable mouth, and a sort of Mediterranean look about her complexion. He walked back towards the gate, and she did not take her eyes off his, which he found both unnerving and exciting.

'You must be Bella,' he guessed.

That made her blink with surprise. 'Yes. That's right.' Swiftly she regained her poise, held out her hand, and introduced herself. 'I'm Bella Cassell. And you are...?'

'Keith. Maxted. Alan invited me round this morning, but...'

'...but he must have forgotten to disinvite you. Typical Alan. Rather a dreamer, isn't he? And he was rather upset about being dragged away suddenly to stay with some horrid relatives. The Scotts have been having a difficult time, you know? Alan's grandmother has just been killed.'

Keith shook his head. 'No, I didn't know. We don't know one another well. But he did tell me about you. He wasn't wrong, either.'

Bella was tempted to ask what he wasn't wrong about, but decided it was a flatterer's strategic trap. Then just as quickly she became intrigued: what had Alan said about her?

'Against my better judgment,' she said, looking ahead through the misty morning air, 'I'll ask the obvious question: what wasn't he wrong about?'

They were by now walking slowly up the avenue. Up — not back, the way Keith had come.

Keith seemed on the point of answering her question, then balked, either out of shyness or to keep an advantage. 'I'm sorry,' he smiled, 'I shouldn't have mentioned it. It was said in confidence, after all. Perhaps when I know you better...'

Bella affected not to notice the presumption. It was not impossible that they could become better acquainted. She glanced sideways at him: a nice boy, obviously well brought up, very good looking in a robust way, muscular rather than fat, with wavy hair as dark as her own. And a definite animal-like attraction about him which stirred Bella in a way Alan never had. They quickly established that they were both doing School Certificate Advanced Maths, Chemistry and Biology, which was a surprise to Keith who had not come across a girl scientist before. Any feelings of male superiority were quickly dispelled, however, when Bella revealed nonchalantly not only that she had a far surer grasp of mathematical and chemical concepts than he, but was also doing physics — and loving it — whereas he was finding it tough going.

They arrived at the red gateway to The Fire... The Firs. 'This is where I live,' said Bella. She bit her lip, not knowing what to say next. Keith adroitly said nothing, just went on looking at her, smiling in a way she could not help finding attractive. They gazed into each other's eyes, seeking some clue as to what the next move should be.

'I'd like to ask you in,' Bella finally said, 'but we have to go out shortly, to some boring Boxing Day party.'

Keith regarded this as a sufficient encouragement. 'I'd very much like to meet you again,' he said. 'No strings attached. Just to talk about scientific things.' The expression on his face made it clear that science was not his foremost preoccupation at that moment.

'Hmmm... I'm not sure about that,' she demurred. Then: 'Look, I'm very, very fond of Alan, but it's not as if we're engaged or anything, is it? And he has left me high and dry for Christmas and New Year. So...'

'So... How about coffee at the Kardomah in the city, tomorrow morning?'

Alan would never have thought of inviting her out to coffee in the city, it was far too sophisticated for him. She accepted without hesitation.

It was in the quieter upstairs room of the Kardomah Café in New Street that Keith made the suggestion. 'I've been invited to a New Year's party,' he said, 'and I can take a friend. Would you like to come?'

Bella's first reaction was enthusiastic. Then realism set in. A sixteen-year old daughter in a protective family was still very dependent, especially in dangerous times. 'Oh, but I'm not allowed out at night, because of the air raids.

'That's all right,' Keith reassured her, 'most of us have the same problem, so it's in the afternoon. It's not far away, so I can collect you and we can walk. Or cycle?'

It was a Wednesday afternoon, but all the young people at the party were still on school holiday. The winter's day was short, and by five o'clock it was dark enough for them to play Sardines, which was an excuse to pair off in quiet corners. Keith led Bella to an upstairs bedroom and shut the door. As there was a key in the lock, he turned it.

'What are you doing?' Bella asked, but without a trace of alarm. This brought back memories of Jamie.

'I'm going to have my way with you, then ride off into the night on my white charger!' Keith joked. But she sensed it was only half in jest. 'Come on, let's lie down, at least, while we can.'

Bella wanted both to resist and to comply as he took her by the hand towards the bed. It would all depend on how Keith behaved now.

'Bella,' he said, very seriously this time, 'if you say Stop, I shall. Promise.'

They both removed their shoes and lay down, he with one arm under her head, the other hand resting lightly on her stomach. Then he kissed her gently, and her lips parted as if they had a will of their own. When his tongue touched hers, she felt resistance reaching a low point, and did not object when he moved his hand up to her breasts, or down between her thighs. His fingers were soft as they edged in under her panties, and she knew she was already embarrassingly wet. She hoped he wouldn't mind that. Then she ceased thinking at all as he found her clitoris and gently massaged it. When it came, very soon after, she thought she had never experienced a climax like that by herself.

He lay back, still looking at her face. 'Did you enjoy that?' he asked, almost anxiously.

'Isn't that obvious?' Bella whispered. 'I hope I didn't make too much noise? But how about you?'

She meant, Did you enjoy doing that to me, but he took it another way, guiding her hand down to his flies, which were somehow undone. She knew what to do, but wanted to inspect the male equipment more carefully than she had done with Jamie. With fascination, she examined his penis, stiff and proud, longer and thicker than Jamie's, then extricated his scrotum from his underpants in a matter-of-fact way and marvelled at the size and weight of them.

'It's all very big, isn't it?' she murmured, 'I don't know how my vagina would ever manage one like that. And that,' she added firmly, 'is not an invitation!'

Even though he found her clinical approach deflating, he soon recovered. It took very little time. He had his handkerchief ready.

Afterwards, Bella wished to make it perfectly, absolutely clear that this must never happen again, and they must never let Alan know. Keith gave his solemn promise, but knew he would regret it.

'You really love him, don't you, Bella?' he asked as they put on their shoes and smoothed the bed.

'Love? Oh, I don't know if I'm capable of love,' Bella mused. 'But I'm fond of him in a very special way, and I *am* sure that I must never do anything to hurt him. Even more so now, after... after this. It isn't guilt. I really enjoyed it and I'm glad we did it, but I know now there are more important things, and we have them, Alan and I.'

*

The effect on Maddy of her mother's death was two-fold. She started to smoke, which she had never done before, having been brought up to believe that only fast women did that. And — after several weeks of depression that effectively isolated her from the pain Alan was going through — she found herself in the throes of a strange urge to do something positive about this damned war. She and Dolly Wise got their heads together, recruited a few other people with musical and thespian interests, and formed the 'Four C's Concert Party', Four C's being a brilliantly clever play on Forces, to whom they would donate all the proceeds from takings. A church hall was more or less commandeered. The new vicar, who had been invalided out of the army minus one arm, was defenceless before the combined power of these two unstoppable women; 'My Boadiceas of the Arts', he dubbed them.

Alan persuaded Bella, without much difficulty, to play some Chopin and Grieg, but nothing German, he begged. On the way home after, Maddy said she was very impressed, then delivered the backhander.

'She looked quite pretty up there on the stage. Amazing what make-up will do.'

Bill tut-tutted and said, 'For Heaven's sake, Maddy, give over.'

But she couldn't let it go. 'She studied at the Royal Academy, you say? Well, some people do have all the luck. I don't suppose you'll be wanting to listen to me now, will you?'

Alan tried to reassure her, but she continued to go at him for spending so much time with 'that girl'. In vain — in fact, counterproductively — did he point out how much Bella was helping him, with his music and his French, which she spoke fluently.

It was soon after that that the rumours began. There was a spy, a fifth columnist, living somewhere in the avenue. Maddy brought it out into the open one Sunday morning, just as Alan was going up to see Bella.

'I hear your friends' name isn't Cassell with a C, but Kassell with a K? A German name.'

'No, you're wrong, Mum, it's a C and it's Swiss.'

'That's as may be. But what does he do, exactly? Running around in that big car. Must be getting paid a lot of money by *somebody*.'

'Don't be silly, Mum.'

'Silly, am I? Don't you talk to me like that. You go up to your room this minute, and stay there!'

'No I won't! I'm going to see Bella. We have some work to do.'

Bill heard the shouting and came in from the garden.

'The boy's going mad over that girl,' Maddy exclaimed. 'He's disobeyed me and he won't go to his room.'

'She called Bella's father a spy,' Alan cried, 'and it's not true!'

'Now, hang on a minute,' Bill said quietly. 'For one thing, there's not going to be any gossip-mongering and rumour-spreading in this house. If there was any doubts about Dr. Cassell, I'd have heard about it.'

'Oh, in the secret service now, are you?' Maddy sneered. 'Well, we'll soon have the war won.'

'And as for wasting his time,' Bill pursued, 'have you forgotten his last term's report?'

All his teachers had been astounded by the improvement in Alan's results in all subjects including mathematics and physics, which had hitherto seemed beyond him.

Maddy was reduced to silence. There was no Sunday dinner. Instead, she put on her best coat and went out, slamming the door behind her. In the late afternoon she returned, and nothing more was said about Alan's disruptive but productive love life.

However, the gods of love and war, Eros, Aphrodite, Mars and Bellona, had not finished playing with these two young people. Alan's increasing emotional dependence on Bella had gone far beyond an adolescent crush, and this made him all the more vulnerable in a war-torn world where individuals had even less control over their lives than usual.

Alan's friendship with his pals Tom and Gordon had not ceased because of Bella, but he decided to keep them as separate parts of his life. They were hardly compatible. It was with them that he could share fantasies about spies in their midst, as their families thrived on tittle-tattle in the pub and shopping queues, whilst Bill would not tolerate it. Both the other boys were convinced the rumour going the rounds about Dr. Cassell being a German spy had some foundation, and were as suspicious about the mysterious man as Maddy had been. Alan felt he couldn't be too defensive about it or dismiss it too vehemently without losing their friendship, but when the other two told him about their plan to put him under surveillance, 'keep a close eye on him', he was really put on the spot — especially when they made him swear he would say nothing to 'his girl friend'. All he could do was refuse to have anything to do with it: no, he wouldn't search Dr. Cassell's desk; no, he wouldn't get a list of books in his study; no, he wouldn't quiz him — or Bella — about his work or where he came from.

At was about half past ten a few nights later, when the sirens hadn't wailed for once, that an imperious knock sounded on the Scotts' front door. Bill put out the hall light, opened the door, and in the dim light of his torch recognised one of his fellow Specials from down at the station.

'Hello Ian! What's up? Come in.'

Special Constable Ian Bailey pushed a couple of smallish figures in before him. 'D'you know these two, Bill?'

Bill did. 'Yes, of course, young Tom O'Reilly and Gordon Wiggins. What have they been up to, eh?'

'Breaking and entering.'

Alan came down the stairs from his room.

'What's going on? Oh, hello Tom. Hello Gordon.'

They glared at him.

'These two young varmints reckon they were tracking down a spy, and your Alan knew what they were doing.'

Bill turned. 'Alan?'

Alan realised the only thing was to tell the truth. 'They told me they thought Dr. Cassell was a spy. I said it was nonsense, and that's all I know. What have they done?'

'You must have given us away!' Tom muttered.

'No I didn't, simply because you didn't tell me what you were going to do, whatever it was.'

The constable spoke to Bill. 'They got in from the bottom of the garden, over the fields, and activated one of the trip wires by the house. One of them was trying to force a window. Dr. Cassell's housekeeper apprehended them and telephoned the station. Strong woman, that. I'll have to report this, I'm afraid. It's a security matter, as you can guess. I reckon they didn't know what they were doing. But they're trying to implicate your boy, saying he knew all about it.'

'Well, he certainly never told me,' said Bill. 'Do you want us to report now?'

'No, tomorrow morning will do. I don't think anyone is going to escape from England at the moment!'

The following morning Ian Bailey came round again on his way home off duty, to tell them they should not report to the police station; someone would come round that evening after a few other enquiries had been made. When Maddy heard what had been going on, she said, 'There! I told you those Cassells were trouble. But would you listen to me?'

They expected it would be the sergeant who would come round, but at six o'clock Bill opened the door to a man in a mackintosh and trilby hat whom he'd never seen before. He introduced himself as Detective Inspector Garland.

'Inspector?' said Bill. That seemed a bit high-powered for a couple of kids larking about.

'It would be best if your son and your wife could be in on this as well,' said the inspector.

Mystified, they all trooped into the front room.

'Would you like a cup of tea, Inspector?' Maddy offered.

Mr Garland declined politely, and took out a notebook filled with pages of scribble.

'Now,' he began, 'I'm sure this all seems unnecessary to you, but these are strange and troubled times. On the face of it, what we have is a couple of young lads doing their bit trying to catch a suspected spy. Very good, very patriotic. But the government has become aware of the dangers of rumour and gossip that lead to dissension and defeatism.'

He looked up at Maddy, who was staring at the carpet.

The inspector went on: 'They can tear communities apart if we're not careful, when everyone's nerves are being stretched. There have been a few cases of people taking the law into their own hands and victimising innocent people, especially immigrants who have come here to get away from Hitler. Rumours can also work against our war effort.'

The inspector looked down at his notebook, flipped a page, and then looked up at Alan.

'Alan, you know Tom O'Reilly and Gordon Wiggins quite well, don't you?'

'Yes, sir. We've played together for years.'

'But you've been seeing less of them lately?'

81

Alan frowned. He didn't want to try and distance himself from them just because they'd been stupid. 'A bit, yes. We're not interested in the same things so much.'

'Quite. Your interests are much more in line with a new friend's.'

'Bella? Miss Cassell. Yes, we talk a lot about music and our school work.'

'And what about her father? Do you talk much about him?'

Again, Alan wondered what he was getting at, but felt he had no alternative to telling the simple truth. 'We don't talk *about* him. He sometimes talks *to* me, about music, and maths and science I don't understand, for instance. He's very good at that. Better than the teachers, because he's very patient.'

Maddy was looking increasingly unhappy about this line of questioning, and butted in: 'Inspector, what's all this got to do with national security?'

Bill signalled to her to keep quiet, and she gave him an 'I'll speak to you later' look.

'Now, Alan,' Garland went on, looking at him hard, 'listen carefully: did you make a friend of Bella Cassell in order to find out more about her father?'

Alan's mouth fell open. He was speechless. Turned bright pink. Shut his eyes.

'That's... that's a terrible thing to say. No, of course not!'

'Because,' the inspector continued coolly, 'that's what your friends Tom and Gordon say you did.'

This betrayal was beyond belief. 'They said *that?*'

'Yes. And why did they say that, you're wondering?'

'I certainly am!' Alan suddenly caught his breath. 'Oh!'

Garland put his head on one side and raised his eyebrows. 'Yes?'

'I've just remembered. Soon after I met Bella, I asked her where her father saw his patients.'

'His... patients?'

'I'd assumed that because he was called doctor, he must have patients. I must have looked an idiot, not knowing there are different sorts of doctors. Then she told me he's a physicist. I don't know how anybody makes a living out of things like electricity, and heat light and sound. Unless it's teaching. Maybe he's a teacher? But he seems too well off for a teacher.'

'Yes, Alan, they're underpaid, like policemen. You mean you still don't know what he does for a living?' the inspector asked.

82

Alan shook his head. 'If it's anything to do with physics, I wouldn't understand a word of it,' he said with patent honesty.

'And did you tell Tom and Gordon he's a physicist?'

Alan thought for a moment. Then he nodded. 'I remember Tom saying he must do something very hush-hush, and I said he didn't, he was a physicist. He had even less idea of what that was than me. So why would they tell a lie about me?'

'I'll tell you, Alan. Because they've got it into their silly young heads that you think they're not good enough for you now you have Bella. And what made them think of that to say about you?'

Alan shrugged. All this was totally beyond him.

'Because,' said the inspector, 'Tom's mother told them.' He suddenly turned to Maddy, taking her by surprise. 'You know Mrs. O'Reilly quite well, I believe, Mrs. Scott.'

'Oh, I see her in the shops and round about,' Maddy said. 'We've been neighbours for years.'

'Oh, a little more often than that, I think. You go and have a cup of tea together at Ann's Pantry about once a week, don't you?'

She and Bill were both startled to learn she had been under surveillance.

'Yes, we do. No law against that, is there?'

'None at all, but I'm surprised you didn't mention it, the way Alan volunteered the information about asking Bella. And do you and Mrs. O'Reilly talk about Dr. Cassell?'

'He's not a major topic of conversation. We may have mentioned him.'

'And your son's friendship with the Cassells? You resent that, don't you?'

Maddy turned to Bill. 'I don't have to answer questions like that, do I? What have our private affairs got to do with the police?'

Bill merely shrugged. 'I think we'd all best just tell the truth, like Alan.'

The inspector resumed. 'I'll help you, Mrs. Scott. Did you tell Mrs. O'Reilly you were afraid you were losing Alan to the Cassells?'

Maddy shifted uncomfortably in her seat. 'He spends more time with them than he does with us now. This house has become just a hotel for him.'

'That's not true, mum!' Alan exploded.

Garland held up his hand. 'Please! I'm not here to cause trouble between mother and son. There are far more serious things at stake. As you will find out in a moment,' he added ominously.

This warning had the required effect of silencing them.

'Mrs. Scott, did you or did you not tell Mrs. O'Reilly that Alan had found out some suspicious things about Dr. Cassell, and that he'd seen a letter addressed to him as Dr. Kassell with a K. And that he must be a German?'

It was now Maddy's turn to be speechless, but it was a different sort of speechlessness. Finally she admitted she had said that, not daring to look at Bill or Alan.

'I was only repeating what was rumoured,' she added.

'No, you weren't, you said Alan had seen the letter, and that he was worried about it. Correct?'

Reluctantly, miserably, she nodded. 'I just wanted to have him back,' she whispered. Then it all came out in a great flood of resentment and jealousy. 'What I couldn't stand was when that girl was asked to play solo at the concert, and all I got was accompanying. If I'd had the chances in life she's had, I'd be as good as she is. It isn't fair!' She burst into sobs, and Bill passed her a handkerchief.

But Inspector Garland had not finished with them yet. Still looking at Maddy, he asked, 'How well do you know Mr. O'Reilly?'

Blowing her nose, she replied, 'Hardly at all. I don't like him. He bullies his wife and kids abominably when he's drunk.'

Bill knew that Sean O'Reilly was always up before the beak for D and D. His plea was always that he had a terrible lot o' sufferin' to put up with since he lost his left hand workin' in a factory. Most of his energy had gone into following the priest's instructions to increase the Catholic population as much as possible. Tom was the eldest of five, with number six on the way.

'Has he, O'Reilly, shown any interest in your remarks about Dr. Cassell? Now,' he added, 'think carefully about this. It's important.'

Maddy reflected. 'As I said, he's hardly ever there, not conscious anyway. Now I think about it, he did make remarks like "How terrible," and "The man ought to be thrown out of the country." I thought he was being patriotic.'

'Hm,' said Garland, 'quite clever, for an Irishman. Did you ever ask him what happened to his hand?'

'No. His wife just said he was drunk while working a machine in a factory.'

'Would you like to hear the truth?' Garland asked. 'In fact, we have you to thank for drawing our attention to him, because of this unfortunate Cassell affair. We've been searching for Brendan O'Riordan, *alias* Sean O'Reilly, ever since that IRA bomb went off in Coventry in August 1939. Do you remember that?'

Bill and Maddy nodded. They remembered only too well that five people had been killed by a bomb left in a bicycle carrier in the Broadgate shopping area.

'Your friend O'Reilly lost his hand making bombs for that IRA campaign. Fortunately we had his fingerprints — of his right hand — on one of the unexploded bombs. When the police went round to his house last night with the kids, he was in a drunken stupor and panicked, pulled a gun on them so they took him in and... the rest is history. He'd been trying his best to destroy Dr. Cassell, whose work is, shall we say, very important. So he told his son to leave a parcel in Dr. Cassell's house, telling him it would just make a nasty smell when he opened it and scare him away.'

Alan gasped. 'What! They were going to blow him up?' Then he looked sheepishly at Bill; this was a bit worse than what he'd done, in wishful thought only, to Uncle Reg.

'O'Reilly was. Wiggins didn't know it was a bomb, and young O'Reilly may not have known.'

Alan put his hand over his mouth, then exclaimed, 'Bella might have opened it! She might have been blown to bloody bits too! Why is everyone blowing everything to pieces?'

He rushed out and reached the outside lavatory just in time to be violently sick. Maddy went to help him but he told her in a harsh tone she had never heard before to just go away.

When he returned, white-faced, the inspector stood up and buttoned his mackintosh. 'We'll do our best to make sure you don't have to testify in court,' he said. 'If you do, you may need special protection. So in your own interest, *keep your mouths shut* about this. Especially you, Mrs. Scott. No more rumours. As for you, Alan, Dr. Cassell will be told you had nothing to do with it, and that the boys' accusations against you are without foundation. So don't you mention it either, to anybody. Do you all understand?'

They did.

What they did not understand was that they had become involved in another war, which had been going on since January 1939. On the twelfth of that month the Irish Republican Army issued an ultimatum to the British government: get out of Ulster in four days or it's war. Scotland Yard reassured the Cabinet that the IRA had been pretty well wiped out, and were soon acutely embarrassed by their misjudgement. Most people were so relieved not to be at war with Germany that they paid little attention to the bombings that went on sporadically — Southwark power station, Willesden, Birmingham, Manchester, Alnwick, London

Underground stations, Coventry, Liverpool, the *News Chronicle* offices in Fleet Street, Hammersmith Bridge, Piccadilly Circus, Madame Tussaud's Waxworks, left luggage offices at Victoria and King's Cross. By chance a copy of the 'S-Plan' was discovered at the Harrow Weald home of a labourer, Michael O'Shea, in February. It revealed such a well thought-out, sophisticated military campaign for urban bombing, sabotage of Britain's defences, and paralysis of industry, that MI5 suspected it had been masterminded by the Abwehr. They knew that Jim O'Donovan, an important IRA activist based in Dublin, had visited Hamburg twice in recent months, to cement Abwehr/IRA relations. The IRA, like their Breton counterparts, foolishly believed the Germans would be sympathetic to their demands for independence when they had won the war.

O'Reilly had worked alongside Joseph Hewitt on the Coventry bomb that killed five and injured sixty on 25 August 1939, but despite his injury had managed to avoid being picked up in the house-to-house search of every Irish household in Coventry — because he lived in Birmingham, which was teeming with Irish workers. Maddy had been one of the neighbours who had taken food to help Mrs. O'Reilly feed her brood since her poor drunken sot of a husband had lost his hand 'at work'.

Hewitt had been executed in Birmingham for murder on 7 February 1940. Immediately the attacks were renewed — pillar boxes burst into flames, post offices were blown up, military depots raided.

As they lay awake in the shelter that night, with the bombs and the ack-ack thumping away outside, Maddy asked Bill, 'What will happen to the O'Reillys?'

'Who? Oh, you mean the O'Riordans. Well, you know what happened to Hewitt. O'Riordan made bombs to kill innocent people, Maddy. Like the Germans are doing to us. He was helping Jerry. You'd do better to worry about your son.'

She did worry about him, but he had refused to talk to her since the bitter words they'd had when the inspector left. Miserably she tried to explain: 'I only did it because I love you, Alan. I'd lost my mother and I thought I was losing my son too.'

The cold hardness in his eyes shocked her as he replied, 'Well, you've lost me now.'

She realised she had lost all moral credibility with him, all authority. 'Oh God!' she moaned, 'things couldn't be any worse. I wish we'd all been blown up and out of it.'

Bill was no help either. All he would say was, 'We don't possess our children. We have to earn them. And you'll have to win him back.'

Not far away, in the big house at the top of the avenue, Bella was studying in her bedroom, but finding concentration difficult. The drama of the night before had unsettled her considerably, not only because of the implied danger but because she felt there would be repercussions. She was about to discover how right she was.

Dr. Cassell knocked on her door and waited until she said 'Come in'.

Sitting on her bed, he looked at her seriously, his handsome face suddenly more lined with anxiety.

'*Chérie*,' he began, 'we have to leave.'

She nodded her head. 'I had a feeling...'

'I'm so sorry,' he said. 'Just when you are nicely settled at school and making friends again. Well... one friend in particular.' He smiled, and she went over to sit by him. He put his arm round her.

'Oh, papa, I feel like a little tree without any roots, being blown about by every wind. These people round us, our neighbours, they have their own homes that they stay in, year after year, and the children have mothers and fathers... You might have been killed, and I do miss *maman!*'

She burst into tears, and her father hugged her close.

'I know, *ma petite*, and so do I. But that is war, you see. Many of our neighbours have husbands and sons who are fighting, many were killed or made prisoner before Dunkirk, but at least we are alive.'

At least, he reflected silently, I hope we are.

'So,' he went on, gently stroking her hair, 'we must be brave for a bit longer. And you are making my shirt wet.'

Bella began to laugh. 'That's just what I said to Alan the first time he came here!' she said.

The following morning the telephone rang in the Scotts' house. It was a recent installation, used only by Bill. A lot of his business had to be done by phone, to save petrol; and he was sometimes called to the police station for emergency duty. But this time it was not for him.

'Alan,' he called upstairs, 'it's for you.'

'Me? Who is it?'

'Bella.'

She had bad news. 'We have to leave.'

'Leave?'

'For ever.'

Alan stood there with his mouth open.

'Alan? Are you still there?'

He gulped. 'Yes. When?'

'Tomorrow. Apparently it's not safe for us here, because of Daddy's work.'

'I'll come round and see you now.'

'No, you can't. You're not allowed to.'

'Oh! You don't trust me!'

'It's not that. Of course I do. But nobody is allowed into the house.'

'So... So come for a walk, so that we can talk.'

'No, I have to stay in. Oh, this is terrible.'

They were both in tears by now.

'Surely you can creep out for half an hour. I can meet you by the park.'

A pause. Then she said, 'All right. I'll try. But I can't promise. If I don't see you... I love you a lot, Alan. Go on writing music for me.'

He struggled into his coat and ran to the park, ignoring Maddy's question about where he was going. He also ignored the warning sound in his head, told it to Shut Up, in fact. It was ten o'clock on a chilly Sunday morning. Most people were either in church or having a late scraped-together breakfast after the night's bombing. He waited by the park gate for ten, fifteen, twenty minutes, his feet getting number and number, his breath steaming in front of him. Then he saw her, running towards him, without even a coat on, hugging herself to keep warm. He put his arms round her and held her close, and they kissed, a long warm kiss, one to remember for a long time. He felt her shiver.

'You'll freeze to death like that,' he said.

'I know. I didn't dare to stop to get a coat, May might have seen me.'

He took off his overcoat and put it round her shoulders. She protested, but he said 'I've got a blazer on too, I'll be all right.'

In the field opposite the park three gypsy caravans were huddled in a circle, with their dogs dozing on straw underneath and their horses grazing nearby. As they paused by the five-barred gate a girl who must have been about Bella's age came swinging towards them, a shawl around her thin shoulders and a scarf tied round her head pirate fashion. Her smile was friendly so they did not move

88

away. As soon as she was close enough she held out a grimy hand and said 'Cross my palm with silver and I'll tell you your fortune.'

Bella turned to move away, but Alan reluctantly put his hand in his pocket; Maddy never spurned a gypsy, for she was convinced they had the power to put a curse on you, and although he always laughed at her superstition he found he could not withstand it himself now he was confronted by it. He pulled a sixpence out.

'That's all I have,' he said apologetically.

Bella tut-tutted and muttered something about wasting money.

The gypsy girl took his hand in hers, which he found strangely sensuous despite the dirty finger nails, and peered at his palm, tracing the lines with her other forefinger. Then she looked sharply at Bella and said in a voice of such quiet confidence that she could not refuse, 'Show me yours too.' After studying them intently together for a minute or so, she said, 'You are to do a lot together but not for a long time.' Now holding their hands quite tightly but with her eyes shut, she stood silent, then let go of their hands, opened her eyes, and looked with something very like pity at Bella.

'You are in great danger,' she said, 'and you must go away.'

Then she turned her gaze on Alan, who felt she was looking right through him.

'You know you have a power, but she resists hers. I see an old, old place where you will learn what you have to do together. But before that...'

She paused as if reluctant to go on, then said, '...Wrong roads will be taken.'

Alan was about to ask her to explain, but the girl dug into a pocket and pulled out a piece of wood, roughly rounded, split at one end and the other bound with string.

'It's for you,' she said to him with a warm smile.

'What on earth is it?' Bella asked, not wanting him to touch it, as though it was unclean.

He recognised it; his mother had bought several over the years from old gypsy hags on the doorstep.

'It's a clothes peg,' he said, taking it. 'Thank you.'

The girl seemed pleased. 'I made it myself,' she said. 'It will bring you good luck.'

Then the girl ran back to the caravans, pausing only to turn and wave.

'What a lovely carefree life,' Alan said as they turned away from the gate.

'They are parasites, gypsies are,' Bella disagreed. 'They're dirty, they don't send their children to school, they steal, they won't work, and they don't pay taxes.'

'If they don't earn anything, of course they don't pay taxes,' Alan observed. 'And it must be great not having to do algebra. I think maybe I'll join a circus.'

Bella laughed. 'Yes, you could be a clown playing an accordion, with a red nose and big feet.'

He shivered, suddenly aware of the cold.

'If we sit on that bench, we can both wear your coat,' she said.

The bench was just inside the gate, secluded and sheltered from the wind by a low privet hedge. They sat and watched the ducks.

'I'm surprised at you being taken in by such nonsense,' Bella said, rather crossly.

'Then how did she know you are in danger if it's all nonsense?'

'Oh, I don't know. Perhaps I look worried.'

'That bit about us having to do stuff together, and having some power or other...?'

Bella shrugged. 'That's so vague, she could say it to anyone. Probably does, to make them feel good.'

'Well, she couldn't say that bit about you having to go away to just anyone. Where are you going, anyway?' he asked.

'I don't know. Anyway, I wouldn't be allowed to tell you — or anyone else. I'll write to you when I can, but you may not be able to reply. It may be another country.'

'Not France,' he said, 'you can't go there without me, remember?'

'Yes, I'll remember. And you'll remember to dedicate your first symphony to me.'

He laughed, because that seemed so unlikely. 'Yes, I promise.'

The wind was making the leafless trees shake, but the boughs creaked, so they did not hear the footsteps quietly approaching. They heard nothing until, with a grunt, sacks were thrown over their heads. Alan, by no means a weakling, struggled to free himself, and redoubled his efforts when he heard Bella's muffled scream. Then there was a sickly sweet smell, and blackness...

A voice came to him from far away, soft but relentless. 'Now, Alan, I know this is hard, but I want you to close your eyes and try again. The sack is over your head. Did you hear anything, any voices at all? Even a whisper?'

Alan wearily shook his head. 'No, nothing. He was very strong, I know that. And big. He had his arm right round me, so I couldn't move, and with the other one he put that chloroform thing over my face. And I heard Bella scream, and...' He could not control his sobs. He was about to say, 'If only I'd heeded the warning!' but fortunately stopped short. They'd think he was going barmy.

Inspector Garland was sitting by his bedside, in his own bedroom. 'Yes, all right old chap. I'm sorry to make you go through it again.'

Alan wiped his eyes, blew his nose, and looked sheepish. 'That's O.K. I just wish I could help. Poor Bella! Where could she be?'

'We're doing our very best to find her, don't you worry,' Garland said. But he didn't sound optimistic.

Alan mentioned the encounter with the gypsy girl, and Garland told him the police had already spoken to them and searched their caravans.

'The young girl seemed very upset,' the inspector said, 'and admitted she had warned you about danger, so we are still keeping an eye on that lot. She might have overheard some of them talking about kidnapping Bella. We know there's a network between gypsies here and in Ireland, but so far we've not found them to be anti-British. If anything, they're anti-German because Hitler has been trying to drive them out or imprison them, like Jews.'

Dr. Cassell came round to see him, looking distraught and ten years older.

'I'm so sorry,' Alan cried, 'it's all my fault. If I hadn't badgered her into meeting me...'

'You couldn't possibly have foreseen anything like this, Alan.'

'Why didn't they take me instead of her? If it's the Germans, I'm the one who'll be fighting them in a couple of years time when I go into the R.A.F.'

'It would be me they're after, not you or Bella. By the way, she wrote to you before she agreed to see you. This is yours.'

He handed him an envelope, which Alan opened. When he had read the letter, he handed it to Bella's father.

'You don't have to show me, you know.'

'I want you to see it. The police might want to see it too.'

He read it:

My dear Alan
This is to let you know we are moving tomorrow. All very sudden. I don't really know why, but it's not safe for us here. I'm not allowed to tell anyone where we're going. You must promise me to go on with your music. When we can meet again

after the war, I shall write to you. By that time you will have
written your first symphony for me to come and hear.
With my love,
Bella

When Alan went out for a walk with Caesar the following day, he
was surprised to find Gordon Wiggins apparently anxious to talk
with him as he passed his house.

'Hey, Alan, I'm sorry about what happened.'

Alan didn't slow up, but Caesar had other ideas, and insisted on
greeting his old pal Gordon, so Alan was forced to listen to him..

'I didn't ought to have let Tom talk me into saying them things,'
Gordon went on. 'Can't we be friends again?'

Alan turned to him. 'No, I don't think so. A friend is somebody
you can trust, and I don't think I could ever trust you again. In fact,
I don't think I'll trust anybody again. How could Tom even think
of doing something so horrible?'

'He didn't know it was an effin' bomb,' Gordon wailed.
'Anyway, he said the Irish are at war with us too. I dunno why.'

'But we thought he was our friend, Gordon. He betrayed us
both, you know? With the Germans, we know who the enemy is.'

'Not with spies, you effin' well don't,' Gordon said.

'There you are. I told you we can't trust anyone.' Alan felt he
had suddenly aged fifty years. A world of innocence had
disappeared. He was already listening out for hidden motives in
whatever people said. His History master, old Mr. Teyte, for
example, had fiercely attacked the incarceration of the Fascist
leader, Sir Oswald Mosley, under the new provisions of Regulation
18B aimed at persons having 'sympathies with the system of
government of any power with which His Majesty is at war'.

'Draconian!' Mr. Teyte had thundered. 'It's against the whole
spirit of freedom of speech and association we have fought for, for
centuries!'

Alan had tended to agree with him, but now... Could we have
influential people like Mosley stomping up and down the country
undermining our feeble rearguard action against the all-conquering
Nazis? Which side was Teyte on? Then there were Mr. Kempster
and Mr. Keilher, two young masters he had always liked, who were
always talking about pacifism, because they were Quakers. If they
weren't willing to defend themselves, perhaps it was because they
secretly wanted the Germans to win?

Five days later, the first demand arrived at Scotland Yard,

written on an ancient typewriter and postmarked 'London WC 2':

Relese O'Riordan and put him on a boat to Dublin by Monday next or the girl wil come back to youse in bits. In seven days time youll be getting the first finger. When theyve all gone well find something else to send you. We may keep a finger for Jim Hewitt anyways.

The following day, a telephone message came through, very simple: 'Six days to the first finger.' They couldn't trace it. High-powered discussions went on both in Birmingham and at Scotland Yard. On the third day, agreement had been reached. When the caller came through, he was told straight away, 'O'Riordan will be on his way from Liverpool to Dublin at 8 a.m. tomorrow on a steamer flying the Irish flag. Where will the girl be?'

There was no reply to this.

O'Riordan, with his wife and children, were escorted to Liverpool in the early hours. There was a heavy raid on the city that night, and the convoy had difficulty getting to the quay in time for the boat. The irony of the possibility that O'Riordan might get killed on the way, or on the water, did not escape them. The prisoner was accompanied by a strong armed guard who had instructions not to let him ashore in Eire unless the girl had been returned unharmed. It was certain that there were several covert armed IRA men on board as well, among passengers and crew, ready for a showdown if necessary.

At nine o'clock that morning, the duty sergeant at Solihull Police Station looked up from his ledger to see a dishevelled, pretty young girl standing before him in an overcoat too large for her.

'I'm Bella Cassell,' she said. 'I want to go home.'

News of Bella's safe return was immediately telegraphed to Dublin, and the O'Riordans were allowed to disembark. Having gone through customs, they were escorted to what they imagined would be a welcome-home party, but they had not understood how jealously the Irish Republic guarded its neutral status. Instead, O'Riordan was handcuffed and charged with 'membership of an illegal force' — the IRA. By that time the Cassells had been spirited away to their new abode, beyond the long arm of reprisal — they hoped. Alan remained in the dark, sick with worry and guilt. His inner, silent symphony was now playing non-stop, in B minor, like Tchaikovsky's *Symphonie pathétique*. For the first time — not the last — he felt the simplicity of utter despair.

93

*

However, he had to go through the motions of living, otherwise his mother would become totally impossible. He took Grandad Rogers's French novel to school one day and showed it to Mr. Constable when French was the last period.

'Can you tell me anything about this, sir?' he asked.

The French master took it, looked at the fly-leaf, and whistled through his bristly greying moustache.

'Where did you get this from, Scott?'

'It was my grandfather's, sir.'

'Was it indeed?'

Alan began to wonder what was wrong with it. A naughty French book, maybe, that he shouldn't know about?

Mr. Constable adjusted his glasses and ran his finger lightly under some writing on the fly-leaf. 'Have you read this?'

'No, sir.'

'Well, first tell me, what is your grandfather's name?'

'Rogers, sir. Joseph Rogers. My grandmother has just died, and this was in an old tin trunk under her bed.'

'Ah, I see. Sorry to hear about your grandmother. She was very old, was she?'

'No, sir. She was blown up by a bomb.'

The master shook his head sadly. '*Là là, quelle horreur!* We live in terrible times, Scott. Now, this book of yours... *L'Oeuvre.*'

Mr. Constable, M.A., was pleased to be able to talk about Zola. It always seemed to him odd that having spent three years at Cambridge mastering the whole history of French literature and thought since the Middle Ages, he had done nothing since but teach French grammar to boys who, for the most part, did not want to know about the subtleties of the subjunctive — or ways to avoid it.

'This writing here is a dedication by the author,' he explained. 'It reads: "*Pour notre ami anglais, Joseph Roger, peintre et musicien, en espérant qu'il ne suivra pas le même chemin que Claude Lantier.*" Did you follow any of that, Scott?'

'A bit, sir. 'For our friend... our English friend, Joseph Roger without the 's', something and musician...'

'*Peintre.* Work it out,' Mr. Constable urged, ever the dedicated teacher. 'What does it sound like?'

'Painter. Of course! Grandad was a painter, and he played the violin!'

94

'There you are then.'

Together they translated the rest: '...*hoping he will not follow the same road as Claude Lantier.*'

'And it's signed,' Mr. Constable read, '*Emile Zola, Paris, 1893*. This is a valuable book, Scott, signed by the author himself for your grandfather. How on earth did he get it?'

'He was in Paris that year, sir, 1893. He says so in his diary.'

He fished out his carefully transcribed copy of the diary page, which the French master read with increasing astonishment.

'How much of this do you understand, Scott?' he asked.

'He says he met Debussy, sir, and heard him play! Isn't that amazing?'

Unfortunately, Mr. Constable had no knowledge of or interest in music: Debussy, Délibes and Dorsey were all one to him. It was something else that was causing his jaw to drop.

'He writes that he went to 89 rue de Rome, because he'd been invited to one of Mallarmé's Tuesday reunions, by Toulouse-Lautrec! Do you know who he was?'

'Oh yes, sir. He did a lot of posters. My mother copies some of them for fun. But she didn't know her father knew him.'

Mr. Constable realised this boy was leading a hidden life rarely encountered in the suburbs of Birmingham.

'But what were these reunions for?' Alan wanted to know.

'They were very famous gatherings of writers and artists and musicians, like seventeenth and eighteenth-century *salons*. They took place at the home of a great poet named Stéphane Mallarmé, Scott. He wrote the poem about a faun and a couple of nymphs that your friend Debussy mentions. Pity he doesn't say more about what happened there. Just imagine, your grandfather met Mallarmé and Zola!'

'But what does the dedication mean, sir? Who's Claude Lantier and what road did he follow?'

Mr. Constable raked the smouldering ashes of a literary education lying at the back of his brain. It was twenty years since he had read any Zola.

'Now, let me try and remember. The title means 'The Work of Art', and Claude Lantier is the main character, an Impressionist artist who... yes, that's right, he never manages to paint the masterpiece he hopes to, and hangs himself in despair because he's a failure. Not a very amusing story, I'm afraid.'

Alan took a deep breath and sighed. 'No, sir.'

Mr. Constable's dormant memories of his course on the

Nineteenth-century Novel were now being stirred. 'Zola had a bee in his bonnet about heredity,' he went on.

Alan was surprised. 'That's biology, isn't it, sir? I thought Zola wrote novels?'

'Yes, he did, but novels can have some ideas, you know, Scott. Scientists aren't the only intelligent people, whatever they may think. Zola's characters are interlinked members of an enormous family, driven by the strengths and weaknesses they've inherited. It's a bit depressing, in that they can't escape from their heredity, you see. They're stuck with it. Maybe we all are. It's controversial stuff.' Mr. Constable looked at his watch. 'Good heavens, I must rush. I'm in charge of detention today. Look after that book, and try to read it!'

Alan wandered off, ignoring invitations to join in a game of football in the playground, pondering the implications of the revelations issuing from the tin trunk. Heavens above! Here was an explanation for his own inner music, though he didn't understand it; his obsession with a certain kind of music didn't just come from nowhere, and it wasn't a delusion. Joseph Rogers had been deeply affected by Debussy, even though his music had seemed very strange to him; and those same affectable parts of himself had reacted in the same way. His Grandad had been forced to give up the artistic life, his mother had been deprived of the opportunity to develop her talents. But maybe there was a chance for him, if he took it.

From the local library he got out a biography of Debussy, and was greatly encouraged by the similarities between their background. The great composer had been born in very humble circumstances, above his father's china shop. Good. He was shy, clumsy, and often unhappy. Yes, not sure about the clumsy, but Alan admitted to the other two characteristics. Then came the blow: Claude did have wealthy godparents who recognised his musical talent! They enabled him to begin musical studies with a disciple of Chopin, when he was only nine, and he entered the Paris Conservatoire only a year later. Where was he, Alan Scott, going to find wealthy godparents? He didn't think he had any at all. Once again, he heard that voice behind him: *What's the point, you mediocre little suburban nonentity? Stop fancying yourself.* But this time he found he could counteract it with a self-assurance not unlike the one he had once felt when having to face the school bully: he was not going to be defeated before he'd even tried! There was a way in which heredity could create confidence. But again... what if Joseph

Rogers had got hold of a gun? Would he now have a murderer for a grandfather? Would there be tainted criminal blood in him? Was everybody doomed, or blessed, by what had gone before? Could failure be a built-in feature too?

What, however, about the other branches of the tree? Inheriting Grandad's artistic talents was fine, but Gran's input must be just as strong. That was all right: she was good, and sensible, and hard-working, and strong-minded. But what about his father's side? They must have played an equal part in his heredity? That was rather less encouraging, judging by the little he had been told of his paternal forbears, lost in mists of nondescript poverty. He could only hope.

Alan was overjoyed to hear that Bella was safe and intact, and persuaded Inspector Garland to have a note from him transmitted to her, saying he was all right and very happy she had been released. But he was not allowed to ask her to reply.

The fire had died within him, however. He would not form any friendships with either girls at the youth club or boys at school — except for a chap named Keith Maxted, who seemed to be more understanding than the other crass youths. Day after day he took Caesar for walks through the red gateposts of 'The Firs' and wandered like a pale spectre round the silent, rapidly overgrown garden. He dragged the odd weed out of the tennis court, somehow realising with heavy heart that he would never play on it with Bella. He sat in the old summer house and knew for the first time what he, as an only child, had never known before, absolute loneliness. His inner resources had dried up. And the voice came back, even more cajoling than before: 'That girl was giving you ideas way beyond your abilities, Alan. You are a very mediocre musician, face up to it. Forget all that rubbish filling your head. It's just cacophony, no one will ever want to listen to it!'

Caesar sat at his feet, whimpering, looking up, and pawing hopefully at the old tennis ball he had unearthed. 'It'll never be the same, Ceez,' was all his master said. 'Never be the same again.'

There were only two ropes that he allowed himself to hold on to, to prevent his sliding down to the depths of depression. French and music. His did not miss any opportunity to hear or speak French — films, lectures at the Alliance Française or at the university — and he forced himself to plough through Voltaire's *Candide* and Stendhal's *Le Rouge et le Noir*, meticulously looking up and noting every new word. He understood Candide's distress at being forced apart from his beloved Cunégonde (missing completely Voltaire's ironic insights into the young lady's materialistic worldliness, and Stendhal's into the stupidity of the pious Mme de Rênal). Zola was too difficult. Romantic poetry left him cold. Only sardonic wit and detached 'telling things as they are' could appeal to his wounded psyche. As for music, his attitude changed radically and, to him and Maddy, inexplicably. No longer did he try to decipher Debussy or Ravel, or indulge in those strange rambling improvisations. Instead, he revelled in the austerity and emotional purity of Bach and Scarlatti. His head became totally engaged, but his heart not at all. The effect on his playing was remarkable: within months he mastered the technicalities of the requirements for the music examinations, but his examiners noted that his performances, though technically faultless, were 'mechanical and totally lacking in soul'. The classical rules of counterpoint and harmony no longer irked him, and his composition exercises wholly pleased his teacher, who remained completely in the dark regarding the inner turmoil being masked by this meticulous, fanatical immersion in mental discipline.

Whilst Maddy was pleased at the way Alan had — as she saw it — got over his problems, Bill was worried by the unrelieved tension in the boy. He no longer laughed, or punned, or played practical jokes on them. So he dragged him out to the cinema to relax, and once over to Stratford to see *Hamlet*. This was the only thing that seemed to arouse any interest in him, and he cycled over to see several other Shakespeare plays. These visits were supplemented by regular outings to the Birmingham Rep to see solid dramas by Ibsen and Shaw, and the Alexandra Theatre for more amusing fare such as *Charley's Aunt* or *The Ghost Train*.

Slowly, he began to work on his set texts for the English exams, especially the plays. His School Certificate results were likely to be abysmal, except in English, French, and Music, but maybe just good enough to enable him to go into the sixth form. There were serious doubts among the staff as to whether he would manage to get over the compulsory Mathematics hurdle. Apart from the brief period of encouragement by Dr. Cassell, this subject had been the bane of his life ever since he was eight, when Miss Parsons had regularly sent him outside the classroom because he got sums wrong. This masterly educational practice had ensured continued ignorance of the best way to add together two and five-sixteenths and seven and eight-ninths, an essential skill, no doubt, for a carpenter in a nondecimalised society.

He auditioned for the school play, and landed the part of Malvolio in *Twelfth Night*. His performance, an adroit blend of melancholy and comic timing, had the audience rolling in the aisles with laughter. He had finally found the antidotes to depression: comedy, and the dispassionate world of Bach.

He and his mother arrived at an uneasy truce, but he never showed a flicker of affection towards her. Bill, on the other hand, became his stalwart friend, encouraging him in his work, even though he understood little of it, and cheering him on at rugger and cricket matches. The angles and sides of the family triangle had been changed now; it had always been Alan and Maddy who had so much in common, who did things together, who discussed books and ideas, went for long walks in the country. Bill had been the uncomplaining odd man out. But the balance had suddenly shifted, and Alan discovered his father for the first time.

'When you were at school, what did you want to be?' he asked him one day as they walked home from a school cricket match.

'*Be?* You mean do for a job? Nothing. I supposed I'd be in a factory... But now, I'd say I'd have liked more than anything else to be a doctor,' he replied.

'Why a doctor?' He had been expecting his father to say a successful businessman or manager, but his answer didn't surprise him, as though it had been obvious all the time.

Bill looked uncomfortable, as though he'd been caught out giving himself airs.

'Oh, I don't know. It'd be just be nice to be able to make sick people better.'

'You'd have been good at that, Dad. So, why didn't you? Become one?'

Bill laughed. 'I didn't leave school at fourteen because I wanted to, you know. There was no choice for us. Parents thought of school as an annoyance that stopped kids going out and earning their keep. Our mother wasn't being mean or anything. She got a widow's pension, which was worth nothing, and let out a couple of rooms. So we boys were often three in a bed. We were simply poor.' He looked up at the sky. 'We'd better get a move on, it's going to rain. I'm dying for a cuppa.'

Apart from the occasional glass of beer with Harold, that was all Bill ever drank, tea. His only indulgence was cigarettes, a habit he'd picked up like everyone else at an early age. At the moment he could afford Players, and felt a twinge of pleasure whenever anyone offered him a Woodbine, and he could say 'No, have one of mine.'

He remembered well the humiliation of being offered Gold Flake by Reg; he'd resorted to having a packet of Players in one pocket, solely to offer to others. By himself, it was the acrid taste of Woodbine smoke that coated his lungs with the gooey tar that would eventually kill him and Maddy. Every New Year's Eve both of them would place Giving Up Smoking at the top of their list of resolutions, but they never succeeded. Once Maddy asked Dr. Iskander if she should give it up, and he advised her not to if it made her 'nerves' feel better. He was a chain smoker.

'Perhaps I should get a job after school, or on Saturdays.' Alan was beginning to feel guilty. 'I could get a paper round like Gordon.'

Bill looked at him sternly. 'You will not! Only one thing matters for you, my lad, and that's doing well at school and getting your School Cert. I'm not having people saying I can't afford to keep my son.'

That man-as-breadwinner attitude went for wives too. Only one of the wives in the upper half of Fallowfield Avenue, Mrs. Bowles, went out 'to business'. No one ever admitted to a wife 'going out to work'. 'Business' was genteel and almost acceptable — whatever the job might have been. 'Work' automatically implied manual labour, just as voting Labour labelled you as working-class. Only Mr. Brampton, the school-teacher up at the top, next to 'The Firs', could afford to put a Labour poster up in his front window at election time. As for the Liberals, they were wishy-washy, said Maddy, who was too staunchly individualist to believe in collective action. She had always referred to herself as 'going out to Business' when helping out at the shop. As for Mrs. Bowles, as she was always dressed up to the nines and made up to kill when she went off in the morning, there were grave suspicions about the kind of 'business' she was involved in.

'What did you do when you left school, then, Dad?' Alan wanted to know on another of their after-match walks home. Funny he had never thought to ask before; the lives of his forbears had taken on a new importance for him since the chat about Zola.

'Until I joined the army? We didn't have the money for us to be apprenticed and learn a trade. So I found all sorts of jobs — in a bike shop mending tyres, then in a garage, pumping petrol and learning basic maintenance. As soon as I could, at seventeen, I went into the army and learned how to drive. Pretty soon I was put on to instructing and got three stripes on my arm.'

100

'Yes, I've seen the photographs. You looked very smart.'

'It was a good experience for me, unlike millions of others. Well behind the lines. When I came out in 1919, I had a lot more confidence in myself, and went into selling. But the depression soon came, and pretty hard times again. But I nearly always managed to stay in work.'

'Did you ever wonder what the point of the war was?' Alan wanted to know.

'No, not then. The question often came up afterwards, especially during the depression, in the dole queues. It was the loss of dignity that hit hard. Being treated like people of no account, when it wasn't our fault we couldn't find work.'

'And what about this one? What do you think we're fighting for?'

Bill looked slightly startled. 'Well, it's clearer this time, because the Nazis are such... excuse me... bastards.'

'But that's what we're fighting *against*,' Alan went on. 'It doesn't explain what we're fighting *for*. You wouldn't want things after the war to go back to what they were before the war, would you? Lots of unemployment, and no chance to get on in life unless you were rich?'

Bill glanced at him sternly. 'You're beginning to sound like a communist, Alan.'

Alan had begun to take communism quite seriously after that little run-in with Mr. Teyte over Mosley; but the pact the Soviets made with Hitler so disgusted him he decided they were all as bad as one another. It was different now.

'Well,' Alan reminded his father, 'they are our allies. Maybe because we have a common enemy more than because we're fighting for the same things.'

'What's at stake is our way of life, and traditions, and pride,' Bill said. He'd never had a discussion like this before. Alan was just about to ask 'Pride in what, for instance?' when Bill went on, 'Just imagine what it would be like being run from Berlin. But the Germans would never be able to find people to collaborate with their Gestapo thugs. There'd be no Quislings here.'

Alan shook his head. 'Sorry, Dad, I don't think you're right. I think there are cowards and bullies and thugs in every country. Once they're in a position of power, they abuse it. I've seen bullies at school who'd have made great Nazis. Or will, if the Germans win. And the conchies won't be joining the resistance, will they?'

'Well, I don't know, do I?' Bill scratched his head, unused to speculation. 'There are lots of ways of resisting besides killing people, I suppose.'

*

While the School Certificate examiners were slaving away in the summer of 1942, trying to find the odd mark for Alan in Maths and General Science, Maddy contacted Henry Arkwright, who had been Beth-Ann's solicitor and had helped her and Emily through all the probate problems following their mother's death.

'I wonder, Mr. Arkwright,' she asked, juggling her voice between sweet and business-like, 'whether you could let Alan work in your office during the summer holidays, to see if he could take up the law as a career?'

'Do you mean as an articled clerk?'

'I don't know anything about being articled. I meant just to see if he'd be any good at it.'

He suggested that she bring him along to see him the following Friday morning, when he would not be in court.

Alan received news of the legal path being proposed for him somewhat coolly, but realised that failure to reach Matriculation standard (a pass in Maths being a *sine qua non ne plus ultra* as well as *occasio rarissima*) could make progress to the sixth form an impossibility, for some arcane reason vaguely associated with education. Not only that, he had a secret reason for wanting to make the acquaintance of Mr. Arkwright.

'You'll still be able to go on with the piano,' Maddy assured him. 'As I've always said, music is great as a hobby, to entertain your friends, but there's no future in it to make a living. Believe me, Alan, you can't afford to be romantic about this, just face up to it. If you get into the sixth form, you could go on to university, and get a job in the civil service or teaching. But we have to be sensible, just in case, don't we?'

That was unanswerable, so on Friday morning they took the tram to the city, walked along Corporation Street towards the Law Courts, and turned into the dismal building called 'Corporation Chambers'. Arkwright and Arkwright were on the second floor.

'Why are there two of them?' Alan wanted to know.

'Family firm,' Maddy whispered, though she didn't know why they were whispering, 'the father must be dead by now — I've never met him.'

They walked along the chocolate-brown lino of the dark

corridor, click-clop, click-clop, click-clop, past the frosted-glazed doors behind which they glimpsed the vague outlines of accountants and lawyers plying their trade. A pimply clerk not much older than Alan rushed by them with several files in his hand, muttering to himself, and a pretty young secretary stopped to ask if they were lost.

'No, thank you,' Maddy said frostily, as if she had been asked to purchase a naughty postcard.

The Arkwright office was the last one on the left. Alan looked at his Ingersoll watch; they were five minutes early, but Maddy knocked and walked in. Behind the desk sat a dried-up little old woman who reminded Maddy of her most detested teacher at school, Miss Morris, and Alan of his, Miss Parsons. She finally looked up from the paper before her.

'Yes?'

'Mr. Arkwright, please,' said Maddy, trying to sound like Lady Bracknell.

'Young Mr. Arkwright is busy. Take a seat over there.' She looked Alan up and down. 'Juvenile, is it?'

Maddy took in the woman's thick Birmingham accent and saw there was no need to be cowed by her. 'Mr. Arkwright is expecting us. Mrs. Madeleine Scott and Mr. Alan Scott.'

'Are you sure?' Miss Morris-cum-Parsons frowned and consulted a ledger.

'Of course I'm sure who we are,' Maddy snapped. The similarity with Miss Morris was beginning to work on her ire. 'Aren't you sure who *you* are?'

The deteriorating situation was saved by the abrupt opening of the inner office door by Young Mr. Arkwright himself, a bald, cadaverous man of ancient appearance encased in a shabby ash-strewn morning suit.

'Ah! Mrs Scott!' He advanced with outstretched hand. 'And this is young Alan, I imagine. Tea, Mrs. Hicks, if you please.'

Mrs. Hicks looked less than delighted by the turn of events. 'Really, Mr. A, if you don't tell me about your appointments, 'ow can I know who's walking in? They might of been burgulars for all I knew, after the petty cash.'

The interview initially took the form of a chat about old times between Maddy and the solicitor who had known her mother for many years.

'A fine lady, your mother.' He turned to Alan. 'A very fine lady she was, your grandmother, fine business-woman, very upright. I

103

liked that. Upright Arkwright they call me, young man, remember that.'

Mrs. Hicks brought in two grimy cups with tea sploshed into the saucers.

'And what about the young man, Mrs. Hicks?'

'Oh, 'im too? I'll go and wash another cup.'

Alan held up his hand quickly. 'No, thank you. No tea for me.'

Maddy observed the cup with its stained evidence of multiple usage. 'You can have mine, dear.'

'I'd rather not, thanks Mum.'

'Now, Alan...' Mr. Upright A picked up a pencil and began to write. 'How old are you?'

'Sixteen, sir.'

'And why do you want to be a solicitor?'

'Oh, I don't know that I do, sir. I'd like to know more about what a solicitor does. What exactly is soliciting?'

Mr. A hrrumphed through that one and failed to establish a clear etymological or semantic connection between solicitor and soliciting.

Alan came to his rescue by asking if he had any interesting murder cases on at the moment.

Mr. A was amused. 'No, Alan, most of my work is conveyancing — house purchases, you know — and in court I deal only with civil cases, not criminal. Mainly misdemeanours in the Magistrates' Court. There was a fascinating case of riding a bicycle on the pavement last week. Silly young man knocked down an old lady, then in court suddenly blurted out that he'd stolen her handbag. Made me look silly too as I'd just been saying what an upright young fellow he was. The stipendiary magistrate was not amused!'

Alan could not see this as the stuff even of a B-grade film. Momentary visions he'd had during the previous couple of days of becoming the English Perry Mason were fading rapidly. Nothing about this office resembled *The Case of the Howling Dog* or *The Case of the Stuttering Bishop*. However, Mr. A seemed to be a harmless and possibly amusing old cove, so he agreed to the offer of starting work as a clerk the following Monday, for no wages but three shillings a week travel-and-lunch money plus morning and afternoon tea. He tried to get another sixpence instead of the tea, but without success. Mrs. Hicks's slop was part of the deal.

Over the next few weeks Alan and Mr. Arkwright were provided with ample proof of the undesirability of young Scott's entering the legal profession. He regularly dropped off to sleep while copying out conveyances, and misplaced files, and spent every spare minute reading musical biographies rather than any of the books on Contract Mr. A placed before him. His ignorance of all matters legal seemed to be even more pronounced after a month than when he began.

The closest Alan got to interesting cases were those of the rape and the occluded penis, both eye-openers that widened his experience of the world a little. Mr. A gave him the task of taking briefing notes from a Miss Burney of Selly Oak, a comely secretary who had, she claimed, been forced into 'submitting' to her boss on his desk after office hours. She spoke exceedingly rapidly, so Alan thought he would make use of the Gregg shorthand he had been learning. This worked very well, and he filled several pages with characters resembling Arabic. The problem of his total inability to read any of it back later that day was exacerbated by his failure to comprehend what 'submitting' consisted of. He knew the word as a wrestling term, of course, and tried to make sense of it in this light, but without success. It did not seem to warrant charging the man, even though he had, she said, lifted her skirt up to her waist, which Alan said he imagined would be difficult without her assistance. Mr. A told him off for playing the detective, and warned him to keep to the facts as given to him.

The second was a case of work accident compensation, brought by a young man who had been sat on by a piece of heavy machinery. Nothing broken, but his penis had been squashed and suffered such damage that he had to have what he called 'a cafeter' shoved up it every morning. Alan searched the dictionary for 'cafeter' and decided he must mean 'cafetière'. His inability to explain to Mr. Arkwright why this man had to endure the daily insertion of a coffee-pot into his privates somehow gained wider notice, and resulted in ribald, sniggering laughter among the articled clerks of other solicitors at the law courts.

The one mystery Alan did manage to unravel was that of the tea cups. He could not understand how cups could achieve that degree of encrustation until he witnessed Mrs. Hicks at work on the washing up. As there was no running water on that floor, Mrs. H made it her job each morning, as she arrived to open the office, to call in at the ladies' lavatory on the floor below and fill a small enamel bowl with soapy water. It was in this liquid that the cups were immersed after use, complete with dregs; by the afternoon it had achieved the colour of tea itself. The reason for the similarity between the taste of the tea and Lux was also explained. Alan managed to escape the grisly product by making himself a small thermos full of Instant Postum at home each morning.

'I'm allergic to tea, Mrs. H,' he explained, as he poured his own brew into the screw-on cap.

She found this unbelievable and asked anxiously, 'Are you sure you're English, Alan?'

One dismal morning, when Mr. Arkwright was in court, Alan told Mrs. H he was going to do some filing, and disappeared into the store-room lined with folders and rolls tied with pink tape. He had already spotted some that went back as far as 1900, very high up and very dusty. This time, he set the rickety ladder further to the left and ascended gingerly. Wills, deeds, contracts, full of 'Whereases' and 'Heretofores' and 'Hereinafters', disseminated their dust. He pinched his nose to suppress his sneezes, so as not to fall off the ladder or draw Mrs. H's attention to his foraging.

Finally, assiduity paid off. A thick, yellowing manilla folder, with the words 'ROGERS, JOSEPH, 1890-94' written in fading red ink, was buried beneath a foot-high pile of similar folders. Holding his prize to his chest, he returned to his desk, hoping Mrs. H would not look up from her ancient Remington. Surreptitiously he slipped the folder into his school satchel, which served him as a briefcase, quite sure that this would be a very punishable offence.

The guilty feeling that came over him, up in his den, as he untied the tattered red ribbon, was quelled sternly. 'It *is* my business,' he reminded himself, 'it's my family.'

Ploughing through the grimy layers of legal detritus was an unrewarding task, most of it incomprehensible, until one detail struck him as interesting. The documents were signed 'W.B. Arkwright' — that would have been Old Mr. Arkwright; Young Mr. A couldn't possibly be *that* old? Alan did some mental arithmetic: Would he still be working at, say, seventy? Yes, he decided, more than likely, as many old people had been called back into jobs vacated by young men called up, and in a family firm it would be the natural thing to do, to keep it going. So in 1893 he would have been, say, twenty-one. So he might remember something about what had happened.

From that point on, he perused the documents more carefully, until he finally felt he was getting warm: something about a trust and a transfer of funds. Then the first letter-heading from a French company, Haraucourt et Fils. *Haraucourt!* Laboriously Alan worked out that they were agents of some kind, and that large amounts of money had been involved in something called *hypothèques*. The last letter was signed by Mr. Arkwright, and was surprisingly written in French; in it he used the term *détournement de fonds*: there were two terms he would have to look up.

The problem now was, could he reveal to Mr. Arkwright that he had been ferreting about in his file store without permission? Maybe the file accidentally fell on to the floor? Very unlikely. No: only one thing for it. Tell the truth.

When Mr. Arkwight returned from court, he was in expansive mood, having won both his cases. Alan took in his grimy teacup and saucer.

'Could I have a word with you please, sir?'

'Yes, of course, Alan.' Something resembling a beaming smile fleetingly crossed the old lawyer's craggy face.

'The other day I went through an old diary of my grandfather's, and he mentioned a W.B. Arkwright. Was that your father?'

'Indeed it was. The old boy seemed to go on for ever. He only died in 1930.'

'Were you with the firm in the 1890s?'

1890s? My, that sounds positively mediaeval, doesn't it? The naughty nineties! Yes, I took my articles in... let me see... 1892. Fifty years ago! I did retire, you know, but the war...'

He waved his hand about.

Now he had to take the plunge. 'I'm afraid I've let my curiosity run away with me a bit, sir. My grandfather seems to have had some trouble while he was in France, and I was wondering what your father did to help him, since he mentions him.'

Mr. Arkwright began to look serious. 'Yes?'

'Well, I found the file without much difficulty, and I was wondering if you could explain a couple of French words.'

'You found the file? In the store?'

'Yes, sir. I hope that was all right?'

'No, it is not all right, sir!' Mr. Arkwright thundered. 'That store is full of confidential documents. You can't go rummaging like that!'

'But as you tell me every day to go there and find files and put them away, I never thought I couldn't look at some of my own family's papers, sir.'

Mr. Arkwright thought about that for a couple of minutes, and began to calm down. 'Yes, I see your reasoning, Alan. Your family's papers. Did your mother tell you to do this?'

'No, sir, she knows nothing about it.'

'I see.' He seemed uncertain about how to proceed. Then he said: 'You wanted to ask about something.'

Alan opened the file at the last letter. 'It seems my grandfather lost an awful lot of money because of a Frenchman named Haraucourt, and your father uses the words *hypothèques* and *détournements de fonds*. I don't know what they mean, sir.'

Mr. Arkwright put out his hand for the letter, read it, and nodded gravely.

'I remember now. Yes, that was a very nasty business. Your grandfather was quite a gay spark, very, um, *artistic*.'

He said the word as though it was an embarrassing deviation from normality.

'His father died leaving a tidy sum to him and his younger sister...'

'Alice,' Alan prompted him.

'Just so. Which was placed in a trust fund for them. Arkwright and Arkwright had the duty of administering the funds, seeing they were properly secure. As soon as he was twenty-one, Joseph, your grandfather, had full use of the funds, and immediately went abroad to lead an *artistic* life, and began to run through his inheritance at a rate my father thought was alarming. So he suggested that most of the funds should be made to work, bring in a return, instead of sitting in a bank account. We knew of several sound investments and suggested them, but your grandfather had other ideas. He was convinced he wanted to spend the rest of his life on the continent, and that the money should be lodged in Paris, since the rate of exchange was particularly favourable. Unfortunately, he was introduced to an investment agent named Haraucourt...'

'Gaston?'

'Just so. Gaston, who promised him a quite unreal rate of return if he put his money into some mortgages — *hypothèques* — he was managing. The money disappeared.'

'Can that happen in France?' Alan asked naïvely.

'It can happen anywhere!' Mr. Arkwright replied fiercely. 'There are sharks in all waters. We did our best to bring Haraucourt to book, but he was too clever. The moment we accused him of embezzlement — *détournement de fonds* — he threatened us with an action for slander with enormous damages. We and your grandfather could have won, I'm sure, but it would have cost a fortune to proceed. So we had to apologise, say it was a linguistic misunderstanding, and say goodbye to the money.'

'And what happened to the shark?'

'I have no idea, I'm afraid. There was no point in following it up, and we never do *business in Paris* normally.'

The tone implied that it would be the equivalent of supping with the devil.

Alan apologised for snooping and for taking up so much of Mr. Arkwright's time (hoping he was not going to charge him by the minute). He closed the file and said he would return it to the store. When he got there, however, he carefully extracted a few of the documents, sensing that he had not heard the full story. Who, he wondered, was really responsible for the disappearance of so much money? For the time being he had no way of pursuing any enquiry, and Mr. Upright Arkwright would be extremely cross if he discovered he was doing so. In fact, it would be two or three years before he was able to solve this mystery in a Paris which was for the time being and the foreseeable future under German occupation.

*

The School Certificate results were not as disastrous as had been predicted. The compulsory Everest of Mathematics had been conquered by one half of a per cent above the fail mark. Or to put it more positively, 0.5% within the pass range. Alan proceeded into the sixth form to enjoy the sheer delight of doing only subjects he wanted to study, and of never again, he fervently hoped, having to fail to solve a quadratic equation or to make sense of a chemical formula. Physical Training was optional for Sixth Formers, and several of them chose to spend more time studying or lounging about. Alan was told he stood a good chance of being School Athletics champion if he kept it up, but he would have to excel in boxing as well as gymnastics and games. This he resolutely refused to do.

'I simply will not hit anybody for a game, for sport, sir,' he said to Mr. Gillespie, the P.T. master, a wiry old Scot and former army instructor.

'Tha's a great pity, laddie, ye'll no have a chance otherwise.'

But the following week a notice went up: 'Wrestling is to be introduced as an alternative to boxing for 5th and 6th formers. Anyone interested report to Mr. Gillespie.'

Alan had already done some unarmed combat with the Air Training Corps, and soon mastered the holds and falls: the inside trip, the hip lock, and the standing backheel were easy, and his leg muscles were strong enough for him to get submissions from a simple leg lock round his opponent's middle. If he could hold him down just by sitting on his chest, he was very happy, but he had great difficulty with those holds that involved inflicting pain: wrist locks, head scissors, or leg spreads, and many a bout was prolonged by his determination not to use holds that could result in tearing muscles or ligaments.

When he had won his first few bouts with apparent ease, Mr. Gillespie was puzzled.

'You're a natural, laddie. But where did you learn that footwork? For a lad your size and weight, you're very nimble.'

Alan hadn't thought about it; it just seemed natural for him to sidestep, lean out of reach, feint, never allowing himself to be pushed off balance, using his opponent's own impetus and weight against himself.

'I don't know, sir. It's just like dancing, really.'

'You do a lot of dancing?'

'Not a lot now, just Saturday night hops. But for years I had to go with my mother to the dancing classes she played for, and do the foxtrot and the quickstep and the waltz, with lots of giggly girls.'

'Well,' said the sports master, 'you may not have liked it then, but it's certainly paid off now. The body never forgets early training like that. Keep on dancing round your opponent till you're in the position *you* want to be in, then you can control the moves. Rhythm, that's the secret.'

One day as they laid paving stones for a new front garden path together, Bill was trying to decide whether to broach the subject that was tormenting them both. Finally he decided.

'You know, Alan, you're going to have to forgive her. Your mother. We can't go on like this. It's tearing us apart. She only did it because she loves you so much.'

'I'm not so sure about that,' Alan mused. 'I don't doubt she loved me, but I don't think that's why she did it. It was jealousy, not love.'

'I think it's more like possessiveness, something a lot of only children have to put up with,' Bill said. 'Go and talk to a few. Harold Wise, for example.'

'Mr. Wise? He's too old, he wouldn't remember.'

'Oh, wouldn't he? You just go and talk to him.'

The next time Harold came round for a beer, Bill discreetly left them alone.

'Are you an only child, Mr. Wise?'

'Yes, I am, Alan. Terrible, isn't it?'

'No, I don't think so. When I go round to someone's house they're always quarrelling with brothers and sisters, having to share a bedroom, shouting and telling them to stop doing this and stop doing that. It's a relief to get home to a bit of peace and quiet.'

'But there is a disadvantage, isn't there? I found it was like always having to be in the front of the class. Everything you do is noticed, you can't get away with a thing.'

Alan pondered. 'Yes, that's true.'

'Then there's always the problem of possessiveness.'

'Dad said that too.'

'Usually the mother if it's a boy, sometimes the father with a girl.'

'Did you have a problem with that?'

'Did I ever! Can you imagine, a Jewish mother of an only son! Every girl I took home was scared out of her wits. Yes, she deliberately scared them off. So you can picture what it was like when I said I wanted to marry a non-Jewish girl.'

'What did she do?'

'She refused to talk to me, to us, for nearly two years after we were married. Then one day she came round, just to ask if she had any grandchildren yet!'

'And you didn't?'

'No, we were never blessed. Bit too late now. But we're reconciled, since my father died. She's actually admitted she was foolish. It's a pity when forgiveness takes so long. Especially when the only fault has been misplaced love.'

His English master was Mr. Cooke, who had a very good tenor voice, and sang with the City of Birmingham Choir. He had been aware of Alan's traumatic experiences, and had been unobtrusively encouraging his interest in drama as a kind of therapy. One day, Alan was awaiting the bus home when that premonitory feeling made the back of his neck tingle. So he let one bus go by and waited. Sure enough, minutes after, along came Mr. Cooke. Not entirely surprising, but it had never happened before. They went upstairs and sat at the front, the master complaining to Alan that he was having to perform in Walton's *Belshazzar's Feast* which, although twelve years old, was still pretty avant-garde.

'How can I possibly sing a C when the man next to me is

singing C-sharp,' he wanted to know. 'But I've got an idea,' he continued. 'I've been asked to sing some settings of Shakespeare, and I'd love to do my favourite sonnet:

> *When to the Sessions of sweet silent thought*
> *I summon up remembrance of things past,*
> *I sigh the lack of many a thing I sought...*
> *De-dum-de-dum-de-dum-de-dum-de-dum,*
> *But if the while I think on thee, dear friend,*
> *All losses are restored and sorrows end.*

Do you know that one?'

'Yes, I do,' Alan said. 'It would make a fine song.'

'The trouble is, I can't find a setting. So how about writing one for me?'

Alan was startled. 'What, me? Write a song?'

'Not any old song. Set that poem. For me. I know you've studied a lot of music.'

'Yes, other people's. I haven't composed anything for a long time.'

'Never mind. I'm sure you haven't forgotten how. You can still turn out a song, I'm sure. Will you at least try?'

Reluctantly Alan said he would.

That evening he rummaged under his bed and found his old music manuscript book, and re-read on the back cover notes he had made during that feverish period when Bella and her father had inspired him. One was: 'Music is a living force essential for preserving peace in the world'. That was the great conductor, Serge Koussevitzky. And another was a quotation from his mystic namesake, Cyril Scott: 'Certain composers will evolve a type of music calculated to heal... in the future, the great Cosmic Symphony — Unity Song — Love, Wisdom, Knowledge and Joy...'

He re-read his scores and played the long-neglected *Prélude à l'Après-midi d'un Faune*, the musical part of his brain was stirred into action again, and he began to realise that he had been cutting himself off from the greatest and best source of healing for his troubled mind and heart. His copy of the Sonnets was well worn, and he turned straight to Number 30.

The programme of the next Sunday afternoon symphony concert, according to the notice in the paper, included works by both Debussy and Ravel; and there was a French conductor, Gaston Lemaître. The opportunity to go and chat to a French conductor about French music was too good to miss, so he presented himself backstage afterwards. Fortunately M. Lemaître spoke no English, and was delighted to find someone with whom he could communicate. He invited Alan to come and talk in his hotel room, which was only a few minutes' walk from the Town Hall. There, he got Alan to have tea brought up to them, and for some time he seemed glad to respond to the handsome young man's enthusiasm for modern French music. The tea arrived. It was a small room, with no table and only one chair, so they put the tray on the chair and both sat side by side on the bed. When the cake had all gone, Lemaître pushed the chair away, removed his jacket, and invited Alan to do the same, as it was such a warm afternoon. He did so, and had no sooner sat down again than the conductor placed his hand on his thigh, moving it up and down his trouser crease.

'Why don't you lie back and relax?' he suggested.

Now feeling uncomfortable but not knowing quite why, Alan said he was all right, thanks, and moved away. But the hand followed, this time unambiguously crutchwards. Alan suddenly looked at his watch and gasped.

'*Mon dieu! Il est six heures déjà!*' he exclaimed, grabbing his jacket and hastily donning it. '*Je dois aller voir mon chien, il va mourir de faim.*'

'*Mais non, sûrement pas!* Plizz do not liv me!'

But Alan was out of the door before the randy Frenchman had got his jacket on. On the bus home he began to laugh and had to bury his face in his handkerchief. This was a new angle on the connection between music and love that had not occurred to him. Were music-lovers drawn to one another, irrespective of sex, he wondered? Sitting on the piano stool kissing Bella was one of his most treasured memories, but he couldn't imagine doing that with another boy just because he liked Debussy. What about other arts? He knew about actors, and directors, it was a standing joke. But musicians too? Not painters, certainly; they were always having affairs with their female models. What about writers? He knew about Gide and Proust, but what about, say, Shakespeare? Or Voltaire? The question was now firmly in his mind for future consideration: the link between art and sex. But he knew no one with whom he could discuss it.

When he handed Mr. Cooke the completed manuscript three weeks later, the astute master saw straight away that it was dedicated 'To my love, B.C.'.

'I see you've dedicated it to someone, Alan. Do you mind telling me who it is? In confidence, of course.'

Alan could see no reason why he shouldn't. 'I only put initials because the war is still on,' he explained cryptically. 'Bella Cassell. She's... she was my girl friend.'

'Ah. I see. And you want to be discreet. Do you know what my christian name is?'

'No, sir.'

'It's Bruce. B.C.'

His point got through Alan's naivety. 'Oh! I see!' He was blushing furiously by now. 'I didn't mean...'

'No, I didn't think you did. But others might. Why don't you put 'Miss' in front?'

Alan did better than that. He wrote: 'To my lost love, Bella C...'.

They went through the song after school, Alan accompanying, and Bruce Cooke made one or two suggestions about awkward phrasing or infelicitous notation that Alan accepted. But when he pointed out that his music had not matched the last line, Alan refused to budge.

'Don't you see, Alan, there's resolution in the words, the restoration of loss, the end of sorrow? *'All losses are restored and sorrows end.'*

'Oh no,' Alan replied stubbornly, 'there can be consolation *the while*, but not restoration. There's no end to sorrow until the cause has been removed. So I've left that final chord unresolved.'

The singer nodded. 'Yes, I see. It's very poignant. I see that now. Not at all obvious, avoids triteness. I'll try to do it justice.'

Mr. Cooke had not told him that the recital was a united schools' concert to take place in the Town Hall, to celebrate D-Day. There were rousing pieces by Elgar and Walton, then Bruce Cooke sang some Roger Quilter and Vaughan Williams, and ended up with *Drake's Drum*. Alan was hurt but not surprised he had apparently decided to drop his song. However, when the post-Drake applause had died down, Mr. Cooke said, 'We cannot let this great day go by without reference to our greatest English writer, William Shakespeare. I should like to sing a brand-new setting of one of his sonnets by a young pupil of mine, who will shortly be going into the R.A.F., Alan Scott. I know it means a lot to him, and it does to me too.'

He sang it so brilliantly, and the professional accompanist put so much feeling into the piano part, that the audience rose to their feet and demanded an encore. Then Alan was hauled on to the platform and given an ovation. He saw Maddy sitting in the front row wiping her eyes, and Bill was blowing his nose. There was one face Alan would have loved to see there, but he knew miracles did not happen.

The next day, a review of the concert appeared in *The Birmingham Mail*, which ended:

> *The final item was a surprise, as it did not appear in the programme. I was pleased to have stayed for it, as it turned out to be a most moving experience. Alan Scott, a pupil at the school where Bruce Cooke teaches, had set one of Shakespeare's great sonnets,* When to the Sessions of sweet silent thought, *a demanding undertaking for one so young. But his music, whilst obviously coming from the modern French school of* mélodie *rather than the English tradition of Gerald Finzi and John Ireland, revealed a mature and haunting originality. I particularly admired the ending, where he avoided any hint of over-sentimentality. We shall hear more of this young man.*

When Maddy read it, she put her arms round him and gave him a big hug, to which he was able to respond. 'It'll be an opera next,' she said. Bill took his hand and shook it warmly, saying, 'Well done, lad, we're very proud of you.'

But the best was the letter that arrived a few days later. It read:

> *Dear Alan*
> *I have just read the notice of your concert. Don't worry about* Brioso Calmato molto vivace. *Congratulations! Keep it up. If you are ever in London, look me up at the Academy.*
> *Yours aye*
> *FRANK WALKER*

On first reading it he glossed over the Italian, but he now studied it as a technical comment on his music. *Brioso*: joyful; *Calmato*: quiet; *molto vivace*: very lively. It made no sense as a description of the successive moods the song went through. So what was he supposed not to worry about? Then, why did *Brioso* and *Calmato* start with capital letters?

He went to sleep turning the phrase over and over in his mind. Clearly it was there for a purpose, and the professor did not appear to be a man given to gibberish. On the verge of sleep he suddenly sat up in bed, switched on the light, and went to his desk where the letter lay. *Don't worry: B.C. happy, full of life!* The professor must be in

115

touch with her, or with her father at any rate. And she was all right. Unless his translation was constructed upon wishful thinking.

The euphoria of D-Day gradually gave way to weary acceptance that the war was still far from over. The British, American and Canadian armies in France seemed to be getting bogged down. On 25 July three thousand bombers of the U.S. air force dropped many thousands of high-explosive, fragmentation and napalm bombs on enemy positions around Caen. Rumours flew in pubs and queues that they had been so inaccurate they had killed thousands of American troops; in fact, it was six hundred, but the news was hardly morale-boosting. Just when Londoners thought the war might be over for them, twenty thousand people in and around the capital were killed by V1s, flying bombs launched from the Pas de Calais.

Most of Alan's spare time, what little that remained of it each day after his studies for the impending Higher School Certificate, was taken up by the need to do well enough in his Air Training Corps Proficiency Certificate to enhance his chances of being accepted for the R.A.F. University Short Course at Cambridge. Maddy had pleaded with him not to go into the air force, but into the navy. She had always longed to go to sea herself, ever since those far-off days when she used to go and watch the big ships with exotic names in Poole harbour, when on holiday at Auntie Alice's. The first outfit she had made for her little boy had been a sailor suit with anchors on the sleeves.

But Alan refused point-blank: 'Mum, I can't swim, and I panic whenever I'm out of my depth at the baths, ever since those stupid twits threw me in years ago. So I'd rather go to a quick death from twenty-thousand feet than drown slowly in twenty feet of water.'

This blunt presentation of the alternatives upset Maddy considerably.

Emily was due to visit the following week, to get herself fitted for a new costume by her tailor. As they sat over tea in the Kardomah, Maddy said sadly, 'Alan's going into the R.A.F.,' but Emily thought she was showing off.

'He's a bit late to do any good, isn't he? He should have been out earning his keep by now anyway. Who ever heard of a boy still being at school at eighteen? Is he a bit backward? Look at young Percy Wilkins, you know, lives next door to us, he's got a good job at Lawson's, you know, the timber yard, even though he's only fifteen. Now there's a *bright* lad for you.'

Maddy let her ramble on, trying hard not to get annoyed but finding it increasingly difficult. She and Bill were in any case accustomed to being taken to task for spoiling their boy, letting him get ideas above his station, just doing nothing but read books and fiddling with music when he should be out learning a trade. Indeed, he was the only boy in the avenue to stay on at school after the age of fourteen or fifteen. And as for this airy-fairy notion of going to a university, maybe even *Cambridge....!* Who did the Scotts think they were? Royalty?

But it was not a question of pretentiousness. On the contrary, whilst Bill was fairly happy to be able to give his son chances in life than he not had, Maddy was motivated by a determination that no child of hers was going to have to put up with the sort of exploitation she had had to put up with at his age. She had once used a stronger term for it than exploitation, when she and Bill had responded to a neighbour's invitation to go along to the local Congregational church. The rotund vicar had fulminated against declining moral standards, largely blaming prostitutes, 'ladies of the night, Jezebels all'. Over cups of unidentifiable brown liquid afterwards in the vestry, Maddy had gone for him like a tiger.

'I expect they were forced into it by poverty! All very well for you, a man brought up on easy street, but what I was forced to do when I was fourteen was a similar kind of exploitation,' she railed.

A hush fell. The good ladies stopped talking in expectation of some shocking revelation, and their husbands glanced at each other and winked hopefully. The red-faced vicar just looked poleaxed.

'Mind-numbing, degrading office work for a mere pittance!' Maddy went on. 'Just because it didn't involve sex it was thought to be a 'decent' job for a young girl to do. But the mind can be prostituted too, you know. Come on, Bill, we're going!'

She, and therefore Bill, did not go to the church again, for which the vicar thanked God.

Sitting at her painting, escaping from the present, musing on the past as she did only too often, Maddy was filled with an immense sadness. That image — of a talented fourteen-year old, longing to get art or musical training, capable of a bright future in dress design, for example, and offered a singing scholarship in London, but forced into a series of moronic jobs — that image had always coloured her attitude to a society that failed to give opportunities to its young. What she simply could not understand was why parents suddenly found it impossible to support a child as from a certain birthday — 14, 15, 16, 18? — and forced him or her to go out and quickly earn money for the family, rather than allow the child to acquire the training and education necessary to reach full potential both for earning and for self-fulfilment. Whatever Reg and Emily and the neighbours might say, her son was not going to be job fodder. And that was why she had always refused to have another child, since that would halve the chances for Alan. Well, that was one reason; she had never told anyone about the other.

Only too aware of the inadequate training she had had in music and painting, Maddy had made an effort to learn more. Since dance music provided both amusement and a welcome bit of extra money, she had enrolled in a course at The Billy Mayerl School, which cost a lot and just taught her a few syncopated jazz riffs. Mayerl had been her hero ever since she found out that he had started his musical life playing for silent films exactly as and when she had, with bits of Beethoven for the cowboys and Indians and *Hearts and Flowers* for the love scenes. But there the similarity ceased: he had gone to Trinity College of Music, had given the first performance of *Rhapsody in Blue* in England, and had been greatly influenced by the music of Delius, Cyril Scott, Debussy and Ravel. She knew nothing of this, only that when he was little Alan was always asking her to play *Marigold*, the most famous of his magical, popular compositions.

With his Higher School Certificate exams over in July 1944, the way seemed clear for Alan to enjoy an idyllic summer. After cutting himself off from others for a long time following Bella's hasty and devastating exit from his life, he had latterly renewed his friendship with Keith, who was in the Science sixth. It had scarcely been a friendship really, for Keith had inexplicably avoided Alan after the mix-up over Boxing Day. Alan had supposed he was annoyed because he'd forgotten to tell him that he would be away for Christmas, but thought it rather petty of him to go on holding it against him. However, in the sixth form, with its greatly reduced numbers, they found each other good company. What they mainly had in common was an interest in a couple of girls they met at a Saturday night hop — Rebecca, a lively, sexy, exotic girl, and another pleasant but rather colourless one, Joy. In fact, they had become an inseparable quartet, even though they were remarkably different from each other. Keith had developed into a stocky, handsome, dark-haired boy, still — despite Alan's attempts at indoctrination — with no interest in music or anything literary. He had only one aim: to become a doctor. When Keith told Alan he and his family were Quakers, Alan did not respond — all religions left him cold — but when he read Voltaire's four chapters on the Quakers in the *Lettres Philosophiques* (a set text), he quoted truncated bits to Keith with relish: *'George Fox believed he was inspired and had to speak in a different way from everyone else, so he started to tremble and pull funny faces, hold his breath and puff it out. Soon that was the only way he could speak, and this was his first gift to his disciples who trembled as hard as they could. Hence the name Quakers. They quaked, they talked down their noses, they thought they saw the Holy Spirit. They needed a few miracles so they made them.'*

Keith just smiled and said that was a typically cynical French way of looking at things, so Alan gave up.

Their lives were to change irrevocably that summer afternoon in 1944, their last together, ever. Alan had been strongly recommended for the R.A.F. air crew short course at Cambridge, and Keith was expecting to be selected for naval officer training. Joy had just finished a year at a secretarial college.

Rebecca was already in the outside world, training as a nurse, so she was normally able to join them only at weekends, but she had taken some leave in order to spend this last precious week or two with her friends — ignoring her parents' pleas for her to go on holiday with them to North Wales. So she was staying with Joy at her parents' home.

These few precious days — just how precious and unrepeatable they could not know — were spent playing tennis, cycling along Warwickshire country lanes, queuing up for matinées at Stratford (Rebecca made them go twice to *The Merchant of Venice*), lazing in haystacks in the drowsy afternoon heat, gazing at the clouds and talking about the future as though it was really going to happen. The girls, when alone, talked endlessly, about parents, making dresses out of old curtains, boys (*the* boys), and careers. And the war and sex, but Joy had nothing to say about them. In fact, Rebecca's vehemence about the Germans and her enthusiasm for something called orgasm made her very uncomfortable.

Rebecca had matured a lot in the two years she had been nursing, but she had always liked to try and shock Joy with her sexual precociousness. It showed in the way she dressed and undressed; Joy always turned round when taking off her undies, because she thought it was polite, but Rebecca would simply strip off, and even went to the bathroom like that, with a towel flung carelessly over one shoulder, until the time she gave Joy's father quite a shock as he came out of the toilet. He graciously said he wasn't worried at all, and even apologised; terribly English. He was the kind of man who said 'Sorry' when he got his foot trodden on. Joy noticed he was less grumpy for a week after the full frontal; no doubt, she surmised, he was trying to put Rebecca at her ease by being attentive.

On the Friday evening they decided to play tennis at two o'clock the following afternoon, as Keith had an appointment in the morning. But when they got to the park, they found a stray bomb had dropped overnight right in the middle of the public courts. The groundsman, who had been dragged out of senile retirement to look after them, was furious, threatening them bleedin' Jerries with the direst retribution. Rebecca and Joy began to collapse with laughter as he spluttered his sincere but harmless imprecations in language he had learnt at Ypres. Alan hustled them away, saying he knew another court they could go to. They left a message for Keith with the apoplectic pensioner.

Alan explained that it was quite a grand house in his avenue, unoccupied for over two years, so the garden was very overgrown. Its owner, a friend of Alan's father, was serving overseas, he lied. It seemed the safest way to avoid awkward questions about the Cassells. He felt momentary qualms about invading the garden with another girl, but decided it might help to exorcise Bella's ghost. Almost immediately, as he led the way to the back of the house, portentous vibrations began to awaken in his brain, fragments that tried and failed to come together in their present harmony.

The court was bumpy but not too bad, considering the general state of dilapidation. They found the summer-house, all dry and musty, with a low slatted bench still sound enough to sit and even lie down on. It was a friendly place, with a warm, golden atmosphere. Alan fancied it was pleased to be used again.

'But there's no net!' cried Joy. 'How can we play?'

'Not to worry! Never fear!' Alan lifted the bench seat and revealed the rolled net in the locker beneath, just where he had carefully laid it himself many months before.

They played a few games of two against one, Alan winning against the girls thanks to Joy. Rebecca had an almost male aggression and dashed about grimly, her long dark hair swirling over her lean intelligent face. Joy suggested the other two should have a hard-hitting singles, but then they heard Keith calling.

The girls both kissed him, not noticing he was rather subdued. He was Rebecca's boy friend now, but he had been Joy's, and Alan had briefly been Rebecca's, so there was no kind of possessiveness about their relationship. Rebecca said she always thought Alan was expecting her to be someone else, and was constantly being disappointed. He didn't have any such expectations from Joy, who revelled knowingly in being the quintessential mythical dumb blonde. They were all touchingly fond of one another, and being only children increased their mutual dependence.

It would have been easy for Joy to be jealous of Rebecca, who wasn't quite as pretty as Joy, but had vivacity and confident bodily presence. Joy was very envious of her incandescent breasts, which were not large but perfect half-globes, like those of a burnished Indian goddess. Joy's breasts were larger but remained resolutely pallid, adolescent and (to her) uninteresting, with mortifyingly tiny pink nipples, even smaller than Alan's.

Alan frequently tried to touch Joy's bosom, but she told him firmly she didn't like it (she really meant it wasn't worth it), that it would spoil their friendship and his respect for her, so he stopped, even though he did not share her fears. But he kissed beautifully, and sometimes she found it became very difficult not to be roused when he touched her lips with his tongue, which no other boy had ever done to her. He frequently had to be told to be good. Being good meant not putting his hand more than about six inches above her knee, or actually on her tiny pink bits, or on her bottom. He seemed quite content with that, or so she thought. The fact was that Keith had admitted he had never got anywhere with her either, so Alan saw little point in wearing himself out. With a twinge of envy Alan saw that Keith often put his hand on Rebecca's bottom at dances, but she didn't seem to notice. He had never dared to do that, as Rebecca could be very sharp if displeased, something Joy never was. Life was easier with Joy.

'I didn't know it was this house you meant,' Keith said quietly to Alan as they tried to fix the rotting net.

Alan looked up sharply at his friend. 'What do you mean, 'this house'?'

Keith bit his tongue. *Fool!* 'Ah, well,' he blustered, 'you know, let me see, it was when... that time you invited me round and you weren't at home, I walked up the avenue and saw the name on the gatepost, so I remembered it. But it was occupied then, I think?'

'Yes, it was,' Alan replied. He offered no details, and did not see Keith's fleeting smile. 'Let's go and play! We've wasted enough time.'

They were soon hard at it on the court again. The way they played was an indication of character, even at their basic level of competence. Keith, sturdy and muscular, got rid of his aggression by belting the ball as hard as he could; Rebecca was quite fanatical and would hit the ball right at an opponent up at the net if it would win a point; Joy served with accuracy and played beautiful ground strokes (she had had some expensive coaching), but would collapse in giggles when she muffed an easy return; Alan hared erratically round the court after every ball, thinking how much good the exercise must be doing him, and never bothering about the score. They therefore found it better to play Keith-Joy *versus* Alan-Rebecca, which Alan much preferred because he could watch Joy's assets bouncing under her blouse.

After a couple of sets, one-all, hot and dusty, they retired to the summer-house and spread out on the bench the sweet lemonade and off-ration broken biscuits they had brought. Afterwards, Rebecca and Keith insisted that Alan and Joy push off and play singles, which they did with much winking and joking.

As they finished Joy whispered to him, 'Let's see what they're up to!' She was relishing the thought of catching them necking and springing apart red-faced. She crept ahead to peep round the corner. But she saw they were not kissing. Keith was leaning back against the wall with his eyes closed. Rebecca was kneeling at his feet with her head between his legs. Her tennis blouse was up round her shoulders and her bra-strap undone. Joy could see Keith's hands were massaging her firm rounded breasts, and her head was moving slowly up and down. As she came up, Joy could see what it was her friend was doing, even though her hair was hanging down over his bare thighs. Her head went down again, and Keith gave a sort of groan. Joy swung round to face a puzzled Alan.

'Don't look!' she whispered, 'it's disgusting!'

He pushed her aside. When he turned back after taking in the engrossing — appalling — scene (for far too long), all he whispered was, 'I'd never have thought of doing that.' With a shock Joy saw he was smiling. It was like finding out all one's closest family were lepers or murderers. She felt alien. Or rather, they were alien. They walked back to the court, and Joy confronted him.

'What do you mean, you'd never have thought of doing that?'

'I wouldn't have, that's all. Would you?'

122

She snorted.

'Keith was obviously enjoying it,' he said, envy in his voice.

'And what about poor Rebecca? I expect he made her do it.'

'I can't imagine making Rebecca do anything she didn't want to.'

'I suppose she did that to you too, when you were going out with her?'

'No, she didn't. I wonder why not.' He actually sounded regretful.

'Well, don't expect me ever to do that. And don't let anyone else do it while you're away!'

They returned to the summer-house, this time chatting loudly about the weather and the score (Joy had won, Alan's concentration having curiously evaporated). The scene in the summer-house was very different. They were both decently dressed again and sitting side by side, their faces turned away from each other. Rebecca was weeping. Immediately Joy ran to her, thinking Keith had asked her to do something else unmentionable.

'Rebecca! What's the matter?'

'Ask *him!*' she sobbed.

To Joy's surprise, Keith's eyes were beginning to brim with tears too. He averted his face, and blew his nose hard into his handkerchief.

'Go on,' Rebecca shouted, 'tell them why you were so late.'

Keith turned slowly, and looked at Alan in a way he didn't understand. Guiltily.

'You'll know soon enough.' He took a deep breath. 'I'm not going into the Navy.'

'Oh, tough luck.' Alan pushed back his lock of reddish fair hair. 'They turned you down?'

'No. I turned them down.'

Slowly it came out. When he'd arrived for his Selection Board that morning, he'd told them he was going to be a Conscientious Objector. They were very angry, sent him from one recruiting officer to another to get him to change his mind, asking fiendishly entrapping questions like 'What would you do if a maniac was about to kill your mother and you had a gun in your hand?' But he had been prepared for all this by Mr. Keilher.

'Keilher?' Alan broke in. 'The geography master?'

'Yes, he's a Friend. A Quaker. He volunteered for the Ambulance Unit but was turned down because of some heart defect. But I'm doing the same, unless I have to go down the

123

mines.'

Rebecca stood up and slapped him hard across the cheek. He didn't flinch.

'You are contemptible!' she shouted. 'I've done everything I safely could to show you how much I loved you and admired you, and you have the nerve to tell me you're a coward. Thousands of German Jews, innocent good people, are being rounded up like animals and sent off to camps. You've met my aunt who got out of Munich, Keith, and you say you'll do nothing to beat those bloody Nazis? I hate you!'

'I didn't realise you were paying me in advance for going to fight for your people, I thought you did it because you loved me!'

'I *did!*' she wailed. 'But I can't any more!' As Joy put her arms round her, Rebecca sobbed, 'I'd feel I was letting the whole Jewish race down if I ever saw him again.'

'What about your parents?' Alan asked Keith.

'They're lapsed Quakers. Lost their faith when they ran out of arguments against defending ourselves. But I never lost mine. I did try.'

Pacifism in the abstract seemed to Alan ideal as a philosophy, but in the real world it took second place to self-preservation. 'But we've got our backs to the wall, Keith. What if we all do this? Just lie down and let the Germans overrun us?'

'Nonsense!' Keith said, 'D-Day was a month ago, remember? The end's in sight.'

'Then why are we still being bombed? What about these V-1s? We're bogged down in Normandy. What about the Japs? It could go on for another year!'

'Alan, I'm not just going to sit around doing nothing. I'll be either carrying stretchers or digging up coal, or maybe even I'll go in the merchant navy bringing us food. But I simply cannot kill. Just think, in a few months' time you could be dropping bombs on civilians like your Gran. How will you feel about that?'

Alan thought a moment, devastated by this betrayal, by one he had thought of as his most trusted friend. 'Know what, Keith? I'll think they've bloody well deserved it. My father has always said, Never start a fight, but if you're in one, give 'em hell. And that's what I'll do.'

'But they might be innocent, like her!'

'Nobody's innocent!' Alan protested, his voice rising with emotion. 'A country gets the government it deserves, and the Germans let Hitler become their leader. Maybe soon they'll feel the consequences. I hope somebody you love gets blown to smithereens, and before your eyes. Then try to be self-righteous, you... you... self-indulgent prig!'

This additional insult, coming from a friend who never raised his voice, was too much for Keith to bear. 'Right! You can talk about self-indulgence! I'll be putting people together and curing disease while you're knocking out a few tunes. *You* are the self-indulgent prig. Your life's going to be *useless*, Alan Scott!'

The afternoon ended in tears and anger. As they left the summer house Alan looked back, and muttered an apology. It had offered itself to them as a bower of Venus, and they had turned it into a nest of vipers.

Alan suddenly realised what separated him from Keith and Rebecca. They had been having to face realities like racial hatred, and make tormenting moral decisions, while his worries centred on his footling exam results. They were adults, and he still felt like a child, despite the traumas of Caesar being shot and losing Gran and Bella; but they were all just eighteen, barely afloat in a hostile sea.

That afternoon was one of those sad, plaintive, luminous moments when everything is changed, like listening to Delius's *On hearing the First Cuckoo in Spring* for the first time. That evening he did something he had not done for months, he shut himself in the front room and let his soul pour out on to the piano keys. Maddy crept up to the door and listened; at last she began to have some inkling of what he was trying to say.

Second Movement

Mysteries
PURPLE: B flat major

There are two aspects of life: the first is that man is tuned by his surroundings, and the second is that man can tune himself in spite of his surroundings.

Hazrat Inayat Khan, *The Mysticism of Sound and Music*

TEMPO 1

misterioso

London, 12 January 1971

The afternoon is drawing in over Hammersmith. Keith shakes his head sadly. 'What a devastating last meeting that was.'

'Absolutely awful,' Alan agrees. 'For all of us. The end of a chapter in four lives.'

'I've never forgotten the last words you spoke to me. Do you remember?'

Alan remembers very clearly. 'No, I'm afraid I don't.'

'You were purple with anger, and you shouted, 'I hope someone you love gets blown up before your very eyes!'

'I'm sorry, I was very upset. We all were.'

'I'm not angling for an apology. I knew you were grieving about your grandmother. I just mean that those words cut so deep, and straight to the heart of things.'

Alan pauses before replying, 'Not all words spoken in anger are regrettable. I wonder if you remember your response to mine?'

Keith says he does not.

'It was to the effect that you would spend your life healing people, but I'd just make up a few useless tunes. I've never forgotten that.'

Keith begins to apologise, but Alan stops him.

'No, please, what I'm getting at is that you made me aware of my need to do more than make interesting sounds. I've always been haunted by the fear that what I do is useless. The harmonies have changed that.'

'Hence the symphony of healing?'

Alan gives a shrug of self-deprecation and says, 'It's my small contribution.' For a second Keith interprets this as false modesty, then revises as Alan goes on, 'If you hadn't got back at me that day, I might have made a fortune by now writing rock and pop music!'

*

129

'Hi! How did your lunch go with the infamous Keith today?' Bella asks Alan when she returns in the late afternoon, fed up with London cold and damp, longing to get back to California. 'Gin and tonic, thank you very much,' she prompts him, before he can forget the really important things in life.

Alan gives her a mock hard look. 'Darling, you know I don't think he's infamous. He might have been an interior decorator at some time. Made a remark about the colour of our walls.'

'What remark?'

'About the whiteness. Odd for a man to be so colour-conscious. Oh, and he drank us out of tonic. White wine do?'

When they are sitting, curtains drawn to shut out the sleety dark, glasses and cashews in hand, he gets round to answering about Keith. 'Why was I hostile to him? Simply because he opted out at a critical time. Let the side down, as Rebecca said.'

'Who *is* this Rebecca? Is this someone I should know about? Whose horizon is she still floating around on — yours or Keith's?'

'Answer to questions two and three, No, and neither. She came on the scene during the time when you disappeared. She certainly didn't opt out — but she is dead. At least, that's what I was told many years ago.' He empties the rest of the riesling into her glass. 'How did your day go? I can tell you've been consorting with Americans.'

Bella's speech quickly reverts to Californian whenever she spends a few hours with trans-Atlantic friends: twice the speed, twice the volume and vocal range, and half the self-censoring — Alan puts it down to her being the result of a mixed marriage and so having no inborn speech patterns, to which she always replies Rubbish. Alan, on the other hand, seems to become more resolutely English with each sojourn in Los Angeles.

'We...e...ll,' Bella drawls, 'Lindy was there, you know, the drama professor from San Diego, she's just written another book on Beckett, can you imagine? And someone I've not seen for years, Christina, who now lives in New York working for the United Nations and has to compress herself and her chaotic love-life into a tiny little apartment for which she pays the earth, and... you're not listening, are you?'

He apologises. 'I'm starting to live too much in the past. Very unhealthy.'

The reappearance of Keith has opened up a flood of memories for Alan: images, voices, faces, places, long walks with the dog across fields under wide Midland skies, bitter winds and deep snow drifts by the front door. It is, however, Joy, Joy of the vacuous mind and pneumatic lips and breasts, that he perversely conjures up later that evening as he drifts into sleep. Joy, so wrongly named, and Bella, so rightly, become joined by others in his kaleidoscopiconeiric recreations of the past. Poor, driven Rebecca. Then his mother and father, and dear old Gran, and drooly, devoted Caesar, all dead, and he is back in their cramped little semi-detached, with the piano in the front room, and the avenue with the big house where Bella had come to live and had changed his life for ever.

After breakfast next morning Alan remembers what he wants to ask Bella. 'By the way, I have a question about Keith.'

Her shoulders freeze, hands hovering over the typewriter keyboard. The page is headed *The relevance of cognitive science to the analysis of music.* Then without looking at Alan she says, 'Don't you know by now that when one says *by the way*, it's a crucial topic one didn't dare to mention? By the way, what's the question?'

'He wants to know the story behind the harmonies. Do you think we should tell him?'

She breathes a little sigh of relief. 'Why does he?'

Alan spreads out hands full of ignorance. 'Search me.'

'Well then, tell him. He's your friend.' She turns back to her Hermes portable.

'But,' he reminds his wife and collaborator, 'it's ours, not mine to tell. Mind you, I think it's only natural for him to be interested. After all, he's been devoting his life for years to healing the sick in one theatre of war after another. But the harmonies belong to you as much as to me. I wouldn't want anyone queering your research pitch. On the other hand, it could be useful to have a medic in the field working with us.'

Bella thinks that over for a minute.

'Well, do we need that? I do happen to be working with one of the best neuropsychology departments in California.'

'O.K., I understand completely.'

Alan believes this is the end of the matter, and is about to sit at his own desk opposite when she continues, 'But as you say, having someone working with the sick and dying on an everyday basis, and in different parts of the world, could be very useful. Practical.'

He has always found her matter-of-factness both unnerving and fascinating. She seems to have a short-cut to the future, some kind of visionary decisiveness, strongly contrasting with his own visionary tendencies which are rooted in fantasy and imagination and often lead him to tergiversation. That is why they have worked so well together — plus the fact that he has been reared to accept leadership from a strong-minded woman.

'That's what I like about you,' he says, 'you're smart, down-to-earth, and good to look at. I'm glad I chased after you. Since I couldn't have Audrey Hepburn.'

A little later, Bella looks up and says, 'Tell you what, darling, why don't we ask Keith to dinner so that I can get to know him better?'

Alan laughs. 'Vet him, you mean?'

'All right, vet him. Remember, you haven't seen him since you were boys either...'

He looks at her quizzically and breaks in with 'What do you mean, *either?*'

Bella face shows she doesn't know what to say, but she rapidly recovers her aplomb.

'I... I... I simply mean it's a long time for you as well as for him, so you can't know him all that well. I'm only anxious that... well, I believe knowledge should be available to all, but, as you say, we don't suddenly want to find our pitch being queered by unscrupulous researchers, do we?'

'You think he might be unscrupulous?'

Bella shrugs. 'No, not him necessarily. But once we let the cat out of the bag...'

'But we have already! Have you forgotten the mystery phone calls? It's not only the few hundred people who were there who've heard the concert — it was broadcast by the BBC, so hundreds of thousands have heard the harmonies now. And tape-recorded them for all we know. So we've got to watch out for cheats *and* crazy loons!'

'But not many cheats and loons know our phone number!' Bella points out. 'I hope not, anyway.'

They flip through their lists and are staggered at how many people do know their ex-directory number. Then Alan's mind pinpoints the detail that has been nagging him. 'How did Keith know our number?'

Bella shrugs. Then thinks better of it. 'But I told you, I gave him our card at the Festival Hall.'

'No you didn't tell me,' Alan objects.

'In that case, why weren't you surprised when he did phone?'

It is Alan's turn to shrug.

'You see,' Bella explains, 'I knew you'd regret losing sight of him again, once you'd calmed down.'

They are forced to confront both the potential and the present threat. Such is their innocence, their political naivety, that they have been busily avoiding the fact that by releasing Alan's harmonies upon the world they might be doing something other than simply offering a calming and palliative response to the world's desperate need for relief from ugliness and destruction. Yes, those chords have had a remarkable, mystical therapeutic effect on one poor Frenchman, and on a few in the audience at the Festival Hall, but sceptics would put that down to hysteria — until they were tried out under controlled conditions.

'I think we're getting out of our depth,' Alan says. 'A bit of outside wisdom from our doctor friend won't go amiss. But you're right, we must tread carefully. How about tomorrow evening?'

Bella nods agreement and returns her attention to the typewriter.

Alan goes to telephone from the sitting room and soon returns.

'That's fine with him,' he reports as he sits at his desk and opens the new film script he is writing the music for. Of all things it's a war film, set in England at the height of the bombing raids. After a few minutes, he snorts with rage and bangs the pages shut.

'Bloody Americans! Why can't they bloody well get somebody English to write about the blitz, somebody who bloody well knows what it was like?'

Bella looks up, hands poised over the keyboard. 'That's what I like about you, so articulate, so verbally imaginative, so poised. I'm glad I seduced you — since I couldn't have Charlie Chaplin.'

Alan glares at her, then they both burst out laughing.

Keith arrives on the dot of seven armed with a bottle of burgundy, which they think is generous of him considering his liver. He feels *en famille* right away; there's no formality, for which he's grateful, but suspects they might be indulging him with condescension, not knowing their style is normally unpretentious anyway. He helps Alan lay the table while Bella wrestles with spaghetti.

'This makes me realise the greatest disadvantage of the nomadic life,' Keith says, setting spoons and forks. 'I don't have any roots, any base, anywhere in the world. Have packed suitcase, will travel. The tyranny of personal freedom!'

Alan resolves quickly to broach the unmentionable before it becomes taboo through embarrassment. 'Didn't you have any relationships — after Rebecca?'

Keith looks relieved, in fact, that he can talk about her. 'No. Nothing lasting. Brief flings. No commitment, no hurt.'

'I learned young about commitment and hurt, remember? Bella's disappearance?'

Bella pokes her head round the kitchen door. 'I can't hear you, come and talk in here, or I'll come in there and we get no dinner.'

'She really knows where to hit a man,' says Alan.

Although Alan's initial hostility to Keith has pretty well thawed, he still harbours a nagging feeling of betrayal by a comrade who has... what is the word he once applied to another man who fled from battle? Skived off. Etymology doubtful. Probably from *Esquiver*, to dodge a duty or, in mediaeval times, a battle. However, during dinner he begins to realise that Keith had not used his pacifism and noncombatant status as a way to avoid facing danger or 'pulling his weight', and can begin to accept him. Despite his impersonal and undramatic account, it becomes clear not only that Keith has been in many perilous situations, but that he has volunteered for mission after mission in harrowing conditions.

'It wasn't any kind of heroism, I can assure you,' he admits.

'Was it because of Rebecca?' Alan asks.

Keith nods. 'At first it was, when I saw Auschwitz, the starving survivors, the piles of corpses where she might have been lying. I admit I felt murderous rage for a while. But even before that, if I pushed myself it was frankly because of wounded pride. The worst thing had been losing the respect of friends like you and Rebecca, and in my family too. Oh, I knew they'd never hear about what I was doing, so it wasn't to impress. But I gradually got my self-respect back, a bit more every time I went through some new hell helping to rescue and repair. A lot of us in the Friends' Ambulance service felt the same.'

'You did a hell of a lot more than I did,' Alan says. 'I just wanted to get out and back to music — and Bella.'

'Is that some kind of priority list?' Bella asks.

'Sorry, I meant Bella and music, honest I did! You're inseparable anyway. Have been, right from the start. But then, everybody's connected. Take one away and the whole of one's life collapses. But for Bella, no music; but for my mum, no music; but for Bella's father, no Bella and no music; but for Bella's mother, no mystic harmonies...'

Keith looks surprised. 'Bella's mother? I thought she had gone off somewhere. You know, left you and your father?' *Am I supposed*

134

to know this? 'That's what Alan told me, I think, but it was a hell of a long time ago.'

'Not quite,' Bella says. 'She was behind quite a few things that happened during and just after the war, but we — Alan and I, that is — didn't know it then.'

'Well, before we get on to her,' Alan interrupts, 'there is the little matter of the sudden dramatic disappearance of all that suspicious lot of Cassell foreigners from the big house with the tennis court.'

'It wasn't just dramatic,' Bella cuts in, 'it was horrible. Suddenly the war ceased to be a generalised sort of menace. We were being personally targetted, and I found that very unsettling.'

'Ah,' says Alan, holding her hand, 'you do have a British sense of understatement after all. I shall never tease you about mixed blood again.'

'Mixed blood?' Keith queries.

'French and Swiss and English, in various proportions,' Bella says. 'I'm a walking Common Market. But not being pure English could be rather a hazard during the war.'

Two hours later, with the plates in the dishwasher but the pans stacked in the sink, they relax in armchairs with coffee and cognac, mellow with reminiscence.

Alan waves his glass in Bella's direction with an insouciance rare for him. 'One good thing came out of your disappearing like that. I was able to invite Keith and our girl friends to play tennis on your court. *You* never invited me to play on it.'

'No, I only ever played with Jamie,' Bella ripostes coolly.' And sat in the summer house with him.'

'Now, now, children,' Keith, ever the peacemaker, intervenes, 'you can do your fighting in bed when I've gone. You know, Alan, I always envied you two things: your devotion to music, and your devotion to Bella.'

'But Bella wasn't around when I got to know you.'

'Ah...' *Damn! I must be slipping.* '...b... b... but you may not have realised that when we were together, just the two of us, you used to bore the hind legs off me talking about Bella.'

'I didn't! Did I?'

'Are you saying that just to please me, Keith?' Bella asks, admiring the way he covered his *lapsus linguae.*

'No, certainly not. He was obsessed by you. He almost went to pieces when the lady vanished. I think it was music that saved him.'

Alan looks pensive. 'Well, they were both very hard roads to travel, for a while. Lots of obstacles along the way. My mother being a common factor to both, rest her soul.'

'Oh, I meant to ask...'

'They're both dead. A few years back. I have a short-lived family.'

'But you got that musical gift from somewhere,' Keith insists. 'I mean, your mother, yes, but before that. I'm a great believer in inherited tendencies.' He glances at his watch. 'Good grief! It's 2 a.m.! I must get a taxi.'

'Where do you have to get to?' Bella asks.

'Russell Square. I'm in a... a little hotel near the British Museum.'

'Sorry we can't offer to take you back,' says Alan. 'We don't have a car in London. No point.'

Bella is already a step ahead. 'But do you have to go back? The last tube's gone, and it'd be an awfully expensive taxi ride. You can bed down in the study.'

She looks over to Alan, who has no alternative to agreeing that this is the obvious solution.

'Then we can bore you with the rest of the story over breakfast,' she says. 'It's as much mine as Alan's, especially the rest of it, so we'll share it.'

'You were still safely out of the way, remember,' Alan protests, 'with your father, after leaving me with a broken heart.'

'Soon to be mended by Joy and Rebecca and I don't know how many others!'

'Mended? Well...'

But Keith is already dropping off to sleep on the sofa, so they call a truce to their mock battle.

It is well after ten the next morning when Bella rouses herself, leaving Alan still flat out. She strolls, yawning, into the kitchen, naked as is her wont, to be confronted by a man at the sink. With a cry, she grabs a tea towel with purple flowers printed on it and covers bits of herself.

'Goodness! I'd plain forgotten you were here! I'm sorry!'

Then the ludicrousness of her apologising for giving an almost stranger the pleasure of viewing her body strikes them both, and they burst into giggles.

'Don't worry,' Keith smiles, 'nothing can shock a doctor.'

He says nothing about doctors still being arousable. He appreciates, while he can, Bella's contours, the left breast escaping from its makeshift covering, the smooth line of hip and thigh; tending towards the curvaceous, but she is clearly in good shape, looking a few years younger than forty-four. He wonders if she has had a child. She is a year older than Alan (and therefore than himself); he remembers that Alan had confided in him at school that he was a bit worried about this, as she seemed so much more grown up. Keith could vouch for that.

'Are you sorry you gave me your card?' he asks quietly.

'No, of course not. Why should I?'

'We are deceiving Alan, after all.'

'No we're not,' she whispers urgently. 'We did twenty-odd years ago, but not now.'

She half-turns to go, and Keith cannot help glancing downwards as the towel wafts.

'You're coping very well,' he says, 'at dissembling.'

'So are you. Only one slip so far. It's like walking on a tightrope. Rather exhilarating in fact.'

'How do you think he'd take it if he found out?' Keith wonders.

Bella frowns. 'He'd laugh it off... I expect. By today's norms, it was nothing. But he'd think, if she could betray me once, maybe she could again. I wouldn't want to lose his trust.'

'Yet there you are, chatting with a man as if you're in a Japanese bath house. I'm seeing rather more of you now than I did then.'

She looks down at her negligently attired body. 'Heavens! Yes, I must go and dress.'

'You're quite an adventuress at heart, aren't you?' he smiles. It was that smile that first attracted her, she remembers.

'Maybe I have my mother to thank for that.' She looks down. 'Excuse me, I'll go and...'

'We'll not tell Alan,' Keith suggests.

'What about? Our fifteen minutes of adolescent passion, or this? Pure mistake, both times.' She makes a dismissive gesture and returns to the bedroom.

At breakfast, the nude episode is not mentioned. Keith resolutely pursues the Alan and Bella saga with singular determination, which only afterwards strikes them as odd.

'I've been thinking,' — helping himself to the marmalade — 'that business about your musical grandfather in Paris was intriguing,' he begins. 'Did you ever follow it up?'

Alan looks at Bella. 'You know about this, darling, so you don't have to listen to it again.'

'Yes, O.K., I'll be in the study if you get stuck,' she agrees, clearing the table on to a tray.

Bella, by gender, training and temperament, is much better at being interested in other people than Alan is. Anyway, Keith Maxted interests her for more than one reason.

'How long do you expect to be in London, Keith?' she asks.

Keith wonders what is behind the question.

'I'm not sure,' he replies. 'I've just done a pretty long stint, so I hope to be off the hook for a few weeks at least.'

'Don't you have any family in Birmingham?'

'Oh, no. My parents and young sister moved to South Wales soon after the war — Dad was a civil servant. They never really forgave me for my pacifism, so we've lost touch. I've never been back there. So Alan is about my only link with the past.'

She thinks this is sad.

Alan is struck by the coincidence. 'Both of us estranged from the previous generation.'

'And non-productive of a following one,' Keith surmises. 'Or have you got a child tucked away somewhere?'

They both shake their heads. 'Not through want of trying,' Alan says.

'Oh, yes, the neighbours regularly complain,' Bella adds with what strikes Keith as quite a saucy smile. Alan looks mildly embarrassed.

Keith asks Bella about her parents. 'Still alive and kicking, enjoying retirement in sunny California. Mummy still has her family's apartment in Paris, which we all make good use of. My father is very fond of Alan — regards him as the son he never had, I think.'

'I've just realised,' says Alan, 'you and I have at least one other thing in common, Keith. A dislike for aggression. Physical aggression. Oh, I know you take it to ridiculous extremes...'

'I ought to knock your block off for that!' Keith laughs.

'Now that's an expression I've not heard for years — especially from a pacifist!'

Keith turns to Bella. 'So come on Bella, you haven't got round to your mother's part in all this! She sounds a fascinating lady and I'm dying to know more about her.'

'All right, everything in it's place,' Bella laughs. 'We haven't liberated Paris yet. And it's time for another cup of coffee. Alan?'

Alan goes into the kitchen and rattles and bangs about with

cups and cupboard doors. Almost without realising it, Keith says in a low voice, 'One could easily fall in love with you, Bella.'

To his surprise, Bella merely smiles and acknowledges the compliment with a little nod of her head. 'So many have said,' she replies demurely, 'but it's never done them any good.'

'Do you want me to leave?'

She is struck by the way her coolness has disconcerted him. He's evidently no Don Juan, which reassures her. 'Don't be silly,' she says with a smile. 'We're friends now. We can control ourselves.'

Alan pops his head round the door. 'Where are the biscuits, darling?'

'I don't know, darling. Did you buy any?'

The phone rings. Alan picks up the kitchen extension. Keith and Bella hear him saying 'Tomorrow?... Rather short notice... Yes, I suppose I could... No, she has a conference in London... That's very generous... Till tomorrow then.'

'What was that, darling?' Bella wants to know.

'Marcel, ringing from Paris. He wants me to be on a panel at an international music congress tomorrow.'

'Where?'

'Paris. On new music. Very short notice, but I thought it best to say yes, as he said he'd heard such good things about the new symphony. He invited you too...'

'Yes, so I gathered,' she cuts in, 'but you refused for me. I can understand you'd want to be in Paris by yourself, footloose and...'

'But not fancy free, dammit! Aw, shucks!'

Keith, once more, is confused by these two. Is this bickering or bantering? Their words and their attitudes don't gel. In any case, he feels *de trop*, and stands up. 'I really must go. You'll have stuff to organise for tomorrow, and I... well, I have things to do.'

He stays long enough to drink his biscuitless coffee, then bids them goodbye. He kisses Bella gently on both cheeks. 'Your mother's story will have to wait,' he smiles.

'It will keep,' Bella assures him. 'It's worth it. We are very much part of it, Alan and I.'

Keith takes this parting shot as a statement of the solidarity, the inseparability, of his hosts, whose hospitality he has so very nearly dishonoured.

When he has left, Alan takes his wife by the hands and kisses her.

'Of course you can come if you like, darling. I'd be delighted.

Marcel caught me by surprise. I just didn't think.'

'How long will you be away?' Bella asks, clearing away the coffee cups and walking to the kitchen.

'A couple of days.'

'That's fine. It works out quite well, actually. Apart from the conference tomorrow I've simply got to get this paper finished and I shan't have you to distract me. Will you stay at the apartment?'

'If your *maman* doesn't have any of her formidable American friends staying there.'

Bella telephones Alexi Cassell, and after listening to five minutes of stream-of-consciousness commentary on life in L.A., she manages to get in her question.

'*L'appartement? Mais oui*, of course you can go to it. Whenever you like.'

'But is it free now, *maman?*'

'Now? What do you mean, now?'

'To be precise, tomorrow and the day after.'

'Oh, are you going for a little holiday?'

'Yes. Well, not me, Alan. He has to go for a conference.'

'By himself?'

'Yes, *maman*. Is it free? Is there anyone staying in it?'

'Why are you not going with him?'

'Because I have work to do here. Is it free, *maman?*'

'In Paris, in the apartment, by himself? Ah well. It is Alain, after all. Why not? He won't be tempted to be naughty, poor Alain. *Oui, bien sûr, chérie, il est libre, l'appartement.*'

As Bella puts down the receiver, she is suddenly struck by the contrast between two idealisms: that of the young pacifist who knew nothing of the world, and that of her mother, the middle-aged Frenchwoman who had responded to her country's desperate need, even though it meant sacrificing so much. She finds herself veering to Alan's point of view about his old friend.

TEMPO 2 — ALLEGRO

volando - mistico - spirituoso

Autumn 1944

Even though Paris was liberated in August, and the detested Vichy government had ceased to exist in September, by the end of summer 1944 France had not been entirely cleared of the invaders, and the outcome of the war was far from certain. True, the Germans were threatened on three fronts: northern France, Italy, and Russia; German boys of sixteen were being called up for front line duty; and Hitler was shaken by the abortive attempt on his life in July — but he still harangued his generals, who were managing to slow down the Allied advances towards the Rhine. Eisenhower and Montgomery were at loggerheads. In mid-September the Germans unleashed the second of their secret weapons: long-range rockets, V2s, launched from Holland. By the end of March 1945, nine thousand Londoners would be killed by about two thousand rockets. The war in the Far East could not be brought to a rapid close, as had been hoped, because substantial forces could not yet be moved from Europe.

When Alan went up to Cambridge in October, therefore, it was expected that the R.A.F. would still need air crew for some time. He had been placed in a small college, Trinity Hall, which seemed friendly enough. As he stood in the Front Court on his first evening there, with his short black gown flapping round the legs of his R.A.F. uniform, he had to fight off feelings of disbelief. Until now those long-held hopes of going one day to Cambridge had really been fantasies beyond realisation. Even on the train, and waiting interminably for a connection at Bletchley, he would not have been surprised to wake up or learn there had been a mistake. This was, quite literally, another world reaching back into a past of which, though still remote, he was now a part. The first member of the family, and the first child in the avenue ever to go to university! Maybe a time would come when children would expect to do this if they were qualified, but he could not imagine it.

He had read up about the history of the college in the local library as soon as the Senior Tutor had written to him, and knew it had been founded in 1350. Never before had he been aware of anything that old, except for churches and cathedrals he never felt at home in. The picturesque architecture, the Elizabethan blending perfectly with the Georgian, more than compensated in his eyes for the discomforts and inconveniences of college life: a trip to the bathroom required a freezing run down three flights of stairs and across the windswept court to the basement — and come January, that would involve trudging through a foot or two of snow.

Most of the undergraduates were there on short courses with one of the four armed services — Army, Navy, R.A.F., or Fleet Air Arm — except for a few medical and medically unfit students. The short coursers soon found how gruelling their work would be, not only because of the amounts of material to be mastered, but because (for those reading Arts subjects, at least) the work was in two totally unrelated fields: for the mathematics, navigation, armaments and other technical subjects on the one hand, and academic subjects (history, literature, languages, and so on), all competing for attention every day, seven days in the week. Alan had had to opt for either French or Music, his two strongest suits. He did not want to drop either, but finally music won. Far, far away at the back of his mind was that promised symphony.

The first horror was not long in revealing itself: an Air Squadron maths test! When he had gone into the Arts Sixth he had truly believed that he had finally escaped from the need to do mathematics, which from algebra and geometry onwards had resisted his comprehension as fiercely as he resented its opacity and uselessness. Never again would he have to battle with stupid problems such as: 'A 50-gallon bath is filling from a tap at 20 pints a minute, and the plug-hole is emptying at 10 pints a minute. How long will it be before the people in the flat below start banging on the ceiling?' Never again: so he had believed. But the same ghastly question re-appeared on the test in a slightly disguised form: 'You have 50 gallons left in your Spitfire fuel tank as you fly 10 miles south of Dover. An Me 109 punctures it with a 3mm bullet. Will you make it back to England?' Alan spent fifteen minutes trying vainly to work out an answer, then wrote: 'How do I know there is only one bullet-hole?'

The result of the initial test seemed to indicate he was not as dumb as some of the others who were placed in Flight 9. He was in Flight 8. But now he found that his continued existence at Cambridge depended entirely on passing a maths test once a fortnight! O woe! O misery! It looked as if his only hope lay in Signals, as his ability to receive and transcribe morse code proved to be outstanding. He was quite willing to spend hours listening to the dots and dashes and writing down messages as if in a trance, but the earphones had a bad effect on his ears, which began to suppurate.

On the way back from a frugal meal in Hall, with a small slice of cheese on toast for pudding, he was accosted by a hearty type swathed in a black and white check scarf of enormous proportions.

'Ah, my name's Fothergill. You're a fresher, aren't you?'

'Yes, that's right. Alan Scott.'

'Good man. What is your father doing now?'

Alan felt like saying it was none of his bloody business, but replied, 'The same as before. How about yours, Fothergill?'

'Oh, still pottering about in the Lords. Have you joined a sports club yet?'

Alan had determined he was not going to continue to undergo voluntarily the unspeakable discomforts of the rugger field that had been more or less compulsory at school, especially now his ears were so sore. He was having to tie a handkerchief round them to stop the sticky goo staining his pillow.

'No, thank you,' he replied.

'Good. Then rowing's the thing for a hefty chap like you. Boathouse at two tomorrow. I'll just jot your name down, Scott.'

The following afternoon, after battling with his conscience about simply ignoring the whole business, he cycled to the boathouse in his shorts, and stood about disconsolately while someone explained in the Siberian breeze the intricacies of the sliding seat, the eccentricities of the rowlock, the inadvisability of catching a crab, and how much it would cost you if you put your boot through the bottom of the shell. Then they spent an hour sitting in little mock rowing-boats anchored to the bank, pulling and feathering and going nowhere. Alan decided to give rowing a miss as soon as possible and join the Wrestling Club. He was surprised he had not thought of it earlier:

Cycling back from the river along Jesus Lane, that damned music started up in his head again, loud and insistent. Longing to get a hot cup of rationed tea and a slice of ration-buttered toast inside him, he tried to ignore it. Then he happened to glance at a girl cycling in the opposite direction and nearly fell off.

It was Bella. He was sure it was Bella. He shouted her name, but a noisy car passed between them and she did not hear, even though

143

she had seemed to stop pedalling for a moment. By the time he had turned his steed round in the busy street, she had disappeared, but he had glimpsed one single clue: on the back of her gaudy purple mudguard was a white-painted letter G. Every bicycle had letters identifying the college of its owner. He had TH on his — and G meant Girton.

After Hall that evening, he wrote a brief note on his pad of crested college paper:

Dear Bella
I'm sure I saw you today. Please drop me a note. I must see
you.
Love,
Alan (Scott)

The next week was so hectic, trying to balance the impossible demands of his academic course and of the air squadron, that he sank wearily into his bed at midnight each night without any extra-curricular thoughts. His new relaxation, during stolen moments, was playing the college chapel organ. It took him a while to hit the right keys with his feet, but the years spent as a reluctant partner for the girls when Maddy played for dance classes must have left him with fairly good pedal dexterity. He refused point-blank, however, to play for Sunday morning services; hymns bored him to tears. He also discovered how popular you can be if you can play the piano, and developed a liking for jazz improvisation. Strumming away at the old joanna in the mess, with a pint of beer on the top and a couple of girls leaning over him, began to have definite attractions.

Then he found it in his pigeon-hole one lunch-time: his letter returned with 'NOT KNOWN AT THIS ADDRESS' scrawled over it. But obviously it had been opened. He examined every square inch of the letter and envelope, hoping to find some evidence that she had read it. Some tiny secret mark; a faint whiff of the perfume or soap he still remembered from the times when they had been close together, on the piano stool, holding hands, kissing... Ah! Stop it! Not known? Of course, she might have been visiting, and was riding a friend's bike. Or perhaps it was still dangerous for her to be known and traceable? In which case he'd better not pursue the matter. At least, she now knew where he was, and she could approach him if she wanted to.

A few days later he found a hand-delivered letter in his pigeon-hole at the porters' lodge, with a typed envelope. The note said simply: 'Wait'. He was sure it was Bella's handwriting.

Letter in hand, he spoke to the head porter. 'Excuse me, Mr. Loveday, you don't happen to know who delivered this, do you?'

'Yes, Mr. Scott, it was another of the new gentlemen, naval I think. He said a man had handed it to him just outside and asked him to bring it in.'

There was no way he could track down an unknown naval cadet and ask him to identify an unknown man, so that seemed to be the end of that line of enquiry.

After the reverses of December, during which the German armies were able to go on to the offensive under Jodl and Rundstedt, threatening Brussels and Antwerp with recapture, the Red Army began a major offensive in the east on 12 January 1945. Five days later the Russians captured Warsaw. Bill went down the avenue to tell old Mr. and Mrs. Cooper about this. Arnie Cooper was a very retired, completely bald, almost deaf, one-eyed Black Country cobbler of lugubrious appearance and dry laconic wit typical of the Black Country. Somehow the couple had managed to produce a son, Dickie, very late in life. He was a sergeant in the army, stationed in the Middle East, so they always liked to hear about Allied advances.

'I thought you'd like to know the Russians are in Warsaw,' Bill shouted.

'Cor lumme! 'Ear that Edith? The Russians are Walsall!' Arnie shouted. Then his remaining eye looked, puzzled, at Bill. 'Funny, I thought they were on our side. 'Ave they gone and swapped again?'

Eisenhower ordered the massive Allied advance on the Rhine in early February. It was the beginning of the end — and the beginning of a new conflict with the Soviet Union over the future political control of central Europe and Scandinavia.

The bitterness of that winter was extreme, in northern Europe, south of the Baltic, and west of the Wash. Cycling back from the swimming baths, which he had to attend twice a week in order to pass his swimming test (just in case of a forced landing in the drink) Alan had very sore ears and icicles hanging from his eyebrows. He stowed his bicycle in the basement and ran up to his rooms on E staircase. Shivering, he went straight to light the gas fire, but found it was already burning. A voice said, 'I'm sorry, it was so cold, I turned it on.'

145

He turned round slowly, so as not to frighten the apparition away. But Bella stayed there, sitting in his worn armchair.

'Bella? It *is* you!'

'It is me, Alan. Sorry it's been so long.'

He stood there transfixed, looking at her in disbelief, his heart pounding with excitement. Then he rushed towards her, arms outstretched, and hugged her close for a long time, until she said, 'You're wetting my blouse again.'

But this time, it was melting ice, not tears. And their kisses were not the tentative, furtive ones of adolescence. It was not until they pulled apart, and she placed her left hand upon his cheek, saying, 'Dear Alan', that he noticed the ring.

He took her hand and held it fiercely. 'What's this?' His voice was hoarse with emotion.

Smiling ruefully, she replied, 'My trophy of tragedy. I'll tell you about it later.'

He stepped away from her, cold seeping into his heart. 'No! Now! I want to know now! Please!'

Bella saw from his pleading eyes that it would be cruel to delay an explanation. 'Six months ago, I fell in love with a fine man and got engaged to him. He was much older than me, thirty-two, a naval commander. Immediately afterwards, his ship was sent to the far east. They were bound for Darwin, but never got there. A Japanese U-boat got them in the Pacific. No survivors. But I think it's right for me to wear it for a while longer, to show I haven't forgotten him.'

The news was a devastating blow to him, a betrayal. He could never have asked another girl to marry him whilst his relationship with Bella remained unresolved. But he smothered his emotions. One could not both resent and practise possessiveness.

'I'm so sorry, Bella,' he said finally, with a fair show of conviction. 'But you, engaged! It's funny, I've never stopped thinking of you as a fifteen-year old.'

'All right, go on, tell me I've aged in the last four years!' she smiled.

Of course, it was true. He could now see the faint lines of suffering around her eyes and mouth, but they only added to her radiant beauty.

'Age shall not wither her...' he began.

'Nor custom stale her infinite variety! Of course! We both did *Anthony and Cleopatra* for School Certificate.'

'Have you got over it? Your...' He looked away. '...fiancé? Or is it too soon? It took me a long time to get over my grandmother being killed.'

'Yes, I remember. I was there, have you forgotten? No, I've not got over it, because death is horrible when it's sudden and unnecessary, like that. But the engagement was a mistake, I now realise. I even had doubts then. I was too young, and feeling very insecure with mummy gone and daddy often away. Daddy was dead against it — I think that helped to push me into it. The whole world seemed to be disintegrating round me. Tony seemed so solid and dependable and sensible, but we had very little in common. He would have wanted me to spend my life as a wife and mother of six children, definitely no career. But I chose to forget that, or thought I'd be able to change him when the time came. But it would have been a disaster, I think.'

Huddled close to the little gas fire, mugs of hot tea in hand, they could at last begin to fill in the gaps of the last two years.

'Where did you vanish to?'

'Up to Scotland. They talked about sending me to Canada or Australia, but I convinced them I'd be in more danger from U-boats than from bombers.'

'I... we never understood why you were whisked away like that. We knew it was something to do with your father's war work. Was that why you couldn't write?'

'It was partly that. But there was a more urgent reason, which not even I knew about... To do with my mother.'

'Your *mother*? But she was hardly ever there.'

'Exactly. I was simply told she was doing some secret job buried in the country somewhere. I thought it must be code-breaking or something.'

'But it wasn't?'

'Do you remember what nationality I said she was?'

'Um, Swiss, I think.'

'Yes. That's what I was strictly ordered to tell everyone. But she was French, with a German mother. So she was completely bilingual, trilingual, and very useful. Right up to about a month ago. She didn't come back until all the Germans had been cleared from French soil.'

'Come back? Where from?'

'From France. Although Paris was liberated last summer, pockets of Germans held out in certain areas until December.'

'And she was involved with that?' Alan asked incredulously.

'Yes. So I learned at Christmas, when we were reunited at last.

147

She'd been parachuted back to her own region, Les Maures. A very wild and mountainous area inland from Saint-Tropez. Very active resistance country. The *maquis* leader of the Brigade des Maures was called Marc Rainant, and she was his contact with the Free French.'

Alan was puzzled, again. 'But why did all that mean *you* had to leave Birmingham?'

'Because of a man named Krikker. The head of the regional SS. A monster. He ordered a whole village behind Cavalaire to be exterminated and burnt to the ground as a reprisal because they wouldn't betray my mother and Marc. The British decoded messages to agents in England showing the Germans intended to use me as bait — kidnap me, take me to Germany, and say I'd be tortured and killed if she and Rainant didn't give themselves up. That Irish idiot rather messed things up for them, fortunately!'

'I suppose that's why you know the south of France so well, even though you're Swiss. Les Maures? It sounds Moorish, Arabic.'

'The ancient Greeks called the region *maouro*. Sombre, overgrown. Menacing. Like the Black Forest. But I think the name *Maures* must have come from 'Moors'. After all, the Saracens built the village down the road from my grandparents' house, over a thousand years ago.'

'So you had foreign invaders way back then? Did they leave any mark on the place?'

'Daddy thought so. He used to tease mummy about her dark hair...'

'Dark? But she was blonde!'

'No, not really She's where I get my dark hair and skin from, though I'm darker than she is. "A bit of the old tar, you two have got," Daddy would say. And he'd pretend to be Krikker ranting about the locals round Sainte-Maxime and Cavalaire — mummy had told him what he'd written and said in speeches. "Lazy runts," he'd bellow, doing a Hitler salute, "good-for-nothing layabouts, nasty swarthy little people, decadent, diseased, their skins dark with dirt that never washes off. More North African than European!" Krikker once said he was sorry for Rommel, having to cope with all those natives. "The only good thing about Arabs," Krikker wrote in the Vichy press, "is that they hate Jews as much as we do." Mummy would wipe the tears of mirth from her eyes. She said laughing at Krikker helped her to cope when she was being hunted by him.'

'What's happened to him now, this Krikker? Did he get away?'

'Oh, no. That's why she has only just got back; she had to testify against him at the war crimes tribunal. At first he denied all the charges, then claimed he was only carrying out orders, then foolishly tried to justify them as witness after witness appeared, with scars on their bodies and minds to prove him guilty.'

'And that's why you pretended you're not in Cambridge?'

'That wasn't hard. I'm enrolled under another name — my mother's name, Crispin. Isabella — that's my real name — Crispin. It can sound like an English name too.'

'Isabella,' Alan savoured the name. 'That suits you. Shall I call you Isabella from now on?'

Bella did not look all that happy with the idea. 'I'd rather you didn't.'

'Why not?'

'I feel it would change things, change me. I've always been Bella to you. I'd never want to call you Alain. My mother's the only one who calls me Isabella, and that's when she's displeased with me.'

Alan saw her point. 'So your mother's free to come home now, is she?'

Bella shrugged. 'I don't know. There might be more people she has to testify against — Vichy *collabos*. Your letter created quite a stir, you know. It went to the Principal first — she knows about me.'

'I see. Sorry to break your cover. And what are you reading?'

Bella smiled. 'Oh, a few novels.'

'I mean what...'

'I know what you Cambridge types mean! I'm evacuated here from University College, London, where I'm *studying* psychology and physiology.'

'Not music?'

'No, I realised pretty quickly that playing the piano was just a bit of easy fun for me. I never had the passion you have. I'm afraid I have my father's scientific genes, but I want to know how the mind works.'

'Oh dear, does that mean you'll be psychoanalysing me all the time?'

'No, you're far too normal to be interesting. And what makes you think I'm going to see you again?'

As he was visibly stunned and hurt by this, she relented and took his hand. 'Sorry, Alan. I must stop teasing like that. It's a defence mechanism I've built up. Of course I will. See you, I mean. And you are interesting — in a very normal kind of way!'

149

He chased her round the room and into the bedroom, where they lay giggling and panting on his narrow bed; the first time they had been so close, and in private. His hand on her breasts betrayed no shyness, and her response left him in no doubt that she wanted to make love as much as he did. For Alan, who had wondered so often if he would ever know what she looked like naked, this proximity was overwhelming. Hedy Lamarr could not have looked as beautiful. His hand reached for the top button of her dress, finally succeeded in undoing it, and the next two. He was surprised to see that her breasts were a lighter shade than her shoulders, but still golden. Every inch of that smooth skin and the firm roundness would remain in his memory for ever. The top of her silk bra was edged with violet lace, which he gently lowered until the pink-brown of her nipples was revealed. These he kissed reverently, then took them between his lips, and licked them, all the time saying to himself, *This can't be happening, it must be a dream.* Her breathing became more rapid, and her hands moved down his back and pressed him to her.

'Mr. Scott?

They shot up.

'Blast!' Alan whispered, 'it's Charlie. My gyp.' He called out, 'Just getting dressed, Charlie. Been for a swim. Five minutes?'

Charlie's eagle eye had spotted Bella's coat, scarf and bag on a chair.

'I'll make it ten, shall I, Mr. Scott?'

'Thanks. That'd be fine.'

Once again they collapsed with suppressed laughter, but the moment for lovemaking had passed.

'Actually, it's freezing in here,' Bella said. 'And you're still dripping on me.'

Charlie came back half an hour later, said 'Good morning, Miss' politely to Bella, made the bed and tidied up perfunctorily while Alan made more tea (with powdered milk) out in the gyp room. Back by the miserable gas fire with their hands round more hot mugs, they shared the same chair for warmth. Not only for physical warmth, but for the sheer luxury of being close.

'What would have happened in there if Charlie hadn't come in?' she asked dreamily.

Alan told himself not to retreat into shyness. 'I suppose... I'd have ripped your dress off, and your...'.

He suddenly visualised the first time he had seen her. 'Do you remember the first time we spoke?'

'That historic occasion? When your dog tried to rape me? Yes, of course.'

'I couldn't take my eyes off your bra. It was showing through your blouse.'

'I know you couldn't. So I knew you were terribly normal! Would you have made love to me? Gone all the way?'

'What, then?'

'No! Just now, I mean?'

'It was certainly my intention at the time. Perfectly dishonourable. Would you have let me?'

'Did you have a French letter?'

This practical difficulty had not occurred to him. 'No, I'm afraid not. Sorry. I never was a good boy scout.'

'Don't be sorry, Alan. I'm glad you're not the sort who keeps a packet by the bed ready for the next girl. But it wouldn't have been your first time, would it?'

'Would it have been yours?'

'I asked first.'

'No, I'm afraid not. It was with a girl named Shirley, back home.'

'Did you enjoy it?'

'No, not really.' He closed his eyes and tried to bring her back. 'It was more like an initiation ceremony, or an induction course.'

'Goodness! It sounds like something out of Maupassant. She wasn't a pro, was she?'

'Oh no, a nurse. A friend of Rebecca's. She took me in hand, as it were, and showed me the ropes. Oh dear, I seem to be choosing the wrong vocabulary. It was clinical. Very businesslike. She even had a Frenchie, as she called it, and knew how to put it on.'

'Did you do it lots of times?' Bella was not sure if her curiosity was healthy or prurient.

'No, only a couple of times. I was quite fond of her, but she was too matter-of-fact about it for my liking. Absolutely nothing romantic or even warm. I felt I was being used for some kind of serving.'

'Like a pedigree dog? But you don't regret it?'

'I don't think so. I would have liked you to be the first, but at that time I never expected to see you again.'

'You don't have to apologise, you know.'

'No, I suppose not. At least I can hope you'll be the second. Now, how about you?'

Bella had already decided that her libido must be more active

151

than Alan's, that she must have quite a lot in common with Shirley, and that he might not like it.

'Well, I was engaged to be married, you know. So as *maman* had always told me it was important for couples to know they were physically compatible, I made sure.'

'And were you?'

'No, not at all. It was quite a worry, actually. Tony didn't seem very enthusiastic or interested. I even suspect he thought I was a loose woman. Maybe I am? Or was he just too, too English for words?'

'Spoken like a true foreigner,' Alan laughed. 'And was he the only one?'

'Ah, now... I have committed one or two indiscretions, but I am very discriminating.'

For a second he thought of pursuing the matter, but decided he would rather not know any sordid details. He had severe doubts about that smarmy Jamie character, but did not want them confirmed. But there was something he had to know, connected to her use of the present tense.

'Is there someone in tow at the moment?'

'In toe? Is that a football term, meaning underfoot?'

He wondered, Is she being deliberately obtuse now?

'Do you have a lover at the moment?' he spelled out.

'Oh, good heavens, no! I am *une vieille fille*, an old maid gathering dust on the shelf.'

That, he thought, was very unlikely. Still side by side, entwined in his only armchair, they kissed again. Then he turned and looked at her fiercely.

'Now, Miss Cassell, promise you're not going to disappear again.'

'Yes, I promise, darling Alan,' she said, looking into his eyes. She kissed him, not with the ardour they had just experienced, but with a tenderness that he found totally reassuring, a reminder of her first kiss in those far-off days of uneasy youth. 'But,' she added, 'the war's not over yet.'

That sombre thought brought them back to reality.

'And how about your studies?' she asked, 'what are you *reading?*'

'Huh! That's a joke! Air squadron work takes up most of the time — I'm an R.A.F. cadet too. But when I have a moment or two, music.'

Bella gasped and took his hands in hers. 'That's wonderful, Alan! You've stuck to it! I'm so glad, so very glad. Daddy and I knew you had so much originality. Now, tell me all about how you got into Cambridge.'

As he escorted her back to the porters' lodge, she looked sideways at him and said, 'I couldn't help noticing that your ears are very sore and red.'

He tried to pass it off. 'Perhaps someone is talking about me?'

But the concern in her voice was not to be ignored.

'It's the earphones, and the chlorine in the water at the baths, it has a bad effect on them.'

'You ought to take them to the doctor,' she suggested.

'When I have a moment to spare,' he promised.

Pretty soon the old pattern re-established itself, with Bella helping him with his confounded mathematical and navigation problems: he had nightmares about having to work out vector triangles with one engine on fire and a bullet in his left shoulder. Their tough work schedules, the strict college rules — all visitors out by 10 p.m. — and the problem of trailing from or to Girton College, all meant that socialising was severely curtailed; but their moments together were no less precious for that. Maybe more.

The R.A.F. short course ended in March, followed by three weeks' leave. Alan told his parents that it would be only two weeks, and spent seven blissful days with Bella in London. Her father was in the States, and her mother in France, so they had the house to themselves.

Alan was posted to the Air Crew Receiving Centre at the Grand Hotel, Torquay, where the first of several indignities was a medical examination, also known as the FFI inspection, technically 'Free from Infection' but understood by all erks to mean 'Fit for Insertion'. Alan coughed and bent over and had his knees banged with a little hammer. Then the M.O. peered down his ears.

'Hm. How long have you had this?' he asked, probing with a metal spout.

'The soreness? A few months.'

'Did you report it?'

'No.'

'No *Sir?*'

'No, sir. I never had time, sir, on the short course.'

'You haven't been swimming, have you?'

'Yes, sir. We had to pass the swimming test.'

The M.O. next looked in the other ear, shook his head, and Alan began to take the situation seriously.

'Have you ever been told you had a perforated eardrum?'

Alan had not.

'Well, er, Scott, it looks as though you've had otitis externa for some time, and that might have turned into chronic suppurative otitis media. I'll have to send you to the E.N.T. specialist.'

'Is it serious, sir?'

'Oh, yes,' said the young medic cheerfully, 'you could go deaf.'

And this callous, grinning twit called himself a doctor? Was it really possible that he might go permanently deaf? The thought was too appalling, and yet he could not get it out of his head. He began to feel the world closing down around him as his fear of isolation grew. Every day he tried to assess his hearing, until it became an obsession. In the education hut there was a record player and a few old records, which he put on, carefully adjusting the volume to compare with the previous day's aural impact.

Alan's ears were prodded by the Ear, Nose and Throat specialist a few days later. He tut-tutted even more than the M.O., and inserted yards of tape saturated with silver nitrate, which rendered him almost completely deaf.

They were made to march interminably up and down the promenade, but Alan was excused, as he could not hear the commands to turn left, right, or about, and this created havoc. It was clear that no one knew what to do with this new lot of budding pilots and navigators. Should their expensive air crew training be continued in the expectation that they would be needed in the Far East against the Japanese? Or should they be demobilised, to save the country millions of pounds? Or put into cold storage, in case of need? In the end it was decided simply to hold on to them and employ them in menial jobs, until the global situation had clarified.

On 30 April 1945 Adolf Hitler committed suicide, thus depriving the civilised world of the pleasure of witnessing the most interesting trial for Crimes against Humanity, rivalling others unfortunately never held either, such as Caligula and the Holy Roman Inquisitors. On 9 May the general surrender of Germany was formally ratified in Berlin.

VE-Day was an explosion of joy and relief throughout the country, punctuated by peals of church bells that up till now (apart from a flurry for Alamein) had been a warning of enemy invasion. Alan was by that time in prison, or as good as, at R.A.F. Station, Eastchurch, on the Isle of Sheppey. This was a dumping ground for now unwanted air crew, many of whom had been risking their lives for years. He was no longer a cadet sporting the coveted white cap flash and shoulder 'VRs' of the air crew volunteer, but the lowest of the low, an Aircraftsman Second Class. It irked to be an erk. The only relief from total boredom came from daily visits to the sick bay, where a pretty WAAF nurse extracted the tape from his ears and replaced it.

Alan had already met two or three of the others, ex-university short course chaps, at Torquay, but they were cliquey public school types; as soon as they found he was not at Eton, Harrow, or Rugby, they lost interest in him and he in them. The character who latched himself on to him was a rather unlikely one, a down-to-earth Cockney who spoke like a barrow-boy but had the brain of a boffin. He had, like Alan, achieved the highest cadet rank in the A.T.C., but had left school at fifteen to go to technical college to study engineering. He was unsinkably cheerful, incurably cheeky, and could perform the whole repertoire of Max Miller's jokes and music hall songs. He and Alan provided regular entertainment in the NAAFI in the evenings, with Alan quickly picking up the accompaniments.

'Tell yer wot, mate, Al boy, we orta go on the 'alls when we git ahta this bleedin' dreary lot. We'd make a bleedin' fortune. "Al and Tosh, the Musical Skymen", 'ow abaht that, eh?'

Tosh's only interest in joining the R.A.F. had been to become a gunner. He could strip a breech block like unwrapping butter, and had an unerring eye on the range for a moving target. 'I just wanna git one o' them 'einkels in me sights and see 'im burst into flames! Get me own back for blowin' us aht of 'ouse and 'ome three bleedin' times. Three times, Al! You just drive the bloody Lanc and read yer maps, and I'll keep yer covered.'

Tosh also had an insatiable sex drive, and managed to escape from prison after lights out at 10 p.m., either over or under the high fence, Alan never asked how.

After a fortnight's daily treatment Alan was ordered to report to the M.O. for a check. After a cursory inspection with his auriscope, the doctor said 'Hm' (a stock response, Alan supposed, learned by all medical students) and asked him how the ears were feeling.

'Less inflamed, sir,' he replied.

'Have you ever had any real pain inside or under the ears?'

'No, sir.'

'And the hearing?'

'It's fine, now the wadding is out.'

'Tinnitus? Strange noises?'

Alan knew what tinnitus meant. 'No, no tinnitus, sir. I do hear

155

music in my head — have done for years. That's why I'm a musician. But I don't think I'd call it noise.' He thought it best not to mention the premonitory sounds.

The M.O. smiled. 'That would be a matter of taste, I suppose. Beethoven had tinnitus, you know?'

'Yes, I know, sir. He drank loads of red wine to try and stop it.'

'That probably made it worse. Keep off the strong stuff, Scott.'

Alan said solemnly that he would.

'Well,' the doctor sat back, 'you may have been lucky. Or you may not. I'll give you some silver nitrate drops to put in — no need for the wadding, as you call it. You will need another E.N.T. examination and a hearing test to be sure if there's any permanent damage to the inner ear. I don't suppose you'll be here much longer, so I'll put in a recommendation for that with your next posting. Do you have any idea where you might be sent?'

Alan had none.

'It won't be anywhere exotic, with that little problem of yours. Nowhere hot and sticky, no naked dancing girls! Medically, you're Grade 3, U.K. Only, pending further assessment.'

Alan's face registered what he hoped looked like profound disappointment.

Depression set in immediately after this. It was the mention of Beethoven that caused it. Perhaps the 'noises' Ludwig had heard were like twentieth-century atonal music, but he hadn't recognised them as music. Alan's letters home and to Bella contained no reference to hearing problems — not just because he did not wish to worry anyone else, but because pity would be a natural but very unwelcome response. All that covert watching for signs of deafness, the reluctance to enquire if it was getting worse...

In May 1945 the Victory in Europe festivities in the avenue were typical of what was happening all over the country: a street party was rapidly organised, for which every house brought out tables and chairs and set them in a line down the middle of the road. An effigy of Hitler was made and placed, Guy Fawkes-like, on top of a pyre. As evening closed in, the fire was lit, and a great cheer arose as he started to burn and the sparklers stuck in his eyes burst into flame.

The drama could now be played out in the Pacific theatre; but the bloody conflict would go on for another five months. Dr. Cassell was flown over for urgent secret meetings at Los Alamos, and shortly after that scientists were able to say with certainty that

156

atomic bombs would be available by late summer — 'as a psychological weapon' they were told, to be used should the Japanese ignore warnings.

Bella returned to study in London, and — he could hardly believe his good fortune — Alan was posted to R.A.F. Station, Uxbridge, as a Clerk General Duties. This was the category the R.A.F. used for anyone unwanted who could read and write. He reported to the guardroom and stood to attention before the duty corporal, a regular who could spot one of them unwanted poncy aircrew volunteers a mile off, fuckin' waste of time. The corporal slowly drew a form towards him, and asked Alan his name and number.

'Religion?'

Alan had been thinking about this for some time. One of the most irksome aspects of service life, he found, was the compulsory church parade every Sunday morning. You were either C of E, Catholic, Jewish, or Fancy Religions, which meant cookhouse duty.

'Pantheist,' he said.

The corporal had already started to write C of E as a matter of course; he now, with an accusing look, crossed it out and began to write, 'Baptist.'

'No, corporal, pantheist.'

'Pan what?'

'Theist. Pan-theist. It means you believe God is everywhere in nature, and you have to go and worship him there, not inside in a church. It's a very ancient religion, corporal.'

There was a rapid intake of breath through Corporal Cottrell's tight, thin lips. 'Right!' *Fuckin' smartarse!* 'We'll see about that. Make sure you're on parade at 8 a.m. sharp in the morning. Then I'll inspect your kit and your bedspace, and it had better be spotless.' There was no mistaking the menace in the voice.

Years ago Alan had remarked to his father that English school bullies would make great Gestapo officers. He had no doubt this corporal had been one of them.

Within a week Alan was given an appointment to see a top E.N.T. specialist with a battery of frequency tests at his disposal. He prescribed a new drug which would, he hoped, destroy any lurking bacteria, and told Alan to return in a month.

As soon as it was discovered that he could type, as well as read and write, Alan was made clerk to the crabby adjutant, Flight Lieutenant Gibson. Alan's work was boring in the extreme — typing memos and forms, sticking new amendments into the book of King's Regulations. But it was all made worth while by the proximity of Bella, who had found digs in a house just by Uxbridge underground station. Alan tried to get permission to live off camp, but this was turned down flat. Only sergeants and above were allowed to do that.

He and Bella both went up to town to celebrate VJ Day on the twelfth of September 1945, joining in the merry throng that sang and danced all night in Piccadilly and St. James's Park and the Mall. Dr. Cassell was still away in the States, but Bella's mother was back, living in their house in Hampstead, too far away to interfere with their activities. They had to walk all the way back to Uxbridge, some twenty miles, and Alan only just made it in time for parade. Cpl. Cottrell looked very disappointed, but reprimanded Alan for not having shaved and put him on extra guard duty.

One of the functions of R.A.F. Uxbridge was to be the home of the R.A.F. Symphony Orchestra. Many of its members had been orchestral players in civvy street, and its standard was very high. Alan soon got to know them at the NAAFI, and joined in their off-duty music-making, both jazz and chamber music. They played for dances, but Alan soon saw the danger of leaving Bella to the tender mercies of potential rivals on the dance floor, and opted out of the band. Then they invited him to come along to orchestral rehearsals and, when they realised how competent he was, he was soon roped in to play odd piano parts when scores required it. Then the adjutant got fed up with his absences from the office, and forbade them.

One morning, battling with the ancient Remington with the sticking G, he found an officer standing on the other side of his desk.

'Alan Scott?'

Alan stood up. 'Yes, sir.'

'I am Flying Officer Harrington. Evan Harrington.'

'Oh, yes, of course, sir. I've seen you with the orchestra.'

He was the assistant conductor.

'You haven't been to see us lately.'

'No, sir.' He glanced at the adjutant's office. 'Flight Lieutenant Gibson didn't like me being away so much, sir.'

'I see. Are you happy with that?'

'Not at all sir. But...'

'Right, sit down. Leave it to me.'

Harrington knocked on the adjutant's door and went in. Alan

could hear nothing, but could see the Flight Lieutenant Gibson stubbornly shaking his head. Harrington came out, gave Alan a rueful smile, and left looking cross.

Nothing else happened until the sergeant admin came over to him a few days later and said, 'Scott, you're to report to Squadron Leader Maskell right away.'

'Maskell? The Director of Music?'

Alfred Maskell had been an adjunct professor at the Royal Academy and a rising star in the conducting world when called up in 1940, and had been a force behind the creation of the R.A.F. Symphony Orchestra as an important propaganda instrument, taking it on tours throughout the country and the United States promoting and playing British music. He had managed to recruit talented young instrumentalists like Dennis Brain and Neville Marriner.

'Ah, come in, Scott!' He came round to the front of his desk and shook hands with Alan. The first officer who had ever done that.

'You know Captain Walker, I believe?'

Alan searched his brain. He didn't know any captains.

'You met him through a Dr. Cassell, in Birmingham. Professor Frank Walker, at the Royal Academy?'

'Oh, yes! Of course. Sorry, sir. I didn't make the connection.'

'Well, he's a colleague of mine.'

'Did you say Captain? Or professor?'

'Both. He was in the Royal Flying Corps in the last war. Daredevil pilot. Never uses the rank now, but always has a soft spot for musicians in the R.A.F. He was my professor at the Academy, years ago. I respect his judgement. And he says good things about you. You did some study at Cambridge?'

'Only a short course, sir.'

'But you got a First. Look, I think we can use you, not quite sure what as, yet, there are a few possibilities. But we've got to get you out of the adjutant's clutches somehow. He doesn't seem keen to let you go.'

'Oh? I can't think why, sir.'

'Apparently he's had a bad time with WAAFs who can't spell properly and spend all their time doing their nails. But we've spotted a way we can get you seconded to us. Have you seen this?'

He showed him a notice inviting applications from those with any higher educational qualifications to train as EVT Instructors, with immediate promotion to Acting Sergeant. That meant

159

Educational and Vocational Training.

'If you become an instructor in music appreciation, you can do a bit of teaching and work with us too. How does that strike you? We've spoken to the Education Officer, and he will support it.'

Alan said it sounded too good to be true, which was absolutely right.

He went straight back to see the adjutant, notice in hand.

'I'm sorry, Scott, but you can't,' he replied, obviously not at all sorry. 'You're in a screened trade.'

'A what, sir?'

'Screened. That means you can't get out of it. Not unless you're unfit to do it, that is. And you're not.'

That was where the adjutant was wrong. For the following two weeks, he found his letters strangely misspelt, and he could no longer find the amendments where they should have been. Filed documents were mislaid. Alan apologised, saying he had been very preoccupied and disappointed at not being able to do something more useful for the R.A.F. as an instructor.

The harassed adjutant finally gave in. 'All right, you win. I'll sign your application,'

Two months later, in March 1946, after doing a course that covered most of what normally took a year for trainee teachers, he was back at Uxbridge. He walked straight in through the main gates, as befitted his new rank, instead of going through the guardroom as the lower orders had to. Good fortune had decreed that Cpl. Cottrell was on duty.

'EH YOU, AIRMAN! What d'you mean, goin' through the gates? You report to the guardroom!'

Slowly Alan turned and walked up to the man with two stripes.

'You talking to me, corporal?'

'Yes I effin' well...' His beady eyes travelled down Alan's uniform, hoping to find a button undone, and then latched on to his sleeves.

'Wh... wh... where d'you get them stripes from?'

'I am a sergeant instructor, corporal. Kindly address me properly.'

In his abject confusion and fury, Cottrell actually saluted him, before stumbling back into the guardroom.

'That was a delicious moment,' Alan told Bella that evening. 'I only hope he doesn't get promoted to warrant officer.'

Shortly after, Alan obtained permission to live off camp, on the grounds that he needed to study at night; this also meant no more morning parades. Life was becoming civilised again, and he was able to get on with a worth-while job, teaching music, giving illustrated lectures on Great Composers, and arranging scores for the orchestra.

Alexi Cassell was a great surprise the first time Alan met her. Previously she had been only a shrouded face with blonde hair (now, he realised, a wig) fleetingly glimpsed once or twice through the window of her little car driving down the avenue. He now saw she was a strikingly beautiful woman of strong, not to say, overpowering character. Someone out of a Greek tragedy, he thought, like Electra or Phaedra, or Medea. No, not Medea. He could see why Bella didn't want to live at home. Her years out in the field, living under harsh and dangerous conditions with the *maquis* had made her very, very tough. She spoke English volubly with a marked French accent, at great speed, but with Bella she always spoke French, which suited Alan very well. He had felt he was losing his fluency and was glad to be forced to practise.

'Do you have to return to France in connection with your resistance work?' he asked.

She gestured and looked up at the ceiling. '*Ah, qui sait?* It will take a long time for this horrible story to end. There are still many guilty people, German and French, not yet caught in the net. Some have escaped to Spain and South America, we know that. Franco and Perón are good friends to them.'

'Perón?'

'He has just become the new Fascist president of Argentina. Another Hitler. But as if that isn't enough to worry about, we have new enemies much closer to home as well.'

'Oh?'

But she would say no more, and bit her lip as though she had already said too much. In fact, the whole future of Special Operations Executive was up in the air, and F Section's small office in Paris was trying to wind up the outstanding bits of business relating to the *réseaux* — resistance networks — and collaboration. The Germans had been very successful throughout the occupation in infiltrating the *réseaux* with *Sicherheitdienst* (Nazi security service) agents run by whole teams of collaborators such as the notorious Bony-Lafont gang, and one hundred and eighteen thousand suspects were still being hunted down and prosecuted. Alexi knew quite a lot about them, and had spent some rather uncomfortable days and nights at the notorious SD interrogation centre at 82 avenue Foch. Neither her husband nor her daughter knew about this.

'So, Alan,' she said, wishing to deflect attention from her own activities, 'you are a musician?'

'I hope to become one, one day.'

'And do you not think there are more important things to do?'

Her directness took him off-guard. It wasn't hostile or aggressive; just challenging.

'Yes, no doubt. But I don't think they would be what I'm best at.'

'How do you know that? Look at Bella. She could have spent her life playing Chopin in bourgeois concert halls, but has chosen to do something useful, healing people's minds.'

Bella winked reassuringly at Alan, and smiled, not out of complacency, but because she was used to this kind of needling. It was Alexi, and it was French. Only a couple of hours before, Alexi had been baiting her daughter, deriding the usefulness of psychology. 'A pseudo-science in search of respectability,' she mocked.

'May I ask, Madame, what did you do before the war?'

'I lectured in economics, at the Sorbonne, and Geneva, and at the L.S.E.' she replied.

'Really?' It was his turn to smile now. 'How extremely useful. I always wondered why no two economists ever agree.'

But the irony was lost on her.

'Actually,' Alan went on, then bit his tongue, realising how terribly *English* that sounded. 'In fact,' he began again, 'I think music has a very important healing function. It can be very destructive too. It's a weapon for good or evil. But I don't suppose you had much time for luxuries like that up in the hills of Les Maures. I do admire what you have been doing, Madame, even though I know very little about it.'

Mme. Cassell made a sound like 'Hmph,' and looked pleased.

One evening as he and Bella returned from a concert at the Albert Hall, Alan said, 'Let's go mad and have a cup of coffee over there. We've run out of milk.'

Over there was a rather shoddy milk bar next to the Uxbridge underground station. As they poured brown sugar into their chipped cups to counteract the taste, the door opened and another R.A.F. sergeant walked in, taking a seat at a nearby table.

Alan sipped and said, 'It's time I got in touch with Professor Walker again. It was nice of him to put in a good word for me. I was surprised he even remembered me.'

Bella smiled. 'Oh, we had ways of inducing total recall.'

'We? *You!*'

'It was quite accidental. Mummy and I invited him to dinner one night, when you were visiting your parents, and we got round to talking about that afternoon when you played.'

'But your mother wasn't there.'

'No. She was... elsewhere. All right, *I* talked about that afternoon.'

'Well, thanks. I'm glad I wasn't a fly on the wall. I was so pig-ignorant then. Doesn't she want you living with her now she's back? Don't you want to be with her?'

'Oh, trying to get rid of me, are you? Fed up with me now you've had your way with me!'

Alan grinned. 'I thought I was having *your* way with you!' He still felt he needed L-plates in bed with her. 'But seriously, isn't she lonely with your father so far away still?'

'I did try, you know. Living at home again. But she's a real French *mère-poule*, can't accept that I've grown up.'

'I know all about that,' he said with feeling.

'It's different with boys. They never grow up! Mostly they take a wife to replace mummy. But I was almost a married woman once! Anyway, Daddy's coming home from the States very soon.' Her eyes clouded as she said that. 'I wonder how they are going to get on. *Ce ne sera pas facile.*'

To their surprise the unknown sergeant leant over and spoke to them. A well-built, stocky figure running to fat; dark hair, complexion as Mediterranean as Bella's, round face, horn-rimmed glasses that made him look owlish, and a bushy moustache.

'Do excuse me...' (soft, educated, oddly plummy voice) '...I couldn't help hearing you speak French. *Je n'ai pas souvent l'occasion de bavarder en français, et ça me manque.*'

He introduced himself as Frederick Martin, invited them to call him Fred, and told them he was a bilingual lawyer, just starting up in practice in London and Paris (where his mother still lived) when the war broke out.

'So are you stationed at Uxbridge?' Alan asked. 'I haven't seen you around.'

'I've only just been posted here — from Air Ministry. A little, um, investigation I'm involved in.' He laughed, a rather inane, high-pitched, nasal laugh. 'Are you walking back to camp?'

Alan explained that he was living off camp, but didn't say who with. He didn't like the way Sergeant Martin had been looking at Bella. Reluctantly Alan revealed that he was working in the Education Section, and Fred promised to come and look him up.

Later, Bella said Fred had given her the creeps.

'I'm glad about that,' Alan said. 'I think he would like to creep into your bed.'

'No chance of that,' she replied. 'He's too fat, and I couldn't stand that laugh of his. So long as you go on being interesting, of course!'

He knew it was a joke; but when she teased like that he always felt uneasy. Their relationship, he realised, was still very tenuous. For years he would have nothing to offer but poverty as an ex-service music student, with an uncertain future after that. He might become a new Malcolm Sargent or William Walton, or — realistically — he'd be lucky to find a job teaching the recorder to tone-deaf kids in Wolverhampton.

Evan Harrington, who had been in the R.A.F. since 1939, had now been demobilised and was already working with the Documentary Film Unit. He appeared one day at the Education Centre and asked Alan if he had ever thought of writing film music.

'No, I hadn't, but now you mention it, it makes absolute sense. My mother used to play in cinemas for silent films.'

'I'll tell you why I asked,' Harrington went on. 'We need a score for a short documentary being made about the post-war return to normality in France. We could get a French composer, but I've been struck by your affinity to French music, and I think you might be able to produce something with a French flavour, without making it too much of a pastiche. What do you think?'

'Sounds wonderful to me, if I can do it. Who's the director?'

'A chap named Marsa. Simon Marsa. Hungarian. The producers didn't want anyone British or French who'd be lugging a lot of historical or political prejudices around. And you can't very well have a German or Italian.'

'True. One problem — no, two: I've never been to France, you know. I don't even know what it smells like. And I am still in the R.A.F., don't forget.'

'Oh, don't worry about that. The Documentary Film Unit is an official body. We can get you an attachment over there for a while. But you'll be basing your music sound track on the completed film, here in London. It's very precise, split-second stuff. You can come and see us at work, if you like — learn the trade. I'll be conducting the L.S.O. for it.'

Alan suddenly began to panic. Of course he couldn't do it! It was way beyond him.

'But why me? Surely there are established composers you could get? Even a student who has completed a course in composition.'

'Yes, we could do that. But to be frank, we don't have the money to get Walton or Vaughan Williams, or Alwyn or Addinsell. You see, I'm not flattering you!'

To have one's music played by the London Symphony Orchestra seemed so improbable to Alan that his first reaction was to treat it as a joke. When he phoned Professor Walker and told him, he did not seem surprised.

Harrington had, of course, sought Walker's advice about young Alan Scott before approaching him.

'Do you think he could do it?' the conductor had asked.

'He's very inexperienced, but the Music Department at Cambridge thought highly of his composition work. Lacking in structure, but the film discipline will force a structure on his vivid imagination. And he's very good looking, isn't he?'

Harrington feigned innocence. 'Oh? I hadn't noticed.'

The professor shook his head resignedly. 'Now, now, Evan, you have to be good. He's not like that. He has a beautiful girl friend he's been in love with for years. She's a very good pianist, but went all scientific, like her father.'

Alan was beginning to realise what a tight little world this music business was. Maddy often said, 'It's who you know, not what you know, that matters,' and he had always thought it was just an expression of her jaundiced view of society. But apparently not. Did that mean he should refuse? Not play the game? This latest development about the film was an eye-opener to him, giving him a glimpse of a world in which connections were everything. He had a nasty feeling that if you didn't have friends on the inside, you'd probably be on the outside for ever. That was the way pre-war society had worked; would it be more of the same after? Or did the newly elected Labour government under Clem Attlee herald a fairer system of meritocracy?

Alan had voted to put them in; Maddy had stuck to the Conservatives, out of loyalty to Churchill; Bill had opted for a new Liberal candidate who seemed more likely to stand for people who didn't belong to a union and weren't employers.

The professor invited him to come and have a chat about film music in his room at the Academy.

It was not the first time Alan had been to the Royal Academy of Music. Bella had invited him to recitals by graduate students. It was a direct run from Uxbridge on the Bakerloo Line to Baker Street, then a short walk past Madame Tussaud's Waxworks Museum. Professor Walker's room was open, and he was poring over a score with a student when he arrived.

'I shan't be a moment, Alan,' he said. 'Come in and sit.' Alan chose to sit on the stool by the Steinway, and looked at the music — piano music and orchestral scores — piled on it: Bach, Chopin, Brahms, Walton, Bax, Ireland, and several other works he had never heard by Schoenberg, Berg, Webern, and a manuscript by someone called Messiaen, which Alan picked up. He had never seen music like it before.

Professor Walker turned to the student, an earnest, bespectacled young man with a downcast expression. Alan wondered enviously why he hadn't been called up.

'Mr. Jones, I really don't see how you can simply have the bass line in B-flat minor and the treble line in C-sharp and hope to get away with it just by calling it avant-garde. There has to be some kind of relationship and relevance, some *logic* behind it, and you haven't come up with any. Oh well. Persist if you must, but the examiners won't like it.'

The student left. Walker turned to Alan and shook him warmly by the hand.

'Sorry about that, Alan. One really does have to know the rules before breaking them. Every innovator from Beethoven to Bartók has known that. Now...'

He looked at his watch, and Alan expected him to tell him he had only five minutes. But no. 'Now, the sun's over the yard-arm. Sherry? Not a very good one, I'm afraid, but there was a war on.'

Comfortably settled, with the door shut, Alan felt he could relax.

'How is it you know Dr. Cassell?' he asked.

'Ah, Henry and I go back a long way. One of his specialisms, before the war, was the science of sound. Acoustics. Designing the ideal auditorium for different types of music. But he got into that because he was a fanatical *mélomane* and was fed up with not being able to hear his favourite music properly in most concert halls. So our paths crossed several times, here and in Paris, and we clicked. So did our wives, but mine died young, I'm afraid. Killed in a car crash... together with...' He faltered. '...together with our little daughter. That's why I'm so fond of Bella. She's become a second daughter to me, I suppose, although I try not to seem possessive at all.'

'She's had a hard time, with her mother being away so mysteriously too.'

'Ah, Alexi. A very special person, Alexi. Not easy to get on with, but quite extraordinary. And very courageous. I could never have done what she's been through. I suppose you know about that?'

'A little. I gather there's still a lot that can't be told.'

'And a lot of blood to flow under the bridge, I'm afraid. Reprisals are getting a bit out of hand, I think. Revenge doesn't sit well with justice. Now, how do you feel about this film lark?'

Walker gave Alan some useful pointers about the function of music in film, when it should be heard and when only suggested in the background — and when not at all; not covering dialogue or narration, and so on. Then he asked, 'Do you still have that music going on in your head all the time?'

Alan was stunned. 'Good heavens, you remember that?'

'Yes, I found it quite remarkable in one so young and — excuse me — untutored. Then I remembered that Alban Berg started composing when he was fifteen, before he had any formal training.'

'It stopped for a long time after Bella left. I sort of dried up.'

'Emotional block. But it came back?'

'Oh yes. After that Shakespeare song. Thank you for writing about that, by the way. It encouraged me a lot.'

'Can you describe the music you hear?'

'No, not really. Words aren't very adequate for music, are they? Well, it's all texture, not much sustained melody. Like drifting clouds over a dark grey landscape. There's usually a low, rumbling bass, then complex cross-rhythms slowly develop, like African drums talking to each other across a vast jungle, and flashes in the trees. Then there's a plaintive yearning from the strings and woodwind, and it reaches a climax, and fades away into the mist, over the horizon.'

Walker nodded, and then said, 'Soundscapes. Very visual.' He paused, then said, 'Can I offer you a bit of simple advice?'

'Of course. I'd value it.'

'Be mean — when you're composing, that is. Don't be profligate with your material. Draw ideas from what you've already written, make sure you have fully explored and developed that before threading another pearl on to the string. You have a rich imagination, but it needs integration if your works are going to

167

have unity. Don't ramble, like some of the Viennese, Mahler and Bruckner. They never know when to stop.'

Alan promised to be meaner.

There was a tentative knock at the door, and Professor Walker went over to open it. He told whoever it was to come back in ten minutes. As he sat down again, he asked, 'Tell me, what do you think of Disney's *Fantasia*, Alan?'

'Unequal, but I enjoyed the best parts — the Bach, the Mussorgsky, the Stravinsky. Seen it three times. I suppose it fits in with my visual approach to music. I'd love to... Am I boring you, Sir?'

'Not at all. And don't call me Sir. Prof's all right. No, it's good to let the imagination roam. Go on.'

'I'd love to make an animated film in which the images come out of the music and not the other way round. And it would be my music, of course, written with certain images in mind. I'd dictate the visuals too, only I wouldn't be able to create them.'

'But you would have created them in your brain.'

'Really? Hm. I think ideas have to be shared to complete the creative process. It's no good if no one else can hear and see what I've created.'

'Like winking at a girl in the dark?' The professor refilled their glasses. 'Have you ever wondered what it means? Your inner music?'

'*Musique intérieure!* It sounds very poetic in French. Does pure music ever mean anything other than what it is? That's the joy of music over literature. You don't have to explain it.'

'Only justify it to carping critics like me!' Walker smiled. 'But can you tell me what it expresses for you?'

Alan pondered. 'I suppose... an immense kind of cosmic sadness. I expect it's the effect of just living through the worst war in history, even though I didn't really suffer. I remember reading a chap named Cyril Scott, writing about the Dark Cycle and the Dark Forces and the Age of Destruction. That had a deep impression on me.'

'Yes, dear old Cyril! Very mystical.'

'Don't tell me you knew him?'

'Of course. I mean, yes. He's still around, leading a rather nomadic life. Do you know his music?'

Alan did not.

'I'm not surprised. It's better known in Germany than here. As Delius would have been but for Tommy Beecham. But his ideas on the connection between the history of civilisation and music are very provocative.'

'The ugliness of modern music,' Alan mused. 'Do you think good music can be ugly?'

'People thought Beethoven and Chopin were... well... not ugly, but unmusical and shocking in their time. And your hero Ravel was thrown out of the Conservatoire because he annoyed his traditionalist professors.'

'Yes, I know — you told me that the very first time we met, at Dr. Cassell's house.'

'I'm not surprised you remember it!' the professor chuckled.

'But the really discordant music of the twentieth century — I heard *Pierrot Lunaire* the other night and had to block my ears — is surely far more radical and alienating? The difference between Wagner and Webern is much, much greater than that between Bach and Beethoven. No?'

'It's a question of degree, and we'll all put our own value on it. I happen to agree with you — I don't approve of perversely inaccessible music, it's bad manners — but we can't direct music in our sort of society.'

Alan looked despondent. 'If that's the way music's going, I think I'm doomed to failure from the start. Basically, I think if one note can be replaced by another and nobody in the audience would notice, that's the end of music.'

'Right! Every note should have thematic relevance.'

As he shook hands at the door, Professor Walker said, 'When do you expect to be demobbed?'

Alan said it might be another year.

'And will you go back to Cambridge?'

'If they'll have me, I suppose so.'

'They'll have you all right. But if you decide you'd prefer London, let me know as soon as possible. You'd find us a bit more modern and socially committed, a lot less mediaeval, but none of the college life. It depends on what you want.' It would depend a lot on what Bella wanted, he suspected. 'And don't forget...' — the professor's parting shot — 'Don't throw too many seeds into the pot — it'll come out like green pea soup.'

A few days passed before Sergeant Martin put in an appearance. Alan saw his bulky figure sitting in the back row in his class on The Great Romantics.

'I think these two great first piano concertos,' he concluded, 'the one in D minor and the other in B-flat minor, demonstrate the essential difference. Think what Brahms would have done with all those tunes! Tchaikovsky is so wasteful, and Brahms so inventive! Or do we have to conclude the opposite? That Brahms lacked the Russian's rich melodic inventiveness, and so he had to exploit all his themes to the full by turning them inside out and upside down? Think about this. Next week, the two shoes, Mann and Bert.'

Fred Martin lingered while Alan gathered up his 78s and notes.

'Very enjoyable, Alan. May I call you Alan? Come and have lunch, on me. There's a nice little place just down the road.'

'What's wrong with the mess?'

'Oh... I like to get away from this place whenever I can, don't you?'

Despite his intuitive dislike of Fred Martin, Alan was intrigued by him — especially since he had found he was not listed on the station strength.

'Which section did you say you're in?' he asked, as they tucked into their Toad-in-the Hole, more hole than toad as usual.

'I didn't,' he replied with a cagey smile, 'because I'm not. I'm attached from Air Ministry.'

'So what's this investigation about?'

'Very hush-hush, I'm afraid. Don't want to scare the birds away.'

There was no point in pursuing that line, Alan could see. You couldn't trap a lawyer into answering questions if he didn't want to.

'Tell me about that young lady of yours, Alan. Did you say her name is Bella Cassell?'

'Yes.' He wanted to change the subject. 'What did you think about my conclusion — Tchaik-v-Brahms?'

'Very interesting. I just wonder, she wouldn't be related to an Alexi Cassell, would she? I gathered her mother is French.'

'Oh? Did you? I thought she was Swiss.'

'She looks very like her. That's what made me think of her. Anyway, I'll tell you what: ask her to mention a name to her mother, would you, just out of interest?'

'A name?'

'Someone she may know: a chap called Marcel Grévin. Grévin, like the museum of illusions in Paris. Just say he would like to get in touch with her in Paris before the trial.' Sgt. Martin looked at his watch and stood up suddenly. '*Mon dieu!* I must run.'

He shook hands and disappeared into the Uxbridge Road before Alan realised he had left him with the bill.

Alan decided to transmit the message himself rather than

through Bella, whilst realising that this might have been precisely what he was expected to do. In any case, Alan was intrigued to see what Alexi's reaction would be. In the event, it was interesting, but ambiguous.

When he first mentioned the name Marcel Grévin, she very slightly and momentarily but visibly stiffened. Then she looked genuinely puzzled. Then a strained expression came over her face; not apprehensive, resolute. Anyway, not pleased.

'I can't recall the name,' she said curtly. 'So I wouldn't know where to get in touch with him. Who did you say this sergeant was? Fred Martin?'

'Or Frédéric Martin, perhaps,' Bella suggested. 'His French is definitely *francophone*.'

'And that is all he said?' Alexi asked, 'Just that this man wanted to see me?'

'Before the trial, yes.'

Alexi shrugged, but was obviously perturbed.

'Martin's not on the strength of R.A.F. Uxbridge,' Alan said, 'I've checked. And it's a very odd coincidence that he happened to meet us in that café, and happened to know you. But why would he approach you through us? This has been the Cassell address for some years, hasn't it?'

Bella nodded. 'Yes, we lived here until we were moved to Birmingham.'

'He said he's on attachment from Air Ministry,' Alan recalled. 'Perhaps we could check there?'

Alexi agreed, sombrely. 'Good idea. Leave it to me. I'll get someone at the Ministry to enquire. If he turns up again, try to telephone me immediately, will you? Here is a number you can ring, but keep it strictly to yourself.'

Alan usually had his mail sent to the Sergeants' Mess. At lunch time the following day, he went to the 'S' pigeon-hole. There was one from home, which he put in his pocket. They exchanged letters twice a week, but he had still not mentioned that he had met up again with Bella. The other letter had been addressed on a typewriter, all in capitals, and postmarked Kensington, W14. Something told him it would be better if he opened it in a private place, so he waited till he had returned to his office in the Education Block.

There was no letter inside, only another typed envelope: 'MRS. ALEXI CASSELL'. It had not been sealed, and he knew he had been knowingly placed in a dilemma, which finally solved itself: he threw the envelope to the other side of his desk quickly, realising he was late for his 2 o'clock class, and a photograph revealed itself. Even without touching it to uncover more of it, he could see that it was of Alexi, naked and smiling, lying on a bed with her arms round a man in the same state. They were not looking at the camera, and did not seem to be posing. Alan had always realised she was a beautiful woman, but he now saw that overall she was absolutely stunning, for someone in her early forties; very like Bella in important respects. An out-of-focus wisp across one corner seemed to indicate it had been taken through a small aperture — a hole in a wall, or more probably the ceiling. Reluctantly Alan turned it over. A typed label read, in French: 'THE COPY IS FOR YOUR HUSBAND AND DAUGHTER. OTHERS READY FOR THE TRIAL.' He looked in the outer envelope again and found the copy, in an envelope addressed to 'BELLA AND ALAN, WITH BEST WISHES'.

'Rather perverse, that,' he thought. But at least he would not have to admit he had let curiosity get the better of him.

When Bella first saw the picture she gasped and clasped her hand over her mouth. Then, to Alan's surprise, she began to laugh.

'It must be an old photo, of some former boy friend,' she said.

Alan shook his head. 'I don't think so. For one thing, though she's beautiful, she's not a twenty-year old there. And they're cleverer than that. Take a look at the calendar on the wall. You can just make out the date.'

She squinted at the photo, moving under a brighter light. 'Yes, I see.'

The daily date had been torn off to show

1944
Samedi
10 juin

'So, you think she's beautiful, do you? More beautiful than me?'

He looked at the photo again with pursed lips. 'Hmmm... I'm beginning to think I could go in for mature women.'

'Well,' Bella riposted, 'you already know I like mature men!'

They laughed. 'Then let's open a bottle of wine and drink to maturity!'

Before long the seriousness of the situation returned to trouble them.

'How will your father take this? I can't see how it can be kept from him, can you?'

Bella shook her head. 'At least we can see now why the approach has been through us. Mummy could simply have kept it to herself and hoped somebody in France will stop the scandal breaking at the trial.'

'Who is she testifying against?'

'I don't know. She won't talk about it.'

They judged it would be less embarrassing if Bella faced her mother alone.

'He was a *collabo* named Marcel Grévin — as you've no doubt guessed, *chérie*. A member of the Bony-Lafont gang. He had managed to infiltrate our *réseau* posing as a Free French agent, but he didn't know me. So I agreed to become intimate with him and pretend to be a great Vichy supporter, to find out who his French infiltrators were. If we didn't eliminate them, they would eliminate us, and our sabotage work was vital to the Allied landings soon to take place on the coast at Fréjus and Cavalaire. On that day, 10 June 1944, four days after *le jour J*, D-Day, I drugged his wine — you can see the glasses by the bed — and managed to break open the safe under the floor where he kept his lists. But he obviously liked to keep a visual record of his conquests. I should have been more careful. I'm very sorry you have been exposed to all this, *ma petite.*'

Bella went over and hugged her. 'Oh, *maman*, I am not your *petite* any more. I am proud of what you did. I hope I would have done the same. But I don't understand what they hope to gain by this sordid bit of blackmail.'

'One of two things, I think,' Alexi explained. 'Either they want me to refuse to testify against Grévin, or they hope to discredit me and say I was a *collabo* myself and Grévin was the true *résistant*. This photograph could be read either way.'

'What will you do?'

'I shall inform my superiors in Paris straight away, and see what they say. As Grévin is under arrest, they may be able to get something out of him.'

Then the reality of the situation closer to home hit her. 'What will your father think?'

'Ah!' Bella shook her head. 'Only you can judge that. But does it really matter?'

Alexi looked shocked. 'What do you mean?'

Bella had never had a conversation like this before with her mother, on equal woman-to-woman terms, and found it quite exhilarating.

'I mean that you have never seemed very close to each other. Even before the war. I have sometimes wondered how you managed to have me!'

A sad smile flitted across Alexi's face. 'I suppose you're right. You have always been the glue that held us together. I know he has found other women attractive. But I think we'd be sadder apart. As he has never been possessive, maybe we shall weather this storm.'

Bella looked complacent. 'Well, since I've not been shocked, and daddy isn't likely to be, the steam has rather gone out of that sordid little plot, hasn't it?' A very unpleasant thought occurred to her. 'But in that case, supposing they just decide to — as you would say — eliminate you?'

Alexi smiled. 'They might. But I think they realise that if that happens, Grévin and the other *salauds* will have signed their death warrants. They have now forewarned me — we shall make sure these photographs are presented to the judges beforehand.'

'That's rather risky, isn't it? How discreet are they?'

'That's a chance we have to take. Maybe I shall get the Légion d'Honneur for sacrificing myself!'

'Were you looking at the ceiling and thinking of France?' Bella asked.

'I think not. Only an Englishwoman would have thought of doing that.'

'Now,' said Bella, 'What about this strange sergeant go-between? What does Alan do if he turns up again?'

'Oh, I don't think he will. I'm pretty sure I can place him. A very clever fellow, codename ZOG. A disgruntled Englishman, an actor turned petty criminal, who was in prison in Jersey when the Germans occupied the island. He has fluent, faultless, French and German and is a master of disguise — modelled himself on Sherlock Holmes and Arsène Lupin. He was a star double agent for a while, working with MI5 and the Abwehr, but proved unreliable for us. He'll be back in Paris by now, hoping to escape punishment as a traitor by claiming to have done great work in the resistance. It is amusing to see that suddenly there are forty-two million Frenchmen and women who were brave and loyal *résistants!*'

*

News of the rescinded secondment took a few days to filter back to Squadron Leader Maskell. He got on the blower to Alan in the Education Section.

'It's been turned down, I'm afraid, Scott. I see Gibson's hand in this.'

'Do you know why it's been knocked back, sir? Surely the adjutant wanting to block it wouldn't be enough?'

'That's true.' He perused the memo again. 'It says here 'For medical reasons'. You don't have anything wrong with you, do you?'

Alan's ears had responded so well to the new drug over the past weeks that he had completely forgotten the threat of deafness.

'I did have some ear trouble, sir. Oh!... The E.N.T. doctor said I was Grade 3 U.K.. Only. I'm sorry, sir,' he said miserably, 'I should have remembered.'

'Well, that's that,' said Maskell. 'How's the ear problem now?'

'Cleared up completely, sir. That's why I forgot about it. But surely France isn't hot and sticky?'

'Down on the Med it is, in summer. Hot. Not especially sticky. What are you driving at?'

'I remember the M.O. said I wouldn't be going anywhere hot and sticky. And he said it was 'Pending further assessment'.'

'How long is it since you had a medical?'

'About a couple of months, sir.'

'Right. Leave it to me.'

Maskell spoke straight away to Flight Lieutenant Temple, the station M.O., who was a regular recipient of complimentary tickets to the Albert Hall. He asked the orderly for Sgt. Alan Scott's medical file.

'Yes,' Temple read to Maskell, 'he had severe otitis externa and suspected inner ear damage. I'd better have a look at him.'

'Thanks, Geoffrey,' Maskell said. 'We just need to be able to get him to France for a few weeks, that's all.'

Temple sent an urgent memo to the E.N.T. specialist, asking him if he would please re-assess Scott's condition: was he fit to go to Western Europe for a brief spell? The report came through to Temple within a few days: 'Scott is re-graded Grade 2, U.K. and W. Europe Only. There is still a high risk of re-infection in tropical/insanitary conditions.'

Temple sent a copy of the report to Movements, with a copy to the C.O. and to the adjutant — but not to Maskell, whom, they agreed, had better not be implicated — marked 'For urgent action'.

While Alan awaited this urgent action, he was not the only one wondering why Gibson had it in for him so much. At lunch in the officers' mess Maskell and Temple found themselves sitting alone.

'Rum business about Scott, Geoffrey,' said the conductor, 'why do you think Gibson's got it in for him so much?'

The M.O. shook his head. 'No idea. Could be a natural antipathy, but the lad seems pretty innocuous. Too smart for his own good, maybe, with people of higher rank and lower intelligence.'

Maskell saw a chink of enlightenment there. Yes, the adjutant had been outwitted by a mere aircraftsman second class/acting sergeant over the Clerk General Duties/Screened Trade business — but surely a mature, experienced officer couldn't be so petty?

'Do you know what Gibson did before the war?' he asked Temple.

Temple stared at the wall, which was covered with photographs of Spitfires and Hurricanes, and then said, 'I remember one evening here we were all talking about what we were going to do when this lot was over. I was going back to being a G.P., the C.O. was hoping he hadn't forgotten how to design houses, but Gibson was quiet until someone pressed him. Then he said something like, 'It's all right for you educated chaps, professional types, you've got something worth while to go back to. But I left school at fifteen to become an office boy. When I was called up I was a Deputy Town Clerk. I certainly don't want to go back to that, so I'll hang on to my commission for as long as I can.' He was quite aggressive about it, as though it was our fault he'd left school at fifteen. Maybe he's blaming Scott too?'

In fact, he had not seen the last of the adjutant's capacity for pettiness.

The weekend before he was due to go to France, Alan went back home on a 48-hour pass. He and Maddy got out their bicycles and went for a ride along the Warwickshire lanes to Henley-in-Arden. It was becoming as famous for its ice creams as for its olde world charm. Cornets in hand, they walked their cycles along to the field next to the ancient church and leant them up against a five-barred gate, and gazed out over the soft, green rolling fields towards Stratford. For the first time ever Alan had a feeling that this was part of him, and he was part of it. Being brought up in a featureless

176

suburb was not conducive to a sense of one's place in history or geography, but now, having been away from it for some time, he began to appreciate that if anywhere in the world was home, this was it. The improbable angles of half-timbered cottages, the warm centuries-old stones of the church, the blackbird's song on the gentle breeze, the soft burr of a Warwickshire voice urging plough-horses on across the field, and the blessed peace in the wake of another lot of Dangers Averted, all this now brought him an unaccustomed sense of belonging.

'If you find anything as beautiful as this in France,' said Maddy, 'write and describe it for me.'

To set foot outside one's own country for the first time at the ripe old age of twenty, especially into a country one had studied and admired vicariously for years, was an invitation to experience naive reactions of the 'Ooh-aah!' variety. As the ferry steamed into Le Havre Alan was staggered by the bomb damage resulting from the one hundred and forty-six raids the city had undergone, leaving it the most badly-damaged port in Europe. Both the Allies and the Germans had contributed to the destruction of three-quarters of the town — it had not been liberated until 13 September 1944, three weeks after Paris. It would be two years before the ruins could be cleared.

Alan was struck by the brigade of porters infesting the quay, rascally, stubbly, garlic-and-*Gauloises*-reeking pirates in blue overalls waiting to board the ferry and march off with whatever luggage they could hang by thick leather straps from their sturdy shoulders. With great difficulty he found his reserved seat. Longingly he saw that the train on the opposite platform was going to Paris, but this was not yet his destination. He had been ordered to report to the Documentary Film Unit in Rouen; hence the itinerary *via* Le Havre rather than Calais.

The Normandy scenery that welcomed him as the train rattled painfully south-east could not have been more familiar and more different. Superficially the rolling fields of wheat and grass were indistinguishable from those of the south of England, and yet the marks made upon it by human endeavours were quite different. From the stonework of the farmhouses and outbuildings — many of them shattered and abandoned — to the shape of the haystacks, the style of the telegraph poles and the station platforms, it was clear that a different culture had been at work here for a long time, despite the shared history and geographical proximity binding the

177

region to England — and, not so long ago, a common language. Alan was exhilarated by this; many people felt disorientated by dissimilarity, but this was precisely what he had come for.

The Film Unit was still working in Normandy when he joined them, working southwards towards Paris, documenting the efforts to return to something like civilised life after the horrors of being used as a battlefield. Villages destroyed, woods laid bare, fields pitted with shell-holes. The smells emanating from disinterred sewers were an education in themselves; utterly mediaeval and full of character. No tapwater was safe to drink. The black market in food was rife. Worst of all, for the French, was the shortage of coffee; the housewives would do almost anything to get their hands on a tin of Lyons coffee, which sent Alan's mind off on a little fantasy: had the positions been reversed, would the good ladies of Fallowfield Avenue have given their all for a packet of Lyons' Green Label?

The Assistant Director, Albert Corcoran known as Corker, a wiry Yorkshireman in his mid-twenties with a lugubrious sense of humour, cast a pitiless eye over the ravaged scene.

'If t' Frogs 'adn't given in so easy to start with, maybe this wouldn't 've 'appened,' he suggested.

Alan disagreed. 'And maybe it would've happened in 1940 instead, with hundreds of thousands of Allied soldiers buried here now. No Dunkirk, no D-Day.'

'Well, p'raps you're right. But it'll do'em no 'arm to know what it's like bein' blitzed, seein' as 'ow we 'ad years of it.'

'Oh, yes?' Alan raised his eyebrows. 'How much blitz did you get in Harrogate then?'

'Oh, I don't mean up 'ome. I were workin' in London. Emigrated, me mum said.'

Alan thought of Le Havre being blasted by both friend and foe.

'Same with the Jerries,' Corker went on. 'Dresden gave 'em their own medicine back. I were there, you know. Aerial photographer. Snapped the 'ole bleedin' lot in 3-D. Loovely sight, seein' it all goin' up. You missed a treat not gettin' in the R.A.F. a bit sooner.'

Alan was far from convinced by this, but just nodded.

The attitude of the locals was captured in a number of interviews with mayors, shopkeepers, housewives, and priests, for which Alan found himself being used as interpreter as the French girl they had employed used a type of English not easily comprehensible to the film crew, whatever her other charms and uses. There were few young men; they had all been removed as

178

slave labour by the Germans, and were only now reappearing from camps far away in Germany. Continually, using all his senses, Alan was trying to seize the music of post-war France, ravaged France, humiliated France, liberated France, but at times whining, sullen France. For there were those who blamed *les Américains* for all this destruction, and the historical dislike for *les Anglais*, the traditional enemy of the French, was never far below the surface. The embers of Agincourt, fanned by the winds of Waterloo, had burst into flame with the abandonment at Dunkirk. Perfidious Albion! He soon realised that he would have to suggest something much more complex than variations on *Frère Jacques* and *Cadet Roussel*. He did not realise it, but already he was storing away ideas for the four movements of his first symphony: *Dissonances - Threnody - Liberation - Triumph*. Dedicated 'To Bella, with love'. At that very moment, Vaughan Williams was writing the film music for *Scott of the Antarctic* that would become his 7th Symphony; all was grist to the creative mill.

With Bella still in London, Alan was left with Corker for company during their first weekend off. Corker had a 1938 Austin 10, so they pushed off into the blue eastwards to Lyons-la-Forêt, which Alan had read about in an old *Guide bleu*: the favourite hunting ground of the Dukes of Normandy, the most beautiful wooded part of Normandy. They had not taken into account that it had recently been the scene of a horrendous battle, which had taken its toll on the state of the road. It was on a fine Friday evening in June. At around nine o'clock they decided to find a lodging in the next village, but fate stepped in in the form of an empty petrol tank. From the roadside where they were stranded they could see lights in the distance.

'I'll go and try to rustle up some juice, and you stay an' guard the car,' Corker ordered, 'otherwise it'll be stripped naked by midnight. I wouldn't trust this lot any more than the kids in the next street.'

Alan had never before seen such an array of stars in such a black, worryingly endless sky, so he sang to them to keep himself company. The wind was turning chilly, and he donned the raincoat he had sensibly brought. After an hour or so, he heard the chug-chug-chug of an underpowered car in the distance, then a couple of faint lights. Eventually a little Citroën 2CV squeaked to a halt beside the Austin. Corker peered through the window flap.

''Ere we are lad, a can o' petrol and a bed for the night.'

The car was being driven by a stony-faced man who stared ahead and said nothing. From the passenger side a woman emerged and held out her hand to Alan as she approached.

'Meet the countess, Al,' said Corker, fighting his way out of the back seat. 'Countess, my pal, Al, courtesy of the Royal Air Force.'

The Countess was a sturdy woman of about forty-five, who gave Alan a horny, unaristocratic handshake and addressed him in heavily accented English. 'I am Suzanne de Lomilly,' she announced. She seemed relieved when he responded in French.

'I offer you the hospitality of *mon pauvre château*,' she went on. 'Follow us.'

Without waiting to see if they accepted or not, she got back into the *deux chevaux*. Corker quickly refuelled the Austin. The château was well off the main road, and the basic Citroën with its perambulatoresque suspension seemed to be coping with the potholes and ruts better than the English car, accustomed to less arduous surfaces. After about ten minutes, lights twinkled through the vast beech trees of the forest, and the ancient, dilapidated pile stood before them.

'We had some trouble getting the Germans out,' their rescuer said, waving her hand at the shattered wall of the panelled hallway. 'As this was a Resistance centre, they did not treat it with much respect when they made their last stand here.' She took an oil lamp off a shelf and beckoned to them to follow her to a decaying room through the hole in the wall. A tattered Aubusson carpet lay on the floor, still covered with plaster and bits of stonework.

'There!' She pointed triumphantly at a dark brown patch. 'That is the blood of the *boche* who raped me and gave me syphilis. I shot him with his own pistol. Not bad, eh? If we ever get the place repaired, I shall hang it on the wall, just like that.' That was communicated with enough graphic re-enactment for Corker to understand.

'Tell 'er I don't blame 'er,' said Corker. 'If I'd been 'er, I'd 'ave 'ung 'is balls up on the wall too!'

Since Alan didn't know how to translate that sort of balls, he didn't try. But she knew she was missing something.

'Wat did you say about bols?' she asked Corker.

'*Il a dit*,' Alan proferred, '*qu'il aurait suspendu les testicules du boche au mur aussi*.'

She burst into laughter. 'Ah! *Ses couilles!* Do you want to see zem? I 'ave zem in a metal box hupstairs.'

They declined politely, claiming fatigue as an excuse, and

hoping they would not turn up as an exhibit, a trophy, on the breakfast table. Alan wondered if he would be relating this gory episode in his next letter home to his parents. He certainly intended to tell Bella, thinking Suzanne de Lomilly and Alexi had quite a lot in common. Her story, together with those of the dozens of people now interviewed, all added up to a precious insight into different experiences of war, an eye- and ear-opener for Alan. Being blitzed night after night required and even promoted a certain type of dogged fortitude; living month after month, year after year, with the visible enemy all around you — and the invisible enemy, the collaborators, skulking you knew not where, at work, on the bus, in the bar — developed a quite different sort of courage and resilience. Distrust was a terrible cancer in a society, and its scars were still very active in the France the Unit was documenting.

The trial was to take place in Paris in a week's time, a few days after the Unit moved into the capital on 10 July 1946. Since Alexi was a prime witness upon whom the fate of three alleged collaborators largely depended, she was to be met by an escort at Calais and kept in a safe house until called. It was strongly recommended that Bella should stay in London, but she protested so volubly, saying she was a free adult citizen with a valid British passport and visas, that they shrugged their shoulders. However, after her previous traumatic experience at the hands of an enemy, she did see the sense of taking precautions. A seat was booked for her, in her name, on the overnight sleeper to Edinburgh, but she was in fact flown, with her mother, by R.A.F. plane, organised by MI5, to Le Bourget, and then they were taken by car to a safe house in the Marais — at that time still the dilapidated, unfashionable *quartier* it had been since the aristocracy moved out in the eighteenth century. An armed lookalike agent occupied the sleeping compartment to Scotland in the hope that some attempt would be made, but nothing eventuated.

With the arrival of Bella in Paris, everything seemed set for a romantic reunion, but the security services had other ideas. The ladies were pretty safe, they thought, but it would be only too easy for the ubiquitous and now frantic remnants of the Vichy collaborator network to track Alan if he tried to see Bella. She managed to contact him by telephone at his hotel in the Latin Quarter and give him her number, using a letter code they had already established in London. He then went out to a bar in the Boulevard Saint-Michel, bought a *jeton*, and disappeared into the bowels of the basement to find the telephone. He spoke in French so as not to draw attention to himself, and certain arrangements were tersely made.

*

The next night's production at the Opéra was Debussy's *Pelléas et Mélisande*. Alan persuaded Corker to go to an agency and get two tickets (Corker was certainly not willing to waste the prospect of an evening's proper entertainment at the Folies Bergère for that highbrow muck).

His offer to approach Bella (easily recognisable from the photo Alan was always looking at) in the foyer was not altogether self-sacrificing.

'I love a bit of cloak and dagger stuff, Al. And I want to set eyes on this smasher meself and give you my honest opinion.'

Thus it was that Alan did not meet her physically until she slid into her seat next to him, in the dark, just as the curtain was going up to reveal the most magical scene they had ever seen on a stage: the sombre forest in which Golaud is lost, the well where he comes across the strange young girl weeping. In the protective darkness of the balcony, their interlinked hands responded to each cadence of the music with which Debussy evoked the misty, mediaeval, tragic love story by Maurice Maeterlinck. As the ill-starred love of the two young people — Mélisande and Golaud's young brother, Pelléas — subtly, quietly, but inexorably moved towards its tragic conclusion, they could scarcely breathe, each subconsciously refusing to associate their deaths with anything that could happen to them.

When the final whispers of the music had died away, and the applause shattered the magic — far too soon — Bella turned to Alan, threw an arm round his neck, and kissed him with more warmth than he had ever known from her. Then she said in his ear, 'I'm sorry, I have an escort. A bodyguard. Right behind us — no! Don't look round! But he says he'll be very discreet. I have to go straight back though.'

'Damn! I've been hoping to take you to *Le Procope*.'

Her eyes widened. 'But that's terribly expensive! Why there?'

'Because my grandfather went there in 1893. With a girl named Mitzi. Can we at least go and sit somewhere quiet for a bit?'

'Yes, of course. Let's go.'

Having aisle seats they were able to get out without too much delay, and found a quiet corner in an alcove with a plush red seat to themselves, under a bust of Gluck. Bella noticed Alan was looking strange.

'Are you all right, darling? Not feeling ill?'

He passed a hand over his eyes. 'No, not ill. But odd. I get this feeling sometimes, a kind of sound in my head, and it has always meant that I'm going to see someone I know if I just stay still for a while. Tonight, it's very strong.'

Bella looked surprised. 'Goodness! I didn't know you were *psychic!*' She pronounced the word as if it was an exotic but rather laughable disease.

Alan looked uncomfortable. 'Well, not really, but it's in the blood, I suppose you could say. Celtic feyness. Maybe it's the phantom of the opera trying to communicate?'

'Feyness? Is that a word?'

'It is now.' He looked warily at the crowd passing down the grand staircase of the Salle Garnier. 'Where's your bodyguard?'

She looked around and nodded to her left. 'Over there, leaning against the pillar.'

As they went on exchanging their news, the spectators chatted and thinned out. This meeting was so tantalizing, they were so close and yet so separate, now together and very soon apart again.

'It won't be long now,' Bella promised, stroking his cheek. 'Mummy finishes with the trial in two days time. Then we should be safe.'

Suddenly Alan froze. 'Did you hear that?'

'No? What?'

'That laugh. It came from...'

Vainly he scanned the faces of the well-dressed men as they turned to saunter down the staircase, but without success. No one he knew. Then he heard it again. It issued from a slightly built, blond man, talking to an elegantly dressed woman. But his eyes gave him away, just as his laugh had.

'It's Fred!' Alan whispered. 'He's too thin and the wrong colour, but I'm bloody sure it's Frédéric Martin. What the hell can we do?'

But Bella had been assailed by a new sensation, a feeling that her mind had suddenly become like a searchlight seeking out a source of malevolence to the exclusion of all else. It came to rest on the blond man just as Alan said he was bloody sure. She didn't hesitate. She turned and gave a signal to the watchful man by the pillar, who glided over.

'The blond man with the very blonde woman in the fur coat,' she said quietly. 'C'est Frédéric Martin, l'ami de Grévin.'

The man followed Fred unobtrusively, pausing only to speak to another man on the next floor, who picked up a house telephone. By the time Fred unsuspectingly reached the main exit and descended the flight of steps to the Place de l'Opéra, he was being tailed by two agents of the *deuxième bureau*, and Bella's minder was back looking after his charge.

Bastille Day 1946, the first peace-time national day celebration for seven years, was to be the high point of the Documentary Film Unit's visual record of a society finding its way again: *Renaissance France* was the provisional title; it was not intended to, but it suggested all the pain and trauma of the birth process: the unending recriminations, accusations, counter-accusations, acts of revenge, all the pent-up hostility of millions of French citizens who had been oppressed, humiliated, bullied, terrified, and killed, not only by their conquerors but by so many of their own countrymen who opted for Pétain's flawed line: if we are nice to the Germans, they will be nice to us and treat us as equals in the fight against Bolshevism.

A regrettable hiccup occurred just two days before the *fête nationale*; the unit interviewer was involved in a car crash and was in intensive care. It was Corker who had the brilliant idea.

'We need someone who's bilingual, photogenic, capable of asking intelligent and probing questions, am I right or am I right?' he asked the director, Simon Marsa.

Marsa nodded.

'Then I've got just the person you need. Ask Alan about his girlfriend. *Very* photogenic and lively, French mother, English father, spent years in Switzerland. Can't get more neutral than that. If she'll do it, we're back in business.'

Marcel Grévin and Frédéric Martin were brought to trial at the Court of Justice in Paris on 5 July. Grévin's case was the more important as he had been a high-ranking member of the French Gestapo — *Le Corps d'Autoprotection français*, also known as the Bony-Lafont Gang. The chief was Henri Lafont, previously a French gangster with nine convictions for larceny and embezzlement; holding the rank of SS-Hauptsturmführer. He had been convicted for 'intelligence with the enemy' and executed by firing squad on 19 December 1944. His deputy, Pierre Bony, suffered the same fate a week later.

Grévin now appeared in the same courtroom and on the same

charge, and tried to argue that he was under orders from his German superior, Krikker, who would have been much more ruthless but for him. He was also sentenced to execution by firing squad, largely on the basis of Alexi Cassell's meticulous evidence of atrocities and offences committed against civilian populations, mass murders, and deportations he had ordered on his own authority. His counter-charges of Alexi's own collaboration were rebutted by so many highly reputable *résistants* from the region of Les Maures that the judges unhesitatingly applied the harshest penalty in view of his 'cowardly and dishonourable self-defence' — execution by firing squad.

When Martin was told of this he panicked and changed his plea to guilty of collaboration. This ensured rapid proceedings, but did not help him: by impersonating a British non-commissioned officer he had incurred an additional charge of espionage, and was sentenced to ten years imprisonment with hard labour, national degradation (*dégradation nationale*) for life and the forfeiture of all property.

The morning after the trials, Alexi spoke to her husband in California.

'Yes, of course I can return, *chéri*,' she said, 'I'm a free woman now. We can pack up and come over right away. By ship or plane, I don't know, whatever is available. You could meet us in New York.'

She looked forward to telling Bella the good news when she returned from seeing that young Englishman, yes, the *la bonne nouvelle* that mother and daughter were both to set sail for the United States as soon as possible, maybe to a new life there as Dr. Cassell had been offered a senior research job with conditions unmatchable in England or Europe. At last they would be a family again. She felt the war had deprived them all of precious years together, and now it was time to reap some peace — and peace of mind.

Alan was already waiting for Bella at Le Café de Flore, making his *café crème* last, trying to keep the seat next to him on the pavement. An ugly-looking professor called M. Sartre sat smoking and writing existentially in one corner, and his mistress, Simone de Beauvoir (unkindly dubbed 'La Grande Sartreuse') held court, in another. The names of those who floated in and out — Giacometti, Vian, Camus, and a lean, hawklike Irishman named Beckett — meant little or nothing to Alan.

Bella kissed him on each cheek and then lingeringly on the lips.

185

It seemed perfectly normal to kiss quite passionately in public in Paris; in London they would probably have shaken hands and given each other a brief peck.

'I have some news for you,' he announced as they sat at the little round metal table.

'Don't tell me. You've finished your symphony?'

'Ha-ha. Much more exciting. You have a job. If you want it.'

He told her about the vacancy.

'But I've never been in a film,' she protested. 'I might not be any good.'

'Look, we're not asking you to be Betty Grable all of a sudden...'

'Oh! So you don't like my legs? From now on I shall wear trousers, even in bed!'

He knew... thought... hoped she wasn't being serious, but played safe.

'Of course I do. I can still remember the first time I saw them, walking away from me after you'd invited me to your garden party. Absolutely stunning! And they still are.'

Bella rewarded him with a slight tap on the cheek. 'You were saying?'

'You'll just have to ask ordinary people questions about how they feel to be free again on Bastille Day, stuff like that. We're due to wrap the whole thing up in four weeks time. Your new term doesn't start till October.'

Bella was really quite flattered and excited by the prospect, and agreed to go straight back to the unit with Alan.

Simon Marsa had been following the trial in the newspapers and knew all about Alexi Cassell's resistance work.

'Do you think we could get an interview with her?' he asked Bella. 'You could do it.'

Bella shook her head. 'I don't mind asking her if she'd give an interview, but I'd find it difficult to question her, I think. I'm too close, too emotionally involved.'

'Can you phone her? Now?'

She did so.

'*Maman?* I'm so glad you are at home. *Ecoute...*'

That was as far as she got. Alexi broke in with her news. 'Isn't it wonderful, *chérie?*'

Silence.

'Bella? Are you still there?'

'Yes, *maman*, I'm here. So you are going to America.'

'No, darling, *we* are going.'

186

'No, *maman*, *you* are going. I don't know why you assumed I would follow you, just like that.'

'But why on earth not? We can be a family again, all together. Your father is so looking forward to it.'

'Yes, no doubt. It would be nice to see him again. But I have my own life now. My psychology course at London University...'

'You can transfer to UCLA, or Princeton...'

'And I have Alan...'

'Oh, really, Isabella, don't be frivolous!'

'Just remember that it is thanks to him we caught that slimy Fred Martin!' She had never spoken to anyone about her own strange sensitivity to Martin's presence, attributing it, in her materialist fashion, to a quick nervous response to Alan's recognition of him.

'And,' she went on, 'I have a job here in France for the rest of the summer.'

'A job? What do you mean, a job? Selling ice cream?'

Bella was stunned by her mother's disparaging tone, and was about to slam the receiver down when a better idea occurred to her.

'My boss would like a word with you,' she went on, trying to keep her voice as calm as possible. She handed Marsa the phone. '*You* ask her!' she said.

'Madame Cassell? This is Simon Marsa, I am directing a film for the Documentary Film Unit of the Ministry of Information... Yes, Bella is working for us as an interviewer. We were wondering if you would agree to...'

Alexi refused, but did have the courtesy to invite the three of them, Marsa, Alan, and Bella, to the celebration party that evening at the apartment of her chief legal adviser, Maître Brissot.

The atmosphere was thick with Gauloises and laughter when they arrived. The courtyard and staircase of 117 rue Lafayette were not prepossessing, but the interior of the first floor apartment revealed an unsuspected elegance, lavishness even. Their appearance went entirely without notice, and everyone was talking at once, so they grabbed glasses of champagne from a swiftly passing tray, and Bella sought out her mother. They kissed each other on both cheeks, Alexi shook hands with Alan and had the grace to smile at him. Simon Marsa immediately charmed her with his Hungarian *élan*, congratulating her on the trial result and showing that he knew a lot about her Resistance work.

An elderly, dapper man with a silver goatee beard approached, and Alexi embraced him.

'Michel, this is my daughter, Isabella. Michel Brissot, the most brilliant lawyer in Paris!'

The others were introduced, very formally — Alan as 'a brilliant young English composer'. Simon wanted to talk more with Alexi, so Alan decided that this was the moment — or never — to ask the question that had sprung to his mind as soon as he learnt this man was Brissot.

'Excuse me, *Monsieur*, I wonder if you have ever heard of a lawyer named Haraucourt.'

Brissot smiled. 'There are very many of us in Paris, you know. Nevertheless, I have been haunting the corridors of the Palais de Justice longer than almost anyone else, so you have asked the right person. Now, let me see, Haraucourt...'

His slender fingers tapped his lips. Bella, watching him, was sure he recognised the name but was hesitating.

'Might I ask the reason for your question, *Monsieur*.'

'Certainly. My grandfather had some dealings with a Gaston Haraucourt, and I was wondering if he could possibly still be alive.'

'Ah, I see. Gaston? Your grandfather... that must have been a long time ago?'

'Yes, in 1893.'

'*Mon dieu!* That is ancient history!'

'But it is important to me, *Monsieur*.'

'Very well, young man. All I can tell you is that a Gaston Haraucourt was a contemporary of mine, but we followed different paths. I was called to the bar, and he specialised in finance and property. Speculation on a vast scale. When he was accused of *malversation*, he asked me to defend him.'

'*Malversation?*' Alan could guess what it meant, but wanted to be sure.

Bella came to his aid. 'Embezzling, I think.'

'When did this happen, *Monsieur?*' Alan enquired.

'Let me see now, it would have been just before the first world war. He was found guilty, he was ruined, his wife and children left him, and he committed suicide in prison. I did my best for him, but there was no doubt... Now, *Monsieur*, perhaps you will confide to me your grandfather's connection with him?'

'Certainly. He was a victim. He lost all his money.'

'Like hundreds of others, alas. Do you find it a comfort to know that Haraucourt was brought to justice?'

Alan pondered. 'Not that way. I would have liked him to be

alive still, to have met him, and I could have somehow made him feel guilty.'

Brissot laughed. *'Comment dit-on en anglais?* Ze best of Breeteesh luck! What would you have done — challenged him to a duel? He was entirely without remorse. He tried to blame me for the judgement against him. It was anger and hurt pride that made him end his life, not conscience. I hope you can eventually draw some comfort from this moral story. Good luck with your career, young man.'

The old lawyer shook hands with them both; as he sauntered away to join in the celebrations, Bella turned to Alan. 'Well? How do you feel about it?'

'I'm glad Gaston didn't get away with it. That's some comfort, I suppose. And I have to admit that my grandfather was partly to blame. Impulsive, pig-headed, ignoring advice, greedy...'

'Aren't you glad you don't take after him, then?' Bella laughed.

That brought Alan up with a jolt. 'Maybe I do? I've always *wanted* to take after him, and now it looks as though I had better not. What a disappointment.'

'Perhaps,' Bella said thoughtfully, 'you should concentrate on being yourself, and not what your ancestors might have contributed to you. As these new existentialists say, you are what you do, not what your forbears have been!'

Much later that night, his last night alone for some time to come, he hoped, Alan reviewed what he had learned and tried to make sense of it. He had been driven to find out about Haraucourt, as the embezzler had become, in his mind, a destructive monster figure. All he was left with now was a vague sense of retribution. Presumably, Grandad never knew about Haraucourt's undignified end, but he could at least tell his mother about it.

He tried fitfully and unsuccessfully to sleep, with the dawn sounds of an awakening Paris filtering through the window: ancient cars impatiently honking, engines revving and pinking on impure petrol, dustbin lids unsympathetically clattering, voices being raised in greeting and anger. As he drifted off, mind still moiling away, he took stock of the twists and turns in the road he had followed to get to this place at this time: meeting Bella, and through her, Professor Walker, his grandmother's death, separation from Bella because of the IRA and his mother's jealousy, seeing her again in Cambridge, finding out about his grandfather and Debussy, being posted to Uxbridge — the one place in the R.A.F. he could pursue his music —, helping to capture the slippery Fred Martin, and closing the chapter on the man who had caused his grandfather's ruin.

Maybe all these experiences, some pleasant, some unpleasant, all influential, would one day find expression in his music? He remembered odd details of composers' lives (before they took music seriously): Borodin was a medical scientist and Rimsky-Korsakov and Roussel were naval officers; Delius grew oranges in Florida; Tchaikovsky worked at the Ministry of Justice. Biographers did not ignore these experiences, extraneous though they might appear to be. If, he mused, someone was foolish enough to write his biography in, say, 2001, surely what was happening to him now would have some bearing on his life-story? Unfortunately, even the most sympathetic account of his life so far could not disguise the fact that, outwardly at least, it was about as interesting as lawn mower instructions. He imagined his brief obituary in *The Times*:

> ...studied at the Royal Academy of Music, passed with difficulty the requisite music examinations, taught music at various schools, wrote strange, unperformed symphonic works, and died a doddering disappointed dodo at the age of fifty-two. Failed to fulfil his early promise.

Then, in that no-man's land between wakefulness and sleep, no doubt under the influence of the grainy French films he and Corker had been seeing, added to indelible memories of his many childhood visits to the Odeon and the Rialto cinemas, he visualised a list of film titles scrolling up, each with fragments of trailers showing what might have been:

COMING SOON TO THIS CINEMA!

Scott, the Scourge of Suburbia!
Scott and Caesar Win the War
Scott and the Secret Weapon!
Scott, Hero of the Sixth!
Scott of the Jungle!
Scott and the Blue Lagoon
Scott and the King's Enemies!

Tiger Scott and the Messerschmitts
En garde! Scott, Master Swordsman
Scott and the Sewers of Paris
Scott and the Gestapo
Scott in Love
La Belle et le Scott

(All written and directed by A.S.
Music by A.S.)

His rambling mind churned on from imaginative mode to analytical: should a composer's non-musical life be considered as having no relevance whatever to his music? The death of loved ones, failures and depressions, triumphs and romances, all irrelevant? What he did know was that his own music could only be an outpouring from his inner self — whatever that was. What could it be if not the sum total of all those experiences, some pleasant, some unpleasant?... And what next?... what... next?... next... next...

He slept until noon, and awoke feeling more elated than he had for a long, long time.

*

Bella moved into Alan's rickety little left bank hotel, and life became idyllic. To be young, free, in love and in Paris! They both felt they had been robbed of a childhood, and intended to make up for it before youth deserted them. After dinner they strolled hand in hand along the quais from the Pont Saint-Michel to the Pont Royal, and looked across the Seine to the Louvre, the largest royal palace in the world, with the clusters of lights beginning to twinkle on the Pont Neuf.

'So different from poor old London,' Alan said. 'Of course,' he suddenly remembered, 'I've never seen unbombed London, but it couldn't have been as beautiful as this. London's a working city, all those warehouses and cranes and merchant ships. Paris is so elegant. Delius got it just right.'

'What? Got what right?'

'Paris. *The Song of a Great City.* At last I can appreciate what he was trying to express musically. The excitement, the poetry, the effortless stylishness, the delicate suggestiveness. How can I render anything like that?'

191

Bella was seeing something rather different, however. 'But I get the sense that this is a wounded city too. Not like London with its visible scars and lacerations and amputations, but much more deeply hurt, in its soul. It's licking its moral wounds. Maybe they'll be harder to mend than houses and offices and churches. I sense real collective inner turmoil here.'

Back in their room he showed her the growing pile of manuscript books covered with his rapid notations. She complained that although she was able to read most of them without difficulty, she did not have the imagination to hear them in her head.

'With me, it's the other way round,' Alan explained. 'What I hear in my head isn't being played by instruments I recognise, but I have to allot the inner sounds to staves across the page — flutes in heaven, double basses in hell. What has plucking and hitting strings, or stroking catgut with horsehair, or blowing into tubes, got to with pure music? It seems demeaning somehow. Such a clumsy, clodhopping process! It's making me mad with frustration. Wouldn't it be wonderful if we could just wire up the brain to some sort of celestial cinema organ and cut out the middle man?'

'You'd have the musicians' union on your tail!' Bella laughed. 'Seriously, maybe you just haven't mastered the technicalities yet,' she suggested. 'I'm not being patronising, just looking on the bright side. After all, look what Messiaen managed to write in that Nazi prison camp.'

They had heard a performance of the *Quartet for the End of Time* a few evenings before, and had been reduced to silent tears by it.

'Yes, that was extraordinary,' he agreed. 'To think the only instruments available when he wrote it were a violin, a cello, a battered piano and a clarinet. Out of that misery in a concentration camp in Silesia came that etherial, unearthly beauty. O.K., I'm humbled. I'll stop complaining.'

Of course, Alan was still subject to the whims of the Royal Air Force, but his demobilisation number could not take much longer to come up, surely? He really needed to be free by October, otherwise he would have to wait for yet another year before starting his course at the Royal Academy. He had not been wasting his time musically in Paris. At the Conservatoire he met up with several aspiring composers of his own age — especially a young man named Pierre Boulez, who introduced him to a breed of budding composers the like of whom he had never encountered in

England, experimenting with electronic equipment to produce what they called *musique concrète*: natural sounds and noises, from birdsong to jackhammers, which they transformed into eery compositions, sometimes trite, sometimes strangely powerful and unsettling. Thanks to them, he heard a Theremin for the first time, and the *ondes martenot*, and learned that the spooky frequencies emanating from these new electronic instruments were being used for sound tracks in films. If only, he thought, there were some way of creating pure synthesised sounds with the range and varied textures of a symphony orchestra.

Above all, he met Boulez's professor, Olivier Messiaen. Alan wanted to express the profound effect the quartet had had on him, but simply could not, ending lamely by saying 'There are no words.' But Messiaen seemed to understand, and clasped his hand. What a contrast with Boulez's own ideas and compositions! Alan found them stimulating, fascinating, but totally alienating; the formalistic, rigorous sequences of serialism the young Frenchman was adopting seemed to lack any human qualities. He did not want to go down that road himself; and yet he realised that this arid intellectualism was an aspect of the French mind he could not ignore if his own film score was going to suggest the totality of post-liberation *esprit français*. The young music students he met in cafés in the Boul' Mich were so different from their English counterparts, so partisan, so passionate, so political! Musical taste was predicated upon ideology — young communists cheered Prokofiev and were bored with Berio. When he professed an admiration for the wit of Ibert's *Italian Straw Hat* and the sensuousness of his *Escales*, he was told that was all *vieux jeu* and he should go and listen to the young German student, Karlheinz Stockhausen, who was pinning everyone's ears back at the Cologne Conservatoire. So Alan went to hear some of his pieces, and decided this was the end of music as he knew it. But then, he remembered, people had said something similar when Debussy first appeared on the musical scene.

Bella proved herself to be a natural: unaffected in front of the camera, able to put interviewees at their ease straight away and tell their stories of fear, terror, brutality, and courage. She found it a sheer joy to work with Simon Marsa and his chief cameraman, Nicholas, a white-bearded Russian trained in Leningrad (or St. Petersburg as he resolutely referred to it). They were both enviably multilingual. Marsa had particularly requested Nicholas, which remained a mystery to Bella for some time, as their relationship seemed to be constantly on the verge of conflagration. But soon she came to realise that although they argued incessantly with each other, it was with great mutual respect based on meticulous attention to detail. Marsa was a serious Hungarian in his mid-forties, who had trained in Budapest and in France. Before every shot he would stroke his brown beard and say 'Hm' several times while he thought about shooting strategies. During that time, Nicholas would fiddle with lenses and tell his lighting minion to erect silver screens and remove them again. Corker, with his phlegmatic Yorkshire approach to things, was quite resigned to 'a lot o' time wastin' wi' all that European arty-farty stooff, but so long as they're payin' me...'.

A tricky interview had been set up with a child of about twelve, the sole survivor of a machine-gun reprisal in a village. Bella had gained the confidence of the child, and was ready to begin, having sat the boy down in what remained of his home.

Then Simon said, 'Good, we'll have a two-shot, moving up from table with machine-gun on it, to the child's face, there pull back to a two-shot of boy and Bella.'

Nicholas shook his beard. 'Then I'll have to change all the lighting.'

'No, you won't. Why do you change lighting?'

'Because you told me it was to be one-shot close-up. Lighting values for table-top and gun are quite different from lighting for face.'

'No it isn't.'

'Yes it is. You come and look. See, there is red in corner making Bella's face too red.'

Simon peered into the viewer. 'I see no red.'

'Look up in top left corner.'

'Hm.' Stroking of beard. 'Then have white table cloth.'

'If you have white table cloth, I have to reset it all, because too much bottom light.'

' All right, move reflector to not pick up red of table cloth.'

The reflector was moved six inches. Nicholas pronounced himself satisfied. Simon had provided the solution. Honour was saved. They shook hands solemnly, and the interview could begin, forty-five minutes late, but what did that matter when one's art was at stake? By that time, the boy had disappeared with a couple of other lads, with a good meal inside him and two hundred francs in his pocket, and was never seen again.

Bella was in Vichy trying to interview wartime local government officials (who had without exception been stalwarts of the Resistance and should all get medals, they claimed) when the bombshell burst. The letter had been forwarded from Birmingham to Scotland, to London, to Paris, and thence care of the Film Unit, Somewhere in France. The moment she saw the battered envelope, with its Australian stamp and multiplicity of redirections, she knew what it portended. She read the letter and took the next train back to Paris.

Alan was sitting morosely in their little room in the Rue Racine when she came in. Surprised and delighted, he embraced her, noted her distraught face, and said, 'So, you've heard, then?'

She looked astounded. 'You know?'

'Yes, of course. First thing this morning. Did Simon get in touch with you?'

She was nonplussed. 'Perhaps. I don't know who sent it on. But how...?'

'Sent what on?' They were both as bewildered as each other now.

'The letter. This.'

She threw it on the table. Gingerly Alan picked it up. 'Do you want me to read it?'

'Yes. Yes, of course. Is there any wine?'

'Over there. By the bed.'

As she poured herself a glass of Sancerre, he read. It was from the naval hospital at Darwin. Commander Anthony Borland had clung to wreckage and had been picked up from a beach in New Guinea, naked, unconscious, and wounded, by native tribesmen. They had managed to hide him from the Japanese, but it was some time before news of the Japanese surrender reached their remote island. When he was discovered, he was flown to Darwin, but he could not be identified because he was suffering from amnesia caused by the explosion when the ship was torpedoed. Slowly, fragments of fractured memory had returned, and he had been identified six months ago. The only name he could or would repeat was 'Bella Cassell'.

'However,' the neurosurgeon's letter continued, 'perhaps more disturbing is the strange condition Commander Borland still suffers from. It appears that although the brain is continually making new links with his past, and recall is improving, his injury has affected that part of the brain that enables us to recognise faces. From one minute to the next, he will forget the face of the person he is talking to, will look at him or her, and ask, 'Who are you?' This is bound to be distressing, and I thought it best to warn you before he returns to England. He has himself tried to trace you, without success, and I do not know if this letter will reach you. Apart from being understandably depressed, he is otherwise fairly fit physically, and is being repatriated next week. He is due to disembark in Southampton on 26 July. For more up-to-date information, please contact...'

July the twenty-sixth! Alan glanced at his copy of *Le Figaro*. *Le 19 juillet*. Then he went and sat beside Bella. For some time they said nothing.

'I suppose I should be glad for you,' he finally forced himself to say.

'And I suppose I should be glad. Yes, I am glad, for him, for his family. But...'

'I think I know how you must feel,' Alan took her hand. 'I've had my own bit of news as well. Recalled to duty. The country can't do without me any longer. I have to report back to Uxbridge by 8 a.m. Tuesday.'

'The end of a dream,' Bella murmured. 'Maybe the beginning of a nightmare. Oh, Alan!' She burst into tears and buried her face in his chest. 'What on earth am I going to do? I don't love him, I love you, but what if he needs me? He's lost so much already!'

Suddenly she pulled away from him and said accusingly, 'It's all your fault! I never cared about anyone else till I met you! And now...' She began to weep again, but this time silently, her shoulders heaving as she pressed close to him.

Gently he stroked her hair. 'I can't bear the thought of losing you, darling Bella. But I don't possess you. The important thing now is for us not to let the problem come between us, to remember we're on the same side.' He lifted her chin and forced a smile. 'Anyway, you're the psychologist, you'll soon work out what's best.'

She smiled back, but weakly. 'I think psychologists are better at working out other people's problems than their own. But I've certainly never heard of a bit of the brain that remembers faces.'

'There you are, you see. You're already taking a professional interest in his case.'

*

Corker was almost as upset as they were that both Bella and Alan were to cease to be members of the team that had been working so well together.

'Tell you what,' Corker said breezily, 'why don't you two push off for the weekend. Borrow my car. I'd arranged to go back to Lions-in-the Forest, to see the lady in her ruined fairy castle, 'cos Simon thinks it might be a good setting for a film he's got in mind, about a French countess...'

'Ah, yes, the Countess! Who said she was a countess? I thought the Revolution had done away with all that.' Alan's anti-aristocratic instincts were fully aroused.

'She did,' Corker replied. 'She told me she 'ad the title but didn't use it, even though she could, because what the sovereign gave only the sovereign could take away, and Louis the Fourteenth 'ad bequested it. I saw the coat of arms carved over the doorway, see, and asked 'er. It's no skin off my nose what she calls 'erself, only she don't because she's got no side on 'er like a lot of jumped up common as muck people I've met.'

Half-mollified, Alan told him to carry on.

'Right. A countess what gets done by a Nazi and chops 'is balls off. I've told Simon it'd never get past the censor, but will 'e listen or is 'e deaf? I know she wants to forget it, so I wouldn't think she'd be interested, unless we could pay 'er a lot for the location and give 'er a job as an extra. But it don't matter, I can go next week.'

They looked at each other and realised intuitively they were thinking the same thing.

'Couldn't we all go and see the château de Lomilly? It's a lovely part of the country, and Bella's never seen it,' Alan suggested.

'Nor met the *châtelaine*. I've been intrigued ever since you told me about her,' said Bella.

'Nay,' Corker shook his head, 'You don't want me gooseberryin'. Go off by yourselves and 'ave a good time.'

'Nonsense,' Bella said, patting him on the head, 'you'll stop us getting all miserable and morbid.'

Corker was pleased they hadn't taken his objection seriously.

Alan tried to hide his sadness. 'Right then. You can drop me off in Rouen on Sunday afternoon. Then I'll get a train to Le Havre and the night ferry — while you and Bella have fun back in Paris for a few days.'

Bella made a face at the thought of the ordeal awaiting her at Southampton. How was it that the joy she should be feeling was not making her heart sing? Whenever she closed her eyes, her mind was invaded by the tolling bell of Debussy's *La Cathédrale engloûtie*.

It must be the effects of *Pelléas* and Alan's mention of the night ferry.

Corker telephoned the château and managed to communicate (despite a succession of crackles and unmotivated silences) the information that Alan would like to come too — '*Bien sûr*, with pleasure' — with his young lady — less enthusiasm here, but noblesse obliged with 'Of course, *si vous voulez*. Provided, 'the comtesse added, 'that you bring with you some good coffee and a bottle of whisky.'

They piled into the Austin — the boot full to the brim with the luggage of the reluctant repatriate, sundry bottles and black market victuals, and Corker's personal movie camera — early on Saturday morning, and headed north. The distance was only about ninety miles, but they did not expect to arrive much before lunch time.

The heavily rutted, pitted lane taxed the springs of the heavily-laden Austin despite Corker's deft swings of the steering wheel. Bella spent most of her time trying to stop hitting her head on the roof, and finally lay down on the back seat, abandoning her attempts to view the spectacular beech forest, the Forêt de Lyons, around them. When they finally came to a halt, she had almost fallen asleep, half-dreaming that she was lying huddled in the bottom of a little boat being tossed and battered in a raging tempest.

Corker's cheery voice roused her. ''Ere we are, lairdies an' gentlespoons, ler shartoh di lah contess dee Low-milly.'

Then he jammed on the brakes and swore in a way he usually reserved for male company as a large van raced towards them and forced him to spin his steering wheel to the right and go up a grassy bank. By the time he and Alan had got out to vent their anger, the van had disappeared, leaving a blanket of dust behind it.

Severely shaken, all three pulled and pushed the Austin back on to track, and were relieved that no damage seemed to have been done to suspension, axle or exhaust. Gingerly they covered the last hundred yards or so to the main entrance.

Repeated knocks on the thick, studded oak door, followed by calls and whistles, failed to arouse any response. Alan turned the black iron lock and slowly pushed open the door. Again they called out. Silence. Or so they thought at first. Bella was the first to hear.

'Sssh!'

Alan and Corker both said 'What?' in chorus, the way people do when asked to keep silent. Then they also heard the muffled sounds — rappings and grunts — issuing from an indeterminate source.

'It's coming from upstairs,' Corker decided.

'No it isn't, it's from over there.' Bella pointed to a small door under the staircase, hardly distinguishable from the surrounding panelling, and they ran towards it. Alan pulled the bolt sideways, and a body fell out on to the bare brown floorboards. It was, however, well and truly alive, wriggling furiously. The arms were tied behind the back, and a gag was firmly in place over the mouth. Bella removed the gag and stood back as a volley of abuse was projected.

'Cor flippin' 'eck!' Corker peered at the woman. 'She's dropped twenty years!'

Still struggling to free her arms lay the comtesse, looking about twenty. Only then did her elder double make her presence known, lying in the depths of the space under the wide staircase.

Liberty restored, rapid and breathless introductions made the identity of the young woman clear: Suzanne de Lomilly's daughter, Corinne. Recourse to the bottle of Chivas Rigal helped to restore frayed nerves, but the Lomillys did not seem anxious to explain their mysterious and undignified incarceration.

'I presume it was something to do with whoever it was nearly wiped us off the road,' Alan said.

'Yes, no doubt.' Corinne looked at her mother with an expression very like hostile accusation.

'You must tell the police,' said Corker, 'you could 'ave starved to death in there!'

Suzanne shook her head. 'No, no police. We can settle this little difference by ourselves. It is, 'ow do you say, a long story.'

'What's happened to your man?' Alan wanted to know, suddenly remembering the odd silent character who had driven the Citroën.

'My man?' She looked puzzled. 'Ah, he is his own law. Now, this is no way to welcome you...'

Bella had been watching the daughter carefully, puzzled by her silence, and putting it down to shock.

'Are you all right, Corinne?' she asked.

The girl nodded and smiled. 'Yes, thank you. Maman and I must go and prepare lunch.'

'I'll come and help,' Bella insisted. Suzanne and Corinne insisted more vigorously, however, that she should not enter the sacred culinary domain, and installed their visitors in the ancient, once opulent sitting room with a bottle of Chablis. Alan just caught sight of the comtesse attempting to shut a door — which she had said on their previous visit led to an uninhabitable, unsafe and unused part of the château — but failing because the door frame had been splintered round the lock.

Over lunch, during which Suzanne continued to be strangely withdrawn, Corinne explained that she had recently returned from staying with friends in Spain, and would shortly be returning to Paris, where she was studying English and Spanish. Corker took to her immediately and offered to give her a short course in colloquial English after lunch while walking round the grounds. Alan asked her how she found Spain.

'Horrible!' she exclaimed. 'It was rather like going back to the Occupation. Franco's Spain is run by Fascists as bad as the Nazis. I was in Barcelona, which is very anti-Franco, and sometimes I felt nervous when my friends said things in public. You never know who is standing behind you.'

'So your friends are quite courageous?'

'Oh yes, sometimes foolishly so. They make it obvious they hate the church and the régime. They even hold séances!'

'You don't mean spiritualist séances?' Bella laughed.

'Exactly. In Spain that is very dangerous. The church regards such practices as consorting with the devil.'

'Then that is one good thing the Catholic church is doing right,' Bella said approvingly, 'if it discourages stupid superstitions like that.'

Corinne smiled. 'I was just as sceptical as you at first. Maman has brought me up to be a true French analytical rationalist in the spirit of Voltaire and the Enlightenment. But...' She made a gesture that indicated something had changed her attitude.

'I've no idea what a séance is like,' Corker broke in. His French accent was still appalling, but he persisted cheerfully, unashamedly sticking in an English word when his vocabulary failed him; however, he was following conversations very well now. 'Did you 'ave ghosts coming at you through the wall or what?'

'No, nothing so dramatic,' Corinne said, glad the subject has not been allowed to drop. 'Or at least, not visually dramatic.'

Alan broke in, annoyed by the look of intellectual superiority on Bella's and Suzanne's faces and the derisive glance they had exchanged. 'My grandmother used to go to a spiritualist church. When she was killed in an air raid, my mother said she was going to try and contact her, but I don't think she ever did. But I remember about a year afterwards, a new neighbour came round, went into the dining room, and said to my mother, 'There is a lady standing by you, dressed in a long black dress with jade trimming,' and she described my grandmother exactly. Gave a message about being happy, the usual vague stuff. But the description shook us. It was spot on. It turned out that this newcomer was a medium.'

Bella nodded. 'Quite explicable,' she said, 'your mother would still have been emotionally upset by your grandmother's horrible death — she was blown up in the blitz, I remember — and her thoughts could have been picked up by a person with telepathic sensitivity. But that doesn't make it anything psychic or supernatural.'

'I don't think telepathy can explain what I saw in Barcelona,' said Corinne.

Suzanne suddenly stood up. 'I'm sure our guests don't want to be bored any more with bizarre stories. Let us go for a walk before the sun disappears.'

Corker looked at his watch. 'Well, we ought to be going if we're going to find rooms in the town.'

Suzanne looked shocked. 'But what are you thinking of? Of course you will stay here. I hope the beds will not be too damp. I was going to air them, but... some other visitors took up my time. There is one small problem.' She looked at the three of them. 'There are only two beds, big ones. It is up to you to decide who sleeps with whom!'

That was one decision that took no time.

Their walk in the crisp autumn air took them through dappled glades and along winding lanes in which tank tracks could still be seen imprinted in the mud. Alan, Bella and Corinne walked ahead, while Corker tried to persuade Suzanne to take the film project seriously. Alan was puzzled that Suzanne had never mentioned having a daughter on their last visit.

'Oh, I am not surprised,' Corinne said. 'When France collapsed in 1940 I was staying with relatives in Montpellier, which was in the unoccupied zone. So it was decided that it would be safer for me to stay there, and better for my education.'

'What about your father?' asked Bella.

Corinne's expression sadly revealed what she was going to say even before she told them that he had been killed on the

201

Normandy beaches.

'That left my mother to fend for herself here, together with her *intendant*, her estate steward, René, until they took him away to a labour camp in Germany. An officer promised he could get him back if she was 'nice' to him, but she refused, so René had a very bad time. He lost his power of speech. Then this German officer got to hear about me and threatened her. So even now she tries to keep quiet about me.'

Bella took her hand. 'We have that in common,' she said. 'They tried to coerce my parents through me as well. It's the oldest trick in the blackmailer's repertoire: attack through the most vulnerable emotions, one's desire to protect defenceless loved ones.'

Corinne was astounded. 'But how could they attack you like that? England was not occupied!'

Bella and Alan told her about O'Reilly and Fred Martin. It was a complete revelation to Corinne that the English had been subjected to such internal threats and domestic bombings.

'The French have heard about the blitzkrieg on London, but we think that is all you suffered.'

Bella decided to try and push the confidences a little further. 'So, was that unpleasant visit you had earlier today anything to do with the German officer?'

Corinne looked round at her mother and saw she was out of earshot.

'I really can't tell you much, but I don't think it is finished yet. They promised they would return.'

'But what do they want?' Alan wanted to know. 'There can't be Germans on the loose, now, surely? Are they *collabos?*'

Corinne sighed, suddenly looking very anxious. 'It is a cartel, a gang, who think Maman has something they want.'

'And what is that?' Bella asked.

But Corinne had said enough, maybe too much. 'You will have to ask her. I cannot say more.'

When they got back to the château, old René had returned, agitated and very anxious to communicate, by scribbled notes, in private with the comtesse. So once again the three guests were left on their own for a while. They took the opportunity to go upstairs and make up their beds. The large iron stoves had been laid ready for lighting, so they assumed it would be all right to start warming the now chilly damp air.

It became immediately clear, when they returned to the sitting room, that Corinne had persuaded her mother that they could be trusted, and that she should be more forthcoming about the attack on them.

'I must apologise,' she began, 'I feel I am still surrounded by possible enemies.' She turned to Bella. 'You have been threatened also by these monsters?'

'*Oui*. So has my mother,' Bella said. 'You have heard of Alexi Cassell?'

Suzanne's eyes widened. 'That is your mother? Oh, *mon dieu!* But of course I have heard of her! She should have the Croix de Guerre!'

By the time dinner was over, the whole story, or what they thought was the whole story, had been told. Apparently 'being nice' to the German officer, Goetz, consisted not just of sexual favours but of providing a hiding place for works of art looted from other large properties in Normandy and Brittany. Not many, but carefully, expertly chosen. And not large: easily transportable but priceless Corots, Watteaus, Fragonards. As soon as the war was over, and Goetz dead, Madame de Lomilly ought to have declared the paintings and had them returned, but did not know whom to trust, as everything was in a state of turmoil and chaos. The months went by, she remained indecisive, until it was too late: by revealing that these valuable works of art had remained in her possession for so long, she would have inculpated herself. So they remained in an unused part of the house, which she now claimed had been rendered unsafe by shellfire.

Then those thugs appeared, armed with a list in Goetz's handwriting, and began to search the place after tying up the two women. It had not taken them long to find the paintings, load them on the van, and depart at speed. That is where Corker and Co. came in.

'So what can I do now?' Suzanne wailed, 'I have been so stupid. If they are caught they will say where they got them from. If I go to the police and say I had stolen property stolen from me, what can they do but arrest me for complicity?'

Alan's immediate reflection was that even if she had revealed the hoard the moment the war was over, she would still have been a prime suspect as an accomplice, since she had been intimate with the German, willingly or unwillingly. But he said nothing.

'Have you any idea who those men were?' Bella asked.

'No, there were two, they wore masks, they said hardly a word.'

'I remember some of the van's registration number,' Corker said, 'photographic memory, you know.' He wrote it down on a piece of paper. 'But I don't imagine it'll help much. Anyway,' he went on,' I want to know more about those psychic doodahs in Spain, Corinne.'

Suzanne seemed quite relieved at the change of subject, but Bella began to look sulky. Alan was surprised at her intolerance.

'Very well,' Corinne began, 'I will tell you precisely what happened, then it will be up to you to tell me how I was deceived. You had better refill your glasses — it will take some time.'

The bottle of cognac was passed round the table, but only Alan and Corker took any.

'The house of the Perez family,' Corinne began, 'is in the suburbs, quite big, with a garden round it. They are a rare species in Spain — merchant middle class. On a Tuesday, at 11 p.m., all the shutters in the house were carefully locked, the two dogs put out into the garden and trip-wires set across all the garden paths to warn us of anyone prying.'

'It is amazing how these things have to be done at dead of night!' Bella mocked. 'Why not do them at midday, when there is plenty of natural light to see the tricks?'

Corinne nodded. 'In a free society that would be possible. In Franco's Spain, it would be most unwise. These precautions are absolutely necessary, as the whole family would undoubtedly be thrown into prison if it were found out by the police that they were indulging in spiritualism. Such is the immense power of the Catholic Church there. Only the previous week, the Bishop of Toledo had said it was a pity heretics could not be burnt at the stake any more.'

She paused and looked to see if Bella had any other objection, but she just looked down at the table. Then she asked: 'If it's so unknown and dangerous, how did this family get interested in it? And why did they trust you?'

'The daughter was studying English at university, and one day happened to see a copy of a work by Madame Blavatsky on a street stall. So they decided to try it out, as a bit of fun to begin with. As for trusting me, I was not Spanish and I had made my anti-Fascist, anti-religious attitude clear to them before they even mentioned séances.' There were no more questions, though Bella was having to bite her tongue. So Corinne went on: 'A small, three-legged table was brought out from a dark corner where it normally stands covered with books. I should say that on top of the table was fastened a triangular card on which were written the letters of the alphabet, nine on each side. Each letter had a corresponding number, from one to nine. So if the table rose twice on one side, it meant 'B'; twice on the second side meant 'K', etc. Even if one of us was deliberately manipulating the table, he or she could command no more than nine letters of the alphabet. Of course, all the communication was in Spanish.'

'Which you understand well?' Alan asked.

'Yes, very well. There were five of us. Each of us put both hands very lightly, almost negligently, on top of the table. After a few seconds only, one side of the table lifted about two inches off the ground. Sr. Perez — he is the father of my friend, Nuri — asked, 'Is there a guide?' One sharp rap, which meant 'Yes.' They have three guides, known as X, Y, and Z. X's function is to find particular people or spirits; Y is a very strong one who brings people with important messages; and Z is a general information service, as it were. Needless to say, I was still fairly sceptical at this point. There are also two other spirits, Cook and Holmes, who come regularly.'

Bella barely suppressed a snigger.

'This night, it was Cook. He began to write with great speed and precision while Nuri (who was as usual acting as copier of messages) wrote each letter in an exercise book.

'No one but Nuri, who did not have her hands on the table, was looking at the table (but I, for one, was registering in my mind what the message was). Yet not one mistake was made in the writing. Sr. Perez said their friend visiting from a foreign country would like to hear from 'Juan evangelista'. Cook tapped out 'Tomorrow night'. Then a strange thing: Cook wrote, 'You must be here too...' Then the table tipped RIGHT over into my lap.'

'Which could have been pushed down by the person next to you,' Bella frowned.

Corinne seemed to welcome these interruptions. 'Yes, quite right. Now, I had intended to go to Mallorca the following day, and it would have meant changing my arrangements and tickets. Cook evidently sensed this indecision, for he wrote: 'If you wish to succeed, you must begin with sacrifices,' and the table pinned me to my chair. 'O.K., I stay!' I said.'

She paused and looked at Bella, who looked disbelieving. 'Why did they want to keep you there?' she asked. 'Where you a paying guest?'

'No, not paying. Nuri was my pen friend since school days.'

'And you exchange visits?' Bella was clinically relentlesss — this was what had made her such a good interviewer.

'Nuri will visit us here when she can get a passport. That is not easy for known dissidents. The family are all lapsed Catholics, whom the local priest vilifies regularly to the neighbours as lepers.'

'So they wanted to impress you somehow. They obviously succeeded with their séances.'

Corinne still remained calm and unoffended by the inquisition. 'On the contrary, they were very reluctant to even talk about them at first. Only when I convinced them I could be trusted, politically and religiously, did they agree to let me participate. Thank you for letting me make that clear, it is very important.'

Bella remained unconvinced and muttered, 'The usual strategy to arouse curiosity — pretend reluctance.'

Corinne nodded again. 'Maybe. We were again at the table at 11 p.m. the following night. After receiving little messages from sundry people, at about 11.10 the table rose slowly and lowered itself gently to the floor again. 'Is that John?' asked Sr. Perez. There was one gentle but firm tap. Immediately began a message, of which I have the complete text, written in the most beautiful classical Spanish. Remember that the family round the table were Catalans, who speak Castilian or pure Spanish only as a second language.

'The table began to write: *'Me aquí...* Here I am again among you to teach you the good tidings of Jesus. Of all that was beautiful and extraordinary engendered in the body of the Master, there was nothing to compare with his eyes; and concerning them, I shall relate the story of the rich young man. We were between Galilee and Samaria...' And so on, in perfect Biblical Spanish.'

'Which you have read?' asked Bella.

'I have now,' Corinne replied, 'but I'm afraid my upbringing was rather secular, *n'est-ce pas, maman?* This Juan entity told the story of which the key sentence is: 'It is easier for a camel to pass through the eye of a needle than for a rich man to enter the Kingdom of Heaven.' Even I had heard that phrase.'

'Now, when Juan got as far as '...for a camel to pass...', I thought I would speed things up a bit by completing the phrase, so as to save Juan havi'ng to write it out. So I said aloud, "...through the eye of a needle...". Immediately the table began to roll from side to side. Then two sharp raps, which meant 'No!'

'The others did not know the parable at all. Like nearly all Spanish Catholics, they had never read the Bible.'

'I find that difficult to believe,' Bella interrupted. 'Why not, if they were Christians?'

'I don't know how it is in England,' Corinne said, 'but the church in Spain, and in heavily Catholic parts of France like Britanny, does not encourage ordinary people to read the Bible in the vernacular for themselves. It is the priest's job to read bits to them in Latin and translate if he feels like it.'

'So things have not changed much since the days of George Borrow,' Alan said, recalling passages from *The Bible in Spain* he had been encouraged to read for his English Literature exams. 'He took copies of the Bible to Spain a hundred years ago, because he was so appalled at their total ignorance of the scriptures. He found that all they knew were doubtful stories about the lives of the saints.'

Corinne nodded in agreement. 'That is interesting. I met a French Methodist missionary who had just been referred to by the local priest as "the emissary of Satan"!'

'That's stranger than you think,' Alan replied, 'It is exactly what George Borrow called the pope! Oh dear, what hope is there for world harmony when religions foster hatred?'

'We young people must not be pessimistic,' said Corinne. 'Now that Germany and Japan have been subjugated, the future is bright! Nobody will want to fight another war for many, many years. Don't you believe so?'

Alan did not have time to express his doubts, as Bella chimed in, having been following her own train of thought and suddenly realising why she was puzzled.

'Ah! Of course! In Protestant Geneva the Bible is as widely read as in England. My father has a French Bible, but it was published in London by the Huguenots after the Revocation of the Edict of Nantes. But I apologise, Corinne. You were talking about the eye of the needle.'

'Yes, thank you. Juan went on writing: "Verily, verily, I say unto you that it is easier for a camel to pass *over the bridge of the needle*, than for a rich man to enter *the Kingdom of my Father*."

'One detail that struck me so forcibly I recall it vividly, is the emphasis the Juan entity placed on Jesus's gaze (*la mirada de Jesús*). The rich young man almost fainted when he found Jesus looking directly at him, and it was only then that he ventured to ask his question. A very powerful moment that has no equivalent in the Gospels.

'The entire story is in very beautiful language, which this very ordinary family (Sr. Perez is a coal merchant) would have been incapable of writing. And the personality of Juan came through even in the table-raps. Cook, for example, always rapped in a blunt, staccato manner, like a soldier writing out a report. John wrote in slow, graceful, regular taps, making hardly any noise at all. Well,' Corinne looked round, expecting to find them all asleep, but they were very wide awake, 'there is a lot more to it, but I have gone on long enough.'

The silence was broken by Corker. 'I don't know what you think, but I find the whole thing staggering. Getting messages from ordinary dead people is strange enough, but this...!'

Alan had a question. 'What about this camel and needle's eye reference? Have you had time to look anything up, Corinne?'

'Yes, it is an important factor, because no one there knew about this, not even me. But I did some research in the university library last week, and apparently it is a matter of controversy among commentators of the Gospels whether the reference was really to 'the Gate of the Needle' — a narrow gateway into Jerusalem. But nowhere have I found a suggestion that it might have been a narrow bridge. If ancient fortified Jerusalem had a moat around it, it is quite possible that the narrow gate could have been reached only by an equally narrow bridge. After all, in 445 BC Nehemiah built a Water Gate; *and* a Horse Gate, which seems to indicate that horses (and therefore camels) wouldn't be able to get through every gate.'

Corinne then went on to spike Bella's guns by posing the very objections she wanted to raise.

'I suggest that we start by assuming it was all an elaborate trick, so we have to ask these questions:

'One. What could the motivation have been? Remember the family had nothing to gain. In fact, they were running considerable risks.'

Bella raised her hand. 'You're making two assumptions there: first, are you sure they were taking risks? Or did they dramatise the situation for your sake?'

Corinne answered solemnly, 'It is a sad fact that any spiritualist practices are regarded by the church as a form of blasphemy, or heresy, punishable by prison. I have already mentioned what the Bishop of Toledo said, didn't I?'

They nodded.

'Yes. Well, a neighbour only has to mention such dabblings to the local priest, and you receive a visit as frightening as one by the Gestapo. I have lived for four years, even though it was in unoccupied France, with people who were afraid of the knock on the door in the early hours, and I can read in the eyes when such fear is genuine. Either my Spanish friends were all very good actors, or they were really worried about letting anyone outside the family know what they were doing. They questioned me at length about my political and religious beliefs first. If I had not been a foreigner, I doubt if they would have trusted me.'

Bella was not wholly satisfied. 'Very well. Then, to the second assumption you have made: that the family were sincere. Maybe they were indeed good actors, and compensated for a boring life — amused themselves by fooling their friends?'

'Very well,' Corinne replied without annoyance, 'let us admit that is a possibility, although an extremely dangerous one. That leads me on to my second point. Two: if they were tricking me, how did they manipulate all three sides of the alphabetical triangle? Remember the writing was fast, unhesitating, and in a literary language (pure Castilian) that they were not at home in. Except for the daughter, Nuri, who was the amanuensis.

'Three. Was Nuri making it all up? But I remembered the general drift of this remarkable and memorable text very clearly, as you have just heard. The odd word could have been changed, but not the whole message in any material way.

'Four. Am I making it all up? Am I lying? Making fools of you? That's the easiest solution, and you only have my word that I'm telling the truth.'

Bella opened her mouth again but Alan got in just before her: 'All right, let's assume it was coming from some supernatural source. Was it John the Evangelist, or some evil spirit pretending to be him?'

Corinne smiled and nodded. 'A very good question. The family were very worried when an entity calling herself *La Madre negra*, the Black Mother, turned up occasionally, and Juan had given them a kind of exorcism prayer to send her away. She turned up while I was there, and I annoyed her a lot by saying she did not exist any more than a shadow does. The table rattled a lot, and she finally went off spelling out obscenities that the family found too shocking to explain to me.'

'Bella, is there a psychological explanation?' Alan asked.

Bella took a deep breath. 'Well, assuming, as you say, that you are not a mythomaniac, and assuming that you are not subject to delusions yourself, there does seem to be some kind of collective psyche at work there. If one person had memorised the text and managed to use suggestion on the others, for example. But I don't see any feasible motivation for going to those lengths. No money passed?'

Corinne shook her head.

'No other transactions? No. Well then, the daughter was not a young adolescent, but apparently a down-to-earth young woman in her mid-twenties. No apparent hysteria?'

'None that I could discern,' Corinne replied. 'Nuri seems to be a woman of common sense and strong ideals.'

Bella acknowledged the assessment, thinking the same applied to Corinne. 'Was there any other young person?'

'There was a younger son who seemed to have some psychic powers — I mean, the table was more active when he participated. But he could control only nine letters of the alphabet, remember.'

Bella turned to another aspect of the experience. 'It is curious that the whole subject-matter was Christian, even though the family are lapsed Catholics, and you are an atheist. The picture you were given of Jesus gives him great powers of mesmerising — hypnotic powers, if you like. The sort that could make simple people think you were walking on water or had turned water into wine. I rather like that!'

Corinne's mother had remained stonily silent, as clearly hostile to the whole subject as Bella, but resorting to mutism rather than aggressive questioning. But now she asked, 'Why was everyone 'on the other side' writing or speaking in Spanish? Why not Hebrew?'

Corinne shrugged and signalled ignorance on this point. 'Maybe if there is such a thing as pure thought, pre-Babel, it exists above and beyond the tongues of humans, and the receivers translate it.'

'So if we tried it, would it come out in French or English?' asked Alan.

Corker, who had been generally understood to have gone to sleep, suddenly came to life. 'I think I've got the gist of what you've been saying, and I vote we give it a go and find out,' he said enthusiastically. Whether out of genuine interest or to ingratiate himself with Corinne was not clear.

Bella agreed readily, certain that her scepticism would triumph. Suzanne pleaded a migraine and went to bed. Corinne quickly found a suitable three-legged table, and Corker fashioned a triangle from a box lid, on which the alphabet was inscribed, A-G, H-P, Q-Z on each side. 'Yes/Oui/' and 'No/Non' were written before the Q, so that they would require only one — or two — taps. They agreed to put questions in both French and English, and force a linguistic choice on 'the other side'.

It was 11.15 before they were ready.

'At least there's no need to put trip wires up,' said Alan.

'Unless your art-lovers come back,' Corker added, and immediately regretted it. 'Sorry, stupid thing to say.'

'Don't worry,' Corinne said, 'this time we are prepared.'

She lifted her jacket to show the pistol nestling under her belt. My, my, thought Alan, what a long way we are from Hampstead.

First they tested the extent to which one or two people alone could create a message involving letters from all three sides. It proved impossible. Then they agreed to try and spell out 'Now is the time for all good men to come to the aid of the party,' but that also proved beyond them, except agonisingly slowly, as two thirds of the alphabet were upside-down to each of them.

'Well,' said Bella, 'that shows only that we can't manipulate the table here. It doesn't prove anything else.'

They then all joined in to write '*Allons enfants de la patrie,*' and were surprised how slow it was.

For about ten minutes absolutely nothing happened. Wrists were beginning to ache, eyes to droop. Then they were all alert at the same moment as something like a slight electric shock and tremor was felt. The table was undoubtedly stirring, as if gently waking up. The Q-Z side bumped twice: No, or R. Then it fairly quickly rapped out B-I-E-N-V-E-N-U-E, and continued without a pause: G-R-E-E-T-I-N-G-S.

Embarrassed, like Unborn-again Christians having to say 'Peace' and shake hands with strangers, they responded. Corinne took the lead and asked, 'Do you wish to speak English / *ou voulez-vous parler français?*'

Quickly the table rapped out, 'ENGLISH.' Then almost without stopping continued to write, so fast that they could hardly keep up: 'Alan make my girl happy.'

He looked at Bella, who smiled. 'I try to make Bella happy but others rule her life.'

Reply: 'Not Bella. Maddy.'

Alan paled. 'Good God! Gran?'

'She loves you very much.'

'Yes. I know. I will, I promise. How are you, Gran?'

'At peace. Died in my own bed.'

Droplets had appeared on his forehead, which he wiped with his handkerchief. 'Well, that's true,' he explained to the others. 'She refused to go down to the shelter.'

There was a little more to come: 'Dodge forgives...' At this point, the message became confused: 'Harry... haricot...'

Alan shrugged. The names meant nothing to him. Dodge? Harry? As for *haricots* what did beans have to do with anything? Silence. Impatience was setting in once more when the table stirred into life again. They read out the letters as they rapidly spelled out a message.

Bella felt the hair rise on the back of her neck and swallowed hard. 'I tried to stop it, but I couldn't.' She was breathing quickly. 'My side went down time and again but I wasn't pushing at all. Oh, write it down, someone, before we forget it.'

They pieced together the message: 'BELLA YOU MUST STOP BLOCKING YOUR POWERS TO WORK AND HEAL WITH ALANS MUSIC VITAL MANY YEARS TO GO TO SAVE ALL.' Alan read it out loud. The table rapped out an emphatic 'YES'.

'That's what that gypsy girl said,' Alan remembered.

'Ah, yes,' — Bella clutched at a rational straw but was obviously troubled — 'you remembered her saying that, so maybe you were somehow dictating it.'

This statement of residual scepticism seemed to goad the table into providing a more incontrovertible manifestation; it rose of its own accord, with all their hands on top of it, and began to dip in a circle, without turning. At the same time, a curious humming sound emanated from it, a sequence of seven notes, with subtle harmonies in which, despite their complexity Alan unconsciously distinguished seven strands. Slowly the music subsided and the table came to rest.

Alan grabbed a piece of paper, drew a stave roughly on it, and transcribed the notes, humming to himself. 'It's difficult,' he muttered, 'there are loads of quarter tones in there.'

'What is it?' asked Bella. 'Do you recognise it?'

'No. Never heard anything like it.'

'It were sort of out of this world,' said Corker, whose idea of music was normally limited to pop songs and dance music that enabled him to joggle his head up and down and wave his arms about.

Corinne was more specific. 'It made me feel quite faint, but in a pleasant kind of way. Hypnotic. I felt it was speaking to my soul.'

Instinctively Bella wanted to sneer at this, but was reduced momentarily to silence, remembering Corinne was not given to religiosity. She too had been profoundly affected by the sounds, but was not going to admit it. Here was something she could not immediately begin to explain by rational means, and it undermined her hitherto unshakeable faith in a scientific explanation for every phenomenon. She felt like a nun who has just received proof that her religious faith was a psychological aberration.

Eventually Bella said, 'Well, it seemed to do more than just soothe the savage breast,' (which sounded odd in French) 'but I expect we'd be able to account for the affective response if we worked on it. What mystifies me is the source. Do you mind if I look under the table...?'

She never managed to do so, however, for at that moment the table lifted itself to the ceiling, turned on its side, and moved over the Aubusson carpet where it hovered for about a minute, visibly quivering as if with anger. Then, without warning, it was dashed to the ground with such enormous force that the splinters reached the walls and hit the astounded witnesses. Fortunately they had time to throw up their arms to shield their faces. When they opened their eyes, they saw that the table had landed exactly on the patch of Goetz's blood. The scream from upstairs brought them all to their feet.

They reached the foot of the stairs, but went no further, for Suzanne was already rushing down, her nightdress streaming behind her.

'*C'est lui!*' she shouted. 'It's Goetz! I saw him! I thought he was going to attack me!'

Then she looked at the shattered table on the bloody patch. 'I knew something like this would happen,' Suzanne said, white and shaken. 'But I couldn't say anything. It would have sounded stupid.'

They looked at one another guiltily, conscious of having played with forces they did not understand.

Then Corker broke the tension by saying 'By Goom! That were a right bit of excitement! I wish I'd had my camera out.'

Bella decided a show of scientific detachment was called for, before someone had a nervous breakdown.

'There was certainly a sudden release of power, call it psychic if you like, or electric. The temperature dropped very rapidly, did you notice, while the table was hovering. That is consistent with poltergeist activity... I don't think it was your German, it was a release of left-over violent emotion. Have you noticed anything odd about this area before?' she asked Suzanne.

Suzanne, still shivering, said, 'I have felt uncomfortable, especially by myself at night, and try not to come in here.'

213

Alan saw the logical outcome. 'So, now it has been released...'

'It should have dispersed. I think it was the German's last stand — but not a conscious one on his part. Purely mechanical.'

'But I saw him, by my bed!' Suzanne shouted.

Bella had thought about this. She really wanted to ask where his body was buried, but decided she did not really need to know. Maybe it was under the floorboards. 'Naturally,' she pursued, trying to sound as if she knew what she was talking about, 'there was a link between the spot where you shot him, and yourself upstairs. You felt the force of the emotional release, you were already nervous, and your imagination immediately conjured up a vision of the man — a self-induced hallucination.'

Bella's attempt at a rational explanation went some way to quietening everyone down, but even so Corinne offered to spend the night with her mother. Corker complained that no one was offering to sleep with him, but was told he was too brave to need that.

An hour later, huddled together in the chilly bedroom and feeling the damp rising up from the knobbly straw-filled mattress, Alan asked, 'What did you make of it all?'

Bella, half asleep, determined to try and forget the disturbing manifestation, murmured, 'There's something not right somewhere. Something she's not telling us.'

'What? You mean about the Spanish business?'

'No, not that rubbish, I mean about the paintings.'

'Have you ever thought of becoming a barrister? Or an insurance claim investigator? If I'm ever up for being drunk in charge, or go in for a bit of arson, I hope I don't have you quizzing me. I think I shall call you Bellona when you're in that ruthless frame of mind.'

'Bellona? What does that mean? I've heard the word, but I can't place it.'

'The Roman goddess of war. You know, like bellicose and belligerent.'

'I am *not* belligerent!' Bella protested fiercely.

He burst out laughing. 'There! You see?'

She turned her back on him, then after a few moments admitted: 'I didn't like that manifestation at all. There was definitely something evil there, though I hate admitting it. I just hope we haven't let some awful force into the house that will go on haunting them. But I don't believe in hauntings. Did you lock the door?'

Alan looked through the flickering shadows at the door. 'That wouldn't make any difference if it was after us.'

He was sitting up in bed, a spluttering candle by his side, and a pad of music manuscript paper on his knees. He wrote in the main sequence, then hummed to himself over and over again, filling in harmonies of the sonic landscape until he thought he had captured all the tonal nuances of the chords. Eventually he was able to look at the picture-score with its seven columns, and found it good. Then he put down the pad, blew out the candle, and snuggled down with a shiver.

'As far as I'm concerned,' he said in the dark, 'we'll never know what happened in Barcelona, and the paintings are none of our business. That's all in the past. Let it lie, these people have suffered enough. Anyway, I think all that was just a prelude to what we really had to hear about: you suppressing your powers, and us working together in years to come... and this strange music... What is it that makes it so utterly haunting? Why do certain sounds have such a deep psychological effect, Bella? Bella?'

But she was asleep. Sound asleep. He listened to the old house creaking, and the wind soughing through the ancient forest, and drifted away floating on a sea of visible harmonies never heard before, soaring heights and plumbing depths all at once in a universe outside time without extension. He finally dropped off to sleep, humming the strange sequence of notes, feeling somehow that they would ward off any malevolence in the air about them.

By next morning, Bella had not forgotten what was troubling her about Suzanne de Lomilly's account of the paintings, and Alan had not forgotten the music. On the contrary, he felt as though it would be there, in his head, for ever, to be appealed to like a mantra in times of trouble.

After a frugal French breakfast of *biscottes* made from toasted stale bread and weak milky coffee in large bowls, Bella deliberately buttonholed Suzanne and silently warned off Alan and Corker. Corker was only too glad to chat up Corinne in the kitchen, where he astounded her by knowing how to prepare vegetables, a female occupation no self-respecting Frenchman, other than a professional chef, would condescend to perform. Alan was left on his own, and was happy to prowl. His first target was that door with the splintered frame. It was a large moulded door, clearly intended to lead into a once impressive *salon*, now supposed to be uninhabitable. Its vast hinges complained audibly, so he opened it

215

inch by inch, and stepped into semi-darkness the other side. After closing his eyes for a minute to accustom them, he could then make out vague shapes of sheet-draped furniture. The air was heavy with musty dampness, and he could detect the unmistakable odour of rotting woodwork. The only way to get more light was to open the door wide, and this allowed him to see that the room had been ransacked, chairs and tables thrown over, sideboard drawers and their contents strewn over the floor. As he stood there, to one side of the doorway so as to let in as much light as possible, softly humming to himself the seven notes followed by several of their harmonies, he suddenly became aware of a shadow beside his own. He turned slowly, hoping it would not be a man in a mask.

It was René. Seeing him properly, in daylight, for the first time, Alan realised he was not as old as he appeared, but worn away prematurely, his face skeletal, like so many he had seen during the past weeks, still ravaged by years of forced labour, starvation and brutality. Alan smiled and held out his hand.

'*Bonjour, René,*' he greeted him, 'I am Alan, do you remember, *l'anglais?*'

Very slowly, never taking his enormous eyes off his, René extended his hand. The grip had no strength, and Alan immediately understood that Suzanne de Lomilly had taken this human shell back into her service out of pure kindness, not because he would be able to do anything much.

'This is a bit of a mess, isn't it?' he said, pointing back to the ransacked *salon.* I hear Madame had some unwelcome visitors yesterday.'

René nodded slightly and opened his mouth to make a sound. With a shock Alan remembered he was dumb, so he gestured to indicate that he understood this. The Frenchman looked relieved, and then, as much to René's astonishment as to Alan's, hummed the same seven notes. An enormous smile spread over his face, revealing several broken teeth, and he repeated the notes. Alan signed to him to do it again, and he joined in with the harmonies. Again, with more harmonies, joyously, almost laughing through the music. Without realising it, they had joined hands, and stood facing each other, humming, with tears coursing down their cheeks.

Finally, Alan said, 'Something miraculous has happened here.'

René nodded and made more sounds. No words, but clearly a greater range of sounds than he had been able to utter ever since whatever terrible, traumatic experience had rendered him

216

speechless. Alan led him over to a sofa, sat him down, and sang simple words on the sequence of 'magic' notes: *'Le, la, les'*. At first, René's tongue refused to respond, so long had it been since the muscles had been exercised. It sounded like a Japanese trying to master an L. So Alan tried him on *'Me, ma, mes,'* and that worked beautifully.

Suzanne de Romilly was not accustomed to being dominated by anyone, least of all another woman, but found herself unable to resist Bella's suggestion — almost a command — that they should go for a walk. She seemed to realise that it was necessary, and that matters could not be left as they were. The morning air was alive with birdsong; the tranquillity of the forest began to relax her, and she took deeper breaths.

Bella said, with characteristic directness, 'I want to reassure you that you can confide in me. You know about my mother's work with the Resistance, and I also know who can be trusted in Paris. Please tell me what is troubling you. I'm sure I can help you.'

Suzanne shook her head. 'No, it is all right now, they have what they want.'

'Then why did they say they were coming back?'

Suzanne looked startled. 'Who told you that?'

'It's true, isn't it? It's not finished yet.'

The temptation to confide in someone was finally too great, and Suzanne told Bella the whole story.

'When Goetz first suggested bringing the works of art here, I refused point blank. So he offered me half of the proceeds of sale when the war was over. Again I refused, but he threatened to bring Corinne back and do horrible things to her if I did not. So I agreed, but on condition we had a written contract listing the works and their provenance. I thought that if I had something on paper, that would incriminate him and make him keep his side of the bargain.'

'But of course,' Bella said, 'it incriminated you as well.'

'Exactly. That was the risk I had to take. I had no protection. If I had killed him earlier the Germans would have exacted terrible penalties on me and Corinne.'

'Where is the contract now?'

'Ah! That is what those gentlemen want to know. That is why they will return.'

'But why did they leave so abruptly?'

'Because they heard your car coming. They had us tied up and gagged, and were about to torture us for the information. So they threw us under the stairs and rushed off, saying they would be back. If you had not stayed the night, they might have come already.'

Bella's mind had been figuring out the best way to deal with the situation in the short time she had left in France. Alan had to leave, but at least Corker would be around.

'If you want me to help, we must tell my friends here, now,' she said. 'I can't do it on my own, as I have to go back to England in a few days.'

Suzanne was beyond refusing help. They returned to the house and walked into the sitting room to find Alan sitting on the sofa making strange noises to which René was responding. René stood up guiltily, but with a strange gleam in his eye.

'*Mon dieu!* What is going on?' Suzanne exclaimed.

Alan looked up, excited and smiling. 'Just listen to this,' he said. He gestured encouragingly at René, who uttered a complete sentence as though he was singing in an opera on seven notes, while Alan hummed softly in harmony: '*Je m'a...ppe...lle... Re...né Ponge*'. Then he looked very pleased with himself.

Suzanne stood transfixed on the bloodstained Aubusson, her mouth open with astonishment. '*Mais... c'est incroyable!* They said he would never speak again!'

Alan explained what had happened, and looked at Bella, silently asking, 'Well, how do you explain that *rationally?*'

She shook her head in disbelief. 'There is obviously something very therapeutic about those intervals and harmonies,' she said, 'but I can't explain what.'

'At least, you can't deny it's happened,' Alan said, only half joking.

Suzanne went over to René and put her arms round him. '*Mon pauvre ami!* 'she whispered, 'I am so happy for you.'

'Of course,' Alan said, 'it is only a beginning, and I don't know how it can be followed up, but it proves René is capable of speech again.'

'You must find a good neurologist,' said Bella. 'May I make some enquiries on your behalf?' She did not want to take things out of the hands of Suzanne and René. They both nodded enthusiastically.

Then Bella said to Suzanne in a low voice, 'Can we speak of the other matter in front of René and the others?'

Suzanne nodded. '*Bien sûr.*'

Corinne and Corker were prised out of the kitchen and Bella

quickly outlined the problem.

'I'm quite willin' to help,' Corker said, 'but I don't see what use I can be.'

'Just by being around and guarding my back,' said Bella, 'as Alan won't be here.'

Alan cursed the R.A.F. and particularly the adjutant who, he suspected, was behind his sudden recall to the colours.

'All I am going to do,' Bella went on, 'is bring Suzanne and some trustworthy *deuxième bureau* people together, but if word gets out that I am involved, there might be an attempt to apply pressure to stop me. Corinne is very vulnerable too. Neither of you should stay here,' she advised, and made a telephone call to the emergency number in Paris she had been told to ring if she had encountered any trouble during the trial.

René wrote on a notepad that he refused to 'abandon ship', which in French is appropriately the same as to 'abandon the building', and brought out a rifle with several rounds to show he was ready to defend himself and the castle that had been his home ever since he was a boy. Within an hour they were all ready to move off. Suzanne had a briefcase which she kept very close. Corinne placed her revolver on the dashboard shelf, and took the wheel of the Citroën, with Suzanne beside her. It was agreed that both cars should keep together, to discourage any attempt at highjacking, so the first stop was Rouen railway station, to drop off Alan. There was not much time for farewells. Sadly he waved to them and turned to wait on the draughty platform for two hours, for the next train to Le Havre.

As he walked up and down, dejectedly dragging his suitcase, he felt that this was a sad and unsatisfactory way to close the most exciting movement yet of the symphony of his life, a damp squib of an ending. And precious little to look forward to in the next movement either; it would not be a scherzo, he was pretty sure of that. More Mahler than Mendelssohn.

Third Movement

Revelations
GREEN: F minor

*I think that in the lives of all men there must be fleeting moments invested
by the imagination from some intangible cause with a vast and awe-
inspiring significance out of all proportion to the actual event.*

Arnold Bax, *The Lifting of the Veil*

TEMPO 1

alto ma più profondo

17 January 1971

Alan catches the airport bus to Heathrow in plenty of time for his plane leaving at nine. This is one of the advantages of Hammersmith: not the most sought-after area, but only twenty minutes to Piccadilly and half an hour to Heathrow.

At nine o'clock Bella begins her investigation. She has already found out the telephone number of *National Pride* from a journalist acquaintance — both of them being surprised it is not in the phone directory. The office is somewhere in Southwark, near Waterloo Station, not a particularly salubrious area. She dials the number. A female voice says something incomprehensible.

'Is that the office of *National Pride?*' Bella asks in her best Californian.

'Who wants to know?' Distinctly unwelcoming.

'My name is Cassell, like the dictionary. Dr. Cassell. I was very interested by your music reviewer's comments about a concert at the London Festival Hall last week, and I was wondering if I could speak with...'

'We don't reveal names of our reviewers,' the voice cuts her off.

'Wow! Just like the *Times Literary Supplement*,' Bella says in her sweetest tones, 'my oh my, but you do keep high class company. Now, ma'am, can you do me a teensy liddle favour? Can you ask your wunnerful reviewer to call me back on...' (She gives the number of their second phone line, which Bella uses only for her work — colleagues and patients.)

'She's very busy, I doubt it she'll have time. Anyway she's out of town covering other gigs.'

'I'm sorry, what was that? Did you say Gigs? Or Pigs?' The word is new to Bella.

'You tryin' to be funny? The voice has suddenly gone down a couple of classes. 'Stop wastin' my fuckin' time!.' The receiver is slammed down.

That, Bella says to herself, could have been better handled. At both ends. But at least the female reviewer of that rag can be ruled out. Unless she has a boy friend who does her heavy phone work?

She settles at her desk with a second cup of coffee to read through the paper she is due to give at a conference on *The healing forces of music: history, theory and practice*. When the phone rings she sighs. She knows that if she really wants peace and quiet she has only to take the receiver off, but she can never bear the thought that she might miss some urgent message.

For a few seconds there is silence, and she thinks Alan must be using a faulty public phone at Heathrow to say he's forgotten his passport. Then the same low, muffled male voice as before says, 'Take care. Harmony can be put into reverse and destroy everything.' Then the mystery caller replaces the receiver.

This time there does not seem to be the same underlying menace as before. It is certainly a warning, but not a threat like the first one: 'Tell Alan Scott he has released something and he'll wish he hadn't'. Or is she perhaps naively trying to kid herself that there is nothing to worry about? Then the implications begin to swarm into her mind. It's odd that the caller has kept silent until she's by herself. So who's known Alan was going away? — Marcel and other organisers of the Paris conference. Her mother. And Keith. So far as she knows, Keith is the only person in London privy to that information. Not only that, but the caller has not called all the time Keith was in the flat with them. And he was anxious to know about the harmonies. She now thanks God that — inadvertently? — they never got round to that part of their story.

So... what is she to do? Tell the police? She imagines the interview with some bemused young copper from the Bill, and rejects that idea. Go and stay the night with friends? But that would involve explanations she wants to avoid giving to anyone at the moment. Ring Alan and bring him back early? She cannot admit to herself, never mind to Alan, that she's frightened by some telephone crank uttering vaguely sinister messages. Her bottom shoots three inches from the chair when the phone rings again, this time seeming to be twice as loud and strident.

'Stop it! Get hold of yourself!' she mutters, takes a deep breath, and lifts the receiver. This time she says nothing. Silence the other end. Then a tentative 'Hello?'

It is Keith. Why isn't she surprised? He could be ringing for one of two reasons: to see if she's rattled by the Mystery Man; or to take advantage of Alan's absence. So she decides to be very matter-of-fact.

'Keith. Yes? I'm just about to go out. What can I do for you?'

'Oh. Right. I won't keep you. But if you can free yourself for an hour or so about lunch-time, we could have a bite together. No strings, I promise.'

Such promises, she knows, are rarely binding — and it certainly wasn't, the last time she heard Keith say it, only hours before they rumpled someone else's bed. But curiosity is beginning to assert itself. What does he want from her, exactly? She doesn't dislike him, quite the contrary; and with her trained eye and ear she might be able to read something in his eyes or hear a timbre in his voice that will give him away if he is the mystery caller. But best not to appear too keen.

She speaks at last. 'Yes... Keith?'

'Ah,' says Keith, 'I thought you'd gone to sleep, so I was just reading *The Lancet*.'

'I have a conference at Imperial College this morning, but I'm pretty sure lunch will be all right. I'll ring you back when I've checked the programme.' She checks her watch: 8.30. 'In ten minutes. What's your number?'

To her surprise, Keith seems to be flummoxed. 'Oh... ah... that... um... might be difficult. I'm not sure where I'll be. I'm at the British Museum, you see, just outside the Reading Room. Doing a bit of medical history research. So I'll call you again. In ten minutes.' He rings off before she can object.

He was not using a public telephone, she's pretty sure: one always hears the coins going down. And there was no background noise at all, quite unlike the ambient sounds of the British Museum. She knows the telephones only too well in that corridor: they are open booths, and one can always hear the callers either side and the noise of readers walking past. Not only that, she is sure the British Museum Reading Room wouldn't be open yet. Far from putting her off, these little mysteries intrigue her and strengthen her resolve to accept the assignation.

Bella has suggested the rooftop garden restaurant of Derry and Toms in Kensington, because it seemed an attractive neutral public location, and not far from Imperial College.

Keith is astounded by the greenness and vastness of the garden. 'I'd never have imagined such a place! Ducks and flamingos, classical statues and fountains on a roof in Kensington High Street!' His boyish enthusiasm is endearing.

'If it stops raining we can have a walk round after lunch,' Bella

225

suggests. She has ordered the veal and salad, Keith the steak and kidney pie. She declines wine as she has to be on a panel at four-thirty. Keith also sticks to water, without giving a reason.

'So... what have you been researching on at the B.M.?'

He looks momentarily puzzled. 'B.M.? Oh yes. Sorry, I immediately thought of B.M.A. It's just a little hobby of mine, while I'm close to books. How's your conference going?'

Bella is not so easily shaken off. 'A hobby? How fascinating. Something to do with tropical diseases, I expect.'

He nods. 'Yes, in a way. An early medical missionary, a Quaker. I heard a lot about him when I was in India. But it's not really research. Not what you'd call research. Just reading, really.'

The uncertainty and vulnerability that Bella first noted about Keith suddenly comes to the surface again, breaking through the gay Lothario he affected briefly with her.

'What,' she pursues, 'did you find interesting in the latest *Lancet*? I haven't caught up with it yet. Can I take a peek?'

She has noticed that he's come empty-handed to their tryst.

'Sorry,' he smiles. 'It was the B.M. copy. I couldn't bring it out.'

And you couldn't have taken it out of the Reading Room to the telephones either.

Bella is becoming confused by the bits of Keith that ring true and the bits that don't. So far, the doubtful bits have been trivial. But, why are they there at all?

'Talking of hobbies, Keith, have you ever done any acting?'

'Acting?' He looks either wary or pensive, she's not sure. 'I took a small part in the Med Revue as a student, that's about all. Look, Bella...' He shifts nervously on his chair. 'We can't go on skirting round *us*.'

'Us? There isn't any *us*.'

'I don't mean we have anything now, but really, I wish we could just acknowledge the fact that once we made love.'

Bella closes her eyes and sets her mouth. She looks just like her mother. 'Keith, technically, we didn't, and anyway there's no point...'

'Yes, there is a point, Bella, to me anyway,' Keith goes on earnestly, 'and it doesn't mean I want that to start again.'

'You said you could fall in love with me,' Bella reminds him. 'That's quite enough of a warning to me.'

'Then why did you come today?'

'Pure curiosity.'

'The point, to me, if I may say this, is that you were important to me then at a very impressionable age...'

'Oh, come off it, you were quite happy when I said I didn't want to see you again.'

'Only because I feared what might happen to Alan if you moved over to me. I know I shouldn't have responded to you the way I did, but hell, I was sixteen.'

'What do you mean, responded? You led the way!'

'Oh, no, Bella! You were irresistible, and you knew it. I really feared Alan was going to get terribly hurt by you, but when I saw you were getting truly fond of him and might not let him down, I backed off.'

Bella says nothing, not knowing where they can possibly go next.

'What do you want of me, Keith?' she finally asks, so low that he barely hears her. She knows she should not have asked, that it could be dangerous to go on straying in this minefield, but some devil in her can't let it go.

Keith shakes his head. 'I don't know, Bella. I really don't. It's not just... the sex thing. I realised that when I saw you naked yesterday morning.'

She simulates mortal offence. 'Oh, thanks! Really put you off, did I?'

'No, far from it! Any more than you did all those years ago.'

Ah! Here it comes. 'We promised to forget that, Keith, for Alan's sake.'

'No we didn't. We promised never to tell Alan, and we've respected that. I still intend to. But we can't just pretend it never happened. I've never forgotten it. Or what you were like. Your strange mixture of precociousness and analytical observation. I've often wondered since what you turned out to be like in bed. Properly, I mean.'

Bella has never forgotten that episode of pure youthful sexual passion either, innocent though it was by the standards of the nineteen-seventies, but opts for deflation.

'Well, it was no big deal, was it? Not as though we were lovers? A bit of adolescent masturbation, that's all. It's *when* and *where* rather than *what* that matters. When Alan was sad and vulnerable, and behind his back.'

Keith nods his agreement with Bella's down-to-earth assessment of the situation, both then and now. 'It doesn't alter the fact,' he insists, 'that the view... my first view of your frankly delectable body yesterday helped to define the need I feel for closeness.'

She ignores the compliment; the truth is beginning to dawn on her. 'And I'm not the one you need to feel close to?'

'No one is. No woman, no man. But all the time I'm searching in everyone for...' He can't go on.

'For Rebecca?'

'Forgive me.' Keith pulls out a handkerchief and blows his nose loudly. 'You are dark and vivacious... maybe I was looking for you when I took up with Rebecca in the first place! After all, you did precede her.'

'True. I wasn't the first, I suspect. But wait a minute... Didn't you and Alan swap partners? Rebecca was his girl friend, the dumb blonde Joy was yours, and you swapped. Right?'

'Yes. So?'

'So... Nothing, really. It's just an odd repeated pattern: Alan has a dark-haired girl friend, you follow him, but each time you lose her.'

'I never *had* you, not really. And *I haven't lost Rebecca*, Bella. I can't accept that. I have to hold on to something.' He pauses before going on to an intimate confession. 'I still write to her, you know?'

Bella is professionally unsurprised. 'Ah? What do you write?'

'Things that happen. Telling her helps me to maintain some sense of... of...'

'Meaning?'

'Oh no. Certainly not that. There's no meaning. Sense of humour.'

'Yes, I can understand that,' Bella smiles. 'No wonder Jews have that special brand of desperate humour.'

Bella is beginning to realise Keith's obsession with a love lost a quarter of a century ago might be morbid and unhealthy. This was an adolescent crush, and crushes can be very potent, but it was cut off in a particularly brutal way. Fighting off impatience with professional curiosity, she decides to probe a little deeper before trying diversionary tactics.

'Can you tell me how Rebecca died, Keith? Do you know?'

TEMPO 2 — ANDANTE

lagrimoso

FUGUE

con dolore

Waterloo Station, London, October 1947

He did not recognise her. She hardly recognised him. The beard he now sported was grey, nearly white, he had lost most of his formerly black and plentiful hair, and was painfully thin. Despite herself she was driven to take him in her arms and cry, 'Oh, you poor darling!'

It was not the best thing she could have said.

'Yes, a pretty poor specimen, I'm afraid. You are Bella, are you?' His voice was cold, distant.

She was about to ask him if she had changed that much, but stopped just in time.

'Yes, it's me, Tony. It's been a long time. I've heard what you've been through.'

He laughed. A sickening, hollow laugh. 'Oh, you've *heard*, have you? Well, that's all right then.'

Tony's parents were there too, and they took over, distraught but glad at least to see him alive, for they had given up hope — as Bella had — months before their son was finally identified. He did not know who they were either. They all drove back to the family home in Berkshire, in silence.

Dr. Borland was a G.P. in Reading, a slow and pleasant man she had always liked. Mrs. Borland was a pretty, jolly little soul, rather fluttery and, Bella judged, somewhat useless as a doctor's wife.

'I know you're in a difficult situation, my dear,' he confided as soon as they had a moment to themselves. Tony had gone up to his old room to rest, and Mrs. Borland was preparing dinner. 'I've seen several cases like this, men presumed dead turning up. Some find their wives remarried with kids by somebody else. Terrible traumas. Legal minefields too. At least you're still single. I just wanted to say to you that you don't have any obligation towards Tony.'

'No, but...'

'Just hear me out, Bella. He is going to be hard to cope with, for months, maybe years. Probably unemployable. His old firm will take him back, they say, but God knows what he can actually do. That can only make his depression worse.'

Bella nodded. 'Depression is bad enough, but it's the inability to recognise faces that's really distressing. Have you ever heard of this?'

'I'm not a psychiatrist, so I wouldn't expect to have, necessarily. But I know people in Oxford and London who might help. It seems that he's lost the ability that we take for granted, to distinguish facial variations. We manage it just by automatically sizing up minute differences in features, length of nose and chin, width of cheekbones, space between eyes, and so on.'

'But we can't always do it,' Bella recalled. 'To us most Chinese look alike, and I think they say we do to them.'

Dr. Borland nodded. 'That's a good point. The ability depends to some extent on familiarity. So it might be connected with his amnesia.'

'Surely he can recognise people by their voices, like blind people?'

'Yes, of course, but just imagine seeing every single person wearing a blank, featureless mask. He might get used to it, but it's going to take a long time, I think, considering his generally depressed state. And a lot of love and patience.' He paused, then asked, in the undramatic way he would ask a patient he suspected of having heart disease if he had been having any chest pains or dizzy spells lately, 'Do you still love him?'

She realised he was simply being honest and expected nothing less from her, and considered her reply with eyes closed for several moments. Then she slowly shook her head..

'I don't think so... The fact is, there is someone else...'

'Ah! I'm not surprised. You're a very attractive girl.'

' But suppose Tony needs me? I *do* have a moral obligation, you know. He tried so hard to trace me, he must need me.'

Dr. Borland took her hand. 'There is need, and need, Bella. You were the only signpost he had through the fog to his past, apart from me and his mother. We are essential parts of his self-identity — at the moment. But that will probably change, as he begins to rebuild his self again on the basis of new experiences. He has a lot of re-learning to do, and it's going to be painful for all involved.'

When dinner was ready Mrs. Borland went up to wake him, and came down again with tears in her eyes.

'He's already forgotten who I am,' she said, finally forced to confront the reality of the situation in all its bleakness. Up until now her reaction had been based entirely on gratitude to God for returning her son to them. She had had a thanksgiving Mass said for him, and they had all three knelt at the altar at St. Michael's where not so long ago they had had a memorial Mass to commemorate his passing. Bella had refused to attend the thanksgiving, which had upset the Borlands, so she had to explain that since the traumatic IRA episode anything to do with the Catholic church made her feel physically sick. Yes, she knew it was irrational, but there was nothing she could do about it.

What opened up before them all now, as they heard Tony slowly descending the stairs, was the prospect of having to remind him, every morning, maybe several times a day, who they were.

It was Alan who suggested they should not see each other for the time being, and Bella who protested. A curious reversal of rôles, for hitherto he had always been the more dependent.

'It wouldn't be right if I was trying to influence you all the time, and I don't think I could stop myself trying,' he explained.

'But I need you, to talk to, to hold me, to tell me this nightmare can't go on for ever,' she cried. 'I don't have anyone else, Alan.'

He had returned to duty at Uxbridge, where the adjutant had taken a sadistic pleasure in signing him up for several nights as Duty Sergeant in the guard room — in addition to his daytime duties.

'You've been having an easy ride, sergeant,' he said disapprovingly. 'We've been carrying your load for you.'

He just hoped he would not be put on with Corporal Cottrell.

The enforced separation did at least allow him and Bella to move beyond the emotional turmoil churning them both up. She stayed with the Borlands for a few days, then returned to open up her parents' house, musty and neglected since Alexi had flown off to the States. His tour of night duty completed, Alan agreed, not too reluctantly, to spend an evening with Bella at the house. She was looking drawn and had lost weight.

'You're looking tired,' she said. 'And you've lost weight.'

He laughed. 'I was just thinking the same about you. We're both fading away.' The engagement ring, he noticed, had re-appeared on her wedding finger. A diamond surrounded by emeralds. The hardest, and the easiest to shatter.

She said the situation with Tony seemed hopeless, but just as she had been on the point of taking what she called the coward's way out, Mrs. Borland had unwittingly upset everything by telling her that Tony had confided to her how much he still loved her, Bella, and wanted her to be with him, but couldn't tell her face to face because he wasn't sure if she was the right one, the same one. The Bella he loved was the one he vaguely remembered loving, as if in a lost dream; but she could not, after that, pretend that she counted for nothing in his life and was free to go.

'I'm tied, Alan,' she wailed. 'Why can't I just be a selfish bitch and do what I want, for me?'

'Because you wouldn't be the lovable person you are if you did,' he said. 'If I was Tony I wouldn't want to lose you, so I know what he feels. No, I don't *know*, but I can imagine.'

Slowly, over the ensuing weeks, when Bella returned to Reading at weekends after trying to concentrate on her courses on cognition and behaviourism and philosophy of mind, a new rapport was created between her and Tony. He could even laugh at his inability to recognise her after an absence of more than an hour. Bella began to wonder if she should suggest trying out Alan's Magic Notes, which he had now fully scored, but she quailed before the prospect of explaining it to a neuropsychologist: 'You see, a composer friend of mine heard a sequence of strange harmonies, and he hummed them to a traumatised aphasic victim, and he got his speech back.' She could imagine only too well, and with great discomfort, what his reaction would be, because it matched exactly what her own reaction to Corinne's Barcelona story had been.

Alan's parents benefited from the unhappy turn of events in their son's life: to avoid sitting in his room by himself, moping and unable to contact Bella (he could hardly ring the Borlands) he began to go home for weekends. The first visit was strained.

'We were beginning to think you'd forgotten us,' said Maddy.

'How could you think that?' He was irritated by the constant reminders of how much they missed him. 'I've written you once or twice a week, even when we were travelling round France. Anyway, Caesar didn't think I'd forgotten him, and he can't read.'

Caesar had indeed gone berserk as soon as he'd heard Alan walking up the flagstone path to the front door. Alan was shocked to see how much weight he had put on.

Bill was anxious to prevent the simmering resentment of wife and son erupting to the surface, as he had to put up with Maddy's moods and tempers all week.

'And very interesting they were, those letters,' he chipped in.

'When shall we see the film at the Odeon? With your name up there on the screen! Music by Alan Scott! My, we'll be proud of you, shan't we, Maddy?'

Unable to keep his anxieties to himself, Alan told his father about finding Bella again, her mother's espionage activities in France, and Tony's tragic condition, making him swear not to breathe a word to Maddy. Bill was very pleased to be the chosen confidant of his son, after so many years of being excluded from the bond that once existed between mother and son.

'Sounds like a right old mess,' he said. 'What's this fella like, this Tony?'

'I don't know, Dad. I've never met him. But he's had a very rough time. If only he'd come back earlier or later, either before Bella and I fell in love — again, in my case — or when we'd been permanently and securely settled together, married perhaps. As it is, we were just beginning to think we might be happily spending our lives together, and bang! Back comes someone from the dead, like a ghost from the grave.'

Bill was having his own troubles, which he was glad to share with his son; he hardly ever dared to confide in Maddy, because she got so upset and emotional and depressed about things. Robin Hood had sacked him a few weeks before, without notice. He had gone along to head office in Evesham for what he thought was going to be a sales meeting, and they had simply said 'Thanks, Mr. Scott, but we're obliged to re-employ returning servicemen, so just leave the car keys on your way out.'

He had had to catch a train back, at his own expense. The disappearance of the car could not be explained away, so he had to admit he had been sacked. To her credit, Maddy had refrained from commenting that if he had made himself a bit more indispensable it would have been a different story, but her lack of sympathy was fairly palpable.

Fortunately, they were not in a bad position financially. Maddy had found a job in the rag trade, which was going well, expanding even, as a wider range of materials was becoming available for dresses, and housewives were once again becoming fashion-conscious after years of making do. Her advice was being sought increasingly on both design and marketing: it was important, she said, to get in with the department stores, as they could shift stock so much faster and in such bulk. Yes, they expected much bigger discounts than the small suburban dress shops, but production costs should be less if they could mechanise and mass produce

233

quality stuff. She was scathing to the production manager if she found sub-standard models being returned by buyers.

'There's no excuse for skimping now,' she shouted one day in frustration, so loudly that the whole factory heard her, 'times have changed, just forget we had a war on, there's no war on now, except for me. I'm out there in the front line, and the least I can expect is that you'll provide me with good stuff to fire at them.'

She was respected because although she had a managerial position that could entitle her to sit behind a desk all day, she insisted on continuing to go out selling as well, for two or three days a week. 'I know what reps are like from bitter experience,' she told the director. 'If I can sell this tat, they can.'

Only one week before, Maddy had pulled off quite a coup with one of the major stores in Birmingham which had been fire-bombed during the blitz and was now rebuilt. They had placed a very large order for mid-range dresses which they advertised as being 'Massively reduced', even though they were lines specially bought in for the sales. Imaginative prices were written on labels and crossed out, and replaced with impressively reduced ones. Maddy objected to this on principle, but knew that if she rocked the boat, no one would fish her out of the water.

'So what will you do, Dad,' Alan asked. 'Are you going for other jobs?'

'Oh, yes, I've got a few irons in the fire,' Bill replied, but with a vague look in his eye and tone in his voice that meant 'few' was an exaggeration.

'In the meantime, maybe you could take Caesar out for more walks. He's got fat, and that's not good for him. It would do you good too. Make yourself more useful round the house now Mum's the breadwinner.'

'I'm not going to be a bloody househusband!'

Alan realised this was dangerous ground with his father. He might just as well have suggested castration.

'No, I'm not saying that, Dad, but Caesar needs the exercise, even if you don't, which you do. Once a week with me isn't enough.'

A possible temporary solution occurred to him. 'I may be wrong, Dad, but the part of being a special you enjoyed most was the St. John's Brigade stuff, studying for the First Aid exams. Wasn't it?'

Bill looked at him warily. 'Yes, I suppose it was. What's that got to do with the price of parsnips?'

'You could do some voluntary work with the St. John's. They always need people, at football matches and cinemas.'

The idea was clearly not a complete dud. Bill nodded slowly, then shook his head.

'But I can't get anywhere any more. I don't have a car.'

This was the worst part of being unemployed, apart from the cessation of the weekly pay packet, and the one that affected Bill most. His self-worth needed a vehicle to prove itself, just as a knight of old needed a steed. Not for nothing did commercial travellers call themselves Knights of the Road.

Alan was not to be discouraged so easily. 'You can use my bike. It wouldn't mind, so long as you didn't race it too fast.'

Bill's prowess as a cyclist had always been a joke; his thin little legs found it hard to propel him up the slightest incline, and he grew rapidly out of breath thanks to his nicotine addiction. But by the end of the war his physical condition had improved considerably. Peace had brought about a return to a sedentary life-style he found wholly satisfactory.

'Just think of the free matches and films you'd see,' Alan went on. 'It's not so different from being a doctor, and you said that's what you always wanted to be.'

'No, not *always*. I'll think about it.'

Hopes for early release in time for the start of the year at the Academy were diminishing as October went by. Professor Walker was very accommodating.

'As you've already done the equivalent of first year at Cambridge, we'll be willing to take you in in January,' he said, when Alan went to see him in a state of despondency. 'But it would be risky after that. We don't want you failing anything. You can send work in, if you like, and we'll mark it. And you can sit in on lectures and workshops, if you can get away during the week. Some of them are evening classes. Let's just hope you don't get posted to the Shetlands.'

Bella had to write an essay on 'The Creative Functions of the Brain', and chose to do it on music.

'Will you be my guinea pig?' she asked Alan one evening.

'It depends on what you expect me to do,' he replied.

'Just sit there and create and tell me what's going on in your head,' she said. 'Easy really.'

He sat for several minutes, while the familiar structures and textures of sounds began to form in his mind. Then he sighed. 'It's no good. It's simply not possible to communicate what I hear in words. Colours maybe, but even those images change too rapidly to be seized. Can't you just plug me into one of those brainwave things and watch it on a screen?'

Bella laughed. 'You've been watching too many science fiction films,' she said. 'That'll be one of the things to come.'

The door bell rang. Bella looked up from her notebook, mouth open with surprise.

'I wonder who that is?'

'There used to be a well-known method of finding out. Now,' he scratched his head, 'what was it?'

She put her tongue out at him, then rectified the gesture by kissing him — the first kiss on the mouth since Paris.

Alan barely listened to the voices along the hallway until he heard them approaching. Then he caught the anxiety in Bella's raised tones. A genial-looking man in his sixties came into the sitting room, followed by a thin, balding man with a grey-white beard. Bella came last, rolling her eyes up towards the ceiling and mouthing 'Ooooh!'

'Dr. Borland, and his son, Tony — this is Alan Scott, an old friend of mine from Birmingham days. He's helping me out with some research I'm doing on music, you know, how composers' funny brains work.'

The reference to funny brains did not go down well. The lost and dissociated expression on Tony's face gave him the appearance of a sleepwalker. His response to the introduction was a faint grunt, then he turned his attention to pictures on the wall.

'I apologise for interrupting you without notice,' Dr. Borland said to Bella, ignoring or failing to see Alan's proferred hand. Alan was having to retrain himself to English diffidence about hand-shaking after the automatic effusiveness of the French.

The doctor continued, 'We had a surprise call this morning from Tony's specialist to see a visiting American naval neurosurgeon. He returns to the States tomorrow morning. So I thought we might as well...'

He waved his hand about, to finish the sentence for him.

Bella made appreciative noises. The thought suddenly struck her that this was the ideal opportunity to mention the Magic Notes! All she had to do was suggest to Alan that he play them on the piano, and see what happened. Only, of course, there were no quarter tones, much less microtones... Then she noticed that Tony was

236

gazing intently at Alan's face, then at hers. Bella followed his gaze, took one look at Alan, and swallowed hard. Tony might not be able to tell one face from another any more than she could tell one Chinese from another, but he could, apparently, tell when a man's mouth and cheek were besmirched with lipstick, and deduce how they got like that.

Unaware, Alan excused himself, saying he had to get back to camp.

'I expect you'd like to wash your hands before you go,' Bella said, pursing her lips at him in a very curious way. She had never used that funny euphemism before.

'No, I'll be all right,' he said obtusely.

'I don't think so. Sometimes you have to wait and wait for a train at this time of night.' She dragged him along to the bathroom. 'And wash your face!' she whispered fiercely, 'even though it's too late.'

There was no chance of introducing the Magic Notes now.

It was with some trepidation that Bella visited the Borlands in Reading the following weekend, but Tony gave no sign that he had noticed the lipstick, merely continuing to be as remote and unresponsive as ever since his return. Never the most outgoing of men, his new disabilities seemed to reinforce the negative aspects of his personality.

She went out to help Dr. Borland to pick some of the big, red, juicy apples growing at the bottom of the garden, catching them as he snipped them off with secateurs as deftly as though they had been soutures.

'Here's a beauty!' he said, reaching forward on his ladder. 'Catch it, it'd be a pity to bruise it.'

She caught it and put it in the overflowing basket.

'That was your young man, the composer, was it?'

Despite herself, she blushed, angry at having been caught out and at having caused pain so foolishly.

'Yes. I'm sorry your first meeting couldn't have been more civilised. But I want you to know that...'

'You don't have to explain anything, Bella,' he interrupted, looking down. 'As I said before, you're a free woman.'

'Yes, I know that. Thank you. But it's important for me that you should be clear. Alan and I... our relationship is frozen. There's been no... intimacy... since Tony came back. Should I tell him that? Does he suspect?'

Dr. Borland shook his shaggy head sadly. 'I really don't know. He is becoming more and more impenetrable. The American neurosurgeon was less than hopeful, I'm afraid. When he saw the X-rays of Tony's head injuries, he just shook his head and said he was lucky to be alive. I'm beginning to wonder.'

'So there's no hope of relieving or releasing anything by intervention? For instance, there was one curious...'

'It may come to that anyway,' Dr. Borland interrupted. 'Apparently a clot may be forming, and that could lead to a stroke... or worse.'

'Does Tony know that?'

'Oh, he's no fool. When we started talking about possible surgery, he realised straight away it wasn't with the hope of a cure or even an improvement.'

'I did hear of one...'

'So the choice is either slow then accelerated decline into a vegetable state, or an operation that might stave that off for a few months or years — or kill him.'

Well, dammit, she had tried twice, and he hadn't wanted to hear, so that was that. The natural had won over the supernatural. They both stared sadly at the figure of Tony lumbering like a lost dog towards them from the house. At that moment Bella knew she could not abandon him. She went up to him with the apple in her hand, and offered it to him. He took it gently, looked at it, then at her face, puzzled. She put her arms around him and hugged him. Her mind flipped back to that day, a lifetime ago, when a young boy with a wounded dog had taught her to feel compassion for the very first time.

*

'Sergeant Scott speaking.'

He was sitting in his office, preparing a talk on 'The Englishness of English Music'. A self-interested exercise, as he hoped it would help him to excise traces of Englishness from his own score.

''allo! Zat Alan? This is your ol' pal Corker, sergeant. Commong allez vouz, ol' sport?'

'Corker, you old devil! Where've you been?'

Corker chuckled. 'You left at the wrong time, me old son. We 'ad a grand time on the Rivee-aira we did. Cor, you should see them bathin' suits they wear, only you can't 'cos they aren't there, if you follow my drift!'

'So you got some good shots of them, did you?'

'You bet!'

'I'll expect a private view, then.'

'You're goin' to get one o' them right enough, lad. The rushes are ready.'

'Eh?'

'The rushes. The film. Unedited first prints. You're to 'ave a look at them and get yer brain workin' on the music. Bella's being invited too, of course. 'ow is she? You spliced yet?'

'No, not yet. Corker. It'll be a while yet.'

'Well, don't 'ang about too long, or I'll 'ave 'er meself!'

And the best of British to you, Alan thought.

The screening took place at the Ealing Studios, which meant a short trolley-bus ride for him from Uxbridge. Even the unfinished version gave him something to work on, conveying the spirit of a great but humbled nation trying to recover from a long illness, still with warring viruses vying for power and threatening to tear its body apart. Bella's interviews were, in his opinion, the highlights, but he admitted he might be prejudiced. Whenever she appeared on the screen, she put her hands over her eyes, muttering 'This is terrible, I don't want to look'.

There were a few French people there, brought in as advisers; the moment the showing was over they began to disagree vociferously with one another and with the director, Simon Marsa, about political and philosophical implications they found in simple aspects of life that had never occurred to his *perception anglosaxonne*. Sensitivities were clearly still very raw. The balance was too far left; it favoured the right. Collaboration was exaggerated, and collaborationists were let off too lightly. There was too much emphasis on the black market, and not enough criticism of unregulated capitalist exploitation of shortages. Urban problems were treated more sympathetically than the devastation of rural areas in the battlefields of the north and east, but the vast challenges of re-establishing France's ravaged industries were treated inadequately. Alan was amused by this typically French wrangling in which everyone talked at once and listened to no one, until they began to criticise Bella's contribution: she was too intellectual — but her questions were too simplistic; she lacked warmth and sympathy, but she was too emotionally affected by tragic stories. As she sat there, hands clasped, eyes shut, he wanted to shout that she had done a wonderful job, coming in with little or no preparation, but realised that would appear to be excusing her; and she needed no excuses. He just thanked goodness he hadn't written the music yet, or they would have torn that to shreds as well. Was it possible, he wondered, to love France but not like the French?

Simon was greatly encouraged by this reception. 'It's when everybody's happy with what you've done to them that you have to worry,' he said. 'That means you've been too bland. I think we got it just about right.'

Afterwards, Bella and Alan went with Corker to a nearby pub. Glasses in hand, they toasted their hopes for a successful film.

Then Corker said: 'It was a shame about yon fella up at the sharto, wasn't it?'

They asked him what he was talking about.

'Lor', I thought you'd 've heard. Those boogers went back and set fire to the place, and old wotsit was in it.'

'You mean René?' Alan asked.

'Aye, that's 'im. It seems 'e was firing at them from an upstairs window, so they lobbed an incendiary in there. He went on firing, apparently, 'cos 'e got 'em both in the legs. When the police and fire brigade arrived, they were still crawlin' about in the undergrowth, tryin' to escape, wi' masks on but no kneecaps, so they couldn't pretend they were Jehovah's Witnesses. His body wasn't found till well after.'

They bowed their heads in silent tribute. Then Alan raised his glass. 'Here's to René's last stand.'

They gave him a copy of the rushes so that he could begin work, for which he needed constant access to a film projector and screen — and time. The equipment problem was easily solved, as the education unit put on educational and training films regularly. But the adjutant, still irritated that Alan had been allowed to slip from his administrative grasp, was agitating for him to do additional night duties and to appear on early morning parades, which did not fit in well with late-night screen-and-score sessions. Alan threw caution to the winds and went to see Squadron Leader Maskell.

'You say the Academy would take you in January?'

'Yes, sir. Professor Walker said it would be all right. But no later. Otherwise I shall have to hang around till next October.'

'At least that would give you time to get the film score finished.'

'But they'll want it long before that. And I'd have nothing to live on, sir, until my grant started up.'

The thought of returning home to live, dependent on parental support, was less than appealing. Caesar would be pleased, but that was the only attraction. No, at least the R.A.F was feeding him and paying him ten shillings a week and enabling him to stay in London.

Maskell said he would see what he could do. Unfortunately, his intervention immediately threatened to have precisely the opposite effect from the desired one. When the adjutant heard that that bloody Acting Sergeant Scott had gone over his head, he put in a request for him to be posted overseas as a Clerk General Duties, reverting to his substantive rank of Aircraftsman Second Class. The request from the adjutant arrived on the desk of the Commanding Officer at the same time as the Director of Music's request that Scott be recommended for special release from the service.

They were both called in to explain themselves; both realised that a decision would depend on the personal preferences and priorities of Group Captain Collard, DFC with bar.

Maskell was asked to make his case first.

'He's a young man of exceptional talent, despite his comparative lack of formal training,' he began, knowing this would rile that little pen-pusher, Gibson. 'There is no point in making him waste another year of his life when he could get back to his studies in January. A gift like his is vulnerable, and can go stale and be lost forever if it loses impetus.'

He just hoped that the C.O. would not have heard of Messiaen, who somehow drew creative strength from his ordeal in a German prison camp.

'We have all sacrificed years of our lives,' said Collard, 'many more than Scott will be expected to.'

Service: 1, Music: nil.

'Gibson?'

'With respect, sir, I agree with you about sacrifices and lost chances in civvy street. Scott hasn't done his whack yet, by far. Had it much too cushy.'

'And why do you want him demoted?'

'He wangled himself accelerated promotion, then secondment on some junket in France, and has got too big for his boots. Some of my best clerks are still corporals.'

'I don't see that's at all relevant,' said Collard. 'Many of my best crews got killed over the Middle East and Germany, but I don't hold it against those who were too young — or had safe jobs on ground staff,' he added pointedly.

Service: 1, Music: 1.

Collard then asked Maskell to tell him about the 'French junket'.

'He was selected to write the music score for a film being made by the Ministry of Information's Documentary Film Unit, and he would just have time to complete it by January if he was released now — or at least, relieved of all other duties here at Uxbridge. The idea of posting him overseas to do a dogsbody job as a clerk is plain ludicrous.'

The adjutant went red, opened his mouth, and snapped it shut again.

The C.O. frowned. 'The R.A.F. isn't intended to subsidise the arts, Maskell, even though it has done so in your case.'

Service: 2, Music: 1.

It was the Director of Music's turn to keep his mouth shut, which was just as well, as the Adjutant made the tactical error of opening his.

'Damn' waste of time and money, having musicians flouncing around in the air force!'

The C.O. went on, 'On the other hand, I concede that the symphony orchestra has done a splendid job as a morale-booster, and promoting the British cause in America.'

Service: 2, Music: 2.

His next question was to the adjutant. 'When is his number likely to come up for normal scheduled release, Gibson?'

'For Clerk G.D.s, only about twelve months, I should say.'

'Hm,' the C.O. pulled at his moustache. 'That's a hell of a long time to hang around. But there must be hundreds of young men in the same situation as Scott. Why should we make an exception for him, Maskell?'

'Precisely because he is exceptional, sir. I don't think there would be any risk of setting a precedent. He has a job of national importance to complete urgently, and he has a place at the Royal Academy of Music which will entitle him to an ex-service grant. So he's not going to flood the civilian job market.'

The C.O. was making detailed notes as Maskell spoke. Finally he looked up and said, 'You've convinced me.'

Unfortunately, he was looking right between them, and neither knew who had won. The adjutant gave a polite cough.

'Excuse me, sir, you mean he should be posted?'

'No, you blithering idiot, let him go, for God's sake!' Collard thundered.

Service: 2, Music: 3.

Later, in the officers' mess, the C.O. said to the adjutant, 'If you hadn't asked for him to be demoted, you might have got away with it. Stupid, that was. Punitive agenda of your own, eh? You haven't done yourself much good there, Gibson. Get the boy out pretty damn quick and keep me informed. No sitting on it.'

The next week was a whirlwind. Having lost the battle over the troublesome AC2/Acting Sergeant Scott, and not wishing to incur further opprobrium and totally scupper his already slim chances of promotion to Squadron Leader, the adjutant wanted to get rid of him as fast as possible. He expedited the release papers to Air Ministry, with a supporting memo from the Ministry of Information, and Alan was picking up his demob suit and £50 gratuity on the Friday. Bella said he could live free of charge in her parents' house, as they were in California, providing he didn't try too hard to seduce her, and the Film Unit put him on their payroll for £5 a week from the following Monday, for two months.

He knew his parents would be expecting him to spend some demob leave with them when he finally escaped from the R.A.F., so he went up to Birmingham for only a week, claiming that he had to begin his course at the Academy straight away after that. It was with the best of intentions that he greeted his mother, feeling the need to re-establish something of the love that had once been so strong between them. But with unconscious perversity Maddy wrecked his reconciliatory project almost immediately.

'By the way, Alan, I ran into the head of the music department at the university the other day.'

'Ran into him? In your car?'

'No, don't be daft, I just happened to be near there.'

'Which university are you talking about?'

'Birmingham, of course. I went into the offices and told him what you've been doing, at Cambridge and the film music. He said they'd be glad to consider you. He actually remembered your song being sung at the Town Hall! And then...'

'But you know I'm going to the Acad...'

'...and then you could come back home and live. That'd be so much cheaper than finding some awful bombed-out digs in London. They've got some very good people here. If you really are going to go on with music, that is. You have thought properly about languages, or law, haven't you, Alan? They'd be so much more likely to get you a proper job. You could get into the diplomatic easily with your international experience. Anthony Eden says they need more recruits from the grammar schools.'

Before he could recover the initiative, she changed tack in her well-planned strategy for repossession of her son.

'Guess who's coming round to dinner this evening?' Maddy said mischievously.

Alan declined to make any suggestions beyond Winston Churchill.

'Your old flame Joy,' she announced. 'I happened to bump into her yesterday.'

All this running and bumping into people.

He laughed: 'Flame! She wasn't even a flicker.'

'Well, try and be nice to her,' Maddy said. 'She's a nice girl.'

'Be nice to the nice girl, yes Mum,' Alan mimicked.

Maddy gave a little snort. 'I think you've been getting into some bad company over in France. French girls, I shouldn't wonder.'

'There are certainly a lot of them about,' he replied with mock seriousness. 'It must be something to do with the water over there.'

Joy sailed in about a quarter past six, sporting a dress moulded to her curves. His mother's hand was apparent in this. He had forgotten that evening meal time was an hour earlier than in London, a cultural phenomenon he could only attribute to the fact that in a predominantly manual worker society, everyone either got up earlier or finished work earlier. Or both. She gave him a limp handshake and said 'Nice to see you again, Alan,' a nice thing for a nice girl to say.

The two of them were ushered into the front room, and Maddy went off to do things in the kitchen while they 'caught up'. Joy sat down gingerly on the settee and tried unsuccessfully to pull her tight skirt to somewhere in the region of her rounded knees. She really was a very pretty girl, like a pre-war wax doll with flawless pink complexion, large cow-like eyes, and what looked like long spiral bedsprings of hair descending on each side of her cherubic face. She did not ask him anything about what he had been doing since they last met, so he felt he ought to set an example and show some interest in her intervening activities.

'So, what have you been up to, Joy?'

'Nothing much,' she replied. And that, apparently, summed up a couple of years of life on earth for her. She was heavy going at first, but once the floodgates were fully opened, the flow of suburban trivia was relentless.

'Of course,' she went on, 'I know you've been away in the

services and that, but it hasn't been easy for any of us. There's still the rationing, and we can't get the brass.'

'The brass? You mean money?'

'No, silly, the brass for the furniture. You know I work for Porsons?'

'No, I didn't know.'

'Oh, really?' She shook her curls in disbelief, clearly not impressed by his lamentable failure to keep up with the important things in life.

Porsons were the oldest established undertakers in the city. For a moment he allowed his imagination to toy with the idea that she was employed as a gravedigger, or an embalmer, or maybe an entertainment officer at laying-out ceremonies, making sure everyone was miserable.

'Oh, yes,' she said airily, impatiently, as if he had just admitted he hadn't heard the war was over, 'I started as a typist, and now I'm in charge of ordering. It's very complicated, everything in triplicate, but we can't get our hands on enough brass. For the handles on the coffins, you see. And the hinges, though they don't show. People like the best, we have a very select client-eel, very nice they are, on the whole, although some of them can get stroppy when I have to tell them there aren't any brass handles till the end of the month. 'How can we wait till the end of the month?' they say, as if it's my fault hubby chose the wrong time to die. I mean, I say, there has been a war on. Very selfish some people are, but on the whole they're very nice.' She shook her ringlets. 'You still in the R.A.F. then?'

Good God, so she didn't think he'd been living under a stone! 'No, I've just been demobbed.'

'Oh. Funny word, demobbed. I never thought of the R.A.F. as a mob, not like the army, some of them can be awful at dances and things, hands everywhere. One of my colleagues was in the R.A.F. An accountant he is. Keeps the books beautiful, lovely hand he's got. Copperplate. I keep telling him he ought to go in for engraving, he'd do wonders on the brass plates. When we get them, that is.'

Desperate to move off coffins, he asked her, 'Have you heard anything about Rebecca or Keith?'

'Oh,' she simpered, 'I'd have thought you would have heard.' Translation: *That just shows how completely you've lost interest in your old friends.*

Clearly she was going to play hard to get for whatever news she did have, so he decided to play the game.

'Do tell me whatever it is that I ought to know.'

'We...ell... Keith... I suppose you remember Keith?'

Of course I remember Keith, I was the one who mentioned him, you silly bitch.

'I do recall the name. Do go on,' Alan smiled.

'We...ell...'

The story, finally extracted from her and re-assembled into something like coherence in Alan's mind, amounted to this: Keith did indeed go off with the Friends Ambulance Unit, and led a charmed life in the midst of battle through to the end. When he heard about the horrors of some prison camp, Ouch-something or other, he volunteered to go there and help with the surviving prisoners. He said that if he'd known the thousands Rebecca had talked about that day in the summer-house were in fact millions, he might have changed his mind about being a conchy. While he was there he felt, every day, that Rebecca's contempt got a little less.

She, Rebecca, had volunteered for overseas service immediately after that 'horrible experience' by the tennis court, and was on board a hospital ship in the Atlantic, on her way to North Africa or Italy, when it was torpedoed. She had been taken prisoner and had not been heard of since. Keith had searched through lists of prisoners rescued from concentration and P.O.W. camps, but had failed to find any trace of her.

'The other nurses said she was kept separate from them the moment they were disembarked,' Joy concluded, 'and when they asked why, all the Germans would say was 'Juden'. That means Jewish in German, I think.'

'Yes, it does, Joy,' he reassured her, no longer able to mock. So, Alan thought, Good, Auschwitz had eventually forced Keith to face the enormity, the obscenity, that he had been unwilling to compromise his precious religious ideals to help combat. But he doubted whether Rebecca would have been impressed or forgiving. Any more than he, Alan, was.

'It's sad, in a way, isn't it?'

'Not in a way. It is sad, full stop.'

At that moment Maddy knocked discreetly on the door of the front room, having judged they had had time to revive the old flames.

'Dinner's ready,' she announced. 'Bring another chair in, will you Alan?'

The meal was dominated by animated chatter between Joy and

246

Maddy, who seemed to attune herself effortlessly to the trivialities that poured unselfconsciously from Joy's unquestionably beautiful lips. Bill and Alan glanced at each other now and then and smiled.

'See you got your demob suit then?' Bill remarked.

Alan nodded. He was wearing it. 'Not much choice,' he said. 'You can have the hat if you like, Dad.'

'Oh, I'll see if it suits me. Thanks.'

Joy was staring vacantly at one of Maddy's flower paintings on the wall. Bill took advantage of the momentary silence. 'Alan's been working in France, you know, Joy. On a film.'

Joy came back to something resembling mental activity. 'Oh, really? I thought you'd been shooting down Germans, and they'd forgotten to tell you the war was over.'

They laughed.

'Did you meet any film stars?' she asked.

'Oh yes, Joy.' Alan sat back in his chair. 'They were all there, in Gay Paree, Gérard Philippe, and Louis Jouvet, and Jean Gabin, and Arletty, and Pierre Fresnay, and Jean-Louis Barrault, and Josette Day, and Jean Marais, and...'

Joy pouted. 'I've never heard of any of them. I think you're making them up, you're a terrible tease, Alan Scott, isn't he, Mr. Scott, a terrible tease?'

'Yes, terrible. You mustn't tease Joy, Alan,' his father said with mock reproof. 'She hasn't had your opportunities to get about.'

'Not that any of us have,' Maddy added.

Faint tone of reproach there, Alan thought. But he could hardly be blamed for the fact that before the war only the wealthy ever thought of crossing the English Channel, and during the war it was strictly by invitation or royal command only. He remembered he must tell his mother about Haraucourt and grandad.

Gallantly he offered to walk Joy home, hoping she would say No it was all right thanks, but she accepted. As he left her at her gate, she said, 'Would you like to come in for a moment. Mum and Dad are out at the pictures.'

He refused politely, saying he'd better get back, so she advanced her lips to his. There was no denying that she had an extraordinarily kissable mouth, generous, soft yet muscular, lipsticklessly pink. So he kissed it and found that she had made considerable progress since the last time, pressing not only her tongue between his teeth, but her now even more impressive bosom and previously unattainable pubis into him.

She pulled away, for which he was grateful. Temptation, the one

247

thing he couldn't resist — who wrote that? Oscar, of course, poor devil.

'It's lovely seeing you again, Alan. I could come and visit you in London if you like,' Joy suggested.

No thanks, Joy, you're very sexy but the thought of a whole weekend listening to your concerto for brass handles and hinges lacks immediate attraction. On the other hand, the Bella theme (solo violin) is becoming weak and discordant, so maybe I should welcome the reappearance of the discarded Joy motif (clarinet) with its enhanced development and unsuspected sensuality.

'Oh, yes, that would be... nice,' he said, ashamed — half ashamed — of his willingness to take advantage of Joy's offering up of hitherto withheld favours for unwitting sacrifice in the ritual of rebound.

'Here's my phone number.' She had it already written on a slip of paper. 'Night!'

She ran lightly up the garden path.

The following day he brought up the question of Grandad Rogers's misspent youth.

'By the way, Mum, I think Grandad wasn't as bad as you think.'

'I never said he was bad,' Maddy replied, mystified, intrigued. 'What do you mean?'

'I mean, he didn't just fritter away all his money. It was stolen from him by a shark in Paris.'

He told her and his father the whole story, from the day he raided the filing store, but not about the séance.

'Well, you are a dark horse, son, keeping your cards close to your chest all this time,' said Bill.

'Yes, why didn't you tell us before this?' Maddy wanted to know.

'Because there was nothing to tell. I only found out what had happened to the French embezzler just before I left Paris. But the important thing — for me, anyway — is that Grandad was gullible, but not a wastrel.'

Maddy nodded sadly. 'Yes, I suppose that is comforting. Pity your Gran isn't here to know that.'

Alan had a sharp intake of breath. 'Wait a moment. What did Gran call Grandad?'

'Why, Dodge, of course. That was his nickname. He was Dodge to everybody.'

'Why?' he wanted to know. 'Dodging what?'

'No idea. Sorry. Well before I was born.'

'Then Gran does know,' Alan murmured to himself, but Maddy pricked up her ears.

'Know?' she asked, frowning. 'What do you mean, 'She knows'?'

He decided to tell them the rest of the story. 'You see, I was at a séance in France, and a message came through from Gran...'

Maddy turned bright pink with excitement. 'What! She came through? But how? Did she materialise? Who was the medium? What did she say? Did she talk French?'

'Hold on, Mum, hold on. I was just going to tell you. No, she wasn't visible, there wasn't a medium, and she wrote in English. She spelled words out.'

He described the method, and Maddy nodded, obviously acquainted with it.

'She said Dodge forgives somebody she called Haricot, which is French for bean. It meant nothing, but it's beginning to make sense now — I didn't know then who Dodge was. Perhaps she meant Haraucourt? Or Arkwright, come to think of it.'

'We'd better tell young Mr. Arkwright,' Maddy suggested when she had calmed down.

'No, I don't think so,' Alan said hastily. 'He'd be very upset if he got the idea I'd suspected his father. Oh, and Gran said she is at peace because she died in her own bed.'

He did not say anything about the instruction to make his mother happy; she could use that as emotional ammunition in her campaign to get him home again.

The next morning he took a delighted Caesar for a long, long walk, first up to the windmill field. To his intense sorrow, the old mill had been demolished, and a row of prefabricated houses erected in the meadow. That seemed to be a sign that nothing was ever going to be the same again, however much his mother might desire it.

'Remember that field, Ceez?' he looked down at the dog, who panted heavily and wagged his stumpy tail. 'You nearly met your Waterloo there. We both did. You ought to get a medal: 'Wounded in Action'. Maybe they'll put up a plaque one day.' He looked round sadly. 'On one of the prefabs.'

It was during that week's separation that Bella, after sleepless nights, decided on the course of action she must take. She wrote and rewrote a letter many times in the early hours of Friday morning. She then had to decide what to do with the letter. It was too late to send it to Birmingham — Alan would have left before it arrived on Monday morning. She could not trust herself to telephone; and anyway, his mother might answer. There was only one way out.

Just as Alan was getting packed up ready to return to London on the Sunday there was a telephone call. Bill took it — this was the one thing he insisted on doing, even though most calls were now for Maddy.

'What? A telegram? Yes, you can give it over the phone. To Alan Scott? Wait a minute.'

He handed the phone to Alan, who wrote down the message: 'Called away. Don't forget your key. Make yourself at home. Letter in hall explains. Yours truly, Mrs. Beesea (landlady).'

Bill and Maddy were hovering.

'Everything all right, son?' asked Bill.

Alan didn't hear him.

'Alan?'

'What? Oh, yes, fine, just a message from my landlady about where to find the key. She didn't want me to be locked out.'

'That's very thoughtful of her,' Maddy said. 'I must write and thank her for looking after you.'

'No, please don't, Mum. Mothers don't do that for grown men.'

She bit her lip and went back into the kitchen.

*

When Bella arrived at Reading station, she was greeted by a very perturbed Dr. Borland. He took her case.

'I tried to ring you, but you must have just left,' he said as they walked out to the darkening car park.

'Why? What's happened, Dr. Borland?'

'Tony's disappeared. After lunch. Gwen was out shopping and I had a house call.'

'Has he taken anything with him?'

'Just an overnight case. Bare essentials. And his Bible. Maybe that counts as an essential.'

'Have you told the police?'

'No, not yet. I still have to contact a few friends he might have gone to.'

Gwen Borland met them at the door and handed two envelopes to them.

'This is for you, dear,' she said to Bella. 'He left one for you and one for us. I'm afraid Mrs. Bates had tidied up Tony's room and placed a copy of *The Catholic Herald* on top of them.'

As her husband took the other letter from her trembling hand, he said, 'You haven't opened it, Gwen?'

She shook her head. 'No, I didn't dare. I didn't have the courage.'

'That blasted housekeeper, I keep telling her never to touch papers.'

'I expect she thought you just meant your papers, dear,' said Mrs. Borland, ever forgiving.

They digested the contents in silence in the chintzy sitting room, then looked at one another. Then they exchanged letters and sat in silence again.

Finally, the dismal reading over, Bella said, 'The main thing is he doesn't seem to intend to do anything silly. But he's clearly gone through some sort of mental crisis.'

Dr. Borland looked slightly shocked. 'Oh, one doesn't have to be mental to devote oneself to God.'

'No, of course not,' Bella agreed, hypocritically. 'What is a lay brother anyway?' she wanted to know.

'A lay monk is one who undertakes lowly tasks and abases himself in the service of God and his fellow brothers. He has opted for total self-sacrifice.'

Bella was both relieved and angry, but not impressed. 'Well, yes, good for him, but why couldn't he have explained to you what he was going to do without scaring everyone to death?'

Dr. Borland nodded. 'It would have been the rational thing to do, but rationality drowned with his shipmates.'

Looking at the Borlands' letter again, Bella asked, 'But who is this Michael? Who's he gone to be closer to?'

Gwen Borland began to look tearful, and her husband took her hand. Both of them suddenly looked old and frail, and she felt very sorry for them.

'For years after Tony was born we hoped for more children,' Gwen began. 'But I kept having miscarriages. Then, when Tony was seven, I went full term, and a baby was born. Tony was so excited, longing to come to the hospital and see his new brother or sister. But... he was stillborn. He was so beautiful, I felt that if I just breathed into him he would come alive. But the breath needed to come from our Lord, and it didn't come.'

It was the most articulate and sustained statement Bella had ever heard her make.

'It was probably my fault,' Dr. Borland said sadly. 'I thought it would help Tony through grieving if he viewed the body... the baby... with us.'

Bella had always regarded the 'viewing' of dolled-up, mummified corpses as a morbid and oddly materialistic practice for spiritually-minded Christians who should be rejoicing in the progress of another soul towards heaven.

'But instead,' Dr. Borland went on, 'he became obsessed with baby brother Michael. He wrote him letters — the way kids write to Father Christmas — and put them in the letter box. The sorting office knew what was happening and returned them to us.'

'But above all, he drew him,' his wife continued.

'Drew him?' asked Bella.

Gwen went to the bureau and picked up a folder, which she gave to Bella. Inside were sheet after sheet of pencil drawings of babies and children, the early ones rudimentary, but progressively more exquisite.

'But they're beautiful! Who are they of? They look like Tony.'

'His imaginary brother. Every birthday he did another.'

'Yes, I see. 'Michael, 3 today... Michael, 4 today...'

'And every Christmas and Easter, and special occasions,' his mother went on. 'Here's Michael starting school, Michael's First Communion, Michael at Oxford, Michael Borland, M.A. Oxon...'

'He created a whole history for him!' Bella sat back, dazed. 'Rather morbid, isn't it? He never mentioned anything of this to me. I thought he was an only child.'

'Well, he was, in fact,' Gwen Borland replied. 'This was part of his secret world. But that world seems to have become more real to him now.'

'Perhaps it's for the best,' said Dr. Borland. 'He sounds happy for the first time since he came back. Oh, I'm sorry, Bella! I didn't mean you didn't make him happy.'

Bella smiled. 'I understand. I'm quite sure I wasn't making him happy. In fact, I'm only just beginning to understand Tony.' She glanced at her letter. '"Perhaps I was never intended for the married state." That explains a lot. We were never... you know... intimate. In fact, he never really kissed me. I don't know if I should be talking like this, it seems a bit of a betrayal.'

If she had been asked later why she lied about her intimacy with Tony, she would have been at a loss. Was she protecting the illusion of her own innocence or the secret of his inadequacy?

Dr. Borland made a comprehending gesture. 'I think we can talk quite frankly. So if we add that obsession to his religious fervour... You see what he wrote to us.' He took the letter from Bella. '"I now think that my blindness to faces is a blessing, for it has opened my eyes to God. I do not need to see God's face to recognise Him. In any case we can never see His face, because He is always behind us, keeping an eye on us, stretching out His hand to help us when we stumble and despair. And I see so clearly what Michael looks like now, I feel so close to him and shall pray with him every day at the monastery."'

Bella wiped the tears from her eyes. 'That is so sad,' she said.

'On the contrary,' said the doctor, 'it is joyful. His faith has brought him a peace of mind he could never have found with us. We were delighted when he announced his engagement to you, but very surprised, you know. When he was younger we always thought he would end up as a priest, but I must say, a Franciscan monk was far beyond...'

Bella suddenly looked at her watch. 'Oh, Good lord! May I make a phone call, please?'

'Of course. Go into my study.'

Alan knew the house would be empty, but even so he rang the doorbell before inserting his key. He had occasionally been in it by himself before, but now he felt uncomfortable and strange. To ward off the shadows he switched on the light in every room as he went into it, the wide, elegant hallway, the tidy kitchen, the landing, his bedroom. They kept separate bedrooms so as not to shock the cleaner, Mrs. Glover, who was a Methodist and tut-tutted a lot. He was just about to sit down with a cup of tea, to recover from the slow, jerky, delayed journey to Euston, when he saw her letter on the dining table.

My Dearest Alan,

This terrible situation cannot continue. I am being torn in two by my feelings for you and my duty to (and affection and pity for) Tony. I think I shall go mad myself if I don't do something. You are by far the stronger of the two, you have your sanity, your health, your future blossoming before you. Tony has nothing but the woman he remembers as Bella. Perhaps he will die before long, but I cannot be callous enough to say I hope it will be soon.

I said you can stay in the house, and I'm not going back on

253

*that. But I shall stay in Reading. Please do not try to contact
me there, unless there is some kind of emergency. Mrs. Glover
will continue to come and 'do' for you, and Mr. Glover knows
how to deal with the plumbing. Send the household bills on to
me.*

*This is awful, Alan, but I can't think what else to do. I
can't study at all at the moment, but shall try to catch up next
term.*

Goodbye for the present at least, my love.

Bella

*P.S. Maybe I'm not capable of love either? Not the sort of love
you seem to feel. That's a terrible thought. — B*

He had barely read it when the phone rang. It was Bella. Before he
could say a word, and there were several on the tip of his tongue,
she was talking rapidly, urgently, quietly.

'Alan, listen. Something terrible has happened.'

What else could happen that's so terrible?

'Oh. What?' Despite himself he added, 'What's happened? Are
you all right?'

'It's Tony. He's disappeared. He may have done a fugue.'

'A *fugue?*' Bitter laugh. 'Do you mean a Moonlight Sonata or a
Moonlight flit?'

'*Please* be serious, Alan. Not written a fugue, done a fugue. He
does have some memory impairment so it may technically speaking
be a fugue. Or maybe he's simply run away from an impossible
situation.'

'Sensible chap, I wish I could,' he quipped, but not entirely in
jest. 'Where's he gone?'

'He has taken himself off to a monastery in the west of
Scotland. He went there on a retreat once before, apparently, just
before he joined the navy, so it's quite understandable.'

'A retreat sounds a sensible idea.'

'No, not just a retreat this time. He wants to be a lay monk,
Alan. To withdraw from the world.'

'Oh. I see.'

The implications for both of them were obvious, but neither
wanted to explore them at that moment. He must have read my
letter, she thought, and will know I had chosen Tony rather than
him, so maybe that's the end of Alan for me. I have lost them both.

'I don't think I should stay here by myself,' he went on. 'It
doesn't feel right. Suppose your parents came back and found me

here?'

'Alan, please, *please* don't let's make any decisions at the moment. Everything is up in the air.' She lowered her voice so that he could barely hear her. 'You know I want to be with you.'

No, I don't know that.

'Let me know when you come to another decision.'

His voice was cold, detached. He could not get over the fact that she had taken that decision, made that choice, all by herself, without discussing it with him. He did not like being taken for granted, like an old coat that could be picked up and discarded. He might write that in a letter and leave it for her on the dining table.

She was still speaking when he slowly replaced the receiver. *Done a fugue*, eh? *Fuga.* Flight. You didn't have to lose your memory to put an L in fight and skive off — a term and activity he had found basic to survival in the R.A.F. Tony had fled from a situation he could bear no longer. Or perhaps he had done it as a kind of emotional blackmail, to draw attention to his plight? Could one join up as a monk just like that? Supposing they wouldn't take him? Supposing he changed his mind — he seemed unstable enough to do that. Alan's mind raced along several roads of possibilities: How would Bella react — by feeling guilty, or at least responsible in some way, because of the lipstick? How long would it be before Bella would feel free again? Would she ever be free of Tony, or would he haunt her conscience? Only then did it occur to him that neither of them had referred specifically to her letter. He went into the sitting room and re-read it, then crumpled it up and threw it across the room. The telephone rang again, but he ignored it. The telephone ring gave him an idea, however, an idea which he put into immediate and impulsive action. The piece of paper bearing Joy's phone number was in his wallet. He extracted it and looked at it for the first time. Not only was her number there; underneath she had written (during her sojourn in the bathroom, he supposed): 'Alan — Please phone me! — Love, Joy'.

As emotional blackmail was on his mind, it occurred to him fleetingly that perhaps Joy had concocted that whole story about Rebecca, just to make sure the pitch was clear for her. Oh, yes? — and perhaps Bacon wrote *Hamlet.* He dialled her number.

*

When Bella decided to return to Alan, it could and perhaps should have been the signal for a happy ever after ending, but real life and live emotions do not obey the dictates of romantic fiction. They lay in beds only fifty miles apart, but might just as well have been separated by an ocean and felt closer. Doubt, recrimination, hurt, all combined to estrange them.

The seven harmonies tried to establish themselves in the forefront of Alan's troubled mind, and eventually he succumbed to their calming influence, only to wake again and again to the churn of emotions.

Whereas his mind revolved mercilessly around the single issue of Bella, her distress during that sleepless night had two sources — Alan and Tony. No, actually, three: Alan, Tony and religion. Basically, the situation was simple: he was hurt by her action, she was irritated by his reaction.

Alan, green with jealousy, tossed and turned with increasing violence as the soul-searching became more and more destructive and self-justifying. Reviewing the evolution of their relationship from his new standpoint, he convinced himself that he had never counted for much in her life, right from her first flouncing-off before the garden party. She had felt momentary pity for him for Caesar's shooting, but since then she had treated him with what he now saw as callousness and manipulativeness. Clearly when she got engaged to Tony she had forgotten all about him, whereas she had never been replaced in his heart. When he spotted her again in Cambridge, she sailed blithely off without so much as a covert sign of recognition. And she had made the decision to leave him and put Tony first without having the sensitivity — not even the courtesy — to talk to him, face to face and heart to heart. And he was definitely not going to be second choice if she had changed her mind again. He wondered if his father knew that if his mother's other *beau* hadn't been killed, Bill Scott would probably have been second choice. Maddy had made him swear he would never tell his father.

As a church clock struck four, Alan had convinced himself he was better off without Bella Cassell, and even looked forward to having fun with Joy next Saturday.

In Reading, Bella was going through her own hellish turmoil. One thought kept revolving in her head: 'I made it clear in my letter that this was a conflict of love and duty, and that I really loved him.' It was childish and insensitive of Alan to think only of how he was being affected, so maybe it was a good thing this egotistical side of his nature was being revealed now. He had admitted to her that he hoped she would have been as loyal to him if he had been in Tony's position, so how could he hold that loyalty against her now?

But what of Tony's loyalty to her? Rather than turn to her for comfort, he had turned to the church. The more she thought about the importance of religious faith in the lives of the Borland family, the more it rose up, like an alien barrier of whose dimensions she was only just becoming aware. She had tried on two or three occasions to broach with the Borlands the subject of the rôle now being revealed of the Catholic church's active collaboration with the occupation forces in France. She had tried to be fair, giving credit to the nuns who had sheltered Jews, and defining the whole messy subject as high-level complicity combined with low-level compassion. But the subject had met with glacial dismissal. It was, they said, quite simply nothing to do with them. For the first time, she was able to visualise a future as the young Mrs. Borland, in which she would not only be forced to adopt a faith she did not believe, for form's sake (she had accepted that without much difficulty, since she had no competing faith) but — and this was infinitely more serious — be expected to impose a faith upon her children before they could make informed decisions for themselves. This was most unlikely anyway, but the principle was still obnoxious.

Another unpleasant thought assailed her: when she had told them about the way the IRA had tried to use children to plant a bomb in her father's study, and had kidnapped her and threatened her with mutilation and death, neither Dr. Borland nor his wife had shown the slightest degree of outrage. He had merely responded by saying, 'We have to remember they feel very strongly about the attacks on the faith in Ulster.' No doubt they were secretly pleased that she had, apparently, been rejected by Tony; but surely they must realise that it was the height of impropriety for him to have absconded without formally breaking off the engagement? It was really looking as though she counted for very little in this family.

By 4.30 a.m., she was quite pleased to be free of the two men in her life.

As dawn appeared, after an hour's fitful sleep, both she and Alan had arrived at certain decisions.

Bella knew that Alan had to be at the sound recording studios in Wardour Street at 9 a.m. to put in his first full day, and thus would have to allow for the idiosyncratic behaviour of the Northern Line to Piccadilly. So at seven-thirty she went downstairs to the hall

257

telephone. This time she did not ask if she might use it.

Alan was up at seven, showered and shaved by seven-thirty, at which time he reckoned that a doctor's household must be awake. The number was engaged. Right. That gave him another minute to compose his mind for what he was going to say: he was sorry he had put the phone down on her, he should have at least given her a chance to explain what was going on. His hand was already on the receiver when it rang. With a reflex action he jerked it up to his ear.

'Hello?'

'Goodness! That was quick!' Bella gasped.

'I was just going to ring you. You were engaged.'

'Yes, quite right, I *was*: *fiancée* in the past tense; and I was *occupée* because I was ringing you. Oh, good morning,' she added, changing tone.

'Oh, good morning,' he replied, puzzled.

'No, not you, I mean, good morning to you too, but I was just saying good morning to Mrs. Borland.'

'Ah, I see. It sounded a bit frosty. Everything all right there?'

'Far from it. I'm coming back this morning.'

'I shall be at the recording studios.'

'Yes, I know. That's why I'm ringing so early. Just to see if you've remembered to wake up.'

'Is that all?'

'No. Not all at all.'

'That sounds Irish. Look,' — he shifted from one foot to the other — 'I'm sorry I rang off last night. It was a tantrummy thing to do.'

She gave a short laugh, surprising herself; she had thought she might never laugh again. 'Is that a word, tantrummy?'

'It is now. I shall send it to Oxford. What else, if that wasn't all?'

Mrs. Borland was hovering near the kitchen door, pretending to clear out a cupboard by the sound of it.

'I just wanted to say that I need to have my head tested. I shouldn't have written that letter. I had allowed myself to get totally confused. I'm sorry.'

'So we're both a couple of sorry specimens, aren't we? I suppose I'll be back about six. I love you.'

'I'll be waiting. I do too. I mean...'

'I know.' He slowly replaced the receiver and did a little dance.

She had her bag packed and ready, and had brought it down. Dr. Borland tripped over it at the bottom of the stairs.

'Oh. You're going? I was just going to try and telephone the monastery to see if Tony is all right.'

'That's a good idea, seeing that no one there has thought of trying to get in touch with you. I suppose monks aren't brought up to think like human beings.'

'Oh, I don't know...'

'So if you get in touch with your son, would you kindly tell him I'm glad he's made a decision for himself and I hope it will bring him some sort of contentment.'

Dr. Borland looked affronted. 'Shouldn't you be telling him that yourself?'

Bella ignored the suggestion and went on, 'If it's any kind of comfort to you, I shan't be suing for breach of promise, and I have left the engagement ring beside the bed. You could sell it and give the proceeds to a home for unmarried mothers, perhaps.'

Mrs. Borland was shifting from one foot to the other and wringing her hands. 'Oh dear, this is all so impulsive,' she wailed. 'Shouldn't we...'

'No, I really don't think we should,' Bella cut in. 'Could you ring for a taxi, please?'

'I'll take you to the station,' Dr. Borland offered.

'Thanks, but I'd rather take a cab.'

The doctor and his wife exchanged a glance that was part contrition, part relief: they had probably not treated the girl with as much sympathy as a jilted fiancée deserved; but she was no further use to them now as a potential producer of grandchildren, so it would be best for all concerned if she simply withdrew.

The taxi arrived and turned round in the driveway just as the telephone rang. The driver got out, took Bella's case from Dr. Borland and put it into the boot. She was about to shut the car door when Mrs. Borland appeared on the doorstep and called out, 'It's Tony. He wants to talk to you, Bella.'

Bella hesitated for a mere fraction of a second, and then decided she had not heard her.

'Drive on, please,' she said with a royal wave. 'Fast as you can, to the station.'

*

Alan found himself immediately embarking on a Himalayan learning curve, with Corker sitting on one side of him and Evan Harrington on the other, watching the film again almost frame by frame, deciding by the second how much music would be required

259

for which scenes, what the style and function of the music would be, the instrumentation, and the atmospheric impact it would be trying to contribute.

He was glad Corker was there, as it made it more difficult for Evan to keep putting his hand on his thigh. When he persisted, Alan jumped so suddenly that Evan spilled his cup of hot coffee into his own lap.

'So sorry, Evan,' Alan smiled disarmingly, 'I'm terribly ticklish anywhere near my crutch, except when a girl touches me. Isn't it odd? How about you, Corker?'

Corker knew exactly what was going on as Evan's proclivities were notorious and widely shared in the industry. 'I bet you don't mind that smashing girl of yours rovin' around yer bollocks,' he laughed.

Evan got the message and behaved very professionally after that, giving Alan precise information on the process: the music editor would take Alan's score and insert the clicks into the sound track that would indicate to the conductor when to begin and end a musical segment.

Towards the end of the day Simon Marsa came into the studio.

'Sorry not to be here earlier, Alan.'

Alan had not expected him to be there at all. 'Oh, that's fine, Simon. I've been well looked after by Corker and Evan. But I'd be glad to talk over a few things with you soon.'

'How about now? I have to go to New York tomorrow.'

Alan looked at his watch: five o'clock. It would take him an hour to get back to Hampstead. 'Could I make a phone call?'

Bella was there, fortunately. Alan suggested that she should come into the city. 'I should be through by seven, so why don't we meet at the Lyons' Oxford Corner House at seven thirty? The Tottenham Court Road entrance. We can gorge ourselves at the Salad Bowl.'

For the next couple of hours Marsa and Alan went through the schedule of scenes, which Alan could now visualise clearly.

'I see you have established three acts, in dramatic terms, or three movements in musical terms — tell me if I'm wrong,' Alan said.

Simon Marsa nodded thoughtfully, so Alan went on..

'*Devastation:* the aftermath and legacy of Occupation and destruction. German martial music, Wagnerian textures, faint, subdued French themes, maybe broken fragments of Maurice Chevalier songs.'

260

'Ah, be careful there,' said Marsa, 'he's a bit suspect at the moment. Possible collaboration.'

Alan had not heard about that. 'Right, I'll take note. Then, *Stirrings of Revival*, the painful beginnings of reconstruction, both moral and material, with all the inner conflicts and dark pessimism we witnessed vying with the euphoria of liberation — that will need some careful musical irony. Finally, *Future Directions*, the hope for better things to come, definitely heroic, bright, major key stuff.'

The director sat back and stared at the wall. Then: 'I think you've got the hang of the overall pattern pretty well. But don't be tempted to make it too heavy and symbolic. See the film again, several times, let the images speak to you with their own music. Work out the relationships between the background noises of life, the dialogues, the narratives. And see if there are psychological characterisations to be reinforced by your music. But don't be too generous with your material! I suggest you work out a basic theme and use variations on it. The audience isn't going to be made up of music fanatics, remember.'

Alan got the message; he was being tempted to be too portentous, maybe treating the film as an accompaniment to his music.

'There's one other thing I should tell you,' Marsa said as he donned his coat. 'We shall have to record the music sound track in four weeks time.'

Alan gulped. '*Four weeks?*'

''Fraid so. The distributors are being very demanding. So you'll have to be satisfied with a fairly simple score. Maybe it will gain from not being too complex. Keep in close touch with Evan — he can be a bore, I know, but he knows the technical ropes backwards and is good on shortcuts in scoring.'

He got to the Oxford Corner House dead on time, but Bella was already at the entrance. They went up to the Salad Bowl, their favourite eating place, where, for a modest sum, one could not so much eat one's fill as fill one's (rather small dinner-sized) plate to the rim with a wide variety of cold dishes. Each Corner House had several restaurants, catering for different pockets, appetites and tastes. A small orchestra was playing in the background, and the atmosphere was very cheerful and noisy.

'How did it go?' Bella asked.

'It's an irksome process, but I suppose it will be a useful discipline for me,' he answered, with his mouth full of potato salad.

261

'But Simon came up with a bombshell at the last moment. They want the music in a month!'

Bella did not respond with so much as a 'Good gracious!' or a 'Whew!' Simply nodded and said, 'Good. Then you'll have to get it out of the way before Christmas.'

He found her unperturbed reaction somehow reassuring. If she thought he could do it, then he bloody well would. Just as he was about to ask her about the latest in her saga, he became aware of an increase in violin volume behind him, and turned round to see that they were about to be serenaded by an elaborately mustachio-ed Italian-looking fiddler.

'I hope he won't want a tip,' Alan whispered to Bella.

The violinist stopped playing. He had overheard. Then he said, 'Don't worry, Al old pal. This is for your beautiful lady, on the house from me and the boys.'

Alan looked behind the mustache and recognised him. 'Alf! You old... Good heavens! What are you...!' He made a gesture of introduction. 'Bella Cassell, Alf Maloney of the R.A.F. Symphony Orchestra.'

Alf gave her a courtly bow, then turned back to Alan. 'Demobbed a month ago, my young friend. Me and two others from Uxbridge got straight in here. Good wages too. Only...' He bent close to Alan's ear. '...It's Alfredo now. Starting up our own band soon, touring, records, sky's the limit. *Per ardua ad astra* and all that! Name up there in lights before you can say *da capo!*'

With a flourish of his bow, Alfredo led his crew into a spirited rendering of *Jealousy*.

When they had settled down again, Bella gave Alan a blow by blow account of what had happened at Reading, and told him how she now viewed the Borland family.

'I realised with a shock that they saw me simply as a means of providing them with grandchildren they could bring up as good little Catholics,' she said. 'I must have been blind not to see what was on their minds when they talked about baptisms and first communions and catechisms. Anyway, I am no longer engaged, and am in imminent danger of being left on the shelf.'

'Oh, you don't have to worry,' he replied with a smile at her false modesty, 'Corker said he would take you on if I didn't want you.'

When they got home that night, they were both exhausted, emotionally and physically, but realised they would have to clear the air. Each clutching a mug of tea, they sat stiffly side by side on the sofa in the sitting room. Then together, without cue:

{'Alan, I think I should...'

{'Bella, we ought to...'

They laughed.

'Ladies first,' he said.

'Well, I have been doing a lot of thinking about myself,' she said. 'I realise I am too impulsive and I don't always think things through or consider how what I do will affect other people. In other words, I'm a typical spoilt only child.'

'No, you're...'

'Let me finish, please. There, you see, and I'm bossy too. But that's the disadvantage of being brought up to be independent. I've had to make decisions for myself for quite a long time, and I shall have to learn now to take you into consideration if we are going to survive together. On the other hand...'

'On the other hand, I'm probably too sensitive, and insecure, and quick to react to what I see as slights,' Alan responded. 'So I have to adjust too — if, as you say, we're going to survive. But I do want us to, Bella. I'm nothing without you.'

Bella turned on him with surprising vehemence. 'That is *not true*,' she said firmly. 'Alan Scott, you are a man of original thought and talent in your own right, and if I die tonight, you will continue to be! So don't you ever talk about being nothing again! Promise?'

He nodded, with a rueful smile. 'Yes, miss. I *do* love you, Bella.'

She kissed him gently, as she had done that first time, like a butterfly. 'And I love you too, Alan darling. We're meant to be together. But there is one thing you ought to know.'

'Oh dear. What now? Not another husband tucked away somewhere!'

'No, this is serious, darling. You know I had a spell in a sanatorium for T.B. when I was a girl?'

'Good heavens! I'd forgotten that.'

'Well, it was eradicated, they think, but there's always a chance it could start up again. If you starve me, for instance. Or when I'm old. But Papa told me there is some promising research going on in America and Switzerland, and they might find a cure in the next couple of years. But I thought you ought to know,' she added lamely.

'So I shan't have to call you Violetta?'

'No. I can't sing well enough, and neither can you.'

'I certainly shan't be able to if I go deaf. You're not the only one with a weakness, so don't think you're going to get all the sympathy languishing on a chaise-longue all day. I shall be as crotchety as old Ludwig when I'm fifty.'

'I shall never be *that* old!' Bella tossed her head confidently.

Alan wondered silently if she meant she would be like Cleopatra, or would die young.

'Oh!' she went on, 'There's another thing you...'

'...ought to know. Yes? What? Not leprosy?'

'Mothers. I don't think I'll ever be able to be a mother. It's too difficult. You and your mother make each other suffer because she loves you too much, and mine never really had time for me. I've always felt she'd rather be doing something else.'

He kissed her forehead. 'Let's cross that bridge if we ever get to it. Shall we go to bed now?'

'Yes, all right. If you have any... um...'

'No problem, back here in England,' he laughed as he switched off the hall light. 'It was tricky in France though, wasn't it? Heaven knows how Corker managed, the amount he must have got through.'

The next morning, Bella, refreshed and buoyant, went off early to college to start rescuing her studies, so before settling down to work at the Steinway, Alan picked up the telephone.

'Hello, Dad?'

'Yes. Alan?'

'It must be. I'm your only child.'

'Ah, yes. Anything the matter?'

'No, nothing. Is Mum there?'

'You've just caught her. Maddy? It's Alan, for you.'

Alan heard her say 'What's wrong?'

Funny how some people think a telephone call must be heralding bad news.

'Morning, Mum. I just wanted to chat with you, that's all.'

'Oh. Oh, good. It's raining up here.'

Yes, it would be.

'I've just had my first session at the film recording studio.'

'How did it go?'

'I now have a much better idea of what's expected of me and the music I'll write for the film.'

'Good. That's nice.'

'And it suddenly struck me, isn't it a turn-up for the book? Here's your son, mum, doing just what you were doing all those years ago, providing music for films! Only you managed to do it all by yourself, and I have a whole symphony orchestra to help me.'

'Oh, I just thumped away at the few pieces I knew.' She was getting into her stride now. 'My first job didn't last long. I played a piece named *Fire, fire!* each time the cowboys rode on, but I got fired myself because I stopped playing at the bottom of each page to turn over. I remember I was replaced by the manager's daughter — my first experience of nepotism.'

Ah, now, I must steer her away from that. She loves blaming somebody or something else.

'What I really wanted to say, Mum, is this: I can't tell you how much I owe to you, Mum, for helping me to become a musician and encouraging me. If you hadn't kept me at it, I'd be nowhere. Even though Swinstead nearly drove me batty!'

There was silence from the other end. Then: 'Well, thank you. I think that helps to make it all worth while.'

There was stiffness still in her voice, and Alan realised what a deep hurt there must be inside her. She went on, 'Not that you ever spent much time on Swinstead!'

'I'll be sending you a copy of the film music score as soon as I can,' he promised, 'so you can have a clearer idea of what I'm concocting.'

'I don't suppose I'll able to understand it, shall I?'

'Oh, yes, of course you will. I promise it won't be as difficult as Debussy. But you will need thirteen hands to play it. I have to get the score finished before Christmas, so I'm going to be working 18 hours a day till then, and I shan't have time to write much.'

'Oh, that's a shame. Mr. Matthews always notices when you don't write.'

George Matthews had been delivering letters there ever since the avenue was created. Alan cleared his throat. *Here we go.*

'There is one bit of news I have to pass on to you, Mum. You remember Bella Cassell who lived at The Firs?'

'The Fire Station? Yes, of course I do.'

'Well, I've met up with her again.'

'Oh. That's nice.'

As if I'd said I had an egg for breakfast.

Another deep breath.

'And we have just got engaged to be married.'

He heard her whisper 'He's got himself engaged,' and Bill say 'What as?' and her say 'To be *married!*' and him say 'Who to?' and her say 'That Bella girl'.

Don't pause, Alan told himself, *get it all over with.*

'I'm sorry I couldn't tell you before, but our relationship has been very, very complicated because of other people.'

'What do you mean? Whose relationship?'

'Ours. Bella's and mine. So we're only just now able to make a decision for ourselves. We hope you and Dad will be happy for us. The wedding won't be for a long time yet, as we both have to finish our studies, but we think people ought to know we're serious. It's telling everyone we have a commitment to one another.'

He did not mention that they were living together, as this would have shocked them dreadfully. Nice young people simply did not do that kind of thing, even when engaged.

There was another silence, then Maddy said, 'Commitment? Sounds like a gaol sentence.'

He heard his father say, 'Here, let me talk to him... Hello, Alan? I heard a bit of that. Why can't they have two earpieces on telephones?'

'They do in France,' Alan said.

'Do they now? Well, I expect you'll be bringing the young lady home soon, so that we can get to know her better.'

That was a prospect to be delayed as long as possible.

'That might be difficult, Dad. Bella isn't at all keen to return to Birmingham, because of the bomb and kidnapping business.'

'But that's all over now!'

'Not for her, it isn't. The mere thought of seeing the avenue and the old house again gives her the shakes. But you must come up to London, and we'll have a good time. Go to concerts and theatres, you know.'

Maddy was just audible as she said in the background, 'We've really lost him now.'

Alan felt himself seized with anger at his mother's capacity for self-destruction, but tried to control it.

'No, Mum!' he shouted, loud enough, he hoped, for her to hear too. 'You'll only lose me if you keep on driving me away!'

But she could not or would not hear. 'Tell him to come and take his stuff, all of it, or I'll burn it!' she said.

Bill was trying to calm her down, she was sobbing, Alan was close to tears himself.

'I'd better ring off, son,' Bill said. 'She'll be all right.'

Yes, maybe, Alan thought, but will I be? Thanks for ruining what should have been the happiest day of my life, so far! As for his stuff, the only thing he wanted was the tin trunk and its contents.

He went to the kitchen to make himself a cup of tea, and to calm down. Women were beyond comprehension. Always splashing about in a sea of emotions of their own making, and threatening to drown their menfolk in it as well as themselves. Even Bella, the rationalist, was not immune from this strange condition; he had always known that life with her would be tempestuous. So here he was, with the two women he cared about most destined to be alienated for ever from each other. And his mother from him.

Fiercely he stirred in three spoonsful of sugar. He never took sugar — years of rationing had got him out of the habit. Glaring at a digestive biscuit, he muttered to himself. If only he'd had a couple of brothers and sisters, she wouldn't even be missing him. The curse of being an only child! Spoilt, my foot! Despoiled more like. Of course it was hard for a mother to give way to another as the main object of a son's affection and admit she had been forced into retirement, but she had her own partner in life. And that, he realised, was where the problem really lay. For the whole of Maddy's married life, her partner, her companion, had been her offspring, not her husband. Ever since his departure, their incompatibility had become increasingly manifest, and the sad truth inescapable: she found her husband boring, uninteresting, uninterested. The only thing they had had in common was their son.

All this, Alan realised. But then, after effectively disculpating himself, he began to have doubts about his innocence. He could have handled the situation better. Suddenly announcing his engagement over the phone like that was pretty insensitive. An act of cowardice, in fact, since he had balked at the prospect of waiting till his next visit to tell them face to face. Perhaps he should have given more consideration to Maddy's idea of his going to the local university? Even if he had not lived at home they would have seen a good deal more of him. But Bella would never have agreed to return to Birmingham; he would undoubtedly have been separated from her, and might have lost her forever.

He had, therefore, placed his own happiness above his mother's. Q.E.D.. Was this justifiable? His immediate response was to admit to himself that he had been selfish and self-indulgent. But then... Surely it was his mother who had created the dilemma, by showing her unwillingness to share him with the woman he loved? It was all or nothing with her. He imagined another scenario, in which she would leave Bill and Caesar to have a bit of peace and quiet, and come up to London to visit them, enjoy visiting the National Gallery and the Tate and going to concerts at the Albert Hall or shows at the Coliseum. They would all discuss things afterwards over a meal in Soho, and her period of cultural starvation would be ended. He had suggested this on the phone, he remembered, but it had fallen on ears deafened by emotion.

That evening, when Bella returned from college, Alan related the stormy reception the news of their engagement had received.

'It suddenly struck me, after I'd put the phone down, what a different relationship you have with your parents, and you hardly ever see them because they're half-way round the world, compared to me and mine, living just a hundred miles away.'

She went over and sat next to him. 'Can you see no way of breaking down this barrier between you and your mother, darling?'

'I've tried,' he sighed, 'but everything I say or do seems to trigger some new disagreement. The only thing that would please her, I think, would be if I went to live back home, and got a job there, and never had a girl friend.'

'It's like a funicular, isn't it?' Bella said.

His eyebrows requested an elucidation.

'In the Alps, the one lift goes up while the other goes down, quite happily. I'm one lift, and your mother is the other. It seems as if your existential funicular wants you to go up both sides at once, so there's a grinding clash of gears. You are not allowed to go *up* and *down* at the same time, to enjoy the love of both of us. Maybe you will always have to choose, Alan. Hop from lift to lift in mid-air. Can you face that?'

He leant over and kissed her. 'Is that the Swiss school of psychology? Fascinating! So long as I have your love and help and support, of course I can. You are all I've got in the world now.'

Even so, she thought, there must be a way to break through this impasse.

She telephoned her parents in California to give them the news, having worked out the time difference. It was Henry Cassell who answered, for which she was relieved. However, he was puzzled.

'But what about Tony? Aren't you already engaged? You wrote and said he had come back.'

'Yes, papa, he did come back... in a way. But he's gone off again. To a monastery.'

She gave him a brief account of recent events, after which her father said, 'Frankly, I am relieved and not at all surprised. I never said what I really thought of that affair of yours, but I can now tell you I believed it would be a disaster. There was something too distant and formally polite about Tony. I suspected that he might have a part-time job as a serial killer. But you and Alan were made for each other from the first time you met.'

'You really think so?'

'Increasingly. He has matured enough to be able to cope with you.'

'Oh! Thank you very much!'

'You know what I mean. He was overawed by you — by us, maybe — for a long time, but judging by what *maman* tells me, he has developed a strong character.'

She laughed uncertainly. 'You make it sound as though I need a lion tamer for a husband.'

'Not at all, *chérie*, but I know you despise people you can control easily. First you enjoy bossing them, then you despise them. Just like your mother. Maybe all women are control freaks?'

To his surprise, Bella agreed. 'Quite right, papa. We have to be — otherwise nothing would ever get done. How is *maman?*'

'She's not in at the moment, in fact she's in Washington, but I'll give her the news.'

'And tell her we are physically compatible. She has always drummed into me that one must be sure.'

Bella looked over at Alan, and was delighted to see that his remnants of suburbanity appeared slightly shocked.

Her father chuckled. 'Yes, I'll tell her. Any idea of a wedding date?'

'Oh no, not for years, I should think. We both have lots of studying to finish. So tell *maman* not to expect to become a grandmother, and she can go on being forty for ever.'

He asked, 'What are you going to do with your psychology? Research? Or therapy?'

Almost without thinking about it, she replied, 'I'm going to find out why the human brain and nervous system are so greatly affected by music, for both good and ill. I'll be working with Alan eventually. When are you coming back to London?'

'I can't say. We are both very tied up here. Why don't you both come to San Francisco for Christmas? I'll pay your fares.'

Bella thanked him profusely and said it sounded a great idea, but she would have to discuss it with Alan.

'Ah, I see you're learning,' he said.

The warm approval Bella's father expressed went a long way to compensate for the chill left by Maddy's hostility, and somehow opened up possibilities of reconciliation. As they lay in each other's arms that night, warm in each other's love, Bella suddenly turned to Alan.

'We ought to go.'

'What? Where?'

'To see your parents.'

'What, *now?*'

'No, tomorrow. For the weekend.'

'But you said you couldn't bear to go back because of...'

'I know, but that's being childish. The best way to get over trauma is to face it and beat it.'

'Well, all right then, if you're sure. We'd better warn them.'

'No, I don't think we should.' Bella could well imagine what would happen if they did that. His mother would disappear for the weekend.

Alan expressed his gratitude to Bella, knowing, or thinking he knew, how grim the experience was likely to be. In fact, she was having to conquer strong feelings of distrust and resentment towards Mrs. Scott for her rumourmongering, which could have resulted in the death of herself and/or her father.

'Oh, don't thank me,' she said, 'it's pure self-interest. I couldn't stand you going through life full of self-recrimination.'

'Well then, thanks for coming up with the idea. By the way, did you mean what you said to your father,' Alan went on, 'about working with me?'

'Of course! I know we haven't spoken about it since the séance, because there has been so much happening. But I have been thinking about it a lot.'

'I'm glad. So have I. I wondered if you had forgotten about it. I took my attempt at transcription along to Prof. Walker. He laughed when he saw it and said I should have done it on a toilet roll.'

It did indeed occupy a whole sheet of music manuscript paper. Middle C was about in the centre, from which the normally used treble and bass staves extended above and below it, but most of the notes were written on ledger lines extending from top to bottom. There were seven columns of notes.

'Now, what on earth is all this?' Walker had asked gruffly.

'What does it look like? Can you read it?' Alan was anxious to establish the seriousness of this weird exercise in notation. Walker was at first slightly taken aback by the unusual aggressiveness of the

270

questions, but then responded to the earnestness of the young student before him. At least he hadn't asked 'Can't you read it?'

'Of course I can read it. It would have helped if you'd used octavo signs.'

'No, it wouldn't,' Alan assured the professor, 'I tried. Every note has to be in a visible vertical line.'

Walker could only respect Alan's certainty. 'Well then, let's see. I can hear some of it, but it's even more difficult for the eye to take in vertically than...'

'...than Mahler. Or Messiaen. Yes. But the effect is totally different, don't you think?'

Scott's enthusiasm was catching. 'So...' — Walker walked to his Steinway and propped up the polytonal puzzles — '...what we have here is a piling-up of thirds, and fourths, but there are all sorts of triads, major, minor, diminished, augmented... and... what are these?'

'Quarter tones,' Alan explained. 'And microtones. But I don't know how to write them.'

'You certainly won't get them on my Steinway,' Walker growled, shaking his white mane. 'Pick me up if I fall off the end of the keyboard.'

He played the notes over three or four octaves, but even his large hands were already having to abandon simultaneity.

'Here, come and sit beside me, Alan. Take the top half.'

Between them they covered the trunk, but not the roots or the branches. Alan kept his foot on the 'loud' pedal so that each chord was allowed to die away.

The professor looked puzzled. 'Hm. Have you been listening to Scriabin's *Prometheus?*

He felt Alan's reaction to the unintentional suggestion of plagiarism. Then Alan remembered that day — how many centuries ago? — when Walker had asked him in Bella's house if he had heard of Debussy, and he realised it was the typical professorial habit, to look for influences.

'No, I'm afraid not. I only know his *Poème d'Extase.*'

'All I meant was that this goes well beyond what the Russian was trying to do with his so-called mystical chord.'

'Mystical?'

'He was heavily involved in theosophy and Madame Blavatsky — you know, the spiritualist woman.'.

Blavatsky again! 'Oh, yes,' Alan said, 'I've heard of her. In fact, she is responsible for these chords, in a way, via France and Spain.'

'My goodness! You have been getting around since Birmingham!'

The professor didn't know the half of it, Alan thought with a smile.

Alan next showed the seven chords to an Indian on the staff at the Academy, and he was absolutely stunned by them. 'They have extraordinary mystical power,' he said, and then he added something strange: 'Be very careful about revealing the seventh one to the world.' He wanted to copy them or keep them, but he had a sort of predatory look in his eye, so Alan made excuses.

'But he had a sort of predatory look in his eye, so I made excuses. And that,' he ended, 'was how the harmonies were received at the Academy. Maybe I'm getting paranoid?'

Bella thought not. 'It kills me to admit this, darling,' she said, 'but I have the feeling there is something of tremendous importance there. The way the music came to us, out of nowhere, and the effect it had on poor old René. I want to be able to account for that. When something is called 'mystical' it's only because we don't understand it — yet!'

'Frankly,' Alan said, 'it doesn't worry me whether we call it mystical or magnetic, so long as we can work out how to use it for some good purpose. But...' He paused. 'It's odd, the seventh always causes me trouble. I can't get it. Nearly, but never quite there. Ah, well, in its own good time.'

When they arrived at New Street station at noon, Alan telephoned home. Bill answered.

'Hello, Dad, it's me. Glad you're home. Is Mum there too?'

'Er... yes, but...'

'That's O.K. Don't go out for the next hour or so. Something will be arriving.'

'Arriving?'

'Yes. A delivery, on your doorstep.'

'You'll be getting one on yours too. Joy has just rung from Paddington saying you weren't there to meet her. So I gave her your address.'

Joy!

'Oh, my God! I forgot!'

He banged the receiver down and turned to see Bella looking at him with an anxious frown.

'This is catastrophic! Look, darling, something terribly urgent

272

has come up, something I forgot to do at work. Why don't you... If you go out of the station, turn left up New Street, you'll see a big Kardomah café. I'll see you there in fifteen minutes. Oh, have you any change?'

Still puzzled and somewhat suspicious, she left him feverishly dialling.

The 29A bus delivered them to within half a mile of the doorstep. On the way he told her about Joy, admitting he had made the arrangement out of pure pique, had used Joy abominably, and had promptly forgotten all about her during all the subsequent emotional upheavals.

'So,' she asked, 'what is the poor girl doing? Camping on our doorstep?'

'I hope not. Thank God, Corker was at home. I dangled the carrot of her beautiful mouth and bosom before him, and he was off like a shot in a taxi. He should get there before her, and will say I was suddenly called away. It's going to cost me a fortune — slap up dinner, two tickets to the Coliseum, and a hotel room for her, but I deserve it. I think they might be right for one another, actually!'

'She's bound to hear you're back home this weekend,' Bella said.

'Yes, well, I was called back to deal with a big family problem, wasn't I?'

Bella tapped his cheek, quite forcefully. 'Alan Scott, you're surprisingly devious.'

'Let's call it resourceful, shall we?'

'No,' she said firmly, 'devious will do nicely.'

As he rang the doorbell, they kissed to reassure each other. They had worked out their strategy. She had quizzed Alan about the things she should and should not talk about: flowers, dress designs, one-way streets, and painting were all right; sons, husbands, fiancées, piano-playing, the IRA, and the joys of living in London were taboo. So were things Maddy did not possess, like a detached house with a drive, a refrigerator and a washing machine. The list grew alarmingly.

It was Maddy who answered. For a moment she just stood there, transfixed, her mouth open.

'Hello, Mrs. Scott,' Bella said brightly, holding out her hand. 'You look as lovely as ever.'

Alan took advantage of his mother's temporary paralysis and

273

kissed her, holding her in his arms. It was the first time he had done this in a long time, he realised, and it was curiously affecting to feel again the body that had given him birth. She drew back as if he had B.O.

'Well,' she said, 'I suppose you'd better come in. This is a surprise. Bill! Look who's turned up out of the blue. Your son and... er... Bella.'

The pretence that she could not recall Bella's name foreshadowed what they might expect. They had decided on the train that on no account was either of them to react or respond to anything unpleasant, cutting, hostile, or provocative that Maddy might say.

As Bill bent down to pick up their small suitcase, he whispered to Alan. 'What about Joy?'

'It's O.K., Dad. It was a misunderstanding. All under control.'

Bill looked relieved. 'Good. Am I glad you've come! It's been a hell of a night! Three plates, two cups and a saucepan!'

Alan smiled understandingly. He and his father had often had cause to be glad of Maddy's inability to throw straight.

Bella behaved magnificently. Smiling, cheerful, chatty, positive, helpful, tactful. She even made a fuss of Caesar, who swooned and did not disgrace himself by being over-attentive to her legs. They had brought extra rations with them, including a roast chicken and a bottle of wine, so that there would be no embarrassment about providing a meal at such short notice.

'Chicken and wine!' said Maddy, eyebrows raised and mouth pursed. 'You don't see much of that round here.'

Clunk!

Gradually the atmosphere began to relax; partly the effect of the wine, to which Maddy, as she had rather churlishly implied, was unaccustomed; and partly, perhaps — they would never know for sure — because Alan went to the piano (which was sadly out of tune) and played the seven harmonies, as well as he could, from memory — first as chords and then as a series of arpeggios. The sustained harmonics faded away. Maddy was standing beside him.

'Is that something you've composed?' she asked.

'No, Mum, it's something I heard. But it really needs a special kind of instrument that doesn't exist.'

'It's very haunting, isn't it? I feel I've heard it before, and yet I know I haven't.'

While Alan and Bella took Caesar out for a much-needed walk, Maddy prepared lunch and Bill laid the table.

'She's quite nice when you get to know her,' she called to Bill from the kitchen, as though he was the one who had to be won over.

After lunch, Maddy took them all out for a drive to Henley-in-Arden. First, the rails over the back seat had to be cleared of the dresses, for which they formed a cheerful chain-gang from the pavement to the front room. It was mid-afternoon by the time they set off. Bill clearly found it difficult not to be behind the steering wheel. His twitchiness in the front passenger seat always made Maddy nervous, so she made him sit in the back with Alan.

'I always feel like royalty back here,' Bill said uncomfortably.

'Look! There's Mrs. Watkins,' said Alan, pointing to the neighbour with the constantly red and running nose. 'Give her a royal wave!'

The milkman's wife looked startled, began to return the wave, but instead wiped her nose on her long tattered woolly sleeve.

The famous ice-cream shop in Henley was doing a brisk trade. Licking and dripping away in the warmish sun, the quartet walked down beside the ancient church and came to the five-barred gate.

'Alan and I came here just before he went to France,' Maddy said to Bella, looking out over the fields. They were just turning hazy in the evening mist. 'Do you remember, Alan?'

'Yes, of course I remember, Mum. We cycled here.'

'I asked you to tell me if you saw anything as beautiful there. Have you?'

Alan thought of the ravaged countryside of Normandy, with its frayed trees and cratered fields. 'This hasn't been a battlefield, like a lot of France, Mum. It's very peaceful.'

'Our battlefields were the cities. They were spared that.'

He wanted to say that the citizens of Saint-Malo and Cherbourg and Rouen wouldn't agree that they'd been spared, but left it at that. Let her go on thinking that the French had only lost a few cows.

Alan slept on the settee in the front room; it never entered his parents' heads that any other sleeping arrangement would have been possible or preferred. Apart from that sacrifice, the weekend was a success. A bridge had been mended. By lunchtime on the Sunday, Maddy was designing a dress for Bella, and saying she ought to be a model with such a lovely figure.

'I'll get it made up for you,' she said. 'It'll be my engagement present to you — and you'll have to come back for some fittings. I don't know what to give you, Alan. A new pair of socks, perhaps?

275

Your fiancée has told me she can't mend socks. Well, you can't do everything, not even a clever girl like Bella.' She looked from one to the other. 'I must say, you make a handsome couple. I'm proud of you both.'

That evening, when the visitors had returned to London, Bill was greatly relieved that harmony had been restored at last, and that he would not be under fire again. Not for a little while, anyway. But as he always said, you could never tell where or when trouble was going to clobber you next.

For the first time in what seemed like years, Maddy was singing to herself in the kitchen.

'Bella says her parents are going to stay in America,' she called. 'So it's going to be a bit as though we'd had a daughter, isn't it?'

'Yes, it is,' Bill replied from behind the *Birmingham Post*.

He silently completed her thought: *And they won't be around to feel they've gained a son!*

'Except,' Maddy went on, 'that ours would have had red hair.'

Bill nodded resignedly. 'Yes, I bet she would.'

The first thing Alan did back in London was to telephone his rescuer-of-awkward-situations.

'How did it go, Corker?'

'Great, Al! She's a smasher. We got on like an 'ouse on fire.'

'Not boring?'

'Borin'? Nah! She's a good listener, just sat back and lapped it up. You know me, switch me on an' off I go. Ace airman, know all the film stars. Shoot 'er a line and she grabs it. Lovely. I like uncomplicated women.'

'There's a lot of wisdom in that,' Alan agreed, with some feeling. 'But what did she say about me not being there?' He wanted to hear about this rather more than Corker's yarn-spinning abilities, which he already knew to be fabulous.

'I told her you'd really invited 'er up to meet me, but you didn't think she'd go for a blind date. She was pretty pissed off to start with, but I soon charmed 'er into submission.'

'Now, you treat her nicely, you old lecher. She's a nice girl.'

'You're right, Al. Don't worry. I'll look after 'er. I might even mend my ways, with that smashin' figure of 'ers. Cor flippin' 'eck!'

Alan reckoned Joy was more than a match for Corker's blandishments, and would lead him to the altar before he got anywhere near her pink bits. A couple of days later, he had a note from her saying she was sorry to have missed him, but was pleased to have made the acquaintance of Albert (*Albert? Oh, yes*), who had been very nice to her, and was such an *interesting* man, and that now she knew from Mrs. Scott that he, Alan, was engaged she understood why he would have found it embarrassing to meet her himself in London, after 'everything that had passed between us'.

Bella wanted to know what this meant, but he just tapped his nose and winked.

'*De la discretion avant toute chose!* You wouldn't want me to destroy the reputation of a girl with such secret, fathomless depths of hotblooded passion! She might even teach dear Albert a thing or two.'

For the time being, then, and for the first time in his life so far as he could remember, Alan was anxiety-free. His mother was appeased; his relationship with Bella was solid, his love for her reciprocated; he could spend his time doing what he most wanted to do, create music; the British people were striving to make society fairer; the monstrous tyrants of the world had been beaten down. All was not yet well with the world, but it would be.

'This is a good time to be young,' he said to Bella as they lay in each other's arms.

'For the time being, yes. I just wonder if we've learned anything.'

Despite her personal happiness, she had a dark foreboding that this paradise was strictly for fools, but nothing could shake Alan's optimism. He felt curiously lightheaded, euphoric even, when he went to sleep that night. No doubt this unaccustomed absence of worry opened up his mind to whatever stimuli account for those dreams that leave us with unforgettably strong and striking images.

'You're in a thoughtful mood this morning,' Bella said to him over the corn flakes.

Emerging from his reverie, Alan replied, 'I can't get a dream out of my mind. It's a long time since I've remembered a dream, but this one...'

She waved her spoon at him impatiently. 'Well? Come on then! What was she like?'

'No, nothing like that,' he laughed. 'Nothing dramatic either, like being chased and unable to run. I was way up above the earth, I could see the details clearly, continents and seas, deserts and forests and clouds. Then it began to fade. All of it, as if it was melting into nothingness. But at each edge of the equator a band of light began to grow. It spread across the planet until it formed an almost unbroken circle. Somehow I could tell that it went right round. The colours became stronger and I saw it was a gigantic rainbow, but the bands were widening till they covered the poles. Just imagine, the whole of Earth covered with a rainbow. But in one place there was a jagged gap, like a bleeding wound, that seemed to be struggling to close itself up.'

'Was the rainbow sinister?' Bella wanted to know, 'menacing? Like some sort of gas enveloping the earth?'

'Oh no! Quite the contrary. Very, very peaceful, as if it was gently trying to bring about a state of universal harmony. Except for that one spot.'

Bella framed her next question carefully, not wanting to impose any suggestion.

'And it was all completely silent, was it?'

He had to think back, eyes closed.

'I was so struck by the image that I scarcely noticed sound. But now I realise there was sound. As the coloured bands grew stronger and wider, there was an imperceptible complex of sounds. What made you ask that?'

Either he's being very slow this morning, Bella thought, *or he's refusing to see the connection.*

'How many colours are there in the spectrum, Alan? Can you take your non-scientific mind back to that?'

'Yes, of course: Richard Of York Gained Battles In Vain, seven.'

'And how many harmonies did you hear that night?'

'At the séance? Seven, of course.'

'And you've never associated a colour with each one?'

He sat, aghast at his failure to see the transference.

'Now, why on earth didn't I make that connection? It's obvious now.'

'No, it isn't so obvious,' Bella contradicted him, 'and it may be a false connection, a false analogy. But let's follow it through, just for the heck of it: if each colour is one of your harmonies, then why would the earth be covered with them from pole to pole?'

Alan was sunk in a new thought. 'Violet was very vague, as if it was fading. Or hadn't yet formed properly. Just like the seventh chord.'

They both pondered for several minutes, but without success.

Then Bella said, 'Violet has always struck me as the most ambivalent of the colours of the spectrum. Very complex. You know where you are with the others, but violet... I think you ought to write the dream down in as much detail as you can, darling, before it fades,' Bella suggested. 'One day something may happen that will make the meaning clear to us.'

Fourth Movement

Resolutions
BLUE: E major

If only the world realised how powerful harmony is.

Wolfgang Amadeus Mozart, in a letter

TEMPO 1

precipitoso, minaccevole

Kensington, 17 January 1971

By now they are strolling round the rooftop garden. He has taken her gloved hand, and she lets it remain in his hand without responding to any of the little pressures he applies by accident or design. Her last question makes him stop in his tracks and grip her hand so hard she almost cries out.

'Yes, I know how she died. I traced a couple of people who'd known her and I dragged the story out of them.' He pauses, but not for effect. He is breathing too fast, distressed. Bella indicates a bench close by and they sit, huddled, like disconsolate lovers. When he has calmed down he goes on. 'I've never told anyone about this before, Bella. It was just too painful.'

'Are you sure you want to?'

Keith nods. 'Yes. It needs to come out.' He takes a deep breath and exhales slowly. 'This is what we pieced together from the evidence. She — Rebecca — was put on medical duties right away and forced to assist with Mengele's experimental atrocities. What she did, in fact, was to help victims to a quick and painless death. It was all she could do. One of the doctors, a particularly brutal man, took a shine to her and said that as long as she let him have sex with her she'd be safe. Otherwise, she'd be next on the operating table. So she agreed, but took her chance one night when he came into the ward totally pissed. As usual he dragged her into the night nurse's room, took down his trousers, and she helped him. In his drunken stupor he didn't notice when she gave him a jab of strong sedative. Then...'

He is hyperventilating.

'Take your time, Keith,' Bella says. 'No need to rush.'

Keith gives her a grateful glance. 'I ought to be used to body parts. Sorry. It seems she took a scalpel off the trolley and removed his balls and penis, so cleanly he couldn't have felt it. His mouth must have been hanging open, so she stuffed the bleeding genitalia into it. Her hands were covered with blood — we assume they

283

were, because she next began to write on the wall by the bed...'

He pauses, fighting for breath again. Bella sits quietly holding his shaking hand. The comtesse, and now Rebecca! She wonders what the statistics are for revenge-castrations by sexually abused women during World War II. At least *maman* had not felt obliged to take the law into her own hand.

Keith is able to go on with the grim story. 'What she wrote, in Nazi blood, was: 'FUCK YOU KEITH.' Next, she pulled his revolver out of its holster and shot herself in the mouth.' Once again, he stops. Then he looks at Bella, eyes filled with tears. 'She died hating me. Her last defiant act was to curse me!'

Horrified though she is, Bella keeps her voice as professional and unemotional as she can. 'How do you know all this, Keith?'

Keith is jolted back to the present. 'From a young French Jewish girl from Unoccupied France who had just been brought in for the sterilization procedure — chemical injections into the womb. She witnessed it all but feigned sleep when the shot raised the alarm. She was still alive — just — when the camp was liberated, but she died a few weeks later.'

So this is why Keith has been driven all these years: haunted by Rebecca's final malediction. How can it possibly be neutralised? He is evidently very close to a breakdown, so the situation has to be handled with great delicacy. It's unlikely that an appeal to reason would work, but this has to be the first step.

'Keith, maybe she was right?' Bella suggests. 'If you had gone into the Navy, you would have saved many Jewish lives at Auschwitz, wouldn't you?'

'No, not directly, but that's not the point...'

'No, you wouldn't. So, is the point that you wouldn't have done what Rebecca did, if you'd been her? That you wouldn't have euthanased victims of torture or killed the torturer? Is that what you feel guilty about?'

'She didn't just kill him to stop him. He was dead to the world, she could have shot him without...' His pause is not embarrassment — he has seen too many mangled bodies to be embarrassed. He is refusing to face up to Rebecca's` being brutal. Right.

Bella puts her face close to his and in a low dispassionate voice says, 'Without mutilating him? What does that tell you about Rebecca? That she chopped off his cock and balls first?' Her choice of language is carefully gauged.

Keith is confused. He doesn't know where these questions are leading. 'It tells me... that she had been emotionally traumatised. A bit crazy, I suppose. Wouldn't you be, if you'd gone through all that... all that humiliation?'

'Possibly. There's no telling what I might have done under those extreme conditions. Or even you? Can you imagine a situation that could so arouse your anger you might act out of character? Say or do something you wouldn't have done in a calmer state of mind? Or do you have such wonderful self-control?'

'No, of course not.'

'And you have, by the sound of it, a more equable temperament than Rebecca. She did tend to fly off the handle, didn't she?'

It is only a guess, but it's right.

'She was not exactly phlegmatic,' Keith concedes.

'Not like you and Alan, say? More like me?'

'I don't know you well enough to say that.'

'Well, I do. And I can tell you that if I'd been in Rebecca's desperate situation I might well have done those things. Including writing a rude final message to the man who'd disappointed me. But... this is the point, Keith... I wouldn't have meant it. I'd have wanted to retract those words when reason returned. Don't you think she would have wanted to as well? Or was she such a flawed character she could never forgive?'

Keith says nothing for such a long time that Bella thinks he might have lost contact.

'Keith? Well?'

His breathing is becoming more regular as he continues. 'I met the parents of that French girl again not long ago — I'd kept in touch. They knew why she'd died, their daughter, what had been done to her by Mengele's butchers. And yet they are quite happy at the prospect of becoming Europeans alongside Germans. They told me, 'One can't go on hating for ever'.'

It is not the moment to push things any further. Keith is no fool. Bella hopes he will be able to think along new lines now, get Rebecca in a new perspective. She decides it's time to try and divert the flow of past remembrance into a more positive channel.

'But you're giving a wonderful gift to the world, Keith, with your dedication to healing. Doesn't that give you any happiness?'

Keith looks shocked. 'Happiness! Bella... my pitiful healing missions have taken me to the most deperate and stricken parts of the world. For twenty years I've seen little but suffering and death, most of it needless and easily avoidable. Starvation caused by others' greed, limbs torn off children, young mothers burnt alive, mostly because of mindless religious and racial hatred. If I were happy it would be based on someone else's misery.'

It is Bella's turn to be shocked. 'Good heavens! You mean we have to feel guilty whenever we're happy?'

'No! I'm not suggesting we knowingly cause misery in order to be happy, though a lot of people do do that, obviously. It's just that deep down there is a hole at the centre of existence, and most of the time we're trying to ignore it.'

'O.K. So you're not a happy person. We've established that. And the world stinks.'

'I'm not clinically depressed, I hope. But I am wallowing in melancholy today, and I'm sorry. I've been very boring. I don't have many friends to bore, I'm afraid.'

'Glad to be of some service! By the way...' She knows he will see through the naïve approach to difficult country, but it's too late to retreat. '...I had another mystery call this morning.' She looks into his eyes, probably for the first time close up, and what she sees makes her recoil slightly. There is nothing there. She is looking into the void that inhabits the centre of Keith, as if he has been hollowed out by some cataclysmic torrent. She recalls her first impression of him as haunted or hunted, and finds it reinforced. Is it only the loss of Rebecca that is ravaging him?

'Mystery call?' His eyebrows go up, but not excessively, and he does not look away.

'Warning me — us — about revealing something forbidden. That's all I can gather, anyway.'

'Something forbidden? You mean, Alan's symphony?'

'Why would you think that?'

Keith's mouth twitches in that little knowing smile, as if he knows perfectly well what is on her mind. 'Because Alan told me you'd had some 'hate phone calls', and he linked it to fears that he was trying to warp people's minds with his music. What were the exact words?' he wants to know.

Bella reaches down to her handbag and pulls out a notebook. 'Here. I wrote them down straight away. I know how fear can falsify memory.'

Keith reads the single sentence. *'Take care. Harmony can be put into reverse and destroy everything.* H'm.' He scratches his beard and nods his head slowly up and down. 'It doesn't seem to be really menacing. Rather... warning you of possible repercussions.'

Bella agrees. 'It certainly isn't as worrying as the first one.'

'What did that say?'

She remembers only too well. *'Tell Alan Scott he has released something and he'll wish he hadn't.* The odd thing is, Keith, that for several days we were left in peace, but the moment Alan had left, along comes this second one.'

'So you think it's you the mystery caller wants to scare?'

'What do you think?'

'And does it scare you?'

Keith is revealing himself as an adept at deflection. But so is Bella.

'Doesn't it strike you as odd?' She's watching him carefully, and he knows it. 'The only person in this country who knew when Alan was leaving for Paris was you.'

His response is completely neutral, unfazed. 'And you,' he reminds her.

'Yes. And me.'

'And who else? In the world?'

'Oh... The travel agent. And my mother, in California!'

'Are you sure? Alan didn't phone anyone else and say when he was leaving?'

'Nnnnn... I can't be certain about that.'

'Then you'd better ask him next time you speak,' Keith suggests, with perfect equanimity. 'In the meantime, why don't we meet again for dinner, and you can tell me the history of these harmonies that seem to be attracting so much attention?'

Bella is thrown off balance by the directness of Keith's approach. No subtle or devious working up to it. Finally, she agrees, but with conditions, and suggests they meet at eight in a quiet little French restaurant in Soho.

'What do you mean by conditions, exactly?' Keith asks, as they take the lift down to street level.

'What I mean, exactly, Keith, is that you first tell me why you lied about phoning me from the British Museum...'

Keith opens his mouth to object, but she ploughs on. 'And I want you to be straight with me about what happened to you and Médecins sans Frontières. It wasn't hard for me to find out this morning that you haven't worked with them for several years. O.K.? If you don't agree, just give me a call at home at seven o'clock, would you?'

She flashes him a smile and disappears into the crowd in Kensington High Street. He stands there without an overcoat, shivering and blue with cold.

*

287

At a quarter past six Bella telephones Alan at the Hôtel Trianon, rue de Vaugirard — the longest street in Paris. It is their favourite hotel, close to the Boul' Mich and the Jardins du Luxembourg. Someone told Bella that Samuel Beckett once lived in the attic as a penniless young writer in the 1930s The phone rings several times and she is about to hang up when he answers, clearly out of breath.

'Just got in,' he puffs. 'I heard the phone through the door, but couldn't get the key to turn. Glad you hung on, darling.'

'How's it going?' she wants to know. 'Have you had your panel yet?'

'Not yet. We're scheduled for tomorrow afternoon at two, but everything runs late, as you might expect with the French. They never know when to stop talking and the chairmen are hopeless.'

'Have you had any comments about the symphony?'

'Oh yes, a few. Quite polite — on the whole.'

'Not entirely?'

'No, wouldn't expect that. The John Cage-Stockhausen types are vicious about anything that sounds remotely accessible. They are immensely infuential with the young.'

Bella senses his discomfort. 'Don't get discouraged, darling. But don't get cross and name names — and don't let them bully you tomorrow. *A chacun sa musique*, remember?'

'I'll remember. *A chacun sa musique* — even if others don't. What have you been up to?'

'I've been talking to your old friend, Keith. I'm trying to decide whether he's responsible for the phone calls. I had another one soon after you left.'

'*What!* I'm coming back right away!'

'No, darling, don't do that. There's no need. It wasn't threatening. The voice said "Take care. Harmony can be put into reverse and destroy everything". You ought to keep your ear to the ground tomorrow for any comments like that,' she advises him. 'Maybe there's some kind of esoteric movement we've got on the wrong side of?'

'O.K. So what about Keith? Can we trust him?'

'I'll make up my mind this evening. We're having dinner.'

'Oh? Where?' Alan's voice is suddenly terse. 'In the flat?'

'No, I'm not that silly. At Chez Margot.'

'Well... Give me a ring when you get back.' He still sounds either worried or annoyed, she isn't sure which.

'I can simply not go, if you like,' she proposes, knowing full well his pride won't let him agree to that, even if he feels he's growing horns.

'Of course not! After all, you let me come to Paris by myself!' With that he laughs; but it is an uncertain laugh.

Keith is already at Chez Margot's when she arrives. He has found a quiet table behind a pillar, and is indulging himself with a glass of Périer. He stands up, and she lets him kiss her on both cheeks. As they get through the arduous task of ordering they chat aimlessly, knowing that is not what they are there for. Bella requests a glass of chablis, Keith stays with Périer.

'I rang Alan just before I left,' she volunteers. 'The conference seems rather heavy going. He thinks he might be in for some flak tomorrow.'

Keith seems genuinely concerned. 'Oh dear. What about?'

'The world of composing seems as vicious as the world of psychology. If you're not in a same school of thought, put on your bullet-proof vest!'

The pause imposed by the service of soup is followed by a pause dictated by tactics. Will he open up, or wait for her to question him? Bella knows better than he how to not break a silence when necessary. Finally he gives in.

'Ahm... About the British Museum... How did you know?'

She tells him, and he blushes at his stupidity. 'And are you going to tell me why?' she asks with a smile, lowering her eyelashes at him. He's beginning to respect that smile.

'It's all part of the same story,' he begins. 'Where I was, why I was there, why I left Médecins sans Frontières.'

He does not dramatise what happened or seek to exculpate himself. 'You know about my guilt obsession with Rebecca. I was also scarred by being branded a coward by the two people I most wanted to be respected by — Rebecca and Alan. For years I tried to expiate this guilt by volunteering to do medical work in the worst places. But I burned myself out and turned to alcohol. A couple of times I was more drunk than usual while operating, and two patients died — a caesarian on a young woman, and soon after, a simple appendectomy on her father.'

Bella pictures the scene: an impoverished family in Africa or India, suddenly deprived of two of their family because of the self-indulgence of an English doctor they would have trusted implicitly. All she can think to say is 'How terrible!'

'No, not really. So I was deregistered, and had a nervous breakdown. Back in...'

289

She holds up her hand. 'Just a minute. What do you mean, 'Not really'? You kill a couple of poor people, and you say it wasn't awful?'

'Oh, you mean for them? I thought you meant for me. For them... well... Let's just say I couldn't feel desperately sorry.'

'No, Keith!' Bella is incredulous. Keith some sort of serial killer? He seemed to have no remorse, anyway. 'No! Let's not just say that. Let's say you have lost all sense of what being a doctor means. Just because of what a girl friend suffered years ago, you seem to think other people's suffering doesn't matter. Doesn't exist!'

Keith says nothing, just looks down at his plate. Then he raises his eyes to Bella, and she is shocked to see the distress in them. Pleading. For what? For understanding? For the right to silence? She decides she is not going to give him either.

They have to wait until their main course has been served before they can pursue the mystery of Keith's past years.

When he seems reluctant to continue, Bella explodes. 'For God's sake, what's going on here? You want to tell me, Keith, otherwise you wouldn't have started down this road. You wouldn't be here talking to me. So tell me.'

He sighs deeply. 'No one else knows the truth. And it could still get me into trouble, so I'm placing myself in your hands, Bella. The truth was suspected, but never followed up. It was in 1961, in a small town in Morocco. One night I was on duty and a white woman of about thirty-five was brought in, insisting on seeing a white doctor. She was heavily pregnant, with extreme hypertension and impending kidney failure. The older man with her said he wasn't her husband, but her father. He looked pretty ill too. They said they were Dutch, but it quickly became obvious they were happier speaking in German. When I started to question him, he became extremely angry and started to order me about. It could have been just anxiety, of course, but I had a hunch he was a clandestine Nazi, so when I'd sedated the woman I went and phoned a pal of mine at the embassy in Rabat. Fortunately, the military attaché was beside him, and he confirmed that they'd been tracking this pseudo-Dutchman for a while. They knew he was Georg Mottl, one of Eichmann's aides, but needed final proof. The woman wasn't his daughter, but his mistress, Amelia Tunder. She'd been a member of the Nazi party too.

'I just didn't know what to do. The doctor in me said I had to do my duty. But Rebecca was in my head, telling me this was my chance. I opened my cupboard, got out a bottle of whisky, and drank about half of it while I battled with my two consciences. When I got back to her, it was obvious she was not going to have the baby by natural means, so I started the procedure for caesarian. My hand was far from steady, and I cut through an artery. I knew I could probably stop the blood flowing, but I just stood there and watched her die.'

'Wasn't there a nurse?' Bella asks.

'No, they were very understaffed, and I'd insisted I could manage by myself. The baby was stillborn anyway. I just said she'd had a massive haemorrhage and there was nothing I could do. When Mottl was told she was dead, he had a cardiac arrest, there in the hospital. Again, I could have saved him, possibly.'

'But you didn't?'

'He was conscious for a short while, so I told him I'd save him if he admitted he was a Nazi. He swore at me in German, so I gave him a dose of morphine to keep him quiet, and left him to die.'

'And that's when your conscience began to prick you, I suppose?'

Keith shakes his head. There's a triumphant smile on his face now. 'Not at all. I hadn't felt happier for years. At last I was a combatant in Rebecca's eyes. I knew she would forgive me.'

Bella is really worried now. 'You don't really think she could possibly know about it, do you?'

Keith nods firmly, repeatedly, as if trying to convince the world. 'Of course. She's alive, you know. I write to her. When I was getting well into DTs, she used to stand at the foot of my bed and laugh at me, but not any more. Those two little executions stopped that!'

His speech is becoming louder and more excited. Other diners start to look and raise eyebrows.

'But you didn't get away with it?' Bella asks uncertainly. If this happened only nine years ago, and he was found out, how come he is free now?

'In a way, I did. There had to be a major enquiry after two suspicious deaths. Any forensic expert would have seen straight away the first could have been avoided with proper medical intervention, and the second possibly, so I pleaded guilty to being drunk and incapable. My records showed I'd been utterly devoted to my duty and had gone way beyond it, many times. So it was put down to mental exhaustion. I had my medical registration suspended for five years pending treatment for alcoholism.'

'Five years? So you're back on the job?'

'Let's not jump to conclusions,' he says. 'What would you like now? Crème caramel for me.'

With coffee before them, and a stiff Armagnac for Bella, she encourages Keith to move his story on to the present.

'Nothing much to tell,' he continues. 'Back in England, I dried myself out, and I've worked as a medical auxiliary for a couple of years now. I could apply for re-registration, I suppose, but I've had enough, lost my nerve, lost my confidence and motivation.'

'And the phone call?'

Keith looks sheepish. 'I was ringing from the hostel I live in. All I can afford on my meagre wage. It's not much of a life, but the peace is welcome.'

'How do you spend your spare time?' Bella asks.

His shoulders go up in that by now characteristic shrug. 'Reading. Mainly Lewis Carroll. *Through the Looking-Glass*. That's where I'll go one day!' He laughs at the prospect, but it is a hollow laugh that Bella does not understand.

'So why didn't you tell us? After all, we're your friends.'

'Frankly, I was too ashamed to tell you how and why I'd come down in the world.'

This puzzles Bella. 'But you must have managed to save a lot during all those years?'

He nods. 'Yes, I did. Like sailors at sea, nothing to spend it on. But I donated most of it to the Jewish Documentation Centre.'

Bella knows about the centre. It was set up by Nazi death-camp survivor Simon Wiesenthal to track down perpetrators of the Nazi Holocaust and bring them to trial.

'I'm still hoping they will find that bloody Auschwitz killer, *Doctor* Josef Mengele. Mossad has traced him to Paraguay. God! I hope they get him and make him suffer like those women and children he tortured. I'd do it myself if they asked me. Inject him with Jewish shit and watch him die slowly.'

There is no doubting the venom in his voice. Bella thinks that if he is still deregistered it is just as well.

Bella sips her armagnac in silence, pensively; Keith broods for a few minutes, then excuses himself. When he comes back from the toilet he looks as if he has had a great burden lifted from him. 'Who was it said confession is good for the soul?' he beams. 'Now it's your turn. I think I've fulfilled your conditions, Dr. Bella, so tell me how those harmonies came into your lives.'

Bella dabs her lips carefully with her napkin and places it

carefully on the table. Then she looks him straight between the eyes and says quietly, 'There are one or two points that puzzle me, Keith.'

His smile stiffens. 'Oh? What about?'

'You performed those executions — as you call them — as a form of expiation or atonement, right?'

He nods. 'Yes! Yes! That's a very good way of putting it.'

'In that case, why is guilt about Rebecca still eating away at you? What happened to the catharsis?'

She expects him to respond in a professional, clinical way, and is totally unprepared for his reaction. His face reddens, he clutches at his napkin, throws it on the table, and stands with such violence that his chair tips over backwards with a crash. The restaurant falls silent, so his words are heard by all. He utters them, his voice rasping, as though they are being dragged out of him.

'You... don't... believe... me!'

Then he turns and strides out, blindly, knocking plates from a waiter's hand.

*

As Alan has predicted, the panel starts late, with musicians and musicologists drifting in from lunch with much noise and little apology. This annoys him as he wants to get away as soon as he politely can, having managed to get a seat on a plane to Heathrow at 7.30 p.m. Gradually things settle down and each panel member gives a short address (long in the case of the French), followed by discussion.

When his turn comes, Alan has hardly any idea what he intends to say. 'I'd much rather you asked questions or made points I can respond to,' he announces, 'then there's less chance I'm boring you! As one or two of you might know, I spend a lot of time writing film music, so you might want to ask about that business — I use the word advisedly! That's why I run the risk — as Korngold did — of not being taken seriously. But it's what allows me to eat, and I was brought up to regard that as good for professional morale. For the rest, I write mainly for small ensembles, for the simple reason that it's more likely than orchestral stuff to be performed more than once. So, like Ravel, Bartók and many other composers, I make my large-scale stuff more accessible.'

'Your new symphony,' a voice pipes up, 'seems to be the opposite in every way to Cage's *4' 33*. *Mini* versus *maxi!* Did you set out to challenge aleatory music?'

Here we go! Into the lions' den.

'No, I didn't have Cage's four and a half minutes of musical absence in mind at all. It was a clever and unrepeatable experiment, but I find it impossible to include random ambient noise...' (he covers his mouth with his hand) 'Excuse me, I can't help laughing. I find it impossible to include random ambient noise in any category of creative music. Surely musicians — and all creative artists — should be suspicious of something that anyone could do if they have enough cheek? Or am I missing something here? Is effrontery now an art form?'

Someone shouts '*Bourgeois élitiste!*', and Alan joins in the laughter, nodding agreement. The spirit of 1968 is still alive and well in Paris.

'All of us composers,' he ventures after a pause, 'who sincerely put our heart and soul and talent for months and sometimes years into creating an original work, hope that somehow we will manage to get it performed during our lifetime. We've heard a lot already about the difficulties of getting a hearing for new or little known music when concert managers seldom dare to move outside the repertoire they think concert-goers are willing to pay to hear — mainly by dead Germans. Now *that's* what I call élitism!'

This gets a round of applause from the large French contingent there, supported by the Italians who start to chant 'Busoni! Busoni!' The Scandinavians respond goodnaturedly with 'Pettersson!' A couple of renegade Romanians shout 'Enescu!' So many *compositeurs maudits!*

The British stay phlegmatically silent, until someone — an Irishwoman, judging by the accent — speaks up: 'Which British composer do you think doesn't get enough of a hearing, Mr. Scott — apart from yourself, I mean?'

Alan laughs at the jibe, which doesn't sound malicious. 'I don't have any doubts about which one,' he replies. 'He died just a few days ago, on New Year's Eve, aged ninety-one. Debussy called him one of the 'rarest artists' of his generation. Eugene Goossens said he was the 'father of British modern music'. He wrote three operas, several symphonies, two piano concertos, a double concerto, concertos for violin, cello, harpsichord and oboe, major orchestral and choral works. Loads of chamber music, hundreds of songs and piano pieces. Much of it has had only one performance, or none at all. Anyone know who I'm talking about?'

A couple of the British contingent put their hands up. 'Cyril Scott,' calls one.

'Yes, Cyril Scott. A visionary of true inspiration, an innovator years ahead of his time. Strangely enough, it was his writings on music that encouraged me to become a composer when I was very, very young. But he probably wouldn't approve of my symphony. Not enough discord in it. He thought that beautiful music was too rarefied to counteract the coarse, destructive musical thought-forms pervading our atmosphere. So he wouldn't have had much time for the harmonies I use, even though they are far removed from the pretty sounds normally called harmonious.'

This opens the way for the next question. 'Mr. Scott — Alan, I mean, not Cyril — your new symphony is based on six curious harmonies, one in each movement. Shouldn't there be seven? If so, could it be harmful?'

Alan is taken aback. No one apart from him and Bella know about the seventh. And, maybe, the mystery telephone caller. He decides to dodge the question.

'I know seven is a popular magic number, but I had enough difficulty with six. I'm told one woman had an orgasm, and I can't hope to do better than that! As for potential harm,' — he knows he has to tread warily now — '...at the present stage of neuroscience we simply don't know how or why music affects chemical brain reactions. In the wrong hands I suppose my healing harmonies could be changed into dangerous musical manipulations — just as a useful drug like opium has been.'

Arms and voices are raised, the war has begun, but, to Alan's relief, the chairman passes to the next speaker.

During the afternoon tea break, a few of Alan's friends encourage him to do his imitation, at the piano, of *Stockhausen looking for a tune in a cage of silence*. When he had performed it at the Savage Club in London, he had prepared the piano by having German sausages laid on the strings, which had a curious dampening effect, but he has to do without these this time. He replaces the item with 'Mein neues Werk, *Wienstück*, or Vienna Steak, vitch I shall play mit mein hands behind mein back.' This cements the hostility of several of the more humourless avant-garde musicologists.

When Alan arrives back from Paris, he is tired and irritable. His flight has been delayed over an hour, and he has had a battle at the Air France check-in desk because his reservation had been lost. So he was allocated a seat, six inches from the tail, normally reserved for cheap bucket seat travellers, next to a vastly overweight member of a football club outing, who kept lurching into his lap and finally spewed his dinner and a gallon of red wine into the gangway. His companions clapped and cheered. But everything is relative: Alan is about to re-classify these upsets as minor inconveniences.

The front door of the flat is open when he gets to the fifth floor, and voices come from within, one of them Bella's. The moment she sees him she walks over unsteadily and kisses him, then gestures round the flat. It has been thoroughly done over: wardrobes and drawers emptied and contents strewn over the floor, papers scattered, books tossed into piles, some of them with their covers torn off.

'Good God! Are you all right, darling?' She's glad to note his first thought is for her.

Detective Sergeant Fletcher notes it too.

'They were still here when I got back,' Bella tells Alan. 'One pushed me to the floor and they ran out. As I've told the police, I didn't recognise them as they wore balaclavas.'

'You ought to have a doctor look at you!' Alan says. Anger and anxiety are in his voice. Bella assures him she isn't injured, just shaken up.

'How did they get in?' Alan wants to know.

'From the back, through the kitchen door,' Bella tells him. 'Took a ride in the service lift, I expect.' Then she adds sheepishly, 'I'm afraid I left the key in the lock. All they had to do was break the glass and reach in.'

Fletcher's attention is caught by that. 'You usually take the key out, do you, Mrs. Scott?'

'Yes. And double lock it after putting the rubbish in the bin. But this morning I was late and rushed out. I was giving a paper at a conference.'

'What time did you go out?'

Bella looks at her watch as if to orientate herself chronologically. 'About 8.30. I got to Imperial College about nine. When I got back about eight this evening, I found this.'

'Have you any idea if they were looking for something in particular,' the detective asks.

Alan and Bella glance at each other and come to the same decision, both shaking their heads.

'I'll need a list of people who knew you would be out,' Fletcher says, then asks, 'The burglar or burglars would have had to go past reception, wouldn't they?'

'Not necessarily,' Bella tells him, 'there's an entrance at the back going into a side street.'

'Is anything missing, so far as you can tell?'

'It's hard to tell with all this mess. There was some cash in a desk drawer...' Bella goes towards the desk and sifts among the débris on the floor. She bends down and picks up several pound notes. Detective Sergeant jots down 'Not after money. <u>What</u> then?' and tells them to report any missing items straight away.

When fingerprint dusting has been completed and the police have gone, Alan opens the bottle of duty free whisky and pours them both a handsome slug. Then they go into the bedroom to check the hidden wall safe. It is untouched and intact.

'We must clear up,' Bella says with a sigh, surveying the devastation.' We've been lucky — at least there's no vandalism or peeing and shitting on the floor. But first tell me about your session. How did it go?'

He takes a swig. 'I want to know about yours too. Mine went not too badly. I suppose. The Cage brigade was in full array...'

As they put things to rights they give one another blow-by-blow accounts of their skirmishes on the intellectual battlegrounds called conferences. Nothing seems to be missing. It is clear to both of them that the break-in was motivated by the desire to access the harmonies. But to destroy them or exploit them? Bella admits she contacted the *National Pride* office and got a pretty rough reception.

Alan is not pleased, feeling she should have consulted him. 'They wouldn't have found it too difficult to trace Dr. Cassell's phone number to this address, so they put two and two together and decided to move in.'

Bella is about to defend her initiative, but before she can Alan is now sufficiently steamed up to broach the subject he's been itching to find out about.

'Now, how about your *dîner intime* with your friend Keith?'

She declines to be baited. 'At least you didn't say 'By the way'! It was more *infâme* than *intime*. Intimate only in that he regaled me with a long confession about his less than professional activities in Morocco. But we parted on bad terms.'

Alan's reaction is strained. His mouth is set in a hard line, an expression Bella has not seen for a long time, and then on another face, not his.

'Dearie me,' he says, 'you had a tiff, did you?' It sounds as though he wants to say *a lovers' tiff*. 'What about?'

'I as good as told him he was a liar. He thought I did anyway.'

He picks up the copy of *The Guardian* lying on a chair and affects to only half-listen as she gives him a succinct account of Keith's story. When she has finished he turns to the next page, noisily shaking the paper straight. 'Amazing what can happen in a couple of days away. What didn't you believe, exactly? It sounds pretty plausible to me.'

'Ah, but you can't see his eyes and body language. All the signs were there: shifty eyes, tension in the throat, sweating...'

'But surely he'd have been tense and nervous just because he was confessing? I know I would.'

Bella's expression doesn't change, but she feels a twinge of doubt. Has she been too quick to judge, too impulsive? 'But they weren't the only reasons. If he'd really done those things and 'become a combatant', as he put it, he'd be over the Rebecca-guilt thing by now. The catharsis would have had some effect. But he's still obsessed. He still writes to her, can you believe it?'

'Well, frankly, yes. If I lost someone I loved under those conditions, I think I'd try all sorts of ways to keep her alive in my mind. Maybe not write to her, but I'd certainly talk to her and ask her what she'd do, what she thinks. Especially if there was some unresolved business, some misunderstanding we'd not had time to clear up. Wouldn't you?'

Bella has to admit to herself that she probably would not, but says, 'Yes, I suppose so.'

Aspects of Keith are surfacing from the depths of Alan's memory now, things he did not know were there.

'When we were in the upper sixth form — he was Science and I was Lit. — he told me one day that a couple of years earlier he'd taken an essay from my desk and used it for his homework. He was no good at all at the literary stuff and didn't even know where to start on a Shakespeare essay. I was pretty hopping mad because I'd taken hours writing it, and had to do it all again from notes. I went round casting dark accusing looks at several suspects. But not at him. He said he hadn't dared to use it in the end for fear of being found out. Then a couple of years later he ups and confesses! Maybe,' he added,' he'll confess in a couple of years time to other bits of cheating.'

Bella knows what he's implying, but decides to ignore it and simply says that it was interesting but irrelevant.

Alan shrugs. 'Maybe. I think it was a bit obsessive — his conscience wouldn't let go, would it? Like with the Nazis — he couldn't be at peace until he'd resolved the situation. He'd committed two murders in the hope of clearing himself of cowardice. Rationally, a foolish thing to do, but the heart has its reasons the mind doesn't know.'

It occurs to Bella that Alan's essay-theft story is, in fact, illustrating something more than what he'd intended: if Keith really was so conscience-stricken about lying, was it likely he would deliberately weave such an elaborate web of untruths?

'Maybe lying is too harsh, I'll go that far,' she concedes, 'although I didn't accuse him directly of lying. When he rushed off I was about to suggest to him that maybe he'd have liked to do all that, wished he had done it, so much so that he was fantasising a false memory that's become a reality for him. But...' she pauses, reasoning her way along, '...but if he really did kill them through deliberate negligence, then he has other big problems. Yes, I can see perhaps his conscience is nagging at him for playing God, for taking life, when all his moral being had been predicated on saving it and respecting it.'

Another thought slides snakily into Alan's mind. 'Bella, do you think there's some reason why you didn't *want* to believe him?'

She looks startled. 'Not want to? No, I can't think of any reason. Such as what?'

'Oh, I don't know — deciding he'd taken up enough of our time already? Fear he was becoming a bit demanding, a liability, or too attracted to you? Or the other way round?'

She very nearly ridicules the idea by teasing him about jealousy again, but realises it is a genuine possibility, from Alan's point of view anyway.

'It's always a risk, Alan, when someone makes himself, herself, vulnerable by opening up secrets. But I really didn't think he'd go to pieces like that. I just wanted to challenge him, as a way to get him to stick firmly to his story. But he didn't. Either because it wasn't true...'

'Or because it was, and he was crushed.'

Bella nods. 'Can I have done him any harm by rejecting him like that? I hope he doesn't do anything stupid.' She is looking less and less happy. 'I must be losing my touch. We don't know where to contact him, do we?'

Alan looks at her sharply. 'We? Leave me out of it. You created the problem. If you hadn't gone off to an assignation with him by yourself...'

'Assignation!' she exclaims, wondering if he is joking. But his expression shows he is not. 'It wasn't an assignation. I told you all about it. There was nothing secret about it.'

But Alan is now being driven by a devil within him, almost but not quite against his will. 'It doesn't prove anything, the fact that you told me about it. A half-truth is always a good way not to tell the whole truth.'

'Alan!' She is beginning to feel she is entering a nightmare zone, afraid. 'I don't understand your attitude.' Then it strikes her. Where she has seen that expression before, the line of the mouth, the hard eyes. 'You're looking just like your mother, Alan. This jealousy and possessiveness, it's her, a legacy from her. She's still haunting us, trying to drive us apart.' She knows it's not a professional, scientific thing to say, but somehow feels that knowing more than most about the workings of the mind does not mean she cannot make the occasional irrational statement under emotional pressure.

He seems not to hear her, and goes on, recklessly, destructively. 'You know, I've sensed there's something going on between you from the moment he blurted out he'd met you before and you said you didn't remember. You have an amazing memory, you'd never have forgotten. Why didn't you want to admit it? What went on between you?'

Bella utters a little laugh, but it is not remotely associated with mirth. 'Going on... went on between us? For heaven's sake, Alan, you sound like a radio melodrama.'

Her response appears to confirm his suspicions. 'Did you,' he goes on, now quietly and slowly, as though each word has to be dragged out of him, 'did you have sex with him while you were going out with me?'

This brutal accusation sobers her up, and she too becomes quite cold, deliberate, clinically blunt. 'One didn't have sex much in those days, if you mean full vaginal penetration.' Jamie didn't count — he was before Alan's time. 'At least, I didn't, though I can't speak for you or Keith or your girl friends. We were born twenty years too early for guilt-free fun.'

He is like a ferret after a rabbit. 'All right, technically you didn't have sex. What did you do?'

Bella stands up. 'This is just too silly, Alan. Embarrassing and in very poor taste. It was twenty-five years ago, I didn't live in a nunnery, I didn't belong to you, and I didn't do anything I'm ashamed of. Keith and I have never had sexual intercourse and are unlikely to unless *you* push us into it! That's all I have to say on that subject. Now, there is something to really worry about concerning Keith, and we don't know where to contact him... Ah! Wait a

300

minute!'

She goes out into the hall and comes back with a dark brown overcoat. 'When he dashed off he left this behind in the restaurant.' In a pocket she finds a diary with an address written inside the front cover. 'We must go and see if he's all right.'

'You can do what you like. I don't have any expertise in the counselling field.'

'But he's your friend much more than mine. For God's sake, Alan, stop being stubborn! He may be in danger.'

'The way I feel, he might be in a lot more if I see him.' He slaps his forehead. 'Wait a minute! He'll be on your list of people who knew I was away and you'd be out! Right up at the top, I'd say.'

'At the top, as you say,' Bella says calmly. 'Now I'll go and see if he has a balaclava stuffed in a drawer, and leave you to come to your senses. While I'm away you can brood about how childish you've been.'

As Bella telephones for a taxi she ponders on her husband's sudden insecurity and vulnerability, and has the vague feeling it has more to do with the relationship between him and Keith than with her.

*

17 January 1971

My Dearest Rebecca
My whole world has been turned topsy-turvy. This won't be a long letter, but writing to you might help clear my head, which is going round so fast I don't know what. I have made it up to you, I swear, you must believe me. Anyone who doesn't, deserves bad things. Bad bad things. It's an insult to you too and I won't stand for that. No. NO. It's all linked with those strange harmonies Alan has produced. I don't know how, but it's a dangerous situation. I have an idea forming in my poor aching head. Yes. This will settle things once and for all.
I'll write again very soon, when I've got the plan sorted out.
You know you have my love, my real love, the deep abiding sort. That's why I'm doing all this for you..
Keith.

*

When Bella has rushed out of the flat, slamming the door behind her, Alan pours himself another Glenfiddich and settles down to a good old sulk. This turns out not to be a simple process. Two irreconcilable themes run through his troubled mind with no apparent possibility of melding into harmonious counterpoint as he tries simultaneously to calm his jealous fears and justify them:

It is obvious to him now that the reason why she gave Keith her card at the Festival Hall, behind his back, was because they'd been lovers and were still attracted to each other.

But he, Alan, had rudely shunned an old friend, for no reason she was aware of, and she had merely tried to make amends with courtesy.

Who suggested Keith should stay the night? She did, certainly, not wanting him to disappear from her life again.

But they couldn't have pushed him out to walk for hours to Russell Square.

Anyway, what does it matter now, something that happened all those years ago when they were teenagers?

It's not what happened then that matters, it's the spilling over of the past into the present that is threatening. Or rather, the contamination of the present by the past.

But many men have found Bella attractive and have made little effort to hide it. What is so different about Keith?

Rebecca! Reluctantly Alan admits to himself that ever since Rebecca showed she preferred Keith he has harboured a certain resentment, but has tried never to show or express it. When they swapped over Keith got the better deal. Maybe Rebecca did too, and that's why he's always felt sexually inferior to Keith, who was undoubtedly more handsome and successful with girls. Alan recalls that he has only once let slip his sense of rebuff, in the changing room after gym. 'I expect she prefers you,' he said to Keith, 'because you're circumcised'.

Added to that, there is something he can't put his finger on, about the way Keith and Bella reacted to each other. Hence the nagging thought that something is going on between these two to which he is not privy. This reawakened vague apprehensions that before and since marriage she has never been as exclusively 'his' as he has been exclusively 'hers'. On the other hand, maybe part of her charm has always been a certain elusiveness.

Almost instinctively Alan walks over to the bookcase and pulls out his much-thumbed copy of *A la recherche du Temps perdu*. How wonderfully Proust captured the agony and the futility of jealousy! To his surprise Alan finds that some time — many years ago, it must have been — he put bookmarks in passages relating to jealousy:

302

> *La jalousie n'est souvent qu'un inquiet besoin de tyrannie appliqué aux choses de l'amour... Jealousy is often just an anxious tyrannical urge applied to objects of love.*

(But am I a tyrannical person? I've always thought of myself as easy-going.)

> *La jalousie... belongs to that family of unhealthy doubts... is a demon that cannot be exorcised and always comes back in a new form... jealousy is considered by the object of it as a suspicion which authorises deceit.*

(Aha! Now that is worrying! Unwittingly I've thrown Bella and Keith together in an alliance, and I have cast myself as the enemy.)

It is, he now supposes with post-Proustian wisdom, natural enough that Keith has revealed so much more to Bella alone than to him or them both. There is great danger in showing jealousy that can so easily prove ill-founded. His relationship with Bella might be harmed quite seriously, given her independent spirit. Perhaps it is already too late, the damage done?

*

18 January 1971

My dearest Rebecca
Odd to think it's only a few hours since I last wrote to you. You and I know the truth, don't we? Oh yes, we have nothing to fear, nothing to explain or excuse. You told me what to do that night, when was it? I don't know. Just now long ago when we were young and gay. Don't let them live, you said, and I didn't let them out of love for you, love and sorrow, so much sorrow my darling Rebecca. But I have to let the world know I killed them. I thought it was enough that you knew, but it isn't, because Alan, you remember Alan of course, and that smart wife of his, don't believe me. Still think I'm a coward! I can't have that, for your sake. You don't want your lover to be branded a coward, do you? So I'll leave a note for them before I come and join you there. We shall soon be together, my love. I am so glad to be out of this hell...

Keith looks up from his simple deal table to the mirror above it.

Above it, but placed so that Keith can look right into it without standing. What he sees is the bearded, prematurely worn and aged face of a man. Just behind him is a young female face shrouded with dark curly hair. Slowly a smile flickers over the lips, and the young girl nods thrice.

He closes the notebook in which he has been writing and opens the table drawer, reaches into the back of it, finds what he is wanting, and withdraws a small phial.

'Maximum dose, I think, one and a half grammes, to speed me on my way, darling.' He half-fills a glass with water, and carefully pours half the potassium cyanide into it. He screws the cap on firmly and places the phial in a pocket of the jacket hanging on the back of his chair. Five minutes later, just as he is raising the glass to his lips, he pauses.

'What? What's that?' He appears to listen intently, his head slightly on one side. Then he looks at the glass and slowly puts it down. 'Yes, I know that. So, what if Himmler and Goering did kill themselves this way? Yes, they used cyanide gas in the gas chambers, but... What? I mustn't use the Nazi way? Find another way? Ah! Get rid of those who don't believe me? Of course! Then my conscience will be clear at last. I can be what *I* want, not what *they* want! *They* are creating my problems — if I get rid of them, I won't be a coward any...'

Keith jerks upright as a loud knock on the door interrupts his monologue. Clumsily he reaches for the glass and pushed it over, the liquid spilling all over the notebook.

'Yes? Who is it?' Keith shouts.

'It's Frank, Keith. The warden. Your friend Bella is here to see you.'

Bella has to use all her powers of persuasion and professional string-pulling to dissuade the hostel warden from ringing the police about Keith's apparent suicide attempt and — probably — illegal possession of a lethal poison. The moment she smells bitter almonds she warns the two men not to touch anything, since the poison can enter the body through the skin. Quickly she opens the window, then finds a pair of rubber gloves under the sink unit, picks up the contaminated notebook and drops it into the sink, letting water run over it to dilute the cyanide. Keith tries to stop her and then watches, stricken, as the writing is obliterated.

The warden immediately understands the dangers, and dashes off to get a mop and bucket and plastic bags. She drags the zombie-like Keith to his bathroom, makes him wash his hands under the tap, and tears off the cuff of his shirt which has been splashed. She asks him if he has any more of the cyanide, and he says no. His face is ashen; with his grey-speckled beard he looks twenty years older.

'Don't worry, I'd already decided not to commit suicide before you arrived,' he reassures her. Unfortunately, she does not think to ask for the empty container.

The warden is still making noises about contacting the police, but she flashes credentials and undertakes to look after Keith and make sure he receives appropriate treatment and counselling.

'You won't forget your overcoat this time, will you, Keith?' Bella suggests as she helps him on with it. 'You left me with it — and your address — and the bill — at the restaurant.'

As she utters this gentle reproach with a smile, it is enough to bring Keith out of his daze. 'Oh! Bella! I'm so sorry! How much was it?'

She tells him not to be silly, as lightheartedly as she can manage, and whispers to the warden. 'Keep an eye on him for a minute will you, please? I need to phone home.'

While Keith packs a small case under surveillance, Bella dials home from the public telephone in the corridor. She speaks in a low enough voice for Keith not to overhear.

'Alan? It's me. Listen, darling, I've found Keith... No... For Christ's sake, shut up and listen! He's in a bad way. Just about to commit suicide... Cyanide. Very nasty. I've said we'll look after him... What? At the flat of course... *No*, there *isn't* any alternative... Well, I'd have to get him into a psychiatric ward. Do you want your friend to be trussed up in a straight jacket because of you? Just think about that for a moment...' She slams the phone down.

As they go off in the waiting taxi the warden stares after them and shakes his head doubtfully, wondering if he's done the right thing. Then he goes to his office, writes out a notice saying 'CLEANER: DO NOT ENTER!', and sticks it on Keith's door.

Keith huddles mutely, his arms folded tightly across his chest, as they make their way out west towards Hammersmith. Bella looks at him covertly but anxiously, trying to judge from his eyes the degree of depression he might be suffering from.

'You gave us a bit of a fright there,' she says. It won't go down in the annals of appropriate one-liners, but is better than ever-deepening embarrassed silence.

Meanwhile, Alan has pulled himself together. He has made up the bed for Keith, and strong coffee appears the moment Bella and Keith get back. Slowly Keith's colour returns. He recovers enough to start apologising, but they soon convince him that is not necessary.

'Keith, it's nearly midnight. Can you face up to talking now, or in the morning?' Bella asks.

He is immediately on the defensive. 'I don't think I've got anything to say.'

'Fine, but I have,' Bella continues. 'I want to apologise for giving you the impression I didn't believe you. There were — are — things that puzzled me, that's all.'

'Such as?'

'It doesn't matter now. But Alan has something to say to you. Haven't you, Alan?'

Alan sits up straight and coughs. Even though going to bed seems a much better idea, he's going to stick to the plan they have agreed. 'Er, yes. The thing is, if I hadn't had to go off to Paris like that, we'd have got round to telling you by now about the harmonies. It's an interesting story... if we can all stay awake?'

*

'So there were seven, not six?' Keith asks.

Alan nods.

'Then why did you put only six in your symphony? Did you get tired?' He is recovering fast.

'Two reasons. Too difficult, and too dangerous.'

Keith is baffled. 'Dangerous? But I thought you said these chords were therapeutic?'

He looks over at Bella for some kind of professional explanation. Alan's tone-world is closed to him, but Bella's brand of scientific discourse he can cope with.

It will be better, she says, if Alan continues.

'Right.' Alan carefully puts down his coffee cup. 'These harmonies, or chords, get more and more complex. We — Bella and I — tried them out in various forms with groups of people under controlled conditions in California.'

'What sort of people?' Keith wants to know.

'A whole range, from "normal" to schizophrenic, and sufferers from various kinds of emotional and mental illnesses. I can't talk about that side of it, that's Bella's field. But I could judge the effects, even though I can't explain them.'

'I don't think anyone can yet,' Bella interjects. 'We have to wait till we can read the brain better. Maybe one day we'll be able to scan it and know exactly what each brain cell is doing.'

'And what were the effects?'

'Mostly positive, but unpredictable,' Alan says, 'which I put down to my inability to render the complete harmonies as they should be heard. I can still hear them in my head with the utmost clarity, but to transfer those ineffable sounds to imperfect human instruments... They become travesties of the originals.'

'But,' Keith recalls, 'that poor old French chap... René?... they had a dramatic effect on him, and you didn't have an orchestra handy?'

'I know. All I can guess is that on that first occasion, the power was enormous, pristine, full force. I felt it was like, oh I don't know, like an audible heavenly vision. And René's nervous system obviously reacted to that.'

'Including the seventh?' Keith has a dogged look about him now, a determination to pursue, that makes Bella understand he must have been a very good doctor, the sort that gets to the hidden causes. 'What has happened when you've subjected patients to the seventh? What sort of effect does it have? You've got me really intrigued now.'

Again, it is Bella who replies. 'It's quite frightening — because we don't yet understand it. It seems to have an extraordinary effect on certain electrical patterns in the brain. If only we could wire people's heads up and see what's going on in there! Very frustrating.'

The implications of this strike Keith as sinister. 'I've seen the results of people having bits of them wired up to reveal what's in their mind.'

Bella glances at Alan and sees he is looking less than happy too.

'Yes,' she concedes, 'in the wrong hands... But that's true of every scientific and technological advance since Prometheus harnessed fire. All I can say is that the effect of the seventh harmony is as if parts of the brain get realigned and blocked channels are cleared. We've had a couple of cases where violent patients didn't just quieten down, they began to see themselves and the world around them in a totally new perspective. I've no proof, but it seemed as though the whole brain, left and right hemispheres, was engaged for the first time, and enabled them to see things using both reason and emotion.'

Alan is unwilling to lose control over this. 'And,' he chips in, 'most interesting from my point of view, they became creative. Their creativity in speech, behaviour and art forms was somehow released.'

'So,' — Bella retrieves the ball — 'we're working now on the theory that antisocial aggression and suppressed creativity go hand in hand. But it's chicken and egg at the moment.'

Keith is getting caught up in their enthusiasm. 'Is this magic sound so different from the others then?'

'The seventh has a much more complex texture than the others. Took me weeks to analyse and synthesise. Thank God for Moog!'

'Who the hell's Moog? Or what?'

'Both,' Alan explains. 'About five years ago Robert Arthur Moog started to make synthesisers, called Moogs. Didn't you hear *Switched on Bach?* All the rage last year. I suppose it's pretty primitive really, but it does mean we can experiment with complex sounds and harmonies that would cost a fortune with an orchestra. I finally got close to what I originally heard.'

'How do you know that? It must have been all of twenty years ago!' asks Keith.

'I don't think I'll ever forget it. It's etched in there.' Alan taps his forehead.

'Lucky for you. Can't you just play the notes on the piano?' He looks over at the Steinway.

Alan shakes his head. 'For one thing, it's too late for the neighbours. And the piano's a percussion instrument. These have to be sustained sounds in finely balanced harmony.'

'So no one else can hear them but you?'

Bella senses acute disappointment in Keith's voice. Alan picks it up too and shoots a glance at Bella, who does some rapid thinking. It would ideally be better for Keith — for them all — to go through the experience fresh in the morning, but she still has grave doubts about Keith's stability. What might he do during the night? They can hardly stay awake as if on guard duty. She nods her head imperceptibly, and Alan goes into the bedroom. There, he opens the wall safe hidden behind the headboard of their bed and takes out a box of audio tapes.

He quickly provides a pair of earphones for Keith to hear the harmonies. Having adjusted the volume and checked that the sounds are the correct ones, he hands them to Keith. 'Now, this will last fifteen minutes. It's the sequence of seven harmonies, with a very short break between them. It would be best if you lie down.'

'Why don't you take your jacket off?' Bella suggests, 'You'll be more comfortable.'

She takes the coat, and Keith lies full length on the sofa.

Alan goes on, 'Some of the sounds will seem slightly out of tune to you. That's because I've had to adjust the microharmonics and our ears are accustomed to standard frequencies. In fact, it was this adjustment process that proved the most complex part of reproducing the harmonies.'

'It'll be wasted on me,' Keith says, 'as I've told you, I'm tone-deaf.'

Alan says he has never accepted that anyone can be irrevocably tone-deaf. 'But I'm glad you think you are, Keith. It means you're not going to be an easy subject. We find that musically trained people and music lovers react more readily, and we need challenges!'

Bella comes back into the study. 'As you'll appreciate, Keith, we can't do any EEG investigation here in the flat. This is just to satisfy your curiosity.' She is still curious about Keith's fascination with these mysterious sounds, but that will have to wait. Keith, of course, may be aware of why she issues this little disclaimer to technical sophistication: to allay any suspicion Keith might have that he's being treated like a patient or a guinea-pig, as this could lead to distorted results. (In fact, Alan does have another discreet tape recorder switched on, to capture the sounds and the responses.)

'Now,' Bella goes on, sitting beside him, 'we'd like you to verbalise what goes through your mind or how you feel, and if you want it to stop at any moment, just take off the earphones. O.K.? Make sure you have them on the correct way — left and right stimuli are different.'

Keith shows he understands, checks Left and Right, and puts on the 'phones. Alan presses the Start key.

For the first three harmonies, each lasting two minutes, Keith's verbalised and visible reactions are normal: enhanced relaxation and awareness, synaesthesia, euphoria. But after the fourth, he murmurs, astonishment in his voice, 'I can distinguish between the tones now quite clearly. Never been able to do that before!'

At the twelfth minute, Alan and Bella begin to take particular notice, as the three-minute stretch of the seventh is beginning. Keith's breathing becomes slower, his facial expression changes, casts off years. They both see the Keith they knew so long ago, before anxiety and torment added more years than he deserved. He is visibly trying to retain a dispassionate, clinical attitude to what he's experiencing, because he is professionally interested in it, but succeeds no more than a normally virile professor of physiology could while making love. He seeks for words to express what is happening inside his head, but gives up when he has exhausted *ineffable*, *psychedelic*, *transcendental*. Finally opting for *fantastic* he bursts into tears when the harmony stops, as if he has suddenly been cut off from a vision of heaven.

They remain silent until he recovers and sits up rather shamefaced. 'Sorry about that, my friends,' he says, blowing his nose noisily. Alan has a fleeting vision of Keith being rejected by Rebecca in the summer-house, beside Bella's disused tennis court, in a previous life.

Keith looks round the room. 'You know, I feel as though I've just woken up after a long, long sleep. I must have been going around in a kind of stupor for God knows how long, not seeing, not hearing, not taking things in properly. How long will this enhanced perception persist, do you know?'

Bella answers. 'We don't know, Keith. It's very individual.'

He looks at them both keenly, as if seeing them properly for the first time. Then he says, very softly and seriously, 'I have to tell you... I wanted to kill you, Bella.'

Alan thinks he is joking. 'Oh, that's all right, then, I thought you wanted to bed her.'

Bella does not laugh. 'I see you've got your sense of humour back, Alan. Why did you want to kill me, Keith?'

'Because you didn't believe me, or so I thought.'

As it dawns on Alan they are in earnest, he turns pale. 'You mean it? How?' he asks.

'With this.' Keith reaches into his jacket pocket and pulls out a phial half full of white crystalline powder. 'Potassium cyanide.'

Alan, appalled, has gone white. 'Good God! But that stuff is... is...'

'Unpleasant and lethal, in that order, yes,' says Bella. 'May I have it please, Keith?'

There is no refusing Bella in this mood. He leans forward and carefully places it in her hand. Alan looks as though he's ready to shout for help.

Bella knows very well what the effects of cyanide poisoning are: paralysis of the respiratory centre of the brain, weakened pulse, convulsions, frothing at the mouth, death within minutes if enough has been taken.

Keith is distraught. 'I am so terribly sorry, both of you. The thought now of killing my two best and only friends... Please, can you ever forgive me?'

Bella, to the horror of both men, unscrews the cap, and dips her finger in the powder. Then she slowly raises the finger towards her tongue.

It is Keith who reacts first. 'Bella! Don't! I'm serious!' He grabs her wrist, sweat pouring from his brow.

'Thank you, Keith,' Bella says, as composed as though she has been handed a cup of tea, 'now I do believe you want me to go on living.'

Alan is still anxious. 'But we must get rid of that stuff quickly!'

'Don't worry,' Bella says. 'I've already done that. I was puzzled not to find any container in your hostel room, so I looked in your pockets and bag just now when you were listening, Keith, sorry. Disposed of it, found a similar empty phial, filled it and placed it in your pocket. But I must confess I thought it was for yourself, not for me.'

'But... what's in that bottle?' Alan wants to know, still not fully convinced.

'Some of our caster sugar. Here, taste it.' She holds out the phial, and Alan takes it to the bathroom. A moment later they hear the toilet being flushed.

After that, they all sleep, each in his or her fashion. Keith out like a light, Bella like a mother with a sick child, Alan with nightmares in which he finds himself in strange, empty places where nothing he knows and no one he loves exist any more. He has an intimation of total bereftness. When morning finally comes, he kisses Bella more passionately than he has for a long time.

It is breakfast time. Outside, snow falls from a leaden sky. Bella is still in her dressing gown, but has pinned it so as to close her cleavage from view. The men have slung on pullovers and slacks.

At table, Alan holds out a bowl to Keith. 'Sugar, Keith? No? Can't say I blame you, old chap. Now, to get back to business: these Nazis — I'm a bit confused about the latest version. Did you deliberately let them die? Or not?'

'No. I thought I should have done. It distressed me more and more in the following days that I'd missed the chance. Or rather, I'd refused to take it, out of pure cowardice.'

'Missed the chance to do what, exactly?' Bella asks. 'I mean, I

311

guessed in the restaurant that you'd in fact missed the chance to let them die, but what did that missed chance mean to you?'

Keith seeks an answer to this, and finally says, as if making a shameful confession, 'The opportunity to redeem myself — in my own eyes.'

'But why did it matter so much to you to perform a... what's the opposite of cowardly? — heroic... a heroic act?'

Keith gestures impatiently. 'As I said, to redeem myself! We're going round in circles, Bella!' He is getting better by the minute.

'No we're not, Keith. We're going in a spiral towards the real centre of the problem. But *you* have to take the journey there, not me. I think your mind is clear enough now for you to manage it. Now, to redeem yourself? ...yes?'

'Well, with Rebecca. Is that what you want me to say?'

'You just say what seems right to you, Keith. I don't matter. You don't have to prove anything to me — to us. So, with Rebecca, O.K. Why was being a hero in Rebecca's eyes important to you?'

Keith begins to flounder and lose focus; Bella sees the ice is thinner than she suspected, and fears he might opt out of going any further.

Alan senses there's a problem and steps in with a question that has been plaguing him ever since Keith told them about the Nazi episode. 'Can I ask, Keith, what happened to those Quaker pacifist ideals you used to have?'

Keith holds out his hands as if something he thought he had firmly in his grasp has dripped away through his curved fingers. 'I lost them. They simply ceased. It was quite a long process that began at Auschwitz. I tried to ignore it and resist it, but it was like falling out of love, there's nothing you can do about it.'

'But you'd based your life on that faith,' Alan says. This is foreign territory to him. 'Your decisions all flowed from it. So when faith fled, what happened to those decisions? They no longer made any sense, I suppose?'

'No sense at all. I still had a professional conscience, but my moral being had a hole torn in the centre of it. A vacuum. The compass didn't work any more, so I lost all sense of direction.'

'Did anything fill that vacuum?' asks Bella.

Slowly Keith formulates a response, and begins to move his head up and down. 'Rebecca's death. That filled the space. It cast a shadow and nothing was clear any more. I moved in darkness. All I could do was anaesthetise myself with alcohol. I went through the motions during each day, on automatic. But when I realised I wasn't safe any more I resigned voluntarily and came back to England. Rootless, homeless, jobless, with nothing to do but feel guilty about letting Rebecca down. That became sheer torment. As I went through the Alcoholics Anonymous hell that delusion became reality. I convinced myself I'd killed Mottl and Tunder and began to write to Rebecca about it. But...'

He shifts uncomfortably in his seat and looks firmly at the floor. 'But when you seemed to destroy that certainty, Bella, I felt the sand shifting under my feet again. I needed desperately to believe I'd atoned, otherwise I was back in hell.'

'And death was not a way out?'

'*My* death was not the way out, Bella.' He lifts his eyes to hers. 'Yours was.'

He begins to apologise again, and they assure him that they bear him no grudge, with hope in Bella's case and without conviction in Alan's.

'It was quite a relief that you handed it over, nevertheless,' Bella says. 'Otherwise I'd have been obliged to admit to taking it from your pocket, and we should never have been quite certain the seventh harmony had worked positively for you.'

Keith picks up on the word. 'Positively? Ah, yes, I was told about possible reversal of power, negative impact.'

Alan and Bella glance at each other, surprised. 'Oh?' Alan asks, 'Who told you about that?'

Keith gives no sign that he has been caught out, and is perfectly relaxed about telling them things he has never even touched on before. In his travels, he says, he met a guru in India who inducted him into the connections between mysticism and music. He, Keith, was very resistant, being tone deaf, but eventually even he began to understand the power of music on the mind.

Alan's suspicions are immediately aroused by this revelation that Keith has all the time been well aware of the mystical sphere they are working in, but Bella is impatient for different reasons: 'Yes, yes. We all know about the electrical patterns in the brain, alpha and beta and theta brain waves, and endorphins.'

'Even so,' Keith continues, unruffled by Bella's interruption, 'the Sufi gave me quite new insights from ancient wisdom. Don't you think, Bella, that neuroscientists might be just reinventing the wheel, and giving it another name?'

Bella mutters darkly that there are wheels and wheels. She and Alan are both beginning to feel that Keith has been deliberately holding out on them, but at least they now understand why he has been so fascinated by the whole harmonic phenomenon.

'I suppose both of you know the many esoteric studies on Eastern music and harmony?' Keith asks.

Alan admits he has no more than a superficial acquaintance with them, as he has been too involved in Western music and his own productions; and Bella proudly refuses credence to anything mystical. 'If anything seems mystical, it's just because we don't yet know enough about it,' she pronounces.

'But,' Alan reminds her, 'you used to talk about the Magic Notes.'

Bella shrugs. 'Just a figure of speech. I must have been overwrought. What about this guru, then, Keith? Did he lie on nails and levitate?'

Keith ignores the jibe. 'It was the Sufi who warned me about the power of music to destroy,' Keith says. 'Its power can be reversed and used to increase discord — he reckoned it is already happening on a large scale. Maybe,' he pauses, then says quietly, 'it is simply too early for the harmonies.'

This is all too esoteric for Bella, who brings the ball back into her own court. 'As the mystery voice said, they could have worked in reverse. If you'd been fundamentally evil, Keith, who knows...?'

'But I wasn't, was I?' Keith jumps up and starts to put on his jacket. 'We must celebrate this! I'm just going to the wine shop downstairs to get a bottle of champagne. I do believe I dare risk a glass now!'

As he goes out of the room, he pauses and looks round. 'Another thing my Sufi taught me — the importance of the colours we surround ourselves with. White gives you the whole spectrum, doesn't it?'

Alone, Alan and Bella embrace in silence, suddenly aware of the dangers averted.

It is Alan who speaks first. 'So he wasn't an interior decorator.'

They laugh, then Bella says, 'We've still a long way to go, darling, but it was a good test case. I really think we're on to something.'

But Alan is pensive. 'Do you think it's possible he was the mystery caller?'

Bella starts to say 'Of course not', but changes her mind. 'Maybe. Let's ask him.'

'If he comes back. Maybe he's done a bunk — I mean, a fugue, too?'

'I hope not. We have to know, for our own peace of mind.'

Just as they are getting edgy, Keith turns up, puffing and pink, clutching a bottle of Moët et Chandon they knew he could not afford.

'You really must do something about that lift!' he complains.

When they have settled back, glasses of bubbly in hand, Bella gives Alan an encouraging smile and nods towards Keith. Alan draws a deep breath.

'So, can we assume now that the mystery phone calls are going to cease?'

Keith stares at him. 'How on earth would I know?' But his blush gives him away, and he knows it. 'All right. I'm sorry, I really am. You see, I could somehow sense the dangers, but my mind was too muddled to play straight with you. I just wanted to warn you and stop you perfecting a potentially lethal weapon until it could be kept under very strict control. We shall still have to be on our guard, you know?'

We? Clearly, as far as Keith is concerned, the new alliance is forged. Alan and Bella have no choice but to accept it; otherwise Keith will either be shattered again, or will become a dangerous enemy. Only time will tell if they are now taking the right step.

TEMPO 2 — FINALE

Scherzo vivace

1971-2004

Some characters fade from this story at this point, but readers might like to have some idea of what happened to them.

Corker and Joy found great solace and satisfaction in each other, even after marriage. His expertise behind the camera, coupled with his ability to get the best out of girls, resulted in a splendid partnership in the Art Film industry, once he had persuaded his curvaceous spouse that it was selfish of them to keep her all to themselves. She admitted she found it more fun than coffins. After five years, during which Joy filled out rather too much to continue working in front of the camera and became quite fluent in Swedish and German, they bought a house in Clapham before it went upmarket as Clahm. There, in quick succession, they raised four cheeky, rowdy, much loved children.

Soon after his rehabilitation, Dr. Keith Maxted took up a G.P. position in the Northern Territory of Australia, where he found the work immensely rewarding. In Darwin he met and married a beautiful, sensible, intelligent, idealistic (and blonde) nurse named Karen, who adored him and took no nonsense from him. They kept up a regular correspondence with the Scotts. In 1979 Keith wrote a sad and emotional letter:

> *My dear Alan and Bella,*
> *I have just read that Josef Mengele has died of a stroke in South America. I cannot tell you how angry I still feel that that evil monster was allowed to die a natural death. One should forgive, I know, and Karen keeps telling me that. He did me no personal physical harm, unlike thousands of others, but he has left his mark upon me by proxy. Do you think I shall ever lay Rebecca's ghost? Don't worry though — I'm channelling my emotions into good work with Aboriginal children. Lots of healing to be done here!*

Karen, my tower of strength, sends her love. Bless you both.
Keith

Maddy died in 1965, by which time she had succumbed to ever-darkening waves of depression for which she blamed several factors: the non-appearance of grandchildren, to whom she had been looking forward with great hopes of renewed zest for living. The endless monotony of life (as she described it in a letter to her son) stuck in that little box with a dull husband who, upon retirement, pottered and dithered to no purpose all day and every day. Above all, the fact that Alan and his wife spent most of their lives either in Los Angeles or Paris, and rarely came to see them in Birmingham, even when they were back in London. Regularly Alan had telephoned twice a week, wherever he was, but grew increasingly impatient with the endless stream of complaints and recrimination. Bella could always tell when he had been talking to his mother: he had that worn, exhausted look about him.

'You ought to go and see them,' she said.

'I know. But you know what'll happen. It'll be going over and over things that happened years ago, dredging them up, and I'll come back feeling like death myself. I keep suggesting they come and visit us here again, but she always has an excuse. Anyway, when she is here she takes every opportunity to point out how unfair life's been to her. She hates it there but won't take up our offer to shift to London. Even the financial help we give them is resented. The last time I spoke to her, she shouted, "We don't want your charity!" I don't know what to do.'

The effect of her death (from pneumonia that her tar-lined lungs could not withstand) on him took him by surprise. As he stood in his old bedroom with silent tears streaming down his cheeks, all he could think about was what he owed her. But for her determination to ensure a better education for him than she had had, even though it had meant sacrifices, where would he be now? Maybe he had allowed himself to 'grow away' from them — his mother's self-fulfilling prophecy? Maybe he was an ungrateful son? Bella had the good sense to let these guilt feelings work their way through and out, merely reminding him gently of the ways he had shown his love, and never reminding him of the disastrous effects of Maddy's possessiveness.

Bill died of a coronary the following year, stricken with remorse that he had never made his wife happy. He was found lying across the bed with a page from the wall calendar clutched in his hand. It

317

was his and Maddy's wedding anniversary. After the funeral, a miserable affair to which no neighbours came, Alan took away only one thing from Horrible Little Suburban Box Number 27: his grandad's violin and bow, which he fixed over the door of the study like a medieval trophy.

The police never found out who broke into the Scotts' flat in Hammersmith. Since nothing was stolen, and the occupants were not very helpful (pushed off back to America soon after, in fact), they let the case go cold.

*

The paths to be taken by Alan and Bella Scott were not to be revealed to them for many years after the performance of the symphony and the near-tragedy of Keith Maxted.

Alan had, of course, already matured both musically and philosophically in the 1950s and 60s. His mastery of composition, from technical innovation to inspired originality, was slowly formed and refined over the following years. Alongside orchestral and chamber works, his compositions evolved well beyond the tentative and crude beginnings of *musique concrète* — creating sounds like dustbin lids spinning out of control — to the increasingly complex and subtle art of mixing synthesised and orchestrated sound design of the *Symphony of Universal Healing* of 1970-71. The recording of the Festival Hall performance sold very well, especially to people with an interest in spiritual healing.

He embarked immediately, with feverish intensity, on his operatic adaptation of *The Insect Play* — the libretto as well — and finished it in just over a year. The revolutionary time was well chosen for a musical version of this entertaining but ironic satire of war, political ideology and capitalist greed, in which each class is presented as insects: the flighty butterflies, the self-immolating Moths doing their dance of death, the materialistic dung beetles, the lovely musical Cricket family murdered by the ghastly Ichneumon fly, and the army of warmongering Ants. Alan judged it was not right for the plush, dinner-jacketed ambiance of Glyndebourne, so it was premiered in 1973 by the Sadlers Wells Opera at the Coliseum Theatre. What Alan Scott did with it was a surprise to everyone, however. Instead of the anticipated orchestral full-blast fireworks, he scored it for a small, versatile chamber ensemble of hand-picked players who could switch, without taking a breath, from traditional but difficult orchestral harmonies to

318

idioms appropriate to the work's action and characters: nineteen-twenties jazz, Kurt Weillish acerbity, and dance tunes. 'In a sense it's a homage to my mother,' he explained in a radio interview, 'who played that style of music in dance bands in the inter-war years, and as early as 1921 when the play was written. I was brought up to it, sitting under the piano keyboard while she practiced.'

A couple of weeks after the reviews appeared he and Bella received a letter from Darwin:

> *Dear Alan,*
>
> *I was delighted to read in The Times (just arrived) that your insect opera was such a success. As you can guess, it's a subject close to my heart, and I'd love to have seen it. I gather I might even have appreciated some of the music! So glad to know you're loosening up a bit in your old age. Flat stick here, loads of work, but good. Very good.*
>
> *As ever, Keith*

The foray into theatre helped Alan finally to realise that the ideal medium for him — of which he had been aware since his early Ronald Colman youth — was that of moving images, for which he had been writing scores for years. The revelation of something to be attained, far beyond present-day music for films, came one afternoon when, for a nostalgic treat, he and Bella went to see a screening at the National Film Theatre of an old favourite, Walt Disney's original *Fantasia*.

Afterwards, they ambled over Hungerford Bridge, relishing the lights dancing on the murky Thames and the illuminated dome of St. Paul's, still visible against the darkening blue sky despite the encroachment of high-rise office blocks.

'What did you think?' Bella asked.

Alan shook his head and pulled a face. 'I can see why I loved it so much as a kid, but it was a disappointment. I couldn't help wondering how Beethoven and Stravinsky would have rated those images compared with what was going on in their own heads.'

This started his mind working on the potential of computer-generated images based on his own thought-forms whilst composing, as part of his own creative process.

'How on earth can we harness my mental images and transmit them?' he wanted to know, confident that Bella would find a way.

'I'm sure we shall be able to,' Bella assured him. 'Just hang on a

319

few more years, darling, and we'll have you all wired up for sight and sound.'

Music still remained, and remains, largely beyond human understanding, despite its universal importance, and this was a source of immense frustration to Alan — and to Bella, who was working primarily in the field of psychological healing through music. The ancient Greeks had known that music not only alarmed the enemy but relieved gout and epileptic seizures. Depression responded well to music. But still no one knew why, as Shakespeare put it, 'sheeps' guts should hale souls out of men's bodies'.

Bella found her work on the positive effects of music corroborated by evidence of the opposite effects, as hundreds of thousands of young people had their nervous systems subjected to the addictive and mentally destructive effects of rock music. Even after Dr. William Sargant, the British expert on brainwashing, revealed in 1976 that Patty Hearst's kidnappers had 'converted' her to criminality by means of continuous and relentless pounding of loud rock music, few people recognised that musical manipulation of the mind was as serious a threat as drugs. Bella's own observations and experiments led her to support the view that over-amplified music can trigger a brain reaction causing epilepsy and suicidal or homicidal thoughts. Believing that this information needed to be known by the people likely to be victims, she wrote up her results in easily understandable terms and sent it to a leading Los Angeles Rock and Punk magazine.

The hate mail started soon after. At first, a trickle of semi-literate injunctions to 'Get fucked', then came letters and phone calls clearly inspired by fears of financial loss if governments got it into their heads to bring in new protective laws.

'Isn't it ironic,' Alan mused, 'when we tried to spread the idea of music as healer, we got attacked. And now, the same thing happens because you've shown music can be harmful.'

Bella smiled and raised one eyebrow, which meant she was going to disagree. 'I don't see any irony, darling. It's logical — just two extremes of the same thing: people defending their patch.'

*

With the invention of M.R.I. brain-scanning, Bella was at last able to benefit from Takashi Ohnishi's research at the National Centre of Neurology and Psychiatry in Tokyo, showing what was happening inside the planum temporale — the brain's music centre — to account for some of the emotional effects of successions of different tones. The therapeutic results of the improved harmonies were not startling, but nevertheless were impressive enough for both Alan and Bella to be appointed to (or, as the unpretentious Americans put it, 'hired by') the Performing Arts program at the Neurosciences Center in San Francisco, as a team. That was five years after they would have been considered geriatric and unemployable in Britain.

In California, at the end of the century, a new method was announced which could measure the brain's response to complex auditory stimuli, but in fact Bella found the research consisted of quite primitive work on single short melodies.

'I think Keith was right,' Bella said, 'it's too early for the harmonies. And we were born a generation too soon.'

Reinventing the wheel was a painfully slow business.

However, someone was getting impatient. One of their colleagues at the Center greeted them at lunchtime in the Faculty Club with a cheerful 'Hey! You guys must be making a mint of money with those magic sounds of yours!'

Alan and Bella looked at one another with a puzzled expression that apparently looked sincere enough for their informant to say, 'You mean you don't know about it? Have a look on the web...' He gave them a location, which they accessed the moment they got back to their office.

A body calling itself 'The Betternow Health Institute' in Tuxedo City, Texas, was advertising an amazing new remedy for almost everything, 'Based on the revolutionary, fundamental research by Professor Alan Scott and Dr. Bella Cassell at the San Francisco Neuroscience Center'. All you had to do was buy a couple of CDs, sit back, and listen to the Magic Sounds. They would not only Alleviate Stress but Re-align the Cells in the Central Nervous System, Correct your body's levels of various Compounds, facilitate Weight Loss, and enable you to live a Happier and Longer Life. Every capital letter seemed like a Guarantee of Authenticity.

Bella and Alan were appalled, and went straight to see Dr. Carl Straub, the President of the Center.

'So you know nothing of these people?' Straub asked.

'They approached us about a year ago, but we wrote back and told them our research was still a long way from being marketable!' Alan recalled, producing the correspondence. 'If they've got a copy of our material, someone here has leaked it to them.'

It took the Center and the anti-fraud police six months to track down the 'Institute', and the technician who had made a few thousand dollars on the scam. Within months it had started up again, this time from 'The Happy Music Center' in Taiwan. Alan and Bella started receiving letters and emails of complaint from disappointed victims, whom they referred to their own website which explained the situation. They placed warnings in major newspapers and health magazines, but still the gullible went on responding to the promises of the auditory elixir of long life and effortless good health.

'Isn't there anything,' Alan wondered, 'that some money-grubbing bastard won't pervert into something bad?'

Alan was invited to be interviewed on Walter Holcroft's prime-time radio programme, *The Controversialists*. At first, he refused, saying it was Bella they should be talking to, but she was not feeling up to it — a bout of 'flu had left her with constant headaches and dizziness. So Alan agreed, but only if it was done live — he had suffered selective editing and distortion in the past.

The tenor of the conversation was provocative and hostile right from the start, but Alan had scrawled on the pad before him Bella's advice: 'Stay cool and in charge'.

HOLCROFT: Alan Scott, you're a classical composer, so you don't have much sympathy with pop music.

ALAN: Is that a fact?

HOLCROFT: I'm asking you.

ALAN: Oh, are you? Sorry, I thought you were telling me. Anyway, I'm not a 'classical' composer — I wasn't around in Mozart's day. Let's say I write art music mostly, but my critics would dispute that for my film music. As for lack of sympathy, I have opinions about most forms of music, but what I think about 'pop' music — I don't know which of the many kinds you mean — would be totally boring and irrelevant to your listeners. I'm too old to belong to any pop culture, so I'm not qualified to pass judgement. Not publicly, anyway, however much I might rant on among friends.

HOLCROFT: What sort of things do you rant on about?

ALAN: Look, I really don't want to get drawn into the never-ending debate about changing fashions and taste, but there are two things I'm sorry about above all: the abysmal attention given to musical education in schools, which means the young still find it hard to discriminate between competence and cleverly marketed rubbish. And I regret the passing of melody in popular music. Not only in popular music.

HOLCROFT: You wrote in an article recently, quote, 'Pop music is just a mechanical thumping noise blasting out of vast amplifiers'. That's a public judgement, isn't it?

ALAN: Yes it is. But it's not what I wrote. I brought a copy with me, just in case you brought it up. This is what I did write: 'A lot of pop music — not all of it by any means — is just a mechanical thumping noise blasting out of vast amplifiers. Very dangerous.'

HOLCROFT: Almost the same.

ALAN: No it isn't.

HOLCROFT: How do you mean, dangerous? How can music be dangerous?

ALAN: Well, decibels.

HOLCROFT: Excuse me?

ALAN: Decibels. Too many make you deaf — hearing aid manufacturers make a mint out of disco-ravers and ageing rockers with battered ear-drums. But that's not the half of it. Did you know that over-amplified music affects the lungs too?

HOLCROFT: The lungs! Do you go in for old wives' tales as well as outdated, unpopular music?

ALAN: No, neither, actually. Researchers believe that the intense pulses of low frequency, high energy, very loud music could actually make your lungs collapse.

HOLCROFT: Another victory for wowsers and party-poopers! No drink, no smoking, no recreational drugs! And now no loud music.

ALAN: It's a sad old world, isn't it? The problem isn't limited to pop music, by any means. I was at a recital of experimental music recently — terribly serious post-Boulez stuff played on new kinds of electronic instruments. The music was interesting, but the amplification was so overpowering I felt physically ill afterwards — dizzy, nauseous, headache. I wasn't the only one either. And I'm used to listening through earphones to a hundred-strong symphony orchestra in recording studios!

HOLCROFT: How unpleasant for you. Do you want to censor music you don't like? Are you a musical fascist?

ALAN: No, you can't stop it in a free society. I'm dead against censorship. I think the musical fascists are the people who force

323

me to hear music or noise I dislike in shops and restaurants —
even in the gym I go to. It's like a constant brainwashing.

HOLCROFT: Brainwashing? I'm glad you mentioned that.
You've been doing some lucrative brainwashing yourself, haven't
you? Your so-called healing harmonies must have made you pots
of money.

ALAN (taken aback): Well... You really should have done your
homework before broadcasting that bit of slander.

HOLCROFT: O.K., let's move on to...

ALAN: No, Mr. Holcroft, let's not move on till I've cleared this
up, in the interests of truth. I'm sure you wouldn't want your
listeners to feel they'd been deliberately misled by you, right? What
happened was this: some unscrupulous shysters got hold of
experimental work my neuropsychologist wife and I have been
engaged on for many years. They started making extravagant claims
for it and selling it on the internet. They were shut down twice, but
the internet is like a breeding ground for the plague. You never
know when stuff is going to pop up or where from.

HOLCROFT: Right, I'm glad we've...

ALAN: I think you'd be wise to let me finish, Mr. Holcroft. The
reason why I've never made public the complete seventh mystic
harmony is that we don't yet know what its effects would be, and I
might not be able to control it. When my wife and other
neuropsychologists know more about how the brain reacts to
auditory stimuli, we can think about using the harmonies for
genuine healing purposes. Not before.

HOLCROFT: It's great that we've cleared that up, Mr. Scott.

ALAN: Yes, isn't it? And just one more thing if I may, about
music and the young — just go to a Prom concert at the Albert
Hall, and you'll hear a lot of 'pop' music — that is, popular music
from Bach to Bernstein — being applauded by thousands of young
people.

HOLCROFT: Not as many as Woodstock!

ALAN: There speaks a true democrat! I wonder how twentieth-
century civilisation will be remembered by the rats and cockroaches
in a thousand years time? Jimi Hendrix at Woodstock or
Koussevitsky at Tanglewood?

HOLCROFT: You know that record companies subsidise
classical — sorry, art — titles with pop?

ALAN: Very kind of them. Wouldn't be anything to do with the
prestige value of so-called classical and post-classical music, would
it? Great musicians understand and respect one another, and often

bring together apparently contrasting genres. Think of Berio's Sinfonia — Mahler and pop in one! Or Gershwin and Ravel, Vaughan Williams and Larry Adler, Yehudi Menuhin and Stephane Grappelli. Jean-Yves Thibaudet's superb arrangements of Duke Ellington. Or Barenboim and the tango in Buenos Aires. Or Leonard Bernstein. Or...

HOLCROFT: Yes, O.K., you've made your point. So, if you see no fundamental difference between your kind of music and pop, what's the argument about? Just a question of personal taste, isn't it?

ALAN: I didn't say I see — or hear — no difference. I'm defending musicianship and true music that's created by serious musicians, be it popular or art music, motivated above all by the need to express a thought or feeling or mood musically, not just to get to the Top of the Pops chart.

HOLCROFT: Shouldn't young musicians be given a chance?

ALAN: Absolutely! The really talented should succeed, and the rest can entertain their friends with extreme karaoke in the local club. It really bugs me to see so many wonderfully talented serious music students who'll have to content themselves with teaching a school orchestra for forty years. It's in performance that you see the difference between the two scenes.

HOLCROFT: What two scenes?

ALAN: I mean music, and entertainment. An incompetent soloist who tried to foist himself on the public playing Chopin or Debussy or Rachmaninov would be laughed off the stage. But a pop singer with insignificant voice and musical skill can be hugely exciting thanks to sheer energy, personal magnetism, and amplified power. I can see lot of visual and electronic values in the world of sparkling-midriff gymnastics, but is that part of the definition of music?

HOLCROFT: Where do you draw the line? Great opera singers depend on energy and charisma.

ALAN: But opera fans are ruthlessly critical about musicianship, and microphones are *verboten!* Surely you'd agree that it's hard to call 'music' the noise made by some cleverly marketed but musically untalented exhibitionist with a hate-filled contorted face screaming to a pre-recorded phat beat on a boom box or drum machine and masturbating a distorted electric guitar or performing oral sex on a hand-held mic...

HOLCROFT *(hurriedly)*: O.K., we had to cut it there, Mr. Scott. My producer had to cut us off before that last bit of yours went out

— a security delay system, you know. Our bosses don't allow the M-word on this show. Before the kids' bed-time, you know?

ALAN: So spreading slander and frying young people's brains, that's O.K., but not the M-word. Yes, that figures.

When Alan got home Bella greeted him with a good slug of Glenfiddich and a hearty kiss.

'You held your own very well, darling,' she said, 'even though you got overheated and fuddy-duddy at the end.'

Alan pulled a wry face. 'Oh dear, more hate mail. Sorry. I just get so bloody fed up with what's going on. All day long, radio stations pumping out...'

'I know, I know!'

Alan's indignation and despair were bubbling away again. '...and even Aunty Beeb spoons out bite-sized morsels instead of complete works on its so-called classical music station.'

'So write them a letter, you don't have to convert me, darling! Anyway, I taped it all. It was a good job it went out live, it was all there.'

'Not quite,' Alan smiled. 'You missed the best bit at the end. But I had my Walkman on in my pocket, so you can at least hear it.'

*

Gradually the controversies ceased to be hot, and the Scotts were able to get on with investigating in depth the psychic impact of the seven harmonies of which Alan had been made the medium and steward. At last it looked as though technology was catching up with mystical revelation. Unfortunately for Alan, this took him on to complicated mathematical ground, and he depended on Bella to make concepts such as compositional algorithms, flow charts, and serial sequences comprehensible.

Between them they eventually perfected the sequence of harmonies and reproduced them far more accurately than was possible that terrible night in their London flat with Keith Maxted. Most significantly, they came to realise that the power lay not just in each separate harmony, but in their juxtaposition. All seven, one after the other, and in something approaching their full potency, would bring about beneficial realignments of cells in the brain and body that would require very, very careful control and monitoring by specially trained neuroscientists. How much easier it had been for cynical purveyors of shattering, destructive musical noise to deafen and desensitise a whole generation.

The harmonies became very powerful towards the end of the twentieth century, in the forms in which Alan and Bella managed to capture them and integrate them. In this they were greatly assisted by increasingly sophisticated synthesisers developed at Pierre Boulez's sound laboratories at IRCAM, the Institut de Recherche et de Coordination Acoustique/Musique, in Paris. Nevertheless, Alan was aware that some kind of block was preventing further development of the most complex of all, the seventh. Until he solved the mystery, the full potential of all seven was like a golden eagle straining to soar but trapped in an invisible force field. How could it be released? He voiced his frustration to Bella one summer morning in London.

'But how do you *know* there's something holding it back?' she asked, ever the practical one.

Alan's gesture betokened impotent impatience. 'I can't say I *know*, not in the way you mean *know*. One doesn't always know what one's ignorant of. Isn't that what heuristic means? Not knowing where you're going until you're there?'

She resisted the temptation to launch into one of her logical onslaughts. Of course, many mathematicians and scientists had had only a vague notion of what they were trying to discover before they had a break-through, a *Eureka*-moment. Artists, poets and composers, similarly, often strove after an ideal of which they had only the vaguest notion until the day, the hour, the split second everything fell into place. Alan, poor chap, was having to work with his intuition and with his memory, both slippery aspects of the mind. How, Bella now wondered, could he be helped along the track?

Alan watched her as she sat back in her chair, lips pursed and eyes focused way beyond the ceiling. Different though her mental processes were from his own, he recognised that they made a formidable team because of those very differences. Somewhere in another flat someone was playing Beethoven's *Hammerklavier*, which poor old Ludwig had heard only in his head.

'O.K., let's go back to the first time we heard them,' she suggested, 'in the château. Have you still got the notes you made immediately after?'

'Yes, of course.' Alan went to the locked filing cabinet where not his original scribbled notes but several photocopies were kept. He had deposited the originals in the bank for safe keeping, not for fear that anyone could be remotely interested in stealing them, but in case of fire, rising damp, leaking roof, mice, and other hazards nature subjects us to. He handed Bella a copy, which she pored over. Her sight-reading had lost none of its sharpness, even though she now played the piano only rarely. Suddenly she dabbed a finger on the page.

'What do those marks mean?'

'Which marks?' Alan peered over her shoulder.

'The ones before and after the seventh harmony. Oh, sorry, I think they're xerox marks.'

Alan stared at the page, trying to reconstruct what he had jotted down all those years ago and to decipher what now looked like a few smudgy crochets with a squiggle under and above them.

'It's not like the other notes — they're firmly written in the spaces or on the lines of the staves I drew. But I don't think they're blotches from the photocopier. Let me see...'

He went to the piano and played the sixth chord — some of it as arpeggio since the range went from the top to the bottom of the keyboard. Then he tentatively played the mysterious notes that followed, eyes shut, trying to cast his mind's ear back to the moment of revelation, humming gently to himself.

'They don't belong to the sixth... or to the seventh,' he murmured. Then: 'No, hang on, they do belong to the sixth. They're a kind of resolution — no, a transition — coming slightly after the full harmony. Or what I had thought was the full harmony but I sense now that it's incomplete. The delayed notes... it's coming back into my head... were beyond the threshold of my hearing, but I just *knew* they were there!'

Bella was on the verge of entering into another discussion about *knowing*, but asked instead, 'And the ones following the seventh?'

'Well, they can't be a transition, there's nothing else to come. So this must be a resolution.'

He played again, using his sketchy blobs as points of departure, desperately trying to recapture the total, ecstatic effect those sounds had had when they first heard them. If only he had thought of doing this nearer the time, instead of concentrating only on the main harmonies!

'So,' Bella said, leaning over his shoulder, 'the full effect of the harmonies can only be recovered by linking the final two with a codetta, and adding a coda that resolves the seventh harmony?'

'Yes, I think so. That would mean a relationship is set up between the sixth and the seventh, and then between the seventh and...'

'...and... the listener's mind?' This was Bella's territory.

The sheer enormity of the task was becoming clearer, unfortunately. With a sigh, Alan tried once again to harness the sounds. 'That's all I have to do. Piece of cake. Apart from extending the codas beyond the range of human hearing. But there's no instrument that could do that with the kind of subtlety we need, way beyond Western ideas of tonality.'

'You mean,' Bella asked, 'you couldn't reproduce those sounds on modern instruments of any kind?'

'No keyed instruments, anyway. They're fixed. Strings, maybe, but we'll need a new sort of training. We must go back to Paris and work with the IRCAM synthesiser again.'

Alan got up from the piano stool, took Bella by the hand as they walked back to the sofa. 'You know, the more I think about this, the more my mind settles back into its receptive state, the clearer it becomes to me why I was given the harmonies that day. It's beginning to be quite scary, actually.'

'What do you mean?'

'You remember when we first met, I told you I had all sorts of weird music going round in my head, which I couldn't ever hope to write down or play? Like nothing I'd ever heard on the radio or when my mother played the piano? Well, it's as if I'm finally seeing — or hearing — what those sounds were.'

'You mean, you were hearing them in your head when you were a boy?'

'Something very like them. Not the same, but like.'

Bella considered this possibility. 'I suppose it could mean that your brain was receptive to them by nature, not by training. So you were made their guardian, as it were.'

It could also mean — she kept this to herself — that you are projecting the harmonies back on to your childhood memories. Or, indeed, that the mystic harmonies were a re-creation in your own mind of that strange adolescent music that haunted you so vividly. But in that case, Bella objected silently, how come we all heard the harmonies during the séance? How come I was so profoundly moved by them myself? Once again she found reason and experience were in conflict.

'To think,' Alan was saying, 'my mother was always going at me for wasting my time on that. 'If only you'd practise Czerny, you'd soon play proper music,' she'd say.'

Alan remembered how her conception of the 'proper music' they could play together had never appealed to him. Predictable, mathematical, formulaic, dull music for instrumental technicians. But his own inner music had been mad, visionary stuff, it had soared and swooped like a skylark in the bright blue inner space of his mind, free above the earth; sometimes it was an immense orchestra, at others a solitary flute or violin floating effortlessly, ethereally shimmering, but with dark swirling menacing rumbles coming from below.

Now he knew why. Not only why he had been plagued by those sounds impossible to make real as a boy, but why the blindingly, deafeningly obvious delayed harmonic extensions were becoming clear to him only now. At any earlier period, even a few years ago, no electronic means would have been available to realise the subliminal, superliminal, beyond-the-threshold harmonies needed to complete the cycle of healing power.

Alan paid a visit to the bank next morning. The bemused Assistant Manager saw him take out of his vault safe nothing but a sheet of paper with lots of lines going across it and columns of squiggles. The young man would later amuse his colleagues at coffee break by saying it never ceased to amaze him what some people think important enough to pay a hefty fee to keep in a vault.

*

One fine June day, early in the twenty-first century, as they sit in their apartment on Liberty in San Francisco, dawdling over the only meal Alan can cook with any semblance of success — omelette and rocket brunch — Bella, now finely aged, still beautiful (and ash-blonde), looks through the window. She sees the mailman stuffing envelopes into their box, and gives a little shiver. This will be it, one way or the other.

'One for you, from the hospital,' Alan says as he walks back into the apartment. 'It'll be those test results, I suppose.'

'Yes,' Bella says, trying to sound indifferent, 'I suppose so.'

She reads. Re-reads. Hands the report to Alan.

'What does it mean?' he asks, 'I don't understand these medical terms.'

'It means the MRI and catscans reveal my brain has been massively invaded by glioma. That's a very aggressive malignant tumour. And it's spread so much that surgical resection is

330

impossible.'

Alan has to sit down, devastated by the news.

'But... but... you've been well, apart from the headaches and a bit of dizziness.'

Bella smiles wearily. 'That's the fiendish way this particular cancer works. It creates few visible symptoms and then *Pow!*, it's got you.'

Alan takes Bella's hands, not bothering to wipe away his tears. 'The letter says something about six months. Does that mean six months treatment?'

Bella shakes her head. 'No, darling, it means I have six months max to live. I've left it too late, you see. For months I've been convincing myself the headaches were just migraine and the dizzy spells too much Californian pinot noir. Treatment would be purely palliative. I went through all this in detail a couple of days ago with the consultant.'

'You mean you've known for days, and didn't tell me?'

She nods a trifle guiltily. 'I'm sorry, darling, but I needed to come to terms with it alone first, and make some decisions for myself. You see, surgery would turn me into a slobbering cabbage.'

'But I don't care about that!' he wails. 'I love you so much, and I'll never stop loving you whatever happens.'

'Then you'll understand that I want to go with some dignity, the way you'd treat your favourite spaniel if he was in constant untreatable pain. I've put a codicil in my will instructing that I am not, repeat not, to be put on a life-support system if I'm unable to respond. *Do you understand, Alan?*'

Alan, stunned by the fierceness in her voice, nods agreement, draws his handkerchief from his pocket, turns away, and blows his nose, admiring Bella's determination but mystified by her underlying, uncharacteristic defeatism. He takes a deep breath.

'Well, until then, if it happens, we're not going to give in just like that! I can't believe you want to let nature take its course, or place yourself in God's hands, or some such superstitious claptrap! Dignity means resistance, like your mother's against those Nazis. Anyway, I simply can't allow you to die before I do.' The expression of petulant determination on his face is that of a child refusing to go to bed. 'You'll cope so much better than I should without you. The answer is obvious. We've got six months to give you loads of home treatment.'

'Home... What do you mean?'

'We'll practise what we've been preaching and plug you into the harmonies, or plug the harmonies into you — for twelve hours a day if necessary.'

'That'll drive me crazy even if the tumour doesn't!'

'Maybe, but at least we'll be fighting it, won't we? I damned if this is going to be another last summer!'

'*Another* last summer?'

He tells her about the previous ones in his life. Four summers that have meant life was never going to be the same.

'First, 1939, the last summer of sanity, Mum called it. Then there was the memorable, never to be forgotten day in the summer of 1941, when you first spoke to me and Caesar humped your leg.'

'Poor old Caesar! I remember you coming to my garden party covered with his blood.'

'And you kissed me. What a day that was! I was never the same after that. Then, that summer afternoon in 1944, the last time Joy, Rebecca, Keith and I would ever be together; the day we were suddenly forced to grow up.'

'What was the fourth?' asks Bella. She doesn't want to hear about Joy and Rebecca now; they were a separate theme in Alan's symphony of life, as discordant as Keith and Tony Borland were in hers.

'The fourth? The summer we heard the harmonies, in that château in Normandy.'

'Of course. They've certainly dominated both our lives ever since,' Bella agrees.

'They've given us a common purpose.'

'And something to argue about.'

'We'd never have been short of something to argue about. You see? We simply can't let this be another last summer, because I'd have nobody to argue with. So — the harmonies? Agreed?'

Bella is touched by the passion in his entreaty. Would she, she wonders, be doing the same for Alan?

'Yes, of course, darling Alan.' She places her hands each side of his face and kisses his forehead. 'Thank you. But only if you let me monitor my progress every day. This has to be the most exciting research project I've ever done.'

They kiss, warmly, affectionately, but it is a kiss of poignancy they have never known before. That night Alan spends a longer time than usual in the bathroom. Bella slips out of bed and presses her ear to the door, checking that he hasn't passed out or had a heart attack, but quickly returns to bed, for what she has heard is Alan's sobs. For both, an unspoken count-down phase has begun, and they must negotiate it with a combination of his English sorely stressed phlegm and her clinical, dispassionate detachment.

A few mornings later Bella, looking even more ravishing than usual — determined to go out with style — draws Alan's attention to something in the journal she's reading.

'This should please you, darling,' she says, 'this guy Tramo — he's a musical neuroscientist at Harvard Medical School — he writes: 'Music is in our genes'.'

Alan seems unimpressed. He lowers the newspaper into his corn flakes and pushes his glasses up on to his forehead. 'M'hm. Sign of the times. It fits in with minimalism.'

A response she quickly tries to decode. Eyes closed, slight shake of head. 'Sorry? Oh!' She cottons on and giggles. 'No, not jeans pants, silly, genes DNA.'

Alan picks up his soggy newspaper, tut-tuts, and wipes it with his serviette. 'Wow! A musical gene? Maybe that explains musical genius? I wish someone would invent a waterproof newspaper.'

Bella sighs, having just read on, and doesn't tell Alan that Tramo is saying *everyone* has a musical gene, *all* humans possess a universal musical instinct. No, no, no, that's not what Alan would want to hear. She knows how important it is to him to believe that he inherited a gift. She understands that his *petit bourgeois* origins, in that grey No-Man's Land sandwiched uncomfortably between sturdy working class and confident affluence, still render him vulnerable. Socially rootless. Underneath his acquired polish and articulate poise still lurks the boy with the grimy hands and bloodstained shirt from the semi-detached little box.

'Who knows,' she says, 'but for your musical grandad you might have been a corporate accountant!'

'Not a chance!' Alan replies, stroking his shiny pate with the same gesture that he always used to make to smooth back hair. 'Not with my head for figures.'

She looks at him with a gaze expressing some complex emotion comprising affection, understanding, tolerance, acceptance, admiration, amusement. Perhaps the word, after all, is love. Yes, Bella has had to learn from scratch how to love. Perhaps because her own mother never showed her more than distant maternal interest? No point trying amateur psychology on Bella. Whatever the reason, she has not achieved the intensity of Alan's adoration, but is nearly there. Especially now. The irony does not fail to strike her: just as they are approaching well-tempered close harmony, the music runs out.

'Anyway,' she says, 'you might as well stick to music now. Your Mum would be proud of you.'

Alan's mind rolls back to that evening, more than thirty years ago, when a man he vaguely recognised approached him at the Royal Festival Hall, and said exactly the same thing.

Da capo al fine.

OTHER NOVELS BY COLIN DUCKWORTH

STEPS TO THE HIGH GARDEN

After the savage murder of an old theology professor in Melbourne it soon becomes obvious it was for something that he knew. Dr. Simon Prescott, a psycho-historian and guest at the house party where the murder has taken place, reluctantly takes on the role of investigator. He is soon drawn into a sequence of supernatural events. We are taken on a global journey and each discovery reveals new intrigues. *Steps to the High Garden* keeps the reader guessing right to the end.

A multiple-murder mystery of cosmic proportions.... out-of-body experiences solve the mystery and rapidly expand the story in time and space...

— Penelope Fitzgerald, *The London Evening Standard*

What starts out as an unexplained bashing murder of an old theology professor in Melbourne quickly builds into an imaginative, entertaining, and very donnish version of Raiders of the Lost Ark.

— Roff Smith, Editor's Choice, *Sunday Age*

A thundering good tale... psychic thriller in the postmodern mode... can have you sitting on the edge of your seat... tenderness and sensuality (which) the author handles with surpassing skill...

— Joseph Johnson, *Overland*

A first-rate thriller. It's a witty and intelligent book.

— Dinny O'Hearn, *The Melbourne Times*

Duckworth's pace and timing are just about perfect... an original and multi-layered plot... makes Steps to the High Garden *an enjoyable read.*

— Rod Beecham, *The Weekend Australian*

Calder Publications U.K., Riverrun Press U.S.A.
 ISBN 0 7145 4229 6
 Order from: Amazon.com; Calder Bookshop, London, UK; Riverrun Press N.Y., USA; Black Pepper, Melbourne, Australia; or linco41@ozemail.com.au.

DIGGING IN DARK PLACES

Janet Crompton, an outspoken, beautiful but emotionally immature graduate student, is faced with unforeseen problems when she travels from Melbourne to London and France to do a Ph.D. in literary history. She meets Roland Beresford in a picturesque Breton town, Tréborden, where they are involved in very different work. Janet is trying to find the truth behind several different versions of a tragic local legend concerning a young girl who fell in love with the village priest in 1791 and, apparently, ended up in the lunatic asylum. Roland is an aggressive, insensitive, materialistic businessman, briefed to rationalise (or shut down) a papermill that has employed many of the townspeople for 200 years.

Conflict between Janet and Roland is inevitable. Her literary detective work brings clues to light that complement the more mundane police enquiries. She digs in dark places: psychological, historical and political. Their investigations confront them with violent death, blackmail, abduction, drug-dealing and art forgery. In Tréborden, with its cobbled streets, half-timbered cottages and dominating cathedral, Janet makes some dangerous enemies as she tries to complete the three-dimensional jigsaw mystery.

I enjoyed this novel immensely... Similar books sitting on my bookshelf do not match this for content, imagination and readability... The characters were credible, strong and, most importantly, developed interestingly.

— Tina Muncaster, *National Book Council Reader*

Digging in Dark Places *is a complicated novel. Labyrinthine. One needs to pay close attention to the people in this ovel, for hardly anyone is mentioned frivolously. The subtext explores the darker side of Janet's psyche, as well as those of revered university intellectuals and civic families.*
Dark Places *is an interesting read and imbued with a good deal of humour, much of it delightfully unexpected.*

— *The Australian Book Review*

Ryan Publications
  ISBN 0958705941
  Order from: Calder Bookshop, London, UK; Black Pepper, Melbourne, Australia; Melbourne University Bookshop; or RACV Club, Melbourne